DARK
DREAMS

DARK DREAMS

A COLLECTION OF HORROR AND SUSPENSE BY BLACK WRITERS

EDITED BY
BRANDON MASSEY

Dafina Books

KENSINGTON PUBLISHING CORP.
http://www.kensingtonbooks.com

DAFINA BOOKS are published by

Kensington Publishing Corp.
850 Third Avenue
New York, NY 10022

All Kensington titles, imprints and distributed lines are available at special quantity discounts for bulk purchases for sales promotion, premiums, fund-raising, educational or institutional use.

Special book excerpts or customized printings can also be created to fit specific needs. For details, write or phone the office of the Kensington Special Sales Manager: Kensington Publishing Corp., 850 Third Avenue, New York, NY 10022. Attn. Special Sales Department. Phone: 1-800-221-2647.

Dafina Books and the Dafina logo Reg. U.S. Pat. & TM Off.

ISBN 0-7582-0753-0

First Kensington Trade Paperback Printing: August 2004
10 9 8 7 6 5 4 3 2 1

Printed in the United States of America

To dark dreamers everywhere

CONTENTS

INTRODUCTION

What you now hold in your hands is a piece of history.

Quite simply, it's the first collection of original horror and suspense stories written exclusively by black writers ever to be released by a major publisher.

Roll up your sleeves and get ready to dig in. You're in for a feast of fantastic fiction unlike anything you've ever read.

For a few years, I'd kicked around the idea of doing an anthology of horror tales penned by black authors. I'm not the originator of the concept. I'd heard of many others who wanted to do a collection like this, but for one reason or another, nothing ever came to fruition.

I'd chatted with my agent many times about this project, but always set it aside, worried that the timing wasn't right and that no one would be receptive to such a book. Relationship-driven novels and urban books dominated the African-American commercial fiction lists, and I knew from my own publishing experiences how much of a challenge it could be to turn people on to something new. It wasn't until spring 2003, shortly after I turned in my vampire novel, *Dark Corner*, to Kensington, that my agent finally said, "Now that you've finished your book, maybe this would be a good time to mention the anthology to Kensington."

I agreed. Much to my surprise, Karen Thomas, my editor, loved the idea and asked for a proposal. I rounded up some writers to contribute work—Steven Barnes, Tananarive Due, and Zane, all good friends who I knew would be willing to participate—and in short time we had a deal. It came together so quickly and easily that it seemed like . . . well, destiny.

It was a tad frightening, I must admit. Here I was, with an exciting opportunity to break new ground. *Dark Matter*, the brilliant collection of speculative fiction edited by Sheree Thomas, was the only project that came anywhere close to what I had in mind. But I was doing horror stories, and the thing with horror is, people either love it or hate it.

There's little in between. I was intimidated by the idea of organizing an anthology that could appeal to horror fans and yet be accessible enough to pull in people with only a casual interest in stories like these.

Yes, I was intimidated—but determined to make it work. I saw a critical need for this book. Since the success of Terry McMillan's *Waiting to Exhale*, the "black book market" has experienced wonderful growth, but a disproportionate number of the novels that have seen print are in the romance/more-drama-for-your-mama/you-go-girl category. Those books clearly satisfy a desire, but they are far from representative of the range of stories that black writers are equipped to tell. Black writers can write mysteries. We can write science fiction. We can write thrillers. And yes, we can write horror, too. It's time to expand our awareness of what black writers can do with a pen. In the end, all readers will reap the benefits of these writers' unharnessed imaginations.

Not only did I want to show readers what black authors could do in this genre, I wanted to give writers an opportunity to be published in a format that could potentially reach a wide readership. The horror market, booming in the late 1970s through the early 1990s, has largely gone underground to the online e-zines and small presses, where it enjoys a loyal but limited following. Here was a chance to give some newcomers a shot for exposure in the big leagues, if you will—an opportunity for them to get a boost of confidence and a professional credit that will hopefully translate into some great novels down the road. New writers are the lifeblood of the publishing industry. It was a key ambition of mine to find talented new voices and collect them in this book so they can captivate us with their songs.

Finally, I just wanted to see how a project like this would turn out. Could a massive anthology of original horror and suspense short stories written by black authors, with no particular theme, be published and actually find an audience? This book is a big experiment—for me, the contributors, and the publisher, too. We are delving into the unknown, creeping into a darkened cave, and no one knows what will happen. Sounds a bit like a horror story, doesn't it?

I suspect this one will have a happy ending.

Definitions

Anytime the subject of horror and suspense fiction comes up, the questions inevitably arise: What exactly is horror, and what is suspense?

For the purposes of this book, I'm keeping it simple. A horror story scares you; a suspense tale places you in a heightened state of tension. With either of them, there may be something supernatural going on, or there may be a nonsupernatural incident fueling the plot. But the bottom line is, you are chilled or gripped (or chilled *and* gripped) by what you're reading.

With that said, I think the best horror and suspense tales go deeper than cheap thrills, superficial shivers, and gross-outs. A great story can not only frighten you and make you clutch the pages between clammy fingers—it can make you view the world in a different light. A skillfully rendered horror story will plumb a fictional character's deepest fear and force this character to undergo profound personal transformation as he or she confronts the terror and plots a way to overcome it, and in the end, when the character prevails over the threat, he or she will be revitalized and changed by the journey. Assuming that you're closely identifying with the character as the story develops and reaches its ultimate conclusion, when the tale is done, *you* might find yourself rejuvenated and enlightened, too.

Such is the power of these kinds of stories.

This Book

In this book, you're going to discover a vast range of stories unlike anything you've ever encountered. We begin with Zane, the bestselling erotica author, and her story "Resident Evil," about a vampire who rules as landlord over an apartment complex—and the devilish, sensual privileges to which his position entitles him. Then, in "But Beautiful and Terrifying," Robert Fleming flips the script and spins a World War II–era story of a black soldier sent to investigate strange deaths in Tokyo. In "The Power," Bram Stoker Award-winner Linda Addison weaves a tale of two gifted girls who, one summer, learn to channel their talents to overcome a deadly foe. Kalamu ya Salaam tells a powerful story of a white man living in inner-city New Orleans, and the unexpected visitor who pays him a house call one night, in "Bras Coupe."

Indeed, there's something here for everyone. Like quiet horror? Check out "The Fourth Floor," by Ahmad Wright, a gem of subtle terror about a janitor who works the night shift at a hospital. If ghost stories are your thing, read "Empty Vessel," by Lawana Holland-Moore, an eerie fictionalization of an actual historical event. Enjoy graphic, extreme horror? Then brace yourself and read "Red," by Rickey George. How about zombies, à la *Night of the Living Dead*? Dig into "Danger Word," by Steven Barnes and Tananarive Due—their first-ever published collaboration.

There's more—much more, guaranteed to keep you reading late into the night.

But instead of going on, I'll get out of the way so we can step into the world of dark dreams.

One tip: Remember to keep a night-light on. . . .

Resident Evil

Zane

Sangue stood in his apartment window watching the two beautiful young women get out of the sport-utility vehicle in the parking lot of the complex.

"Great, it's about time," he whispered to himself.

It had been three weeks—which seemed more like three months—since he had rented apartment 3-C to Laurie Anderson. Petite with a honey brown complexion, a tiny little waist, and engaging amber eyes—he was ready to take her the moment he had laid eyes on her, but she was not enough. He chose to bide his time until she brought a friend home with her. It was inevitable. All women have at least a few close friends. The one she had pulled up with was incredible. Tall and thick with ebony skin—he could not wait to look into her eyes and see into her soul.

He watched as they made their way toward the front door. He had the entire building wired, inside and out, so he could keep track of everything that was said and done.

Sangue had been the landlord—and owner unbeknownst to anyone—for more than ten years, and he relished the fact that he understood human nature so well. Then again, he had had centuries to get it right.

Sangue figured that Laurie had been hesitant to bring someone home with her because of the condition of the building. Granted, he did very little to fix it up, but that was because he liked the dark walls and the dim lighting throughout the corridors. All the current tenants—with the exception of Laurie—loved the decor as well.

He listened to their conversation once they got closer. He could hear

every single word, despite the rain. The taller one—the friend—
seemed to be full of attitude. He would change that—easily.

"Laurie, hurry up! It's pouring down out here!" Skylar yelled out as
they made a mad dash for the front door.

Skylar waited under the awning while Laurie continued struggling
to maneuver three paper grocery bags and close her trunk at the same
time. Skylar had two bags—all that she could handle. Besides, she had
just gotten her hair done that day, and sixty-five dollars was sixty-five
dollars. It was Friday night, and she wanted at least to look good
throughout the weekend.

"Thanks a lot, Skylar," Laurie stated with sarcasm after she finally
made it to the door.

"Hey, don't get nasty," Skylar said. "You're lucky I'm even helping
you bring all this shit in. I had a date with Pete tonight and I canceled
it just for you."

"Well, I guess I should feel lucky, then."

Both of them knew the real deal. Pete and Skylar had been having
some drama lately. Minor problems that had escalated into major issues because of a serious lack of communication. Skylar wanted to concentrate more on her career managing an art gallery, and Pete wanted
her to concentrate more on him. He had always been a momma's boy
and demanded way too much attention. Laurie did not understand why
Skylar even continued to deal with Pete on any level. In her opinion,
men always claimed to want an ambitious woman but would then try to
discourage her from pursuing her dreams when they found one. That's
why Laurie was determined to remain single until she had finished
medical school and started a private practice.

"Laurie, you're taking forever and a damn day to find the keys. Why
don't you have them on the same key ring as your car keys?"

"I haven't been living here long, Sky. I just haven't gotten around to
it."

"You've always been a huge procrastinator."

"Yeah, well, whatever," Laurie said. "I found them. Just move out
my way so I can get to the door."

After they entered the building, Skylar scanned the foyer and
frowned as they started down the hallway toward the elevator.
"Humph, this doesn't look like much. What's your rent again?"

"Eight hundred." Laurie walked ahead of Skylar and pressed the
call button for the elevator. While they waited, she turned back to

Skylar and rolled her eyes as she still juggled the bags. "Don't start talking junk about my place. You know as well as I do that it's hard to find a decent apartment in this city."

"True, I can see the 'affordable' part because eight hundred isn't bad for a one-bedroom, but the 'decent' part is yet to be determined."

They got off the elevator on the third floor and started toward the back of the building. Skylar noticed a camera in the top left-hand corner of the hallway. "Wow, Big Brother is watching, huh?"

"That's one of the things I'm digging about this building," Laurie responded. "At least they have some kind of security."

"Who'd want to break into this dump?"

"Didn't I tell you not to talk junk about my place?"

"Okay, sorry. I was just . . ." Skylar stopped dead in her tracks when she thought she heard a scream. "What the hell was that?"

"What was what?" Laurie asked.

"Don't play dumb with me. Didn't someone just scream?"

"Oh, that's just Agina."

"Agina?"

"Yes, this old biddy that lives in three-G. She does that every night about this time." Laurie unlocked her apartment door, walked inside, and dropped the bags on the counter in the kitchen, which was on the right as soon as you came in. She glanced at her wall clock. "Yep, she's right on time."

Skylar set her bags down beside the other bags. "Are you telling me that she screams at the same exact time every night?"

"Give or take a minute or two."

An eerie feeling shot up Skylar's spine. "Don't you think that's a little strange? Have you ever gone to check on her?"

"For what?" Laurie shrugged. "Sky, the woman is obviously fine if she's still around to do it night after night. Maybe she's off her rocker or something. I don't know and I don't care."

"That sounds lovely coming from a future doctor. Remind me never to admit myself to the hospital where you end up practicing."

"Very funny. Want a wine cooler?" Laurie asked as she took a four-pack of them out of one of the bags.

"Sure, why not. Mind if I check out your place?"

"Sky, don't be silly. We've been friends since junior high."

Skylar went into Laurie's living room and sat down on the sofa.

"So what do you think about my place?" Laurie asked as she sat down beside her and handed her a wine cooler.

"What do I think about what?"

"My place."

Skylar looked around the apartment. "What can I say? It's an apartment. The furniture is nice, but this is the same furniture you had in the last two places you broke the lease on."

Laurie sighed. "Don't remind me. My credit rating is screwed for life, and my growing mountain of school loans is only making it worse."

"I'm surprised they even rented you a place. They must not have checked your ass out good."

They both laughed.

"Whatever, tramp. You're just jealous."

"Of this building? You're tripping." Skylar took a sip of her wine cooler. "Have you ever met her?"

"Who?"

"The old woman who screams."

"Yeah, I met her once. I went door to door and introduced myself to everyone on this floor when I moved in three weeks ago. I decided not to go through all four floors, because I probably won't be here long."

Skylar smirked. "No big surprise to me. Just until you get behind in your bills enough for them to evict you, huh?"

"Hey, I like to stay one step ahead of them. I'll be damned if I'm going to have all my worldly belongings—how little of them there are—sitting on the curb."

"How old is she?"

"Who?"

"Damn, Laurie, are you doing horse or something? I'm talking about the old woman."

"Oh, she's older than just about any damn body I've ever seen. I didn't ask her age because—"

"You don't care. I know. So what about your other neighbors? They cool?"

Laurie picked up the remote control off the coffee table and turned on the television. She could not afford cable, and she quickly grew frustrated flicking through the channels as she replied, "I guess, for the most part. Some of them seem kind of freaky."

"What do you mean by 'freaky?'"

"Damn, Sky, you're full of questions tonight. Did you come over here to keep me company and to help me finish unpacking or to interrogate me?"

Skylar looked around the room. "I don't see any boxes that need unpacking."

"That's because I have them all shoved in my bedroom, Miss Smarty Pants. There's so much shit in there that I can barely crawl into my bed."

"Sounds like we have a long night ahead of us, then. But answer my question first. How are your neighbors freaky?"

"Well, there's Agina the screamer, who you know about already. Then there's Nikki who lives in three-A. She's a stripper by night and a schoolteacher by day. Then there's—"

"Get out of town! A stripping schoolteacher?"

"Sky, loosen up. Everybody has bills to pay, and I'm not one to question how they pay them as long as they aren't hurting me. Know what I mean?"

"I guess," Skylar replied. "So who else?"

"Oh, I saved the best for last. Apartment three-H. Tall, sexy, hopefully not dating anyone seriously."

"Damn, who is he?"

"My landlord, Sangue."

"What kind of name is Sangue?"

"I don't know, but his name could be Vicky and I would still be trying to ride his dicky."

"Um, I don't know if I'm old enough for this conversation."

"You are not even fooling me, Sky. I was there the night you lost your virginity, heifer, and you've been overusing that pussy ever since."

Skylar giggled. "I didn't realize there was such a thing as pussy overusage."

"If there is such a thing, then you're damn sure guilty of it."

"What nationality is this Sangue person?"

"Looks like a brother to me. But he does have this exotic look about him."

"So describe him."

"He's tall, *really tall*, and you know how I love a tall-ass man."

"That's because you're so short," Skylar chided. "Tall women like me just pray to find someone our same height."

"Sky, you're five-ten, not six-six. Imagine how the professional female basketball players must feel."

"They don't have a problem finding men, because they hang out with pro male players who are even taller than they are."

"Good point. Anyway, Sangue is tall; he has this bronze complexion, these black eyes that look like diamonds, and a perfect smile. He's not fat and he's not skinny; he's perfect."

Skylar checked out the way Laurie's eyes glazed over when she spoke of her landlord, and her curiosity was piqued. She had never seen Laurie so mesmerized over a man. Skylar was usually the one who dated a brother solely on the basis of looks.

"Do you think he's home now?"

"Who?"

"Laurie, your ass is either drunk or doing horse or just too fucking tired to think straight. I'm talking about Sangue."

Laurie shrugged her shoulders. "I don't know. He could be. Actually, most of the time I see him, he is going out at night. The same goes for all of my neighbors. It's strange, now that I think about it. I've never seen any of them leaving or entering the building during the day-time."

"Never?"

"Nope, but I haven't been here that long, and you know my tight schedule. Between school and holding down that shitty-ass job at the dry cleaners, I'm hardly home. That's why I still have all that crap in boxes."

"You said that one chick is a schoolteacher. She must leave during the day."

"I'm sure, but I've never seen her. She goes out dressed like a straight-up whore at night, though."

"Humph, you better make sure that you keep her at a safe distance when you do start dating."

"Sky, I'm not trying to date. An occasional fuck? Of course. Dating? I don't have time for it."

Skylar got up off the sofa, feeling a little tipsy after polishing off her wine cooler. She had never been able to tolerate her liquor well. She went to the front door of the apartment and opened it.

"Sky, what are you doing?" Laurie asked.

Skylar moved her head from side to side, trying to make out the letters and numbers on the different doors. "Which way is three-H?"

"Sangue's apartment? On the left. Why?"

"Let's go meet him."

"Are you crazy?" Laurie jumped up, pulled Skylar back inside, and slammed the door. "We're not about to go knock on that man's door at this hour. He might be sleep."

"Laurie, it's just going on nine-thirty. No grown-ass man is going to be sleeping at this hour on a Friday night."

"Good point. He's probably not home anyway."

"Only one way to find out." Skylar yanked on Laurie's wrist. "Let's go."

Sangue let out a deep laugh as he watched and listened to the women go back and forth over whether to come visit him. They had no idea that a miniature camera and microphone were hidden inside various items inside Laurie's apartment.

"Come to me, my sweets," he said. "Daddy's waiting."

He was delighted as the taller one won the debate and they headed his way down the hall. He was aroused by the aggressiveness of the one called Sky. He could do a lot of things with a woman like her in his corner.

Before they arrived, he pumped two sprays of mint breath freshener into his mouth. The one thing he hated about his present state was the everlasting foul breath. He despised it, but he was not about to change his diet to correct it.

There was a timid knock at the door. He knew that had to be Laurie, still probably kicking herself for even mentioning his appearance to her friend. After a brief pause, there was a louder, more anxious knock.

"Ah, you want me, don't you?" he said to himself, realizing that could only be Sky.

Sangue knew that he was attractive. No one had ever been, or would ever be, able to resist him. He could easily have bedded Laurie, whether she imagined so or not, but he had been patient. He had nothing but time, after all, and now his patience was about to pay off.

He took his time going to the door and hesitated briefly as he whiffed the air. They were both in heat. He could smell their wet pussies through the walls.

Sangue grinned as he opened the door. No one said anything. The two women just stared at him with their mouths open and their tongues hanging out once they realized that he was completely nude.

He saw the way they took in his more than ample dick and his perfectly molded body.

"Can I help you, ladies?" he finally asked as they continued to struggle to regain some composure. "Is there something I can do for you?" He glanced down at his dick, which was pointing at them like an arrow. "Anything at all?"

Come on, Sky. You're supposed to be so aggressive, he thought to himself. *Don't be afraid. Make a move.*

As if she had read his mind, Skylar managed to speak. "Um, sorry to catch you at a bad time, but Laurie was wondering . . ."

"Yes?" Sangue inquired. "Was wondering what?"

Laurie remained speechless.

"She was wondering where the closest library is."

"Library?" Sangue laughed. "Both of you came calling at this hour to find out about a library?"

"Um, yes. Since she just moved in, she's still trying to get to know the neighborhood, and being in medical school, she really needs to locate a library close by."

You may be aggressive, but you're not a good liar, he thought. *You came for this dick and you know it.*

Sangue sighed. "Come on in. I'll be happy to write down the directions."

Laurie caught her breath and said, "No, no thanks. I'll find it." She started pulling on Sky. "Let's go back to my apartment, Sky."

Skylar pushed Laurie off her. "No, let's not. Look, we're all adults here. Let's keep it real." She looked up at Sangue, who towered above her tall frame. "Why'd you come to the door naked?"

"Why not?" He ran his long, manicured nails over his torso and grabbed hold of his dick. "I have *nothing* to be ashamed of."

"You damn sure don't," Skylar replied, moving past him into his apartment and pushing Laurie in ahead of her.

Sangue was just about to close the door when he glared across the hall at apartment 3-G.

"Go to bed, Agina. Go lie down in your dirt and stop being so damn nosey." Even though his words were said so softly that they were barely audible, he knew that Agina heard him, and he could hear her, moving away from the door in disgust.

He shut the door and went into his living room, where the two beauties were engaged in a discussion about his elaborate belongings. What they did not realize was that all the items—from the paintings that lined the walls, to the gold trinkets lying around—were authentic.

"Do you like what you see?" He sat down on his antique armchair—his throne—and eyed them seductively. "Other than me, that is?"

Laurie cleared her throat while Skylar giggled and pointed to a painting of a field with a schoolhouse in the background. "Wow, *King's Crossing,* by Abigail Monroe!"

Sangue was impressed. "You know your art."

"I manage an art gallery. The replicator did an incredible job," she commented as she moved closer to it. "It almost looks real."

"Not *almost*, my dear. It *does* look real." Sangue smirked as he thought about the night, many, many decades earlier, when he had made off with the painting like a thief in the night. "All of my paintings look real."

"That's an understatement," Skylar agreed.

"Laurie, can you come here for a second, please?" Sangue held out his hand for her. At first she did not budge, but then he gave her the look that no woman had ever been able to turn away from. Within seconds she seemed to be gliding toward him.

She took his hand, and he pulled her down in front of him so that she was kneeling; his dick was standing at attention at her eye level.

"Laurie, do you know why I rented you the apartment?"

"Because it was vacant," she whispered. "And because you couldn't get another tenant any faster."

Sangue left out a thunderous laugh. "No, not at all. Apartments, even ones such as yours, are easily rentable in this city. I wanted you to rent it, Laurie, so I gave it to you."

She gazed at him in confusion. "But why?"

"Even though you have horrible credit and a tendency to skip out on rent, I wanted you to be near me. I knew this day would come, when you would do what I wished."

"What you wished?"

He nodded toward Skylar, who was leaning against the wall, witnessing their conversation. "My wish was for there to be two of you. I need more than one woman to satisfy me."

Skylar licked her lips. She had never been so horny in her entire life. Until that very moment, the thought of having a threesome with another woman—especially her best friend—nauseated her. But Sangue had changed everything. She knew nothing about the man, but she was willing to do anything to please him.

Laurie was still confused. "Satisfy you how?"

"Sexually," Skylar responded for him. "He wants us both to do him, right here and right now."

Laurie looked over her shoulder at Skylar in shock. Sangue grabbed her chin and redirected her concentration to his face. "Laurie, don't get weak on me now. The night is young."

"I-I—don't understand," she struggled to say. "Skylar just wanted to meet you and—"

"Laurie, shhh! This is what I want you to do. Take my dick into your mouth and devour it. Devour it like it is the most delicious thing you've ever seen or tasted."

"Bu-but, I can't," she said in protest.

Skylar grinned and started toward them.

Sangue was slightly disappointed but could deal with the switch-up. Skylar got down on her knees and roughly pushed Laurie to the side so she could get to his dick. He felt liberated as she took him into her mouth and began to deep-throat him with expertise. Each time she took his dick in and out of her mouth, the intensity of her speed grew as her cheek muscles engulfed him.

He did not even look down at Skylar. He kept his eyes fixated on Laurie, whose eyes were fixated on her friend trying to suck his dick clear off his body. What Skylar did not realize was that he could remain forever hard and explode in her mouth a hundred times without growing limp.

"Laurie, you want a turn?" he asked. He pulled Skylar off his dick by her hair and told her, "You can't be greedy and have it all. Laurie needs a turn." He held his dick, now glazed with Skylar's saliva, steady with one hand as he reached for Laurie with the other. *Game over*, he thought as she took her rightful place in between his legs and took him into her warm mouth whole.

He fed them both dick for nearly an hour and grew bored. They both swallowed—a blessing—and now it was his turn to taste them.

He led them both into his bedroom, where his custom-made, over-size bed screamed an invitation for them to lie upon it. He wanted to be the one to undress them, and he did, taking his time, often pulling off pieces of clothing with his teeth. He wanted to bask in their scents, for they would never be the same—never be so sweet—after tonight.

Sangue entered Laurie first. His large body seemed like a monstrosity plummeting into her tiny one, but she was all his. Her moans and eventual screams of pleasure only served to make him more excited, and he really tried to drill a hole right through her back with his dick.

As he had his way with Laurie in the missionary position, with her ankles wrapped around his neck, Skylar climbed onto his expansive back and licked and sucked everything from his earlobes to his asshole to the soles of his feet.

The three of them became one as the night progressed. After Sangue realized that Laurie could not physically handle any more of him, he moved on to fucking Skylar like she craved to be fucked: roughly. She was a sexy beast that countered each of his movements with one of her own. Laurie lay there spent, watching them out of the corner of her eye, both wishing for and dreading her next turn.

They took turns riding him until around three o'clock in the morning, both equally amazed that his dick was still hard enough to split bricks even though he had climaxed countless times, as they both had. Sangue was pleased with the night's offerings but knew that soon it would all have to end—at least that phase, for it would be time to move into the next one.

He heard his front door opening and thought, *That bitch!*

Nikki came into the bedroom just in time to read Sangue's mind and said, "I told you about calling me a bitch! Even after all this time, it's still rude."

Nikki was dressed like a streetwalker, in a short red leather skirt that exposed half her crotch, and a lace bra that was doubling as a shirt. She had tiny speckles of blood on the corners of her full, juicy lips. Her cinnamon skin was glittering in the moonlight that shone in through the windows as she took in the scene before her.

Sangue never broke his stride as Laurie rode his dick and Skylar rode his tongue. Since he could not verbally speak, he used telepathy. *Nikki, go lie down in your dirt. You've already fed tonight.*

She rubbed her stomach. "Yeah, but sometimes it's like Chinese food. An hour later and you're hungry again."

Skylar and Laurie were so much into the sex, they did not even notice that Nikki was in the room—despite her speaking—until she had climbed on the bed behind Laurie and started rubbing her shoulders, then her breasts.

Sangue sent Nikki yet another message: *You better not even think about it.*

Nikki threw her head back in laughter. "You can't do them both at once, no matter how much experience you have."

With that, Nikki yanked Laurie's neck to the side and buried her fangs into it. Laurie froze in time as she felt the pain. Fighting against it was useless, and she gave in quickly as Nikki started sucking her blood.

Sangue was pissed as he allowed his fangs to stretch out. *How dare that bitch come in and take one of mine!* He bit into Skylar's thigh, right at the verge of her vagina, and relished the mixed taste of her blood and the pussy juices that had been free-flowing for hours. Skylar winced and tried to push herself off Sangue's mouth, but he would not let her go. She could feel her flesh ripping as she struggled harder to free herself.

She looked in front of her at Laurie, who was facing her, and saw the death in her eyes. She knew that she was next.

"No!" she screamed. "I don't want to die like this! Not like this!"

Those were her last words as she toppled over on the bed.

Sangue raised his head from between Skylar's thighs as Nikki tossed Laurie's lifeless body to the floor. He hauled off and slapped Nikki so hard across the face that her neck cracked.

"You ruthless bitch!" he lashed out at her.

Nikki laughed. "You love it."

"What kind of wife are you?"

"I'm a good wife, that's what kind," she said. "All these pretenses we put on, telling people that I'm a fucking schoolteacher, and living in separate apartments so you can seduce these women who could never hold a candle to me."

"Nikki, I do this out of necessity and not desire."

"Bullshit. If that were the case, you would just settle for going out at night and feeding at random. You insist on playing these games, and they're growing old."

Sangue grimaced and decided to divert the attention back onto her. "Don't forget that I hear and see everything." He pointed at Laurie on the floor. "You told this latest one that you strip at night."

Nikki pouted. "I get sick of the same old same-old. I just wanted to make my life sound more interesting for a change."

"Nikki, you're immortal. How much more interesting can your life be?"

She pushed Sangue back on the bed. "Let me show you."

He slightly protested as she lifted her skirt, moved her thong to the side, and mounted him. "We don't have much time. Daylight, our coffins."

"There's time enough."

Sangue and Nikki fucked for an hour and then decided they were playing with fire—and would be, literally, if they saw the sun. They lifted the women and carried them down to the basement, where they kept the coffins for the new ones. It would be a couple of days before they resurfaced. All the other residents in the building were safely tucked away in their coffins except for one.

Sangue banged on the door of apartment 3-G after trying his key and realizing that the dead bolt was on. "Open this door, Agina!" There was no response. "You know if I really want to break it down, it's a walk in the park. I'm tired of replacing these damn doors."

He heard the dead bolt click, and the door eased open. He went inside the dark apartment and followed Agina into her living room, where she retook her seat in a rocking chair. It had been built for her by his father in 1586, the year of his death.

"Agina, why must you treat me so badly?" he asked.

She leered at him with pure hatred.

"Agina? Mother?" he said. "What's done is done, and there's nothing I can do to take back the past."

"I should be with your father. I don't want to be here. This is not right."

Sangue sat down on the love seat across from her. "We go through this every night, when you have those horrific screaming spells. When will it ever end?"

"It will end when I am with Robert. You had no right! You had no right to do this to me!"

"Momma, I was trying to give you something special. Eternal life."

"Well, I never asked you for it and I don't want it! You have damned me for all eternity, and I can't stand you, the one and only child I gave birth to. I was an old woman. You should have just let me go instead of coming into my death chamber and biting me like you did."

"But I love you, Momma. I need you."

"You have Nikki. She never wanted this life, either, but she's become just as appalling as you over time. It's not right to keep killing all these people, son. It's not right."

"I'm not killing anyone, for their deaths are merely temporary."

Agina shook her head in dismay and waved Sangue off. "Please leave me be."

"Not until you eat," he said, placing a jar of warm blood down on the end table beside her. "Not until you eat and get into your coffin."

"So you can lock me in there?"

"That's the only way I can make sure. I can't let you expose yourself to sunlight. I can't and I won't."

As much as she craved to let the sunlight blow her bones away into the wind as dust, she still loved her child. She was torn because, as scary as it was being immortal, she really could not be sure what existed on the other side, in the afterworld.

Reluctantly she took the lid off the jar and drank the blood, hating herself for savoring the taste as it trickled down her throat. After she was done, she obeyed Sangue by climbing into the dirt-filled coffin in her bedroom and allowing him to chain her inside.

One Week Later

"Shit!" Laurie exclaimed as she climbed out of the passenger seat of the silver Mercedes.

Nikki, posted as a lookout at the end of the alley, laughed so hard that she was bowled over in pain.

"It's not funny," Laurie said. "I hate it when the blood splatters all over the fucking place."

"I told you to stop picking the big, juicy ones until you get used to the technique," Nikki replied. "That one had to weigh at least three-fifty."

They had been having a good night; both of them had fed off two men each so far. The more they ate, the hungrier they seemed to become.

"You're a natural," Nikki added. "Sangue will be proud of you."

"Sky needs to be out here with us. It's so exhilarating."

Nikki sighed in disgust. "She's not about to come out here. But she's going to have to get off her high and mighty horse before long. No one is going to stand for her shit."

"Just give Sky some time."

"Well, that she has plenty of."

They both snickered as they headed back to the main street to pick out their next prey.

As Skylar stood in the window that night, watching two young female college students unloading boxes from a rental truck, she was full of hope and despair. What would this new life bring? What pleasures and what horrors?

Agina had just finished her nightly screaming spell. At first, Skylar had to cover her ears because she could not take it. Her hearing had increased tenfold and made the screams seem louder than a freight train making its way across her brain.

One night, her third night as an immortal, she crept over to Agina's apartment and knocked. She had never met or even seen her up until that point. Nikki had let it slip that Agina was Sangue's mother, which made Skylar want to find out about her even more.

Agina opened the door in a white cotton nightgown outlined with lace eyelets that had blood caked into the tiny holes. There was blood caked on top of more blood, and the dirt from her coffin had turned some portions of her gown a dingy brown.

She stared at Skylar for more than a minute in complete silence and then turned to walk back into her apartment.

"So how does it feel?" Agina asked Skylar, who had followed her and sat down while Agina reclaimed her usual spot in her rocking chair.

Skylar knew exactly what she meant. "It feels strange."

"I guess it does feel like that in the beginning. It's been so long for me, my memory comes and goes in spurts."

"How long have you been one? A vampire?" Skylar inquired.

"Since fifteen eighty-six."

"Fifteen eighty-six!"

"Yes, more than four centuries."

Skylar sank deeper into the cushions of the love seat. "You mean this will never end?"

"There are ways—very painful ways—if you are really determined."

"Did you make Sangue a vampire?"

Agina let out a hideous laugh that sounded more painful than anything else. "No, my son made me one. It might sound terrible for a mother to say this, but I wish that I had never had him."

Skylar's eyes met Agina's, and neither of them blinked for a moment.

"I love Sangue," Agina continued. "But the one who made Sangue convinced him that he would be the next master, and he has been believing it ever since."

Skylar thought of all the other people in the building—all of them just like her—and replied, "He is the master of many."

"Maybe, but he needs to stop. All the innocent lives he has taken. Look at you. Did you think you would die last Friday night?"

Skylar shook her head. "No, that was the furthest thing from my mind."

"Exactly; you had a life. What will your friends and family think has become of you and your friend?"

"Good question. That is something Laurie and I will have to discuss. We can't go out during the daytime, so I can't continue to work the same job. Sangue said I don't need to work. Is that true?"

Agina nodded. "Sangue has more money and valuables stashed away than most governments. You can amass a tremendous fortune in four hundred years."

Skylar had not thought of it that way. "So why this building?"

"Because he likes it, and what he likes is never up for discussion. He bought this building ten years ago and started pretending to be the landlord so he could lure people like . . ."

"Like Laurie," Skylar interjected.

"Yes, like your friend."

Skylar talked to Agina for ten or fifteen more minutes, and then Agina told her that she should get back into Sangue's apartment across the hall before he came home and found her in the wrong place.

Skylar felt bad because it was all her fault. It was she who had insisted on meeting Sangue that night, on knocking on his door, on engaging in intimate acts.

She had been fascinated with vampires since she was a child, but was not sure if she completely believed in them. She thought it would be incredible to discover that they really existed, but her feelings had always been mixed. She had often dreamed of a vampire lover, like the ones portrayed in films and books. They always seemed sensual by nature and in command of themselves and their surroundings. On the other hand, she had feared they would be bloodthirsty beasts who went around ripping out throats without a second thought. How ironic that she would end up as what she had always both loved and feared.

Immortality seemed so strange. Knowing that she would never die changed her total outlook on life. She would get to witness things that people could only imagine would be invented. She would witness the future. She would witness forever.

She was still not used to feeding, but assumed it would grow on her. Laurie had taken to it quickly, which was strange, because Skylar had always been the aggressive one. Laurie had been out with Nikki for the past three nights, masquerading as a hooker so she could feed off prospective johns in dark alleyways. They would bring warm blood back for her to drink.

Sangue went out by himself every night and came back grinning as he climbed into his coffin before the break of dawn. He said he loved her, but she knew that he told the other women that as well. There were more than two dozen women living throughout the building, all of whom he claimed to love, all serving him after he had added them to his stable.

She looked at the two moving in and yearned to open the window and warn them to get into their truck and drive away as fast as they could. A man had come calling two days earlier about renting the vacant apartment on the first floor, but Sangue had lied and said it was already rented. He was waiting, waiting for his next trinkets to show up. They had.

But Beautiful and Terrifying

Robert Fleming

It was the time of the American occupation of Japan, the early fifties, and the feeling of anti-American sentiment was growing like weeds among the locals who hated the coming of democracy and the loss of feudalism. There was a reverence for the old ways and traditions, which any foreigner could sense whenever the emperor, Hirohito, was mentioned. He arrived in Tokyo, a slightly decorated black American soldier, a grunt with personal orders from the big man himself, General Durston. Or at least, the orders came from a second louie attached to the general. There were killings of Japanese girls going on in the clubs near the American bases—nasty slice jobs, mutilations—and word had it that some colored troops were doing the butchering. Because of that, the nigger soldiers, as General Ike had occasionally called them when he was off duty, saw their leaves canceled, off-duty privileges yanked, and all fun vaporized with a blanket restriction to base.

"I heard the Nips grabbed two colored boys in Osaka and damn near cut them a new asshole when word about the slaughter of these yella gals got out," the lieutenant said to him, pulling him aside at the airport. "The big boys want you to wrap this one real fast. Things could really heat up."

"I know, sir," he said. "They don't want full-scale riots."

"Where did they bring you in from?" The white man, clad in a starched uniform, didn't look like some of the other soldiers committed to the reconstruction of the vanquished Land of the Rising Sun.

"Kyoto, sir."

"We spared Kyoto because it's some kind of holy place for these pricks," the lieutenant volunteered, twisting his mouth cruelly. "I would have dropped the friggin' bomb on the bastards, too. If I hear another person moaning about how we shouldn't have dropped a second bomb, I'll pull out my forty-five and blow their brains all over the ground. Do you think the Nips would have just dropped one bomb on us if they had it? They would have dropped one on every big city in the States. You know I'm right."

He didn't answer the officer; instead his eyes surveyed the widespread damage caused by the regular night bombing in the final weeks of the war. Much of the place was still in shambles. Sure, there were some reclamation projects going on, but for the most part, the devastation was yet in evidence. Yes, Yank flyboys had hammered the hell out of it, as Operation Iceberg, the battle for Okinawa, drew to a close. Okinawa was in spitting distance of Nippon.

"I know some of the others told you that I hate all colored because I'm white, but that is not the case," the lieutenant said bluntly. "I have nothing against you or your race. Still, I don't think your people could handle the pressure of combat, listening to those bullets whistling overhead, the bombs falling all around. That's just how I feel, and a lot of other whites in this man's army feel the same way."

Again the black soldier said nothing. His eyes flashed with serious disdain while he buttoned his lips and remained mute. He was not going to let the white man ruffle his feathers, regardless of what he might say, regardless of what might be implied by the humiliating words: *Nigger, why are you here?*

"I don't get it, just don't get it," the white man said, shaking his close-cropped blond head. "How did you get Old Man Casey to be your rabbi? You have no combat experience that I know about. Tell me. I won't tell anyone. Are you guys bed-buddies?"

Behind them, a couple of B-29s were coming down for a landing, engines roaring. The pilots loved the fact that they could fly these babies without any flak or small-arms fire zeroing in on them. Their collective noise drowned out the continuing interrogation of Davis by the now red-cheeked officer, who acted as if he would knock the cullud boy on his black ass if given the chance. White officers, both Army and Air Force, walked by on the tarmac, grinning and nudging one another, happy that one of their own was reaming out a lazy, shiftless coon—at least, that's how it looked on the outside. This Davis, a former supply truck driver.

"Answer me, Davis," shouted the lieutenant, the cords showing in his neck. "Remember I outrank you. How in the hell did you get Casey under your damn thumb? Answer me, boy!"

Davis knew this kind of race rage firsthand. He knew not to take the bait, what Command would do if he slapped the taste out of this cracker's mouth, how Old Man Casey would feel if he gave in to the "lower part of his nature," what this would mean to his military career in this segregated army. Negro leaders such Mary McLeod Bethune, Adam Clayton Powell, Walter White, and A. Philip Randolph bitched and moaned about the beatings and murders of colored soldiers throughout the country, some lynched in uniform, others attacked at army bases. Among whites, it seemed only a handful were willing to put it on the line for their dark brothers: political types Henry Wallace and Wendell Wilkie, money man Marshall Field, and novelist Pearl S. Buck. They wanted to see a new world emerge. This redneck was not one of them.

"I saved the general's life in Italy, and he found it in his heart to be generous," Davis answered, straightening his tie.

Suddenly, a jeep with two privates appeared behind them, and one of the men jumped out, snapping off a salute. "Sergeant Davis, you're to report to HQ ASAP," he said, taking his arm down. "There they are to present you with evidence and your new partner. You are to come with us."

Davis got into the jeep, followed by the private. He sat ramrod-stiff on the backseat, never looking back, never acknowledging the lieutenant, who stood there glaring at him with burning eyes. God, he hated niggers, especially those who thought their shit didn't stink.

There was something sinister and evil about this case. The last chief American investigator out here to check things out was mysteriously struck by a bolt of lightning on a clear day as he left the grounds of a shattered temple just outside the city. The bolt shot through him from his head down with such force that it seared away his clothes and knocked him several feet into the air. When onlookers glanced up into the sky, there was no dark cloud to be found, so the talk started that there was a curse connected to the case. The soldier was dead at the scene.

"The guy was a son of a bitch anyway," one of the brass remarked when he was going over the folder of the murders. "He probably pissed off the wrong person."

However, the Japanese said it was another sign that the gods didn't want the Yanks in their sacred country—not even the arrogant Gen. Douglas MacArthur, who was running the whole show. He even bossed the emperor around. He changed the rules concerning their treatment of their women, outlawed the local gangs, came down hard on the black market, and even altered their traditional customs. He was rumored to have said about the murders, "Our boys have got to learn that fraternizing with the enemy, even with their women, has its consequences."

At headquarters, Davis met his new partner, Sgt. Gelb, who shook his hand, looking him square in the eyes, before holding out a manila envelope marked "confidential." He was tall, pale, with brown hair and exceptionally long arms and legs. His uniform fit him snugly, creases almost cutting to the touch, with his black shoes casting off rays. It took Davis several minutes to follow what he was saying. There was an accent, something regional, but he couldn't place where it was from.

"Sergeant Davis, we have a big problem here, mighty big," his white counterpart said slowly. "The general put us together because he thought we would be able to get this thing solved in no time. He has great faith in you and your abilities."

"Can I see the folder, please?" Davis reached for it.

Holding the folder, he walked over to the chair facing the door. The information was startling, even shocking, for it said that four servicemen, one Negro and three white, were missing, and four B-girls, Japanese, were dead. Killed in the most horrible manner. Tortured, branded, and strangled. What raised his eyebrows was that each woman had been sliced open, her heart removed, and the lips of her vagina stitched crudely shut, but not before there had been a great deal of sexual trauma. All the girls, ages seventeen to twenty-two, were found positioned on the bed, body in a natural sleeping pose, legs straight, with her hands folded neatly across the chest. Oddly, there was very little blood at the crime scene.

"Have you read this, Sergeant Gelb?" Davis asked, sweat coming to his forehead. "What do you make of it?"

"Don't know. It's strange as hell. Either some devil worshippers or a lone madman. The brass want this mess cleaned up before it starts an international incident. I don't like it. I think there's much more to this than what is on these pages—much more."

Davis scratched his head, looking at the black-and-white photographs of each female victim, stunned by the brutality of the deed. "Can I ask you something?"

"Yes, what?"

"What in the hell happened to the soldiers?" That was the part that bothered him most—the disappearing soldiers. What was that about?

Gelb sat on the corner of a desk, watching the men walking briskly back and forth, some task in mind. Their movement underlined their efficiency, intent, and discipline. There were no goldbricks among these handpicked guys, not at all. He waited until there was no one near them before he spoke on the most mysterious element of the case, the detail of the murders that had everyone baffled.

"Pretty decent bods on those lovelies," Gelb remarked, giving a leer. "Even if they are yellow. I like them small like that. Compact, bite-size morsels."

"So what happened to them?" Davis repeated.

A look of horror crossed Gelb's pale face, spots of blood appeared on his cheeks, and his hands trembled ever so slightly. Davis noticed the officer's Adam's apple working frantically as if his throat had seized up on him. A few seconds passed before the white man could reply. The officer knew something, something that ate away at his sense of calm, and his eyes widened as if the corpses of the mangled Japanese women were right in the room with him. Whatever he knew, he wasn't saying.

"All I know is that something weird happens every time one of these yellow girls get killed," he said in a hoarse whisper. "There's never . . . never . . . anything left of the men. No body . . . no gun . . . no dog tags. Nothing . . . nothing but their shoes."

"Their shoes?" Davis couldn't believe it.

"Yes, don't you think that's odd?" Gelb said sadly. "Just their damn shoes."

Davis was shaken, mortified for a moment; then he said, "I think we should start with the Tojo, the bar where a lot of these girls worked. What do you think?"

"Sure, you go on over there and I'll join you later," Gelb said. "I've got to talk to a man here. Save me a seat. We'll turn the place inside out until we find out what's what. Stay put until I get there. Okay?"

Davis nodded, reached for his gun, removed the clip, and slid it back into place. "Don't worry. I'll be there when you get there. But don't take too long."

The grapevine said service was first-rate, the girls pleasing to the eye, and the sushi and sukiyaki the best on this side of town. Most of the grunts ate there, watching the nimble Japanese waitresses moving effortlessly behind tables as they carried the hot food with a grace usually reserved for other trades. It reminded Davis of another place, Kyoto, the old capital with its bounty of temples, gardens, inns, and shops. As far as Japanese towns went, Kyoto was special to the men in the service because the women were plentiful and easy. He knew that most GIs only wanted to use the local women there for sex, especially the ones in the bars and the others who hung around the PX, as they counted the days before their tours ended and they could return home to their chaste all-American girls. But to these Japanese women, sex was about GI money—Yankee dollars—and cash meant survival. They flooded the cities from the countryside, where there was no work and life was hard.

"The Tojo is down that street; you can't miss it," a soldier yelled at Davis as he walked across the road. "The shouts and singing should lead you right to it."

He found it with no trouble. Once inside, he stood at the rear of the place, absorbing its boisterous Yank atmosphere, soldiers drinking and hollering, harassing the timid Japanese waitresses. Some older officers drank beer and teased the girls as they walked past, swinging their slim hips beneath the flowered kimonos. A few of the guys danced with each other to the music of Vaughn Monroe coming from an old Philco phonograph, his baritone groaning of love lost and regained.

"Sergeant, who are you looking for?" a white soldier asked, moving close to him.

"Not you," Davis replied, looking around.

"Want a table?" the grunt asked. "Keiko, a table for this dark-complexioned gentleman!"

One of the waitresses, a slender girl in a yellow kimono, smiled and led him to a corner table, which was all right by him. She deliberately sat him away from the others, not wanting any trouble to arise from a Negro mixing with the others.

Davis sat down, and soon the waitress returned with a bowl of rice and turnips, bits of chicken, and a bottle of cold beer. He whispered that he wanted some chopsticks, a bottle of warm sake instead of beer, and a small cup. Two white soldiers in a nearby booth laughed and poked their lips out, making them bigger in a racial slur. He ignored them and turned his attention back to the waitress.

"What's your name?" Davis asked, sounding as cordial as possible.

"Keiko, Mr. GI," she said. "Is there anything I can do for you?"

He pulled out a picture of the last Japanese girl who was murdered in a hotel not far from the bar. It just showed her face; her eyes were closed, and no sense of the horrible crime she had endured was visible. The victim looked so serene, so spiritual.

"Do you know this girl?" Davis asked. "They say she worked here."

Keiko shook her head.

"Look at the picture again," Davis insisted. "Look closer."

Keiko started to say no again, but something changed her mind. "Her name is Miyako. Very sorry I no know her at first. Bad, bad picture."

"What else do you know about her?" he asked. He wanted to be a real cop when he got out—if they allowed Negroes to be cops.

"Miyako, she special girl, not like others," Keiko said, a faint smile on her lips. "What happen her? Is she okay, GI?"

"No, she's dead." He said it with the finality it deserved.

Keiko swayed for a second, stunned by the news, then went on talking. "I know her from before. Her parents killed when American bombs come. I go with her to bury them. She not like the rest of us. Special . . . special."

"Yes, you said that," he said matter-of-factly. "What made her so special?"

"I only know what I hear," Keiko said. "She have powers. She could move things without touching them. Shut off radio without touch. Stop clocks, too. She could read minds even if you say nothing. Special . . . special."

Davis didn't know what to make of that. "When did you see her last?"

"Days . . . days ago." She was still grappling with the news of her friend's death. "A real special girl. She could make you pick up a glass if she wanted to . . . walk a certain way if she wanted . . . Somebody say they see her toss a broom down in anger and it turn into a snake. Real special."

"Did she go out with men?" he asked.

"Sometimes. Always with Americans, soldiers. Nothing but, I afraid."

At that moment, Gelb popped his head into the bar, whistled once, and Davis stood, thanking the girl for her answers. She stood there, still stunned. He walked past her and out into the street. He thought it was strange that this Miyako woman would go out with soldiers, especially after it was American bombs that killed her folks. Gelb was eager to tell him something.

But what Gelb said was nothing new. "The girl's name was Miyako, worked here at the Tojo, and no one had seen her for two weeks," the white officer said in a rush. "The inn where the murders occurred is near here. I got a tip that we should go there around twelve."

They got into the car, pulled out a map, and headed for the inn. Gelb drove slowly, not wanting to miss the address. The inn was in a very damaged part of the city, full of debris, and was one of a few buildings still standing. The soldiers got out, walking with caution, for several robberies had occurred in the area. They stood outside, across the street from the inn, hunched up against the chill of the wind, watching their timepieces.

While waiting for something to happen, Gelb told Davis, with a low rasp in his voice, about a certain Mr. Matsui, an old former priest, who warned him of a legend of a Japanese siren, a strikingly beautiful young girl, who possessed the power to seduce men and seize control of their wills and souls before loving them to death and taking them into the dark world. Davis laughed at the story, calling the postwar fable a fairy tale meant to keep the natives in line. He believed there was a human being responsible for the killings, nothing more, nothing less.

The legend, Matsui had said, went back to the Meiji Restoration in the late nineteenth century, after Japan was emerging from 250 years of complete isolation from the outside world. It seemed the first of such deaths began just after the foreigners started arriving. Hundreds of foreigners, or gaijin, died mysteriously. Matsui added that the siren was a demon clothed in flesh, able at times to assume the appearance of any Japanese woman, skilled in the art of love. She was the perfect instrument of death, the spiritual revenge by the ancestors against the foreigners, especially the American occupiers, for defiling the sacred soul of Japan. Sex with the demon meant death.

"The old man also said that once the seduction has begun, nothing or nobody can stop it," Gelb said, almost convincing himself of the validity of the story. "He said the men no longer wish to live in the present, so they willingly invite this demon into their lives. Furthermore, he added that this evil thing stalked her prey, waited for the most intimate moment, seized her victim, and absorbed all of him until there was nothing left, not even a husk of abused flesh. It was as if she swallowed her victims whole."

"Do you believe that crap?" Davis asked, feeling a bit uneasy.

"I don't know. I guess not." Gelb kept swallowing hard. "I'm tired of all this smiling and bowing—makes me nervous. I can't help but feel we're one big joke to them."

"Lieutenant, do you believe there's a demon who takes control of women and uses them for its purpose?" Davis followed up with another question. "Is that what we're dealing with here? And why GIs?"

The officer laughed. "And why not? First, we bomb the shit out of them with these atomic weapons and then we turn their world upside down. Who knows? Maybe the demon's a Red. Wouldn't that be something if Moscow and the Russkies were behind all of this?"

Davis didn't like anything about the case. Or Gelb. "Don't joke. This is serious. We have a killer out there, and we're no closer to capturing him than we were when we got here. What do you hope to find at this damn inn? It's probably another dead end."

"Ease up, Sergeant."

"I'm ready for whatever happens," Davis boasted, touching the weapon holstered at his side. "Demon or not, this baby will stop it in its tracks." Unfortunately, he didn't really believe what he was saying.

Hours passed. At five to twelve, a jeep pulled up. A soldier and a woman stepped out, hugged once, and went inside. Gelb and Davis let the couple go inside, stop at the front desk, and then go up to their room; then they followed. When they spoke to the innkeeper, he was reluctantly cooperative, saying he didn't know where they had gone at first, but a threat to shut the place down brought the needed answers.

They went up to the second floor, where the room was, careful not to alarm the other women and their clients. As they were about to knock on the door, they noticed that it was open, just a tiny bit. Just enough for them to see the occupants of the room. They stood and watched the soldier shed his clothes while the woman, in her bright red kimono, poured him a cup of warm sake. They could not see her face, only her back.

"All of you GI are in big hurry," the Japanese woman said soothingly, easing her garment away from her body, revealing her small, round breasts and a slender waist. "Me speak beri good, American-san. Make love all night. No rush. Take time. Go easy, Daddy."

"Sure, baby," said the white soldier, his ruddy Irish face obviously the result of drink. "We have a good, good time, yes?"

The woman seemed preoccupied, pouring him more sake. "Good . . . good time. Are you married, Joe? Got wife back home."

"Name's not Joe but Allan," the soldier said, panting a bit, fighting back a desire to toss her on the bed. "And yes, I have a wife back in the States."

"Very good, good to have wife," the woman said, laughing. "You real cute, GI."

He lifted his butt to let her remove his underwear, her hands going through the motions with a practiced grace, and then she took off the rest of her clothes. She was a real pro. Her long, tapered fingers seized his privates, stroked them for a moment, before taking him into her mouth. It didn't take her long to bring him close to climax. When she got him completely distracted with his longing for her, she sat on him, locking her legs around him as she ground almost manically against his pelvis. He moaned and tried to match her movement, but she was too much for him. His mouth opened to scream, but her hands covered it. He bit her, fighting for air, yet her hands remained fast. His teeth drew blood that ran between her fingers, along the back of her hands and onto her wrist.

While both men were excited at first from watching the coupling, they were also afraid, too terrified to run, their fear growing with the increasing volume of the dying soldier's agonized screams, a continuous background noise that perfectly matched the gruesome sight of the man's flesh, bone, and blood being slowly pulled by an unseen force into the spinning vortex of light and evil emitting from the Japanese woman writhing atop him. They also felt something like a strong electrical charge coming from the pair on the bed, powerful enough to stand the hair on their heads on end. Still, they stood there, watching, mouths agape.

"She's killing him, killing him," Davis said, moving to enter the room, but Gelb grabbed his arm. "We've got to do something."

"No, let's watch," Gelb said.

Suddenly, the soldier screamed at the top of his lungs, a tortured, ear-shattering scream, as if he were being turned inside out. The room filled with a blinding light and a fog of some kind. Gelb and Davis fell down on their knees, holding their hands before their burning eyes. There was another scream, more terrifying than the first. It was Davis who got to his feet first, drew his gun, and rushed into the room.

"My God, Gelb . . . Gelb," Davis yelled. "You've got to see this!"

Scared, Gelb ran into the room, where the sight of the woman left him with spaghetti legs. He wanted to run but could not. The Japanese woman lay on the body, her heart ripped open and that feminine space between her slim legs stitched shut, just like the others. Both soldiers stood close to the bed, surprised that her lover was nowhere to be seen. Only the man's highly polished black shoes, government issue, remained.

"Look at her face!" Davis shouted, holding the photo of the dead girl up for his partner to see. "Look at her!"

Gelb snatched the photo from him, surprised. "Damn, it's that Keiko dame. Same girl! Oh, shit, what's going on?"

Davis sat on the bed, found a cigarette from the pack in his shirt pocket, and lit it. "The general won't believe this. This is some mumbo-jumbo shit. Nobody will believe this." He heard Gelb throwing up his dinner in a corner of the room, retching like there was no tomorrow.

The dead woman's face slowly turned toward Davis, the features of Keiko slowly being replaced by those of another Japanese woman, someone they had never seen before. She spoke to him without moving her lips, her voice echoing in his mind: *For you GIs, we Japanese women are all the same, all whores; only our faces are different, and even then you cannot tell us apart. Remember this, soldier. Suffering reminds us we're alive, reminds us of what is right, and even death reminds us that there is a price for what we do to others. Remember what you have seen. And you shall be spared.*

Davis watched the process happen without saying a word, swallowing hard, about to piss his pants. By the time Gelb stood behind him, it was all over. It was the body of a Japanese woman they did not know on the bed, ripped, bled, and stitched. And all that remained of her lover was his shoes, neatly placed on the floor.

Gelb ran from the room, about to heave again, his legs struggling to keep him up. While Davis listened to his partner scramble down the stairs, he lit another cigarette, his hands trembling. He kept shaking his head. This shit was unbelievable. How would he ever explain this? How many Yanks had this thing killed? Why? Her words made no sense to him. Maybe it was because of the A-bombs dropped on Nagasaki and Hiroshima; maybe that was it. A cruel debt being repaid. Karma or some shit like that.

Another flash of light filled the room. He stared at the dead woman on the bed as she sat up, the hole in her chest closing, and the stitching between her legs vanishing. He tried to get up and run but found he could not.

The woman, now whole, placed her feet on the floor, smiled slyly, and asked, "What is your name, GI? You want good time, good, good time? Me make love to you all night."

Davis struggled to get up from the chair, but his body seemed leaden, like a collection of dead flesh, and then he screamed, screamed, screamed.

He Who Takes Away the Pain

Chesya Burke

"Get back in that bed, girl. You go on to sleep," Mama said, clinging tightly to her apron.

Hattie Mae let the curtain fall back into place and ran to bed, her tiny ebony feet patting on the hardwood floor. She scooted in next to her sister, Betsy, and snuggled under the tattered covers, awaiting Mama's kiss.

And of course Mama didn't fail her. Her lips were soft and moist despite the worn, tired look on her face. She sighed as she stood back up, holding her back. Evidence of a long, hard life, Mama always said.

"Now, you go on to sleep, girl."

The girl nodded and closed her eyes. She heard Mama cut off the lights and pull the door shut. It squeaked just before it had closed all the way. Mama hadn't pulled the door completely shut, Hattie Mae knew, or else it would have been too dark. Hattie Mae didn't like the dark.

But when she opened her eyes, the room was almost completely black. Except for the light from the hall and that from the street post outside her window, she could hardly see past her nose. Neither of the lights reached as far as her bed.

The shadows on the walls shifted and changed in the strange way that they sometimes did at night, and she stared, hoping to see him somewhere within them.

"What are you doin'?" Betsy whispered. She held her hand over her mouth as she coughed. "Mama's gonna skin you if she finds you awake again."

"I thought you were sleep. She'll skin you, too."

"Un-um." She shook her wobbly head. "I'm smart enough to play sleep. You ain't," Betsy whispered, elbowing her in the side. It didn't hurt, though; she wasn't that strong anymore.

The shadows on the wall shimmered again, and this time she thought she saw the outline of a man within them.

"I think I just saw him," Hattie Mae said with a smile.

She pulled the covers back and started to get out of bed. But her sister grabbed her arm. "He'll put pepper in your eyes. Now, get to sleep."

Hattie Mae heard Mama cleaning and washing the dishes from supper. She had just turned off the water when there was a loud thumping sound on the roof.

"He's here," Hattie Mae said, with all the excitement that only an eight-year-old could hold. She bounced up and down on the bed, making the springs squeak and moan under the strain.

Just then she heard Mama's footfalls coming toward their room. Betsy must have heard it, too. "Told you." Then she put her head back down, pretending to sleep.

Mama burst into the room, not bothering to turn on the lights, as she made her way over to the bed.

"Thought I said to get to sleep, Hattie Mae. He's comin'. Heard him on the roof just now. You better get on to sleep,' fore he put pepper in your eyes." She put her hands on her large hips. "Now, don't make me swat you, girl."

Betsy sat up, wiping her eyes this time, pretending to wake up. "What's wrong, Mama?"

But Mama knew better. "Don't play with me, girl. If you were really sleep, you would've woke up with all that bouncin' up and down. I heard it all the way in the kitchen."

There was another loud thump from the rooftop, and Mama almost jumped outta her skin. When she looked back down at the girls, Hattie Mae thought she saw fear in the old woman's eyes.

Mama smiled and bent down to kiss them both on the forehead. Hattie Mae reached out to hug her mama.

"Is he here, Mama?" she whispered into her ear.

This time she was sure that she had seen tears in her mama's eyes; the woman, who had grown old beyond her years, wiped them away fast. "I think he is, baby."

Hattie Mae smiled at Betsy. "Black Man's here." Then she looked to her mama and asked, "Will he take it away, Mama?"

"Yes, baby. He'll take it all away. Did you kiss you sister good night?"

Hattie Mae nodded her head.

Suddenly a shadow loomed behind Mama, completely engulfing her dark skin in its blackness, making her a shadow within a shadow. The room grew colder, and Hattie Mae could see her breath as she spoke. "He's here."

The shadow seemed to shrink into itself and form the outline of a man. A very tall, dark, featureless man. For the life of her, she could swear that he didn't have a face. The shadow man glided toward Mama. He moved with an unnatural agility and seemed to float on nothing but the air itself, and for the first time Hattie Mae thought that she should be afraid of him.

The man began to speak, his voice a soft whisper, "I'm here for your sick."

Mama moved aside slowly to let the shadow man by. She seemed to have a mixed look on her face: half mournful, half proud. As if she thought that just by doing this she had blessed them and cursed them at the same time.

And Hattie Mae knew from experience that was just what her mama thought, for the shadow man had taken her father, too.

The man reached her bed in just two steps, whereas it would have taken her more than ten, and slowly bent over and touched Betsy's head.

His fingers sank right into her skin as a sharp, bright light was expelled from the wound.

Hattie Mae closed her eyes. She didn't want to see what would happen.

In a few moments, she couldn't see the light through the cover of her own eyelids anymore. She opened her eyes. The shadow man was gone.

"Did he take it, Mama?"

"He took it, baby."

Hattie Mae sat up in her bed, afraid to look over in the spot where her sister should be—*had* been for her entire life. She slowly turned her head.

Betsy was gone.

Then Mama said, "God bless He who takes away the pain."

* * *

The lady nurse came that next day. She stood at the door with her sharp white pants and white blouse ("You can't trust a woman in pants," Mama always said) and her big black bag.

"Ain't no sick here," Mama said as soon as she opened the door.

"I would be willing to just check out your girl there." She winked at Hattie Mae. "What could it hurt?"

Mama shook her head. "She ain't sick. Don't need no doctor here."

"Oh." The woman shot a big smile. "I'm not a doctor. I'm just someone who wants to ease the suffering. That's all."

"We got him for that."

"I'm sure you do. But"—she smiled again—"what can it hurt? Just some time and a little bit of hope. It won't cost you a thing."

"Look," Mama said, "we don't need no healers here. Gettin' them riled up. Makin' them think that God ain't meant for them to suffer. Tryin' to turn them away from Him."

The woman shook her tiny head. "I just want to help ease the pain a little. That's all. Maybe save a life or two along the way."

"We was put here to die. Now, get. Ain't no sick here." And Mama slammed the door.

When she spun around, she caught Hattie Mae staring at her. "Hattie Mae, you get in there and do them chores. And empty that trash, girl."

Outside, Hattie Mae pulled the can behind her like it weighed a ton—and to her, it did.

Betsy used to do this, before she was gone, she thought. Now I gotta do it. *I hate doin' the trash.*

Just as she picked up the heavy can and tried to lift it into the bend, the weight was lightened and was lifted right out of her arms.

She looked up to see the nurse's pearly white teeth smiling at her. Her dark skin was a strange contrast to those bright whites. "Hi."

"Hey." Hattie Mae looked around. She knew she wasn't supposed to be talking to this woman, but she had to admit that she liked her.

They had lived in a place called Baltimore before they'd come here, and Hattie Mae knew that not everybody lived like this. Now she just wanted everything to be like it was before. She just wanted hope. But there was no hope; Papa and Betsy were gone.

"So what's your name?"

"Hattie Mae," she whispered.

"Oh, that's a pretty name. Boy, I wish I had a pretty name like that."

"What is your name?"

She smiled. "I have no name by which they call me outright. Not to my face anyway." She laughed, and her entire face lit up like the wick of an ignited candlestick. "But you may name me if you like."

"Well, I don't know. Ain't never named nobody b'fore. Papa said that pickin' names for us girls was the hardest thing he ever had to do. Ends up, he just named me after his mama, and Betsy after Mama's mama." Hattie Mae looked at the ground as if she had said something wrong.

The woman smiled. "Go on, you can do it."

"Well, how 'bout Joy? Always liked that name."

The woman thought about it for a moment. "I like that. Joy." She let the word linger on her tongue for a moment. "Joy."

"Maybe Mary, like the mother of Christ. Or Sara. That's in the Bible, too."

"I like them all."

"I really like Mary," Hattie Mae said, just as Mama opened the back door to their shotgun house, calling her name.

"Well, then . . ." The woman bent over so that the two were eye to twinkling eye. "Why don't you get back to me on it. Okay?" She winked.

When the girl watched her walk away, it almost looked as if she were walking straight into the sun itself. Hattie Mae got a warm feeling all over her body.

"Let he who knows pain and fear know him. Those with doubt in their hearts and hate on their minds will not see him." The preacher's voice boomed through the small church room.

Everyone sat motionless and quiet. Every once in a while a loud "Amen!" would ring out from the onlookers, but it did not interrupt the showman's flow.

"And do not be fooled by those she-devils with the short skirts and long legs. For they are the work of evilness. Man was placed here and woman came next to tempt him. But do not be tempted!" He pointed his bony finger into the crowd. "She will DAMN you."

He paused, looked around, eyeing everyone in the humble room. To Hattie Mae it seemed as if he held her gaze for an eternity.

"But He who takes your pain will come. And he will save you. All you must do is ask. Like a child on Christmas, you'll be happy. Sickness comes, and there will be those who tell you to run to those doctors. Those she-devils. Those unholy folk who don't give a damn about your soul, they only want your body. But that's sinful. If God wants you well, he'll heal you."

"Amen!" someone shouted.

"That's sinful. Sinful!" He ended his sermon on a high note, repeating that word with particular vehemence. "Sinful!"

The church members were spellbound, as they usually were when the man spoke. And now they shuffled out of the room, all lost in their own thoughts of sinfulness.

Pastor Zackaria was said to have the gift of sight, as had his father before him. And his grandfather had it, too. Hattie Mae and Mama walked over to the pastor, and her mother shook his hand. He held Mama's hand tightly in both of his.

"He came to us last night, Father," Mama said.

"Praise the Lord," the preacher said. "She's walking with the angels now, sister."

Mama nodded. "And with her father."

The days and months passed. Every now and again the woman without a name would visit, and Mama would slam the door in her face.

The outside world moved along as it always did, while the people stuck together on the tiny island continued to die.

Hattie Mae saw the nurse going to other people's houses, but they all shunned her, just as Mama had.

The girl had begun to overhear the adults' whispering about smallpox. She didn't know why, but that word had scared her.

They had said that some of the deliverymen had brought it over on the boat from Africa when they delivered supplies.

A pregnant cloud of hopelessness hung over the people. Night after night, He Who Takes Away the Pain also took the people's loved ones. One night it was Mr. Carson, the next it was Mrs. Black and her unborn child, and so on.

The schoolhouse was virtually empty now, for only Hattie Mae and three other children were well enough to come. And then it closed when the teacher, Mrs. Carson, went away with him.

That night the girl awoke to find him standing over her bed, his icy hand on her forehead.

She felt the sickness run through her body as he caressed her face. She felt the deadly presence of something older than time touching her soul. And she knew that she, like her father and sister, would be taken away soon.

The next day in church, there were very few people. Most of the five hundred or so people who had originally come here with Pastor Zackaria had either left or were too sick to attend. Hattie Mae knew that they, like her family, would never get better. Her mama had died during the night, and he had come to claim her.

She had tried not to mourn her—like Mama had instructed her before she died—but she'd cried like a baby alone in that house. She hated to be alone.

Pastor Zackaria also showed signs of the sickness, as he sat and spoke, telling everyone not to be afraid, that the end would come soon enough. But now the "Amens" had been replaced by the coughs and moans of the sick.

Just then the doors to the church burst open, leaving the splintered wood to hang freely from the weak hinges, and the lady nurse without a name walked in. She didn't carry her big black bag, since no one here could be helped anymore.

She walked—almost glided—to the front of the church and stood at the altar.

Although her lips did not move, the group could hear her voice clearly inside their own heads.

"The last of you has been infected now. You were offered the opportunity to help yourselves. To save yourselves and your children from the suffering of death and pain. But you refused." Still her mouth did not move, and her eyes blinked wildly. "He who takes away your pain—your children's pain—also takes away their lives. But"—she paused and held out her hands—"she who stands before you now could have taken away your sorrow as well." And with that she was gone. Her beautiful, magnificent light faded into a dull glow and then into a small, pin-size light, and then disappeared altogether.

The small group of fewer than ten people sat in silence for a moment, stunned, unable to speak.

Then the pastor's voice erupted, a hollow shell of what it had once been: "I ask you all now, what is pain without suffering?"

Everyone applauded in agreement, the horrendous coughs echoing throughout the dead room.

Hattie Mae looked up to the sky, hoping somehow to see the unnamed nurse. She dared to name her: Hope.

Bras Coupe

Kalamu ya Salaam

"**K**ristin, I love you," I blurted, sounding like I was trying to convince myself more than Kristin, even though I was sincere. I both wanted her and wanted her to know I wanted her. Nevertheless, like when rotely instructing a client on how to fill out a 941, at the moment I felt emotionally disengaged.

I snuggled closer. "Kristin . . ."

"David, you don't have to say that to get me to do it. I know you love me."

As I pressed close to her, all down my chest I felt her body stiffen. There was no smile on her face as my fingers traced the outline of her lips. She was distancing herself from me like I was the manager of a department where thirty grand was missing. I reached across her head and turned off the lamp on the night table. Almost as soon as the room was dark, she spoke: "I'm not staying tonight. I've got an early meeting and I want to be prepared."

I had been caressing the side of her face, down her neck and moving toward her breast when I stopped. Suddenly, I had the strangest sensation we were being watched. The light was out and we were alone, but it felt like Kristin's conscience was standing by the side of the bed, auditing us. I imagined an unemotional specter with PDA in hand intently and efficiently noting the details of every movement of two overeager people who were groping in the dark, searching for the right words to say to each other, determinedly trying to discover the right touches to unlock passion in each other.

I wanted to say, Kristin, what's the real reason you're not staying? I wanted to say, Kristin, are you tired of sleeping with me? Maybe you want out of this relationship. Maybe you don't know where this relationship is headed. God knows I don't know.

She placed my hand over her breast. "Come on, hurry up. I want to leave before ten."

I didn't want to hurry up. I wanted to take it slow, like they say women prefer in those self-help sex manuals Kristin furtively reads. I don't know why people even read those books—the procedures never work like they say. Even the ones with pictures don't work. It's a case study of diminishing returns. You try all that stuff, and afterward, all you've managed to accomplish is, you've "tried stuff." The profit margin's too thin when you only accrue an extra penny's worth of pleasure for every dollar of time you invest in reaching the ultimate climax.

She reached down and touched my dick. "You're not hard." She gently tugged at it. "Oh, David . . ." An exasperated exclamation, and then suddenly she scooted beneath the thin sheet covering us, and I felt her take me in her mouth.

Please hurry up and get hard, I vainly instructed my dick.

It didn't.

After a minute or so, she gave up, pulled the covers back, and sat up in bed. So instead of me asking her what was wrong, she was checking on me. "Honey, what's wrong?"

I could feel my dick, limp against my thigh. "Nothing."

"Nothing," she softly repeated my lie like a proctor giving you a second chance to admit you cheated on a test. Then, with the adroitness of a prosecution lawyer waving a key piece of evidence before the jury, she reached under the covers and fingered my dick. "Yes, there is."

I felt like I had been caught with a signed blank company check in my wallet. Kristin had the uncanny ability to make me feel guilty about wanting to enjoy sex with her.

"Maybe I'm just trying too hard." Upon hearing my words, she immediately moved her hand.

"Oh, David," she said as she leaned over and kissed me. I didn't respond to her kiss.

I wasn't looking for pity, and besides, it wasn't me taking the perfunctory approach. "I'm all right."

I loved Kristin, but I wasn't fully comfortable in bed with her yet. She would do whatever I asked her to, but I always had to ask. I could never get a sense of what, if anything, she really wanted. Our relationship was humming along like a chain of hardware stores: efficient, neat, well stocked, well managed, and totally without excitement.

The lamplight blazed on. I turned my head into the pillow. The light physically hurt my eyes. After the metallic click of the lamp there was a long silence.

"Did you hear about the shooting?"

So that's what it was that was bothering her. God, somebody was always getting shot.

"They"—she paused briefly to let the weight of the loaded single syllable sink in—"shot this lady's baby. My God, they shot a baby. None of us are safe."

"What color was the baby?"

"What difference does it make?" She misunderstood me. That was precisely my point—color shouldn't make a difference, but I knew that color was what she was really concerned about and not murder. "It was an innocent baby. Somebody has got to do something."

"What color, Kristin?"

"They didn't show the baby on television . . ."

"What was the child's name?"

"Etienne."

I turned my head away and looked at the wall. I knew what was coming next, the same old white-black issue. I didn't feel like arguing about the color of a dead baby and whether color made a difference.

"David, why did you turn away while I was talking? You make me feel everything I say is so wrong."

The words I didn't dare let out of my mouth played loud and clear in my head: because if I turn around and tell you how racist you're acting, we'll end up arguing with each other, and I don't feel like fighting. The truth is, you're upset because the baby was white. If the baby had been black, you might or might not have said anything, but you certainly wouldn't have felt threatened. You . . .

"I know you think I don't like blacks, but that's not it. David, I'm scared."

"I know. I'm scared, too," I agreed, except my fear wasn't for my personal safety. My fear was that blacks and whites would never get beyond being black and white—separate, unequal, and distrustful of each other.

"If you're scared, why did you move into this neighborhood? Something like fighting fire with fire?" I didn't answer, and Kristin chattered on, barely pausing for a response to her rhetorical question. "Soon as the sun goes down, the only people walking around outside are . . ."

I turned over slowly, lay on my back, and covered my eyes with my forearm. "Are what? Murderers? Muggers? Rapists? Thieves?"

"You said yourself that some of these people don't even like the idea of you living in their neighborhood."

"I'm really sorry to hear about that baby." I uncovered my eyes and reached out my hand to touch her knee. She covered my hand with a firm grip.

"My brother says I should get a gun if I'm going to keep spending time with you."

"I bet your brother Mike owns every Charles Bronson video ever made and carries a long-barreled forty-four like he's Dirty Harry, or is it David Duke?" My accusation hung in the air like a fart.

I could see her wanting to recoil, but, like being trapped in one of those small interrogation rooms that IRS agents use for audits, there was nowhere to run and she had run out of documentation to prove her innocence. "Kristin, you don't have to come here unless you want to."

"I want to be with you." Our eyes locked and searched each other until I turned my head and flung my forearm back across my face. Kristin started her well-rehearsed sales pitch. "Besides, it's senseless for me to come pick you up, take you to my place, then bring you back to your place, and then drive back to my place."

"That's right."

"And you refuse to buy a car."

"That's right. My bike and the buses do me just fine."

"So obviously, if we're going to be together, I have to come see—"

"At least until y'all get bus service out there in civilized Metairie."

"David, I'm not complaining about coming to see you. I was just talking about the safety issue."

"Has anything ever happened to you around here, or to me? Has anybody even so much as said something out of line?"

"David, it only has to happen once . . . and then . . . then you're ruined for life."

"You only die once."

Why did I say that? I have to learn to control my mouth.

"Why did you say that? Mike says you have a death wish."

"So your brother Mike has given up the family construction business to become a psychologist, huh?" She flinched at my parry but continued her offensive.

"I told you about Ann Sheridan, didn't I?"

"Yes."

"She'll never be right again."

We were about to get into a bad scene. This was one of those classic dilemmas: You're callous if you don't sympathize with the victim, and you're a bleeding heart if you criticize the routine stereotyping. I felt like I was trying to talk to a client who was also a good friend and who was trying to get me to help him cheat on his taxes. I guess I could say, "Let's not go there; it's not healthy." Or I could sympathize—being raped is a terrible, terrible thing.

"She's seeing a psychiatrist. She stays pumped full of drugs. And she can't even stand to be in a room with a black man." Clearly this was going to be one of those evenings when all our time in bed would be spent talking about the major issues of the day rather than more productive and more pleasurable pursuits.

"Hey, you want a beer?" I bounded out of bed. Two hops and I was in the doorway. "Abita Amber." I looked back; Kristin shook her head no.

When I got back from the kitchen, Kristin was lying still with the covers pulled tightly around her. I stood looking down at the trim form shrouded in my ice blue sheet. I had been so smitten by her from the first time I saw her jogging in the 5K corporate run.

"Hi, my name is David, and I just got to tell you, I think you're beautiful."

"David, I'm Kristin. Your flattery is appreciated, but you said it so easily, I'm sure I'm not the only girl who's heard that today."

"Look, I'm not from here. How does one get to talk to a girl like you?"

"Do you want to talk to a girl like me, or do you want to talk to me?"

"Touché." We had walked in silence for a moment, catching our breath. Then we started talking, and we talked and talked, and talked some more. And now here we are, several months later.

As the immediate past of our getting together jetted through my mind, I concentrated on Kristin's hairline and on the upper half of her face, which was the only visible part of her. Her eyes were closed, but I knew she was awake.

"Suppose it happened to me?" she said, picking up the conversation where we had left off when I tried the let's-drink-a-beer evasion. Her voice was partially muffled by the sheet, but the import of her question came through unimpeded.

I put the beer bottle down on top of Ed McMahon's smiling face on the Publishers Clearinghouse envelope announcing that I had won $30 million. At least the worthless envelope made a convenient temporary coaster. Usually that junk went straight from the mailbox into the front-room trash can, but Kristin insisted that I ought to reply because "Who knows? You can win a lot of money." As soon as she leaves, it's trashville for that scam.

"Don't think like that," was my reply to her question as I leaned over and pulled the sheet down so that I could see her whole face.

"I can't help it. I'm a woman. You're a man. You just don't know."

I sat down facing the foot of the bed, one foot on the floor, my left leg drawn up next to Kristin.

"Every time I leave here after dark, it's traumatic." Ignoring the strain in her voice, I turned, leaned over, brushed back her auburn hair from the side of her face, and lovingly surveyed her facial features. She was ravishing.

The subtle scent of an Italian perfume wafted intoxicatingly upward from the nape of her neck. The milk white orb of a perfect, polished pearl stud earring highlighted her porcelain smooth, golden-colored facial skin, which was cosmetized with a deft finesse that made it almost impossible to tell what was flesh and what was foundation.

New Orleans women, the mixture of French, Italian, English, Indian, black, and God knows what else, gave a new meaning to feminine pulchritude. She had a classic Roman nose and a pert mouth whose corners ended in a slight upturn that almost made it impossible for her to frown. The attractiveness of Kristin's almond-shaped light brown eyes nearly hypnotized me, and made it hard to respond to what were clearly some serious issues that she wanted to talk about.

"Sometimes, when I get home, I have nightmares thinking about whether somebody has broken in and . . ."

"And what, shot and robbed me or something?"

"Yes."

"Is that why you always call in the morning?"

"Yes."

"I'll be sure to phone you if something happens to me," I tried to joke.

"David, what are we going to do?"

"Try to keep on living. Try to love each other. Try to make this city a better place."

"That all sounds so noble, but I keep thinking about that baby and about Ann."

"Don't think about it."

"That baby wasn't thinking about it and now he's dead. Before it happened to Ann, she never thought about it. I'm not an ostrich. I can't just stick my head in the sand and forget about it." I had to smile at that and hold my sarcasm in check. I had started to say, "That's exactly what you're doing by living in Metairie."

After a short pause, Kristin continued, "Why do they act like that? They have to live here, too. Can't they see that . . ."

"Kristin, sweetheart, we're all in this together," I whispered while running the back of my fingers up and down her forearm.

"No, we're not. We're the ones who have everything to l . . ." Her vehemence indicated a real feeling of being wronged.

It never seems to occur to many of us that black people suffer more from crime than we do. "You know the overwhelming majority of murder victims are black. You know most of the rape victims are black . . ."

"I know about Etienne. I know Ann."

"I bet Ann was crazy long before that guy raped her," I said under my breath. Before she could ask me to repeat what I never should have uttered aloud in the first place, I tried to change the subject. "Come here," I said as I slid beneath the covers and pulled her toward me. Outside, somebody was passing with some bounce music turned up to 15. Bounce was that infectious New Orleans variation on rap that featured chanted choruses over modern syncopated beats. I felt Kristin stiffen in my arms as the music invaded the atmosphere of my bedroom.

"I don't know how you stand it," she said into my chest.

"It's just music," I responded while rubbing my face into her hair.

"I'm not talking about the music."

"What are you talking about?" I asked, pulling back slightly so I could read her physical expressions.

"Not knowing when one of them—"

"Them. Them! Who is them? You mean a black person?" I questioned while disassembling our embrace and stretching my arms upward.

She propped up on one elbow and spoke down to me. "No, I mean one of those crazy young black guys, the kind who would shoot you for a Swatch watch."

I looked her directly in the eyes. "You mean the kind who listens to that music we just heard?"

Kristin didn't answer. After a few seconds, I turned away briefly at the same time that Kristin reclined and twisted her head to stare up at the ceiling. I watched her and waited for her reply for about forty-five seconds. Although she didn't say anything, something was clearly going through her mind. Her eyes were darting quickly back and forth like she was checking figures in a set of books against figures on an adding machine tape. I finally broke the silence with a dare. "Penny for your thoughts."

She responded while still looking up at the ceiling, "Honest injun?" That was our playful code to initiate a series of questions and answers with no holds barred.

Now we were both looking at the plaster ceiling with the swirl design—I wish I could have seen how those plasterers did that. "Shoot your best shot," I said, my eyes still following the interlocking set of circular patterns as I reached out to hold Kristin's hand.

"Mike says you probably moved to Treme because you've got a black girl on the side." She paused as the gravity of her words tugged at a question I knew was coming sooner or later. Her grip on my hand involuntarily tightened slightly. "Have you ever done it with a black girl?"

"Yes."

Her hand went limp, and I heard her exhale sharply. I turned to look at her. She frowned, closed her eyes, and spoke softly, barely moving her quivering lips. I wouldn't let her hand go, even though she was obviously a bit uncomfortable interrogating me and touching me at the same time.

"When?"

"Five years ago, in college."

She turned now and focused intently on my eyes. "That was the last time?"

"Yes."

"Do you . . . do you . . . I mean, Mike says . . ."

"I'll answer any questions you have, Kristin, but I won't answer Mike's questions. I'm not in love with Mike."

Silence.

My turn.

"You want me to compare doing it with you to doing it with a black girl, don't you?" Her face tensed. She pulled her hand away.

Silence.

There, it was out in the open. "If you want to know, you have to ask."

Silence. She rolled onto her side, faced me, and used her cherry red lacquered fingertips to outline my short, manicured strawberry blond beard. She started at my earlobe, and when she got to my chin, she hesitated, sighed, lay back squarely on her back, and tried to sound as casual as she could. "Did you ever have trouble getting it up with her?"

"No," I replied quickly, almost as if I didn't have to think about it, but of course I had already thought about it when I discerned the direction her questions were headed.

A terrifying hurt sound escaped Kristin's throat; it sounded like she couldn't breath and was fighting to keep from being crushed. "I can't . . ." Kristin's words peeled off into a grating whine. "David, why . . . ?"

"Why, what? Why did I do it with a black girl? Why did I have trouble getting it up a few minutes ago? Why did somebody shoot Etienne? All of the above? None of the above? What?"

"I'm going home." She threw the covers back and started to climb across me to get out of bed. I grabbed her waist and pulled her down on top of me. She tried to resist, but she only weighed 112 pounds and was no match for my upper body strength.

"No, don't run from it. Let's face this. We can do this." I held her in a bear hug. She vainly tried to push away.

"David, stop. Let me go!" she hissed, struggling to break free as I determinedly tightened my grip. "Let me go."

Her small fists were pummeling my chest while I forcibly retained her in my embrace. She had been momentarily kneeling over me, trying to scamper out of bed when I caught her in midmotion.

"David, you're hurting me." I used my left hand to grab her right wrist and yanked her right arm. As she lost her balance, I rolled over, pinning her to the mattress. "Stop! Stop!" She started pleading, "Please stop. Let me go."

"Kristin, listen to me."

"No, let me go. Stop." She was tossing her head back and forth, trying to avoid looking at me.

"Kristin, that was five years ago. Five damn years. If you didn't want to know, why did you ask me?" We stared at each other. "Five years ago doesn't have anything to do with us to—"

"It has everything to do with us. That's why you can't get it up with me, because I'm not black."

I pushed her away, swung my legs over the side of the bed, and sat up.

"Did Mike tell you to say that?" I spat out the accusation over my shoulder.

After she didn't answer, I pushed my fists into the mattress and started to get up. I heard Kristin crying.

"Why . . . how do you think it makes me feel? I come out here to be with you and . . . oh, shit. Shit. Shit. Shit."

I stopped midway in pushing myself up and allowed my full weight to sink back onto the bed. Now she was really bawling. I looked over at the Abita, grabbed the bottle, and drained it. I sat focusing on the beer label and asking myself how did I let a couple of hours in bed degenerate into this mess.

I had drunk the remaining third of the beer too quickly. A gigantic belch was coming, and I couldn't stop it. For some strange reason, I just felt it would be disrespectful to belch while Kristin was lying there sobbing, but I couldn't help it.

The belch came out long and loud. "Excuse me," I apologized. Afterward, I looked over my shoulder at a heaving mass of flesh and hair—even after our tussle, her long, luxuriant hair flowed beautifully across her shoulders as though sculpted by an artist.

Her back was to me as she faced the wall, silently crying and sniffling. I didn't know what to do, what to say. "Kristin, it's not . . ."

"Give me a cigarette, please," she said without turning around, while making a strenuous effort to stifle the sobs.

I had an unopened pack of cigarettes sitting on the night table. Neither one of us smoked that much anymore, but after we made love, we liked to share a cigarette. I ripped the cellophane with my teeth, peeled the thin plastic from the box, and noisily crumpled the crinkly protective covering. I started to ask, "Why do you want a cigarette and we haven't made love?" but realized that would be a silly and insensitive question at this moment. I flipped the box top open and took out one cigarette. I pushed it back and forth between my fingers. As I lit the cigarette, I felt a sudden urge to urinate, but it seemed inappropriate for me to step away now. I didn't want Kristin to think I was running from her, or didn't want to talk, or whatever.

"Here." As I reached the cigarette to her, she sat up and took it without really looking at me and without saying thanks—or saying anything. She must have really been pissed, because she seldom became so nonplussed that she forgot her etiquette training.

I picked up the empty beer bottle and, at a loss for what to do next, began reading the fine print on the beer label.

I felt movement in the bed. When I turned to see what she was doing, Kristin stepped to the floor, smoke trailing from the cigarette she held in her left hand.

I felt like I was sitting for the CPA exam. Neither of us was saying anything, but I knew I had better come up with the right answers or this deal was off. I looked up as she stepped into the bathroom and partially closed the door behind her.

I saw the light go on in the bathroom. I heard her lower the toilet seat, and then the loud splash in the bowl as she relieved herself. After she stopped urinating, I heard the flush of the toilet and then nothing. Maybe she was sitting there, still crying.

I sat on the bed with an empty beer bottle in my hand. Damn, five years was a long time ago. Linda. I don't think either one of us was really in love. We thought we were. I rubbed the cool beer bottle across my forehead as I remembered those crazy days in Boston. I think what was most surprising was how unremarkable the sex was. I mean, it was good, but it just was. It was no big thing. No ceiling falling on us; the earth didn't move. And there was no scene about it. We did it and enjoyed it and that was it. Not like . . . I didn't want to go there. I looked at the vertical shaft of light paralleling the edge of the partially open bathroom door.

I think Linda caught more grief than I did. A lot of her friends stopped speaking to her. All my friends wanted to know was what it was like. Sex really doesn't have to be all this. I remember how nervous I was the first time and how she just said, "Look, I don't know what you expect and I don't care what you've heard. We're just people. I'm not into anything kinky. You will use a condom, and if I ever hear you talking any jungle fever shit, you'll be swinging through the jungle all by your damn self."

The thing I most remember is that she said thank you the first time I ate her out and she reached a climax. "I don't know what's wrong with me, but this seems like the only way I can get a climax."

I had tried cautiously to ask her what she meant, without being crude or rude.

"Head. Straight sex is okay, but I can only reach a climax when I get some head."

"Is that why you're with me?"

"David, don't believe that shit about brothers got dick and only white boys give head. And for sure don't believe that you're the only one willing to lick this pot."

"No, I didn't mean . . . ah, I didn't mean to im—"

"Shut up! You talk too mu—"

"David, I'm sorry. I kinda stressed out because . . ." As I snapped back to the present, Kristin was standing over me. I hadn't heard her return from the bathroom. I realized I had been sitting with my eyes closed, rolling the beer bottle over my face, thinking about Linda. ". . . well, because I was afraid of losing you. I know you love me. And I think you know how much I love you."

Yeah, enough to come over to the black side of town at night, is what I thought, but of course I didn't say anything.

"You don't feel like talking, do you?"

"No, I feel like it. I want to talk. Let's talk," I answered quickly. I opened my eyes and focused on her petite, immaculately pedicured feet. Her toenails were polished the same brilliant red as her finger-nails. Her feet were close together, and her toes were twitching ner-vously in the shag of my Persian blue carpet. Kristin was standing so close to me that when I looked up, I was looking right at her muff.

I quickly placed the empty beer bottle on the nightstand. I pulled her close to me, embraced her waist, and kissed her navel. I felt her slender hands caressing my head. Where was the cigarette?

"I know I'm not very sexy . . ."

"Kri—" I tried to turn my head upward, but she hugged my head hard to her stomach.

"No. Just listen. I've got to say this. I know sex is important to you, and I'm willing to try whatever you want to make you happy. Anything. Okay? Anything."

"Hey, babe, we're going to be all right. You'll see. We're going to make it just fine."

"Be careful who you love, because love is mad," was all my father ever told me about love. Nothing about sex. Nothing about under-standing women. Just "love is mad." We were sitting in the front room, listening to his Ellington records. He played that Ivie Anderson song where she sings about love being like a cigarette. And he played a cou-ple of other songs. And a concert recording of Ellington, employing his trademark suavity, telling the audience, "We love you madly." I don't know how many other Ellington fans there were in Normal, Illinois, but early in my life my father recruited me simply by playing records for hours as he sat in the twilight on those evenings when he wasn't running up and down the road selling farm equipment.

I guess I just wanted to be around him. He was so seldom there for any length of time, when he was there I did what he did. I listened to jazz. Mostly Ellington, Basie, and Charlie Barnet playing "Cherokee." I remember once Dad played Charlie Parker's "Koko." Dad said Koko was based on "Cherokee," but I couldn't hear any "Cherokee" anywhere. He laughed. "Yes, sometimes life can be complicated." And then it was back to Ellington and all those gorgeous melodies. I still have the record Ellington signed for us backstage at the Elks dance many years ago. Well, not really signed, because his signature wasn't on there. Just a scrawled "Love you madly."

"I believe you when you say that," Kristin intoned without missing a beat.

"That's because I love you madly and mean it with all my heart." It had become easier and easier to reveal that truth to Kristin.

"David, I just heard on the news that the casino is closing. What are we going to do?"

"Well, you're going to hold on to your job with the tourist commission, and I'm going to draw unemployment."

"I guess now would be a good time for us to live together. I could move in with you—I mean, if you want me to—and we could split the rent."

"A couple of months ago you were scared to spend the night; now you're talking about moving in with me."

"Only if you want me to." I detected a note of anxiety in her voice. Both of us were probably recalling that angry exchange we had when we first discussed living arrangements over dinner at Semolina's: "David, all I pay is utilities and a yearly maintenance contract; it would be a lot cheaper for you to move in with me even if you took a cab to work every day."

That's when I had unloaded. "I didn't move down here to live in a white suburb twenty miles away from the center of town. I know your family finds it a lot more practical, i.e., safer, to enjoy New Orleans from a distance, but if I'm going to live in New Orleans, I want to live in New Orleans. Besides, that's one of the main reasons the city's so crazy now."

And then Kristin had exploded with a prepared litany of rationalizations: "There's nothing wrong with wanting to be safe. I love New Orleans. I didn't move to the suburbs to run away. I live in Metairie because it's family property and . . ."

"Because you can't live uptown anymore, because your family sold their lovely hundred-year-old historic Victorian house," I had replied dryly.

"David Squire, you're just a starry-eyed idealist. You have no idea of how neat New Orleans used to be and how messed up it is now. . . ."

"Now that blacks run and overrun the city. Right? Now that they have messed it up and made it impossible for us nice white folks to have a really neat time?"

Kristen drew up sharply, as if the bright-faced college student who was our waitress had put a plate of warm shit in front of her instead of the shrimp fettuccini, which she hardly touched.

"David, let's just change the subject, please," Kristin had said in the icy tone she used when her mind was made up and, right or wrong, she was going to stick to her guns.

"Well, just think about it, David. I'm not trying to push you or anything; it's just that my half would help with the rent." Hearing Kristin's languid voice flow warmly through the receiver made me realize that I hadn't responded to her question, and that there had been several long seconds of dead air while she waited for my tardy reply.

"Okay, I'll think about it, Kristin. You know, this whole job thing has happened so suddenly, I'm not sure what I want to do. So I'm going to just cool it for a while and see how the chips fall."

"God, David, you sound so cool to say you just lost your job."

"Yeah, well, getting excited isn't going to change anything. Besides, I can get another job. Good accountants are always in demand."

"David, I've got to go, but I just wanted to call as soon as I heard on the news—"

"Kristin?"

"What?"

"I love ya."

"And I love you." The worry vanished instantly when I reassured her that our relationship was not in jeopardy. Her tone brightened. "I'm on my way to the gym. I could swing by when I finish."

"No, I'm all right." I heard the disappointed silence, like she was holding her breath and biting lower lip. Why was I being so difficult when all she was trying to do was reach out and touch? Besides, I had really come to enjoy her perky company. "But on second thought, babe, it would be great to be with you. Call me when you get back in."

"I can come now. Skipping one day of gym won't be the end of the world."

"No, no, no, no, noooo. Go to the gym. Call me when you get back home."

"I'll call you from the gym."

"S'cool," I said, slurring my signature sign-off.

"It'll be around eight-thirty."

"S'cool. I think I'm going to walk down to Port of Call and get a beer or something. Later, gator."

It was a near-perfect November evening in New Orleans; what little breeze there was caressed your face with the fleeting sensation of a mischievous lover enticingly blowing cool breaths into your ear. It would have been a waste of seductive twilight to stay indoors. I grabbed my lightweight green nylon windbreaker and ventured forth as though this evening had been created solely for my enjoyment. I didn't have to go to work tomorrow. I would hook up with Kristin a little later. My rent was paid. I had twenty dollars in my pocket and a healthy stash in my savings account. I didn't have a care in the world.

As I neared Rampart Street just before crossing into the French Quarter, indistinct sounds of music mingled from many sources: car radios, bars, homes. No night in the old parts of New Orleans was complete without music.

This is where jazz began. My father the jazz fan had never been to New Orleans. Satchmo and Jellyroll had walked these very streets. I looked up at the thin slice of moon that hung in the sky. "Dad, I'm here."

I knew he'd understand what I meant. He had been a farm boy who never really cared much about the land. What he liked was meeting different people. All kinds of people, but mostly people who weren't living where we lived. Dad would have loved New Orleans and the plethora of street denizens of amazing variety who seemed to thrive in the moral hothouse of licentious and sensual living that was the trademark of Big Easy existence.

Before I reached the corner, a police car slow-cruising down the street passed me. I looked over at the cops, one blond the other dark-skinned, and waved. Their visibility was reassuring.

When I got back from Port of Call it was fully dark. I should have taken my bike. Cycling was safer than walking. Moreover, walking through the quarter was more dangerous than walking through Treme, which was flooded with police once the casino had opened in Armstrong Park. I wondered if they would keep up the policing now that the casino was closed.

It was about twenty minutes to eight. I had casually checked my watch as I turned off Esplanade after crossing Rampart. When I got close to my place, I saw somebody had left a forty-ounce beer bottle on my stoop. I picked it up and routinely checked all around me to make sure nobody was trying to slip up on me as I unlocked my front door.

The alarm beeped until I punched in the disarming code—that was my one concession to Kristin. No, I wasn't going to buy a car, but yes, I would get a security alarm system put in.

I locked the dead bolt and flipped on the front-room lamp. I felt like some Dr. John. I put the empty bottle down, twirled my CD rack, pulled out Dr. John's *Gumbo*, slid it in the CD player, turned the volume up to six, and sang, "Iko Iko" along with the good doctor as I danced to the kitchen after turning off the floor lamp. I was using the empty forty as a microphone and moving with a pigeon-toed shuffle step. I ended with a pirouette and a slam dunk of the forty into the thirty-gallon kitchen trash can.

While pulling off my windbreaker and hanging it in the closet, I heard a faint knocking, but I thought it was one of the neighborhood kids beating out a rhythm on the side of the house. The knocking persisted, only louder. Who could that be? Nobody besides Kristin ever visited me. I jogged into the front room.

"Yeah, who is it?" I shouted out as I detoured to turn the music down.

"I'm Brother Cooper, man."

"Who?" I shouted through the locked door.

"Bras Coupe," came back the indistinct reply.

"I don't want none."

"I ain't selling nothing. I just wanna ask you something."

"What?"

"Open the door, please, mister?" There was an urgency in his voice that I couldn't decipher. I peered out the window next to the door, but the streetlights were to his back, and most of his face was in shadows. I turned on my front floodlight. I still didn't recognize him. His left hand was empty; I couldn't see his right hand.

"I ain't goin' do nothing to you, man. I just want to ask you something."

"I can hear you," I shouted back through the solid wood, dead-bolted door. I continued watching him through the window.

"Look, I'm just as scared as you, standing out here, knocking on a stranger's door, enough for to get shot. I know you don't know me, but I used to live here twenty-two years ago. I left town and I'm just passing through. My people done all gone and I just wanted to see the house I grew up in."

This sounded like a first-class line to me. He stepped back so that he was fully illuminated by the floodlight. "Look, I couldn't do you nothing even if I wanted to—I'm cripple." He twirled around to show me the empty, dangling right sleeve of his sweatshirt. He was probably too poor to procure a prosthesis. "If you got a gun, why don't you get it and hold it on me—I just want to see the house."

I was in a quandary. Suppose the gun thing was a trick to find out if I had a gun. Suppose he was planning to come back later and rob me. He didn't look like anybody I had seen in the neighborhood before. And there was this tone in his voice—it wasn't fear; it was something else. He pleaded with me, "I wouldn't blame you for not letting me in, but it sure would mean a lot to me to see the house."

"The house has been completely remodeled; you wouldn't recognize it now."

"If you don't want to let me in, just tell me to get lost. That's your right. It's your property now. . . ." Renters don't have property rights, I thought as I weighed his appeal. "But you ain't got to handle me like I'm stupid. I know the house don't look nothing like when I lived in it."

I said nothing else. He backed down the steps and stood on the sidewalk. A car passed, and he flinched like he thought the car was coming up on the sidewalk, or like he feared somebody was after him.

"You white, ain't you? And you afraid to let a one-armed black man in your house after dark. I understand your feelings. Can you understand mine?"

It pained me to realize I didn't and, worse yet, possibly couldn't understand his feelings. I had all kinds of black acquaintances that I knew and spoke to on a daily basis, but not one whom I was really close to. I had been here over a year and still didn't have one real friend who was black and not middle-class.

My mind ping-ponged from point to point, searching for an answer to his softly stated albeit deadly question. Could someone like me—someone white and economically secure—ever really understand the feelings of a poor black man? Especially since I wanted honesty and refused to settle for the facade of sharing cultural positions simply because I exercised my option to live in the same physical space with those who had little choice in the matter.

My pride would not let me fake at being poor, walk around with artificially ripped jeans and head rags, pretending I was down. Besides, when you get really close to poverty, you understand that poverty sucks big-time. You see how being poor wears people out physically, emotionally, and mentally.

These neighborhoods are like a prison without bars, and a lot of these people are doing nothing but serving time until they can figure a way to get out, which most of them seldom do. Especially the men. They just become more hardened, callous, and emotionally distant. My stay was temporary. I was not sentenced by birth, but visiting, one step removed from sight-seeing. Regardless of what I like to tell myself about commitment and sincerity, it was my choice to come here, and I always have a choice to leave—a real choice backed up by marketable skills that would be accepted anywhere I may go. I know that most of the people in this neighborhood have no such choice.

As if to distract myself from the meaning of this moment of conflict, I looked at the disheveled man on my sidewalk and wondered, had his father ever played him music and told him that love was mad? Obviously, his father had not sent him to college. Could not have. But the conundrum for me had nothing to do with poverty in the abstract, or even with letting this man into the apartment. For me the deep issue was stark and cold: Was I mad for trying to love the people who created jazz? If this man had appeared at my father's door, would Dad have let him in?

I overcame my fear and my better judgment, pulled out my key, and unlocked the dead bolt. I started to throw the door open, but realized that there were no lights on in the front room and that the hall door was wide open, exposing the rest of the house. "Wait a minute," I said firmly through the door.

I turned around, flicked on my black lacquered floor lamp, turned the CD player off in the middle of Dr. John singing "Somebody Changed the Lock," and then closed the hall door. I quickly surveyed the room to make sure there was nothing lying round that . . . Wait a minute—why was I worried about the possibility of a one-armed man being a thief?

I returned to the door, peeked out the window—he was still standing there—and then released the lock on the doorknob. I cautiously opened the door. "I guess you can come in for a minute." I felt my pulse pounding and struggled to remain calm.

He started up the steps slowly. His hair was the first thing I noticed as he stepped into the doorway. It was untrimmed; it wasn't long, but it was uncombed. As I surveyed him, I instinctively stepped back from him, and then I reached out my hand to shake. "My name is David Squire." Suddenly, I was assaulted by a distinct but unidentifiable pungent odor that I had never smelled before. He reached out his left hand and covered my hand. I realized immediately that it was a faux pas to offer my right hand to a man without a right arm. He seemed to sense my embarrassment.

"I'm Bras Coupe. Lots of people call me Brother Cooper." His hand was rough and callused. His skin felt leathery and unyielding. I looked down at his hand. His clawlike fingernails were discolored and jagged. When I withdrew my hand and looked up at his face, he was examining the room. He said nothing more and just stood there looking around.

Finally, I stepped around him to close the door. The scent that I had caught a whiff of in the doorway engulfed me now and wrestled with the oxygen in my nose. I had to open my mouth to breathe. I was certain I had made a mistake letting him in; now the question was how to get him out.

"You want to sit down?" I asked in a weak voice.

He slowly sank to one knee right where he was. After swiveling around so that he was facing me, he locked into what was obviously for him a comfortable posture. He leaned his weight on his left arm, which was braced against his upraised left leg. It was almost as if he was ready to jump up and run at a moment's notice.

"You do not use the fireplace." He raised his head slightly and audibly sniffed twice, his nostrils flaring with each intake of air. "No windows open." He sniffed again. "You don't cook." He rose in a surprisingly swift motion. And then for the first time he stood up to his full height. He was huge.

I backed up.

He laughed.

"I'm not going to hurt you. If I wanted to, I could have killed you by now."

As I measured him from head to foot, I couldn't hide my shock when I saw that he was barefoot.

"You wear your fear like a flag." He nonchalantly watched me inspect him and laughed again when my eyes riveted on his bare feet. "Show me the rest of my house, David Squire."

I was glued where I stood. I couldn't move. I had never felt so helpless before.

"Do you understand what you feel? You should see yourself. Tell me about yourself," he commanded.

I stammered, "What wha . . . wha—what do you want to—to know?"

"I already know everything I want to know. It's what you need to know about yourself that matters. Why are you here? What do you think is so cool about all of this mess?"

I couldn't answer. Somehow to say "I came to New Orleans because I wanted to get to know the people who created jazz" seemed totally the wrong thing to do. He turned his back to me and looked at my stereo system. "Do you have any of my music?"

"Wha—what?"

He stomped on the floor three times in rapid succession with his right foot, shouting, "Dansez Badoum, Dansez Badoum, Dansez Dansez." Then he spun in slow circles on his left foot while using his one hand to beat a complicated cross-rhythm on his chest and on his upraised left leg. Somehow, simultaneously with turning clockwise in a circle, he carved a counterclockwise circle in the air with his head. His agility was breathtaking. He dipped suddenly in a squat, slapped the floor, and froze with his piercing eyes popped out in a transfixing stare. I felt a physical pressure push me backward.

"I thought you liked my music." He looked away briefly and then returned his full and terrible attention to me. I was quaking in my Rockport walking boots. Neither of us said anything, and a terrible silence followed.

"Talk to me, David Squire."

"It's—it's about life," I stammered quietly.

"Eh? What say you?"

"Black music. Your music. It's about life. The beauty of life regardless of all the ugliness that surrounds . . . usss . . ." Instantly I wished I hadn't said that. It was true, but it sounded so much like a liberal line. Just like when Dad had introduced me to Mr. Ellington, I couldn't think of anything right to say. So, I said the only truth on the tip of my tongue: "I love your music."

"Am I supposed to feel good because you love my music? Why don't you love your own music? Why don't you make your own music?"

I had never thought about that. It didn't seem right. There was no white man I could think of who could come close. Even Dr. John was at his best when he sounded like he was black. When I looked up, Brother Cooper had his eyes steeled onto me like an auditor who has found the place where the books have been doctored. My mouth hung open, but I had no intention of trying to answer that question.

"After you take our music, what's left in this city?"

"I'm not from here." Words came out of my mouth without thinking.

"You're from the North."

"I'm from Normal, Illinois."

"Where did you go to school?"

"In Boston."

"Where in Boston."

"Harvard."

"Sit down, David Squire." Still in a squatting position, he motioned toward my reading chair with his hand. "You look a bit peaked."

I sat.

In a swift crablike motion, he scurried quickly over to me without rising. He touched my knee. There was nothing soft in his touch. It was like I had bumped into a tree. "Harvard, eh? Your people must have a little money."

"Most people think going to Harvard means you're smart," I blurted out without thinking. Putting my mouth in motion before engaging my brain was a bad habit I needed to lose.

" 'Smart' doesn't run this country. Does it?" He looked away.

I began sweating.

"Go relieve yourself," Cooper said without looking at me.

As soon as he said that, I felt my bladder throbbing. I almost ran to the bathroom, locking the door behind me. I turned on the light, the heat lamp, the vent. I unzipped my pants, started to urinate, and felt my bowels stir with an urgency that threatened to soil my drawers. I dropped my pants, hurriedly pulled down the toilet seat, plopped down, and unloaded.

I wiped myself quickly. I washed my hands, quickly. I threw water on my face, quickly. And then I looked into the mirror. My face was pale with terror.

"David Squire, come, I must tell you something before I go." At the sound of Cooper's voice, my legs gave way momentarily and I fell against the wash basin. My hands were shaking uncontrollably. I couldn't go back out there, and I couldn't not go.

"David Squire," the powerful voice boomed again, "open the door."

My hand trembled as I flicked the latch and turned the knob. I pulled the door open, and there he stood directly in front of the door. "Every future has its past. What starts in madness will end in the same again. My name is Bras Coupe. Find out who I am and understand what made me be what I became. Know the beginning well and the end will not trouble you." He looked through me as if I were a windowpane. I couldn't bear his stare; I closed my eyes.

"Look at me."

When I opened my eyes, I was in total darkness. I shivered. I felt cold and broke out sweating profusely again when I realized I was lying on my back on my bed. Now I was past scared. I was sure I was dead.

Then that voice sounded again. "You fainted."

His words wrapped around me like a snake. I felt the mattress sag as if, as if he was climbing into my bed. All I could think of was that he was going to fuck me. All the muscles in my ass tightened as taut as the strings on my tennis racket. From somewhere I remembered the pain and humiliation of a rectal exam when I was young.

My mother was sitting on the other side of the room, and the doctor made me lie on my stomach. The last thing I saw him do was put on rubber gloves. They squeaked when he put his hands in them. And they snapped loudly as he pulled them snugly on his wrist, tugged at the tops, and let the upper ends pop with an ominous clack on his wrist. "This might hurt a little, but it will be over in a minute." And then he stuck his finger up my rectum.

It felt like his whole hand was going up in there. I looked over at my mother. She didn't say anything; she just had this incredibly pained look on her plain face, which always honestly reflected her emotions. "It will be all right, David. Yah, it will be all right," she said, sounding the "Y" of "Yah" as though it were a soft "J"—her second-generation Swedish background was generally all but gone from her speech, except for the stubborn nub that stuck to her tongue whenever she was under duress.

What had I done? What did I have? The pain shot up from my anus and exited my mouth as a low-pitched moan. I was watching my mother watch me. I resolved that I was going to be strong and I was going to withstand whatever this man was going to do to me.

The man with his whole hand up my butt wasn't saying anything. He just kept pushing, and pushing, and pushing. I don't remember him stopping. I don't remember anything else except that, despite my best efforts, I cried.

And now, here I lay in the dark, awaiting another thrust up my ass. The anticipation was excruciating. My resolve to remain stoic completely crumbled, and I started crying—but not loudly or anything. In fact, there was no sound except the imperceptible splash of huge tears flowing slowly down the sides of my face and falling shamelessly onto my purple comforter.

Suddenly the bright light from the table lamp illuminated my predicament. He was standing next to the bed. I recoiled, rolling back from the sight of him. "Are you okay?" he questioned me. "You look . . ."

He stopped abruptly and cocked his head as if he heard something. After a few brief seconds he returned his attention to me. "They're coming." Without saying anything else, he turned and walked away toward the kitchen. A moment later, I, too, could hear a police siren.

And then it seemed like nothing happened. Just hours and hours of nothing. No sound from the kitchen. Nothing at all. My heart was pounding.

I tried to make myself sit up. It was like a dream. I couldn't move. I told myself to get up. But I couldn't move. I wanted to move. I wanted to run. But I couldn't move.

Eventually, I made myself stop crying. It took so much effort, I was almost exhausted. Suddenly, there was a loud knocking at my front door. The rapping startled me. I involuntarily let out a brief yelp of fear: "Ah."

Cooper appeared soundlessly at the foot of the bed. "Go."

I jumped up.

I was in shock.

The knock was louder. I don't know how I got to the front door, but when I got there, I didn't say a word as the insistent tapping started again. It sounded like somebody beating on my door with a club. Suppose this was one of Cooper's friends, come to do me in.

I glanced over my shoulder at the back of the house. Cooper had turned the bedroom lamp off.

I glanced out the front window. Two policemen were outside. One on the stoop, one on the sidewalk. I hadn't done anything wrong. Why were they knocking on my door?

"Yes," I said meekly without opening the door.

"It's the police, sir."

I cracked the door—I had forgotten to lock it when I let Cooper in. "Is anything wrong, Officer?"

"Yeah, I hate to tell you this, but there was a double homicide a couple blocks away, and we have reason to believe the murderer is still in the neighborhood." The officer spoke of two people murdered with the casualness only a New Orleans policeman could evince when discussing the carnage that had now become so common. "Have you seen or heard anything?"

I could have stood there for ten hours and not been able to honestly answer that question. I didn't really know what I had seen or not seen. At that moment I doubted my own sanity. Just then my phone rang.

"One minute, Officer—that's my phone." The phone stopped in the middle of the second ring, before I could answer the extension in the front room. It was too soon for the answering machine to pick up. No, couldn't be—I instantly rejected the notion that Cooper had answered the phone.

I had left the door open, and the policeman stuck his head in and made a quick announcement. "Sir, we're just advising everyone in the area to be careful and please call us immediately if you see or hear anything."

I dashed back to the door as the officer was talking. He was a young black guy, medium build, clean-cut, and he spoke with an air of authority. I was about to say something to him when I heard Cooper call out to me from the bedroom, "That was Kristin; I told her you would call her right back."

"Okay," I said, responding to both Cooper and the policeman. Before I could say anything else, the policeman was backing away from my door. I turned quickly, looking for Cooper, but it was completely dark in the back, and I couldn't see anything. When I turned back to the front door, the police cruiser was pulling off from the curb. I closed the door, pulled out my key, and made sure that I locked the dead bolt this time.

As I started toward the bedroom, I realized that I had locked myself in the house with Cooper. I froze in the hallway next to the bathroom.

I turned the hall light on. I started feeling afraid again. The bathroom door was partially open. I stood away from the bathroom door and pushed it fully open. Nothing.

I turned on the bathroom light. Nothing.

The front-room light was on. The hall light was on. The bathroom light was on. There were only two more rooms: my bedroom and the kitchen just beyond it.

The bedroom was completely dark, as was the kitchen. "Cooper," I called out in a subdued and shaky voice. Nothing.

I repeated the call a little louder: "Cooper." Nothing.

I put my back to the wall and inched into the bedroom. Just inside the doorway, I stood perfectly still, opened my mouth to balance the pressure in my ears, and listened as keenly as I could. Nothing.

The table lamp was only about three feet away, but every time I went to reach for it, something kept me pinned to the wall. Was he in the dark, waiting to waylay me?

"Cooper."

Nothing.

I took a deep breath, pushed away from the wall, and jumped on the bed. I was safe. I hit the lamp switch. Light filled the room. Nothing.

All that was left was the kitchen.

Now that most of the lights were on, it was less frightening. I stepped into the hallway and reached my hand around the doorway to turn on the light in the little combination kitchen-dining room. This apartment was shaped funny because it was really a large double carved up into three apartments.

There was nothing in the kitchen. I ran to the kitchen door, which opened to the side alley. It was still locked with the dead bolt and I had the key in my trouser pocket.

Every room was lit. There was nobody in here.

I walked through every room, growing bolder by the minute. I searched through each room three times. Nothing.

Opened closet doors. Nothing.

Pulled the shower curtain back and looked in the stall. Nothing.

Looked under the bed. Nothing.

I must have been hallucinating.

I turned off the kitchen light and haltingly inched my way back into the front room.

I turned off the front-room lamp.

I turned off the hall light.

I turned off the bathroom light.

I sat down on the bed and turned off the lamp.

As soon as I felt the darkness envelop me, I flicked the switch back on. What was I doing? Where was Cooper? Was Cooper ever here? What the hell was going on?

Then I remembered Kristin.

I picked up the phone and dialed her. Her phone rang and rang and rang until the recorder came on. "Hi, I'm out at the moment, but I'll be right back. Please leave your name and number at the tone and I'll get right back to you. Thanks. Ciao."

"David, get ahold of yourself. This is crazy," I mumbled to myself as I sat on the side of the bed, staring into space.

I got up again, went from room to room, turning on all the lights. Tested the kitchen door. It was locked. Walked to the front of the house. Tested the front door. It was locked. Started at the front room and searched each room in the house again. Nothing.

I turned the lights off in every room except the bedroom. I sat down on the bed.

I got up and walked around.

I turned off the table lamp.

As soon as it was off, I switched the lamp back on.

I called Kristin again. No answer.

I went to the bathroom, splashed water on my face. Dried my face on the green towel hanging from the towel ring, turned off the bathroom light, and went back in the bedroom.

I kicked off my shoes. Lay down on the bed. Turned off the light. Heard something in the room. Turned the light back on. Nothing.

I couldn't go on like this—afraid of my own apartment.

I called Kristin again. "I clearly remember Cooper saying that Kristin called," I said out loud to myself. She still wasn't home.

I turned the radio on. I turned the radio off.

I slipped back into my shoes and walked from the bedroom to the front room, turning on lights as I went.

I walked from the front room to the bedroom, turning off lights as I went.

When I got back in the bedroom, I reached out to switch the lamp off, but I couldn't. So I stood there and looked at my hand on the switch. Finally, my hand moved to the phone and I called Kristin one more time. No answer.

I lay down. I got up.

I got tired of standing.

I sat on the bed.

I stood up.

Then I thought I heard a knocking on the side of the house—Cooper was coming back. I walked through the house and turned all the other lights back on.

I was exhausted. I didn't have the strength to leave the front room.

I looked out the front window, reconnoitering the area in front of my house. I couldn't see anything.

I left the window and stood in the middle of the front room.

For the first time since I had come back from Port of Call, I thought to check the time. I looked at my watch. It was 9:05.

I started to walk to the back of the house; instead, I turned around. I had to go outside. I pulled out my key, unlocked the dead bolt, and threw the door wide open. I didn't think about setting the alarm, getting a jacket, or anything. I just stood in my open doorway and felt relatively safe now that I was halfway out of the house. After a few minutes of deep breathing, I stepped completely out of the doorway and closed the door behind me.

I looked up and down the street. A young guy was walking down the street with his hands in his pocket. Miss Sukky was pacing back and forth, plying her wares at her usual spot down on the corner at Esplanade Avenue. A dog came sauntering toward me, sniffing at the ground between the street and the sidewalk. The street mutt paused when he saw me, snorted gruffly, backed up briefly, turned, and trotted away. A couple of blocks down, a police car's blue lights were flashing. It looked like every other night.

Pow. Pow. I heard two shots in the distance, and I jumped as each one went off. This was just like any other night. I had gotten used to the gunfire. Or so I thought. *Pow.* A third shot.

I slumped down on the top step, and before I knew it, I felt uncontrollable waves of emotion welling up inside me.

For the first time since I arrived over a year ago, I began to question whether living here was worth playing Russian roulette, betting your life that the next murder wouldn't be your own.

The economy, such as it was, was disastrously close to imploding. The gaming industry was a bust. Crime was spiraling out of control. Everywhere you looked, the neighborhoods were disintegrating. Abandoned buildings, vacant property, and housing for sale dominated the landscape—even on exclusive, posh St. Charles Avenue. The whole city was up for grabs.

New Orleans wasn't fun like I had expected it to be, like I had wanted it to be. I couldn't go on pretending everything was cool. It wasn't.

Madness again. That's what Cooper had said: madness. Again. What did he mean by "again"? Was it ever this mad? Was New Orleans ever like this before?

Kristin was always saying she admired my integrity. What would she think if she could see me now? I almost started crying again. I had to keep screwing up my face and rapidly blinking my eyes to fight back the tears—a crying man sitting on a stoop wouldn't last long in this neighborhood—but I wasn't totally successful, and every time I wiped one away, another small tear droplet would form and sit at the edge of each of my eyes.

Why was I crying? I wasn't hurt.

But I was in pain.

I wasn't robbed.

But an essential part of my sanity was gone.

"Kristin, I'm sorry." I had been so condescending toward her. I threw my head back and bumped it repeatedly against the front door. Harvard-educated. *Bump.* Physically fit. *Bump.* And emotionally traumatized. *Bump-bump.* I head-knocked the door a couple more times, partially dried my face with my shirt sleeve, reached into my pocket, pulled out my handkerchief, and, in an almost pro-forma attempt to clear my nasal passages, blew gobs of mucus into the white cotton. I sniffed once more, gave the tip of my nose another cursory brush, and then dabbed hard at my mustache and down the sides of my mouth and over my beard. I folded the handkerchief and stuffed it back in my pocket. As I did so, my fingers touched my keys, and I recoiled with a reflex action. I couldn't go back in there. Not now. Not tonight.

I resigned myself to sitting on my steps all night. Or maybe I would walk over to the Exxon on Rampart and Esplanade and call for Kristin, and ask her . . . ask her what? To come get me. Ask her . . . Somebody was standing in front of me.

I was almost afraid to look the youngster in the eye; he might interpret my gaze as a challenge or a put-down. I had seen him around a couple of times. He unblinkingly looked at me like he was trying to decide what to do with me. I just looked at him.

I could have gotten up and gone inside. I could have spoken to him. He could have spoken to me. But I just sat there and looked at him. He just stood there and looked at me. Neither of us said anything.

Finally, he nonchalantly turned, walked to the corner, and stood there with his back to me. He pulled out a cigarette, lit up, blew smoke up in the air, turned around, and started walking away. When he reached the far corner, he turned and disappeared. I finally exhaled.

Leaning forward, my forearms resting heavily on my knees, I clasped my hands and dropped my head. "I don't want to die. Please, God. I want to live. I'm trying, God. I'm trying my best." I couldn't remember the last time I had prayed to God. Whenever it was, for sure I had never uttered a more sincere prayer in my life than now.

My hands were shaking. Literally shaking. I tried to keep them still. I could feel them shaking uncontrollably. I pushed them under my thighs momentarily, trying to keep them still. It didn't help.

I passed my hands through my hair, interlaced them behind my head, and leaned back against the door. It didn't help.

I leaned forward again, clenching and unclenching my fists. My hands were still shaking. I entwined my fingers and tightly clasped my hands. I had my eyes closed. I was afraid to look at my hands. Afraid to look at myself.

I took a deep breath.

"It's not worth it. It's not worth it," I heard myself muttering a bottom-line assessment I never thought I would be thinking, let alone saying out loud.

"David, what's wrong? Why are you sitting out here?"

I looked up, and there was Kristin, dashing out of her car and racing breathlessly toward me. I hadn't even heard her drive up. Her trembling voice was full of anxiety as she sprinted across the sidewalk.

"Are you okay? I got here as fast as I could. Who was that on the phone?" Her words gushed out in a torrent of concern and consternation.

At that moment all I could do was drop my head and tender my resignation. This business was a bust; it was time to move on while I still could. "Kristin, I'm scared. Please, take me to your place."

Hair Dreams

Joy M. Copeland

No one ever told Zaszou the stories about hair left in combs, brushes, or in the trash, about what could happen if the loose hair fell into the wrong hands. No one ever mentioned anything about the nasty headaches or worse that could ensue if birds got hold of the stuff and used it in their nests. No one explained that the proper way to dispose of hair was to wrap it in tissue before placing it in the garbage, or better still, to burn it. But then, most folks didn't talk to Zaszou unless it was to order her around. And even when giving orders wasn't their purpose, Zaszou only half listened.

With latex-gloved fingers, she picked the hair from the sink. The strands clung to the glove like the threads of a spider web. She laid the hair out on a towel. Wet, it looked a light brown, but she could tell that when it dried, it would be a dark gold. Blond hair was her favorite. It made her think of her Barbie doll, preserved in the shoe box under her bed, with its tiny waist, perfect oval face, slender legs, and long, corn-silk yellow hair. Of all her dolls, it was the one she hadn't ripped apart. It was the doll that looked nothing like her. Not one feature matched her own—not her skin that was the color of freshly plowed earth, not her broad, flat nose, dark kinky hair, or thighs layered with fat that rubbed when she walked.

As she stood at the sink, memories of her father drifted back. She was six. It was the day he'd brought home the Barbie. She'd overheard him talking to her mother.

"I hate to say it, but, woman, you got one funny-looking child."

"Ain't nothin' wrong with Zaszou that growin' up won't fix," her mother replied. "Anyway, she's your daughter, too."

"Kinda been wondering about that. She don't take after me or none of my people."

Those words had never left her. But her father did.

Zaszou became conscious of the time she'd been hovering over the bowl. She patted the hair with a paper towel to hasten the drying, then focused on sifting through the trash can. There was nothing that anyone would pay for, just tissues stained with lipstick, a condom wrapper, a flattened toothpaste tube, and an empty cigarette pack. But then she saw it: a matted wad of hair. It was dark, the shade and texture of her own.

"Don't bring me no wads less than the size of a quarter." Miss Ruby had demonstrated the correct measurement by coiling her pointy fingers. "Gotta be enough to make a hairdo for a tiny doll."

Color didn't seem to matter. The old woman paid the same price for any hair—a dollar-fifty per packet. Blond should've been worth more, Zaszou thought, since it was harder to find. She placed the new wad next to the hair that was drying.

"Zaszou! You 'bout finished in there?" The voice was from outside the room.

Zaszou scrambled to put the hair into the three-inch-by-two-inch plastic bags according to Miss Ruby's instructions. "Separate the hair you collect," she could hear Miss Ruby saying. She stuffed the small bags into her pocket.

"Zaszou! Sleepin' in there or somethin'?"

"I'm finishing this bathroom." She resumed cleaning the toilet only seconds before the woman appeared at the bathroom door. It was Dee.

Dee was much older. She was dressed in the same sea green uniform and once-white shoes. "Yancy's picking me up early. We're going out tonight," Dee said gleefully. "If you want to catch a ride, you best be finished by three-thirty." It was already three.

"I still got twenty and twenty-four to do." Zaszou rubbed her forehead on her sleeve, displaying a wet armpit.

"Well, then, you got a problem." Dee pushed back the shower curtain to inspect the tub. "Humpf. From the looks of things, you ain't finished this room."

"That ring don't come off," Zaszou said.

"I should know. How many times I done this room before you came? Anyway, you better pick up the pace. Stop that daydreamin'! Mr. Russell gonna fire your ass if you don't watch it."

"I'm movin' fast as I can." Zaszou rolled her eyes and picked up the pile of towels. Several months ago, her mother had given her a choice: Either stay in high school or bring home some money. High school was a struggle, even PE. Then there was all that teasing. Her counselor had seemed relieved to hear her choice. The Wayside Inn was the only place that would hire her.

"I ain't recommendin' you for no more jobs. Remember, three-thirty. If you ain't there by then, we're leaving without you." Dee turned and left.

Zaszou took a deep breath and felt the lump in her pocket that was her latest treasure. In three days, she'd collected enough hair for ten small packets. Ten packets meant fifteen dollars. *To think this stuff would have been thrown away.*

Pulling sheets, changing towels, vacuuming and dumping beer cans and trash, somehow Zaszou managed to clean the remaining rooms in less time than usual. Maybe it was because her steps were quicker as the deadline to catch her ride approached. Maybe it was because the occupants of twenty and twenty-four were cleaner than most. Or just maybe it was that these days most of Wayside Inn's patrons only stayed the afternoon, hardly bothering to turn down the bed to do what they came to do. In any case, she didn't find more hair. At least none that met the "size of a quarter" standard. She needed eighteen dollars to add to her savings to pay for braids. Not real human hair, of course. But the other stuff that looked just as good. With what she'd saved and what she had in her pocket, she was still short three dollars.

At 3:22, Zaszou made up her mind. And at 3:23, after vacuuming the last ash from number twenty-four's stained carpet, she took the scissors from her utility cart and cut an inch and a half of her own already short hair. Hurrying, she separated the frizzy clump into two parts and stuffed each into one of the little bags. What was left on her head was stubbly and thick. It fought her efforts to smooth and secure it with a rubber band. She forced the band to hold, but only in the very back, leaving the rest of her hair to feather out all which-a-ways, like she'd just got out of bed.

Zaszou locked the room and ran along the second-floor balcony that overlooked the back of the motel. She spotted Yancy's late-model Bonneville. It was the color of summertime lemonade, cool as it waited in the shade of the willow tree near the Dumpster. She knew that Dee would already be inside. Zaszou shoved her cart into the utility room and bounded down the stairs.

"Only one minute to spare," Dee said, glancing at her watch as Zaszou, dripping sweat, climbed into the backseat.

She caught Yancy peering at her in his rearview mirror. Today his yellow knit shirt matched his car. She looked down.

"Oooh whee. Girl, I do believe you get uglier every time I see you," he said with a laugh as he chewed on a toothpick.

"Now, why you got to go and say that to the girl?" Dee said, slapping his bare arm. "Apologize!"

"What for?" Yancy hollered back. "The truth?"

Dee shook her head and looked out the window. There would be no apology, and Zaszou really didn't expect one. Not today. Not ever. All three sat quiet for the twelve-mile ride from the interstate into town. Zaszou closed her eyes and retracted her neck like a turtle. The warm breeze blew in the open window, bringing road dust that clung to her face. She'd forgotten Yancy's remark. She was thinking about her braids. Tomorrow was her day off, and the appointment that would change her life was at one.

Downtown Rolinville consisted of a Presbyterian church, a diner, a drugstore, a pizza parlor, a coffee shop, a barbershop, a hardware store, a movie house, a gas station, and a funeral home, which stayed busy even if the maternity ward in nearby Cannon River didn't. Five years before, the town council, in a moment of lunacy, had twenty parking meters installed along the town's five-block business strip. Now half the meters were broken, and folks refused to park at the ones that weren't, opting instead to put their vehicles on the side streets and use the meters to tie their dogs. The Piggly Wiggly, the last business establishment to be added, occupied a large space with its own parking lot several blocks away from the main business strip.

When the Bonneville entered downtown, Zaszou broke the silence.

"Yancy, let me out at the drugstore. I'll walk the rest of the way home."

"You still got money to spend, two days before payday?" Dee asked.

"I saved some," Zaszou mumbled.

"Well, stop the car, Yancy!" Dee said. "Didn't you hear her?"

The car was only traveling thirty miles an hour, but Yancy hit the brakes so hard it threw Zaszou against the front seats. She scrambled out.

"What about my gas money?" Yancy said, still working his toothpick.

She'd completely forgotten that she owed for the ride, two weeks' worth. "You're saving bus fare" was the way Dee had put it when they first made the arrangement to ride together on days they both worked. According to her mother, the only thing Yancy did all day, besides play the ponies and chauffeur Dee around, was shine that Bonneville.

"I'll give it to you Friday, Yancy. When I get paid."

He grunted.

Zaszou stepped past a group of men who were gathered near the pizza parlor. They cut their eyes at her, then resumed their conversation. She looked to see that the Bonneville was well down the street before bolting around the corner.

Miss Ruby's house wasn't much different from her own, except it had two windows on the front instead of one. And it had been painted, even though now the paint was peeling. The small porch was uncovered. Excited, she knocked. A man came to the door in an undershirt that stretched across his big belly. He scowled. She'd seen him before but didn't know his name. Men came and went from Miss Ruby's. They always seemed to be men from out of town, who hung around for a while and just disappeared. At least that's what her mother had told her.

"Miss Ruby home?" Zaszou said in a low voice.

"Ruby! Ruby! It's that girl again!" Then he rubbed his belly and stared as they waited. He didn't invite her in.

"What you yellin' 'bout, Frank?" came Ruby's shrill voice from inside. "Oh, it's you," she said when she saw Zaszou. "Frank, go finish eating."

He sucked his teeth and left.

"Step inside, chile," Miss Ruby said, waving the sleeve of her kimono-style robe. "I wasn't expectin' to see you again *this* soon." Her head wrap was the color of canned fruit punch. It didn't match her robe.

No one else in Rolinville wore colors like Miss Ruby—bright pinks, oranges, purples, and reds. Way too flashy for somebody her age, folks would say. They must be jealous, Zaszou thought. It didn't matter that Miss Ruby's clothes all clashed or that staring at them too long could make a person feel queasy. It didn't matter that everyone shunned her place, complaining about the foul smell coming from the backyard. Or was it something about the fact that no birds, squirrels, or rabbits were ever seen in her front yard that kept people away? Or that dogs, cats, and children crossed the street to avoid getting close? Zaszou didn't know why folks didn't like Miss Ruby. But Miss Ruby had always been nice to her.

Zaszou watched the woman's smile. Those two gold teeth, set like twins, fascinated her. One had a star that showed the cream-colored enamel underneath. Zaszou tried to control her stare. But the star tooth beckoned.

The interior of the house was as busy as her robe. Two sofas, at least three chairs, a number of tables, lamps, and rugs, all crammed into the small room, in no particular style or arrangement. The place smelled of chitlins.

"What you got this time?"

Zaszou placed the plastic packets in the woman's large hands. "I got twelve."

"Let me see." Miss Ruby turned on a lamp and held one over the shade. "That one looks good."

"There's two blond ones."

"Maybe. Maybe not," Miss Ruby said, examining another packet. Her hand with its long curved fingernails made a shadow on the wall like a hawk's talon holding its prey. "Most blondes ain't real blondes. I can make a blonde anytime, with bleach." The old woman cackled.

"Oh," Zaszou said, a little disappointed, so sure she'd found the real thing.

"Chile, you think blond is all so special. I favor red hair myself. I mean natural red, of course."

Zaszou wondered about the color of Miss Ruby's hair. She'd never seen her without a full-head scarf.

Miss Ruby checked each packet in the light. On the last one, she glanced sideways at Zaszou. "These will do. Is this really what you want to give me?"

The gleam of Miss Ruby's smile was so bright, Zaszou thought she saw sparks coming from the star tooth. She shifted her gaze to the floor. "Yes, ma'am," she said weakly. She wondered why she was being questioned.

"You swear you didn't mix any hair, one with the other," Miss Ruby hissed.

"I swear," Zaszou choked.

"Good. Long as we have an understanding. We do have an understanding?"

Zaszou nodded. She was agreeing to something but didn't know quite what. Her school counselor had told that she was a little slow. She'd taken that to mean that she wasn't supposed to figure out everything. But she wasn't going to let Miss Ruby know that, by asking her to explain what "understanding" she meant. "Miss Ruby, can I see your dolls?"

"I showed you once. I know I did," Miss Ruby barked.

Zaszou lurched back like she was about to be beaten. Shoulders hiked, her head resumed its turtle position.

"You one pitiful chile. Gonna jump out your skin when I blow steam. You gotta blow your own steam sometimes. Let folks know you ain't afraid."

Zaszou peeked up from her floor gaze to see the old woman's frown.

"Pitiful, pitiful . . . Okay. I'll show you my dolls again, but just for a second. And no touching."

Miss Ruby left the room and returned minutes later with a black tray, the kind used to serve beverages. On it were five tiny dolls, in various skin tones, each about the size of a clothespin, with porcelain-painted face, arms and legs, and a head of human hair in different shades.

"They real pretty." Zaszou sighed as she peered over the tray, her face so close she could've breathed life into the dolls. "What you gonna do with them?"

"I told you. Sell 'em."

"Can I buy one? I mean when I got more money."

"Sorry, chile. But you ain't never gonna have enough money to buy one of these."

"Oh," was all Zaszou could think to say. She didn't think to question how much was too much, a figure that she'd never be able to afford. She didn't think to wonder, if the dolls were so expensive, why Miss Ruby stayed in a house that was like hers with only one extra window and some peeling paint. She backed away from the tray.

Miss Ruby frowned and shook her head. "How much I owe you this time?"

"Eighteen dollars," Zaszou mumbled.

Miss Ruby reached inside the fold of her robe, pulled out a roll of bills, and counted out eighteen. "Won't be needing any hair for a while. Got to work with what I got."

"Oh."

"Come back in a couple of months."

Do braids last that long? Zaszou wondered. She'd have to ask the hairdresser.

On the way home Zaszou thought about her braids. The nose and mouth she'd handle later. She didn't have a clue how, but she would.

All evening and later that night, Zaszou's mind danced with thoughts of getting long hair. She sang a song while washing the dishes and kissed her mother on the cheek before going to bed.

"Why you so happy?" her mother asked.

"Just am," she answered.

The next morning her mother called to wake her. "Ain't you goin' to work today?"

"Don't have to. It's my day off."

"Well, I got things I need you to do. I still got to go to work."

Zaszou groaned at the thought of chores and rolled over.

"And when you get paid tomorrow, I need some money to pay the electric."

Zaszou was glad that she'd kept her dealings with Miss Ruby and her plans to get the braids secret. Her mother would just fuss at her for going to Miss Ruby's, and then claim whatever money she'd made from the deal, plus her savings. Since the diner had switched her mother to part time, things were just that tight.

"Do that pile of wash on the sofa and clean and season that chicken for tonight."

The front door closed with a bang that rattled the glass. Zaszou sighed.

She spent the morning finishing her chores. Then she changed into a white skirt that showed more leg than usual, put on a pair of red sneakers that she only wore when it wasn't raining, and took the money she'd saved from its hiding place, a sock ball. She stuffed the cash in the small red plastic purse with the gold chain.

It was a ten-block walk to Elaine's Beauty Parlor, an establishment operated right out of Elaine's kitchen, complete with a sign in the front yard, and a back porch where, on nice days, she served iced tea and cookies to waiting customers. Zaszou had only heard her mother's friend talk about the place and had never been inside, until the day she decided to make an appointment.

"I'd like to get some braids—the long ones," she'd said to Elaine, a tall thin, dark woman with rough, strong hands, shiny from pressing oil. The place smelled of fried hair and chemicals.

Parting it with her fingers, Elaine had inspected Zaszou's hair with its straight edges and nappy undergrowth.

"I can do it. It'll be an all-afternoon appointment, plus the cost of the extensions." She'd pointed to a line on the price list that made Zaszou eyes grow wide. "For that much time I'm booked."

"I need a Thursday, my day off."

Elaine searched through several pages of her spiral date book. "I've got a Thursday afternoon I can give you, four weeks off. You want that appointment?"

Zaszou nodded. Actually, she was glad that the appointment had been set far off. It gave her more time to come up with the money.

She walked past several stray dogs. Too busy sniffing the Johnson's overturned garbage, they didn't even notice her. A few blocks from Main Street, she broke into a skip, swinging her head as if she could already feel the braids whipping her face.

"What you doing there, Zaszou?" It was Mrs. Peters, on her knees, digging in her petunia bed. "You look like a cheerleader. Practicing or something?"

Mrs. Peters should have known that she could never be on the cheerleading squad, Zaszou thought. Why, she wasn't even in school. She immediately stopped skipping and resumed a normal walk. "No, ma'am," she said as she passed the yard. "Just getting exercise."

Zaszou needed to cross Main Street to get to Elaine's. That's when she first saw the Bonneville. It was parked on a side street not far from the funeral home. To avoid running into either Yancy or Dee, she ducked into the alley behind the funeral home. The tiny street where bodies were delivered was quiet.

"Where you going in such a hurry?" The voice came from behind. "Look at you all dolled up in your little red sneakers and short skirt. Got the nerve to show them big legs."

"Oh, Yancy. Where's Dee?"

"Dee's busy shopping, spending more money. Money we don't have. So why you here?"

"Got some business." Zaszou turned to leave, but Yancy had grabbed the chain of her bag and wrapped it around his forearm

"Wait a second, girl! You got some money for me? You know, what you owe me?"

"I was gonna pay you later, when I get paid."

"Well, you must have some money in this little purse here."

She pulled on the chain, but he jerked it away from her. "Well, lookie here," Yancy said, opening the bag. "Girl, you is rich."

"That money's to pay a bill."

"Well, I'm a bill. Ain't I a bill?" He counted the cash.

"Yancy, you can't take that." She reached out to snatch the money. He waved it higher as she tried to jump for it.

"Calm down, girl." He grabbed her outstretched arm and bent it behind her. "Let's just say you've paid up for your rides for a while."

"No, you can't take my money," she whined.

Yancy just bent her arm higher.

"Oooow!" she screamed.

With the chain and purse still dangling from his forearm, Yancy put the money in his shirt pocket and pulled Zaszou closer. She strained against his whiskey breath. Pain throbbed in her bent arm, but that hurt wasn't as much as the painful thought of losing her savings, losing the chance to get the braids.

"Lemme go, Yancy." She was breathing hard.

"You and I can have a little fun." He snickered, groping under her skirt. "We might even find a new way for you to pay for rides."

He spun her around with her arm still yanked high behind her. She was being pushed down the alley. Hopes for the braids were dissolving in the tears that rolled down her cheeks.

Suddenly, a large bird, probably a hawk, swooped low, just missing her and clipping Yancy's head. "Goddamn it!" he yelled. Blood was trickling from his head, where the bird had scratched him. The bird came at them again. He held onto Zaszou and swung the chain wide, hitting the bird while they both ducked. His swing caught the bird in midair. The creature hovered, stunned if not injured, for a second, like a kite that had lost its wind draft. Then it took off, making a terrible screech.

"That was one crazy bird! You must've greased up this morning with bacon. That bird wanted a bite of you."

"Lemme go," Zaszou whined.

He punched her with the hand that held the chain and pushed her faster. She heard the door squeal, and she found herself on the floor of a shed. She was dazed from the blow to the face, and now afraid. When he shut the door, the only light was from pinpointed rays streaming through several small gaps in the wood. Zaszou could make out his large frame standing over her, but she couldn't see his eyes. "Please, Yancy. Just let me go."

"I can't let you go now. Not after you got me all hot and bothered." She heard him unzip his pants. "It's nice and dark. I don't have to see your ugly face. Yeah, nice and dark. But it don't matter for what I'm going to do."

Her face throbbed, and she could tell that her jaw and lip were swelling. Yancy was busy yanking off her panties. She reached behind her and felt something metal. It was long and rough, with a pointed edge. Something told her to grab it and point it toward him. Just as she did, Yancy came down hard on her. The weapon found a soft place on his body, a place that seemed to welcome it. She thrust it upward with all her strength.

"Aaaahh. Aaaahh," he moaned, but she kept pushing. Then it was quiet. Not a bird, not a dog, not the sound of children, a lawn mower, or an insect's buzz.

Her breath had slowed. She lay there under Yancy's heavy body, with her hands still wrapped around the cold, hard metal. Half delirious, she pictured herself again moving in slow motion, head swinging, with long blond braids brushing her face.

There was another groan from the body. Then nothing.

"I gotta get outta here. I gotta get my money," she murmured.

Those arms that could single-handedly turn a mattress at the Wayside Inn managed to push Yancy's weight aside. She extricated her legs, stumbled over the body, and made her way to the door. Getting her money back was the only thing on her mind. She needed more light to find it. She opened the door, and the brightness of the sun blinded her for a minute. Still-warm blood covered her hands, legs, and skirt. She opened the shed door wider. Again it squealed. She checked Yancy's back pockets. Nothing. Then she turned him over. Yancy's eyes stared into space, and his mouth was frozen in a silent gasp. Poised in a squat, she searched the front pockets of his unzipped pants and, finally, his shirt. The money was there. It seemed to pop out of his pocket and into her hand like a lost bird. She squeezed it tight, leaving a huge, bloody print on the outside bill.

She became aware of someone standing at the door. "What going on in there? Who's messin' around in that shed?" Their eyes met in the half dark. "Hey, what you doing there? What's all this blood?"

Zaszou leaped up, pushed past the man, and sprinted down the alley. She bolted past two ladies strolling with their toddlers. Then she darted into the street without looking. The brakes of a delivery truck squealed as it just missed her. With her wide strides she could feel the breeze between her legs, the place that was now bare, the place that he'd wanted to go. Her legs were taking her somewhere. She wasn't sure just where. It wasn't to Elaine's Beauty Parlor. Elaine wouldn't want to serve ice tea and cookies to someone with bloody hands. It wasn't to the diner where her mother worked. At lunchtime her mother would be real busy and wouldn't want to be bothered. It wouldn't be to Dee's, 'cause Dee was still out shopping, and even if she could find her at the store, Dee would be so upset that Yancy wasn't there to drive her home with those heavy packages. For sure, it wasn't to the sheriff's office. Her mother had once told her that "Those folks put folks like us *under* the jail." No, she didn't know quite where her legs were taking her. It was like her legs had a mind of their own. They were now in charge. But wherever they were taking her, she had to get there soon because she was running out of breath.

Zaszou heard the police siren in the distance. It was an unusual sound for Rolinville. The only time the siren blared was when the sheriff's office tested it to see if it still worked. When Zaszou's legs and breath finally gave out, she found herself on Miss Ruby's street. She limped the thirty yards to the old woman's door and banged on it nonstop.

This time it was Miss Ruby who opened the door. She wore a patch on her left eye, and today's colors were violet, orange, and red.

"Been wondering when you were gonna get here," she said with a half smile. "Look at you. All covered in blood."

"It was Yancy," Zaszou said, panting.

"I know, chile. And that scumbucket got just what he deserve. Was just a matter a time." The siren was closer. Miss Ruby looked up and down the street.

Zaszou saw a rust-colored feather hanging from her purple head wrap.

"Don't just stand there!" the old woman shouted. "Hurry up. Get in here before somebody sees you."

Rolinville moved quickly to fill the gap created by the physical exit of one of its citizens. It was as though the universe set to rebalance what was out of whack.

By 1:30, the town was abuzz. Someone had murdered Yancy Jeffers right behind the funeral home. Gutted him with a stake, like a vampire killing. It happened just about the time Paradise, the pony that Yancy bet fifty bucks on, paid off seven to one. The boys in the back room of the pizza parlor had wondered why Yancy didn't show for the daily broadcast of the race results. They all commented on how Yancy had favored Paradise and would have made a bundle. Only his bookie knew about the win. So when the word came down about finding Yancy's body, he pocketed the money.

* * *

At 1:45, when the town's part-time treasurer heard about Yancy's death, he swallowed two aspirins, held his head, and immediately calculated the financial consequences to the town. Funds were drying up, just like the soil around Rolinville. The town hadn't budgeted for a murder. At least there'd be no costs for transporting the body, he figured, since the funeral home also served as the town morgue and there'd be no charge for carrying him across the alley. It was unlikely that Yancy carried any life insurance. But everyone knew Yancy had that yellow Bonneville. It was possible that the town could recoup any additional burial charges by selling that car. That's if Yancy didn't still owe a big payment on it.

At 2:15, Dee Jenkins heard about the murder. She'd been sitting on the bench outside the Piggly Wiggly, where Yancy was supposed to pick her up. He was already thirty minutes late. A group of women coming to shop were babbling about a black fellow that had been killed over by the funeral home. She had no idea it was Yancy, until they made mention of a long yellow car. Dee ran out of the parking lot and accosted the first black person she encountered. When the person confirmed that it was indeed Yancy, Dee started wailing and jumping around like a child having a tantrum. She managed to return to the bench where her packages waited, continuing to sob uncontrollably. A brown-skinned gentleman in about his late forties came and sat beside her. He brought her a cup of water and offered to drive her and her packages home. On the ride home she just kept repeating, "How am I going to get to work?" But when she glanced over at the man's powerful arms and surveyed the cream-colored leather interior of his car, she went quiet.

By 2:30, everyone knew that it was that slow-witted Zaszou Beale who'd done it. At least that's what they'd been led to believe by all the accounts. Amos Koons, the hearse driver and alternate pallbearer, said he'd seen the girl digging in the dead man's pockets when he looked into the shed. A number of other people in town said they'd seen a wild woman covered in blood running away from the area about the time of the murder. Their descriptions sounded like Zaszou; but then again, nobody was sure. No one seemed to have a picture of her, not the school, not even her mother. When the sheriff interrupted her mother's shift at the diner, she'd already heard about Yancy's death. She didn't believe it could be Zaszou, since her child could never run as fast as everyone was saying. But Zaszou wasn't home. No one knew where she was. Her mother went home that afternoon, fully expecting Zaszou to show up for dinner and help with the dishes the way she always did.

The sheriff alerted the authorities in Cannon River. The search for Zaszou had begun.

At 6:30 the next morning, the sheriff paced the streets of downtown Rolinville. The search party had been out all night. There'd been no sign of the girl. In fifteen years in law enforcement, this was his first real homicide. There'd been hunting and farming accidents, drownings, and even a suicide. But Rolinville folk didn't kill each other.

He hadn't slept all night. He'd figured Yancy Jeffers for a trouble-maker from the first time he saw him. Who could miss that big yellow Bonneville in a population of pickup trucks, midsize Fords, and Chevrolets. Yancy was a lowlife. He was probably doing something he had no business doing. Now they were after this poor teenager. And where was this girl Zaszou anyway? He knew her mother from the diner, but to his knowledge, he'd never laid eyes on the girl. He didn't spend much time with the black folks unless he was locking them up. Sometimes for drunk and disorderly, sometimes for petty theft. Never for anything big. He ran a clean town. There was no trouble. The folks that voted him in every two years liked it that way.

As he made it past the funeral home near the murder site, he spotted a young white woman wandering aimlessly near the drugstore. She was tall and thin with blond hair almost to her waist. She looked confused. The red cloth suitcase she carried matched her red canvas sneakers. She reminded him of his daughter.

"Can I help you, miss?" he asked.

"You the sheriff?" she answered. His badge was a permanent fixture on his shirt.

"Yes, ma'am."

"The one that puts folks under the jail?"

He laughed. "I don't know who told you that. I hope that's not what folks think about me around here."

She scanned the street.

"Where you going, miss? Do you have people here?"

She shrugged.

"You look like you're lost. This is Rolinville." He looked into her eyes, a habit he'd formed as a young recruit in Petersburg before coming to this bump-in-the-road town. Her eyes were ice blue, vacant and otherworldly.

"Yeah, I know. Guess I got off the bus in the wrong town," she said.

"Where did you intend to be?"

"Guess not here."

"You got your ticket to get back on the bus?" he asked, hoping not to have to explain another voucher for an outlay of cash the town didn't have.

"No ticket," she sighed.

He winced.

"But I got money." She pulled out a handful of bills.

"Gotta be careful showing folks cash like that," he said. "Gonna be a while before that bus comes along again. The schedule's posted near the stop. Down the road a piece near the Piggly Wiggly. You can't miss it."

She still looked bewildered.

"There's a big sign that says 'Bus Stop.' That's probably where you got off when it came through about twenty minutes ago." He scratched his head. "Check the schedule. I figure you got at least three hours before the Richmond bus comes through. Meantime, you can go on over to the diner and get something to eat. "

"No, thanks," she said quickly.

"Well, good day, ma'am." He watched as she headed toward the bus stop. Couldn't fathom her standing there for three hours. It occurred to him that maybe Zaszou had got on that early bus, the one that came through twenty minutes ago. No one had been assigned to watch there. He felt a little stupid at the thought that she might've gotten away, right under his nose.

The Track

L. R. Giles

Nash Blanding checked his watch while he rounded the turn in the outside lane. He was making good time, his best all week. His lungs felt like hot-air balloons with each breath; he loved that feeling. Speeding up, he lapsed into a pleasant memory of his track and field days at Commonwealth University; he'd been all-state. Caught up in the past, he only narrowly missed running into a woman and her dog that had stepped leisurely onto the track.

He weaved into the middle lane only to see an elderly couple walking hand in hand, so he veered all the way to the inside lane to reestablish his pace. At Commonwealth, when the athletes were on the field, the track was off limits. Anyone who dared to come up the stadium steps or walk through the gate was subjected to a verbal lashing from Coach Harry. Where was Coach when you needed him?

These people were out every morning; no matter how early Nash tried to be, someone was always there to meet him, and he hated it. Sure, it was a big track, but if *they* weren't going to use it right, *they* needed to stay the hell at home. There should be a sign: "No Resolutionists Allowed."

That's what he called them.

Resolutionists.

Usually they only woke up on New Year's Eve and wandered the earth for a month or two before going back into hibernation, but it seemed in Stepton there was a special breed that stayed up all year long. Most resolutionists are of the fitness variety. They tell themselves, I'm going to walk for thirty minutes a day—as if you don't do that anyway—and that's going to make me healthier. But after that strenuous morning trek, they're at the Waffle House, ordering a double stack with bacon on the side. Well, Nash didn't know that, but judging by the guts on some of them, it seemed like a solid assumption. Then, after a week and a half of walking and not seeing any results, resolutionists become fed up with this myth of physical fitness, and their workout schedule becomes first sporadic, then nonexistent. That's the only thing that kept Nash running at the newly opened Stepton High School track—he knew most of the current crowd would be cut in half by next week, and then another downsizing would take place the week after that.

I'm going to outlast you all in every way, shape, and form, he thought. He stepped his speed up another notch.

Ahead, waddling along in the middle lane, was a flabby, familiar shape in a designer sweat suit. Nash rolled his eyes and shot past the guy like he was the Flash, moving too fast to be seen by the human eye.

"Hey, Nash, wait up," Ray Pudletter called after him.

It seemed Nash wouldn't be invited to join the Justice League any time soon.

He slowed down and felt the muscles in his face tighten at the sound of slow, heavy footfalls slapping the clay behind him.

"Nash, buddy, hold up a second."

With a quick stab of his index finger, Nash reset his watch. After all the interruptions his time was shot to hell anyway. He made an abrupt stop and let Fat Boy catch up.

"Boy, you sure can move," Ray said, winded from the short walk.

Blandly Nash said, "Just trying to stay in shape, Ray."

The corners of the man's mouth turned up in an awkward smile that raised his jowls and turned his eyes to slits. "What's with that 'Ray' stuff?"

He fought a grimace. "Sorry about that, Pud." Actually it was *the* Pud. He even had it in quotation marks on the business cards for his realty company.

"Don't mention it. Ray just sounds too . . ."

"Normal?"

"Well, yeah. The Pud seems hipper, more down to earth, relaxes the clients so I can get in their pockets and they can get in my houses." He laughed and slapped Nash's shoulder. "Get what I'm saying, good buddy?"

Nash was glad he dealt with Century 21. "Pud, it was good to see you again; maybe we can do the social thing some other time, but I—"

"I didn't come over here to be social, Nash, or should I call you the Black Stallion?"

It was his old track nickname from freshman year, the one that had stirred up so much controversy because he was one of the few blacks on a mostly white team. He'd hated that name and so did his parents; they'd written the dean about it, and it was made known that no commentators, announcers, or journalists were to use that name when referring to him. Of course, people still remembered the name, but most had the common courtesy not to say it to his face. Most except the Pud.

Stern, Nash said, "I don't really like—"

"Talking business in your off hours? I understand, but I can make it worth your time. Trust me."

"I already have a house."

The Pud shook his head, "No, I don't want you to buy anything from me; I want to buy something from you."

Nash wrote copy at the news station; he didn't have anything to sell. "I still don't know what you're talking about."

"I want your expertise. I want you to train me."

For what? The Twinkie Olympics?

He went on candidly, "Well, the summer's more than a few months away, but I want to get in shape so me and the missus can go to the beach and have fun, like we used to. But, I've put on a little weight."

No, how about, you put on a big weight? "I'm not a trainer, Ray. You'd probably be better off at that gym downtown. They have professionals for that type of thing."

"That won't do. I don't want people to *know* I've got a trainer. They'll start to talk then. People know you and I are friends, so with you training me, it'll just look like were out running together, casually."

The news that they were friends shocked Nash. "I appreciate that you think highly enough of me to ask, but my schedule's kind of strict and—"

"Five hundred a week," he proclaimed, "cash."

Nash cocked his head, "You're serious?"

"As a heart attack."

He left that one alone. "And what exactly do you want for five hundred a week?"

"Just get me running to the point where I start to shed this weight. Push me and don't let me give up."

Five hundred a week was almost Nash's regular salary before taxes, so that part of the deal sounded great. But Ray was a businessman, a shrewd one at that, so Nash made sure to cover his ass. "I need something in writing—a disclaimer—saying that if you hurt yourself, it isn't my fault. I also want the fee in writing, and that doesn't change if you decide to skip days. Okay?"

Ray nodded. "That's what I like to hear." He stuck out his hand.

Nash shook it, quickly pulled his hand from that greasy palm. "We run at five-thirty on weekdays and seven on weekends."

Ray was smiling.

"That's a.m.," Nash clarified. Ray's smile faltered. "Take tomorrow to think about that and get your mind right and meet me here on Monday with the paperwork I asked for."

Nash didn't say good-bye. He walked around Ray and sidestepped two power-walking women. The terms of the training seemed solid enough, but that five hundred a week wasn't money that Nash would mortgage his house against. Ray "the Pud" Pudletter was a resolutionist, just like the rest of them, and Nash was sure he'd outlast him, too.

He knew what to expect before he opened the door to his one-story rancher on Trenton Street. It was Saturday and cartoons were on; she'd be planted in front of the TV with whatever snack food rocked her boat. No, not his daughter—he didn't have any children—but his wife, Gwen.

The scent of artificial butter assaulted him as soon as he stepped inside—popcorn at nine in the morning. He rounded the corner where she sat Indian-style on the couch with the bowl of kernels cradled between her chubby cottage cheese thighs. "Good morning," she said, and popped some corn in her mouth.

He responded with a grunt and headed for the shower.

In the stall he stood with his palms flat against the wall and his face toward the floor. Water sprayed across his back, trickling fast and hot down his buttocks and fatigued legs. When he met Gwen during his senior year, there were plenty of times after practice when he'd come back to his room and they would go through the shower ritual together, though getting clean wasn't the objective back then. But, as is often the case when people go from lovers to committed, to married, things changed. He remembered what attracted him to her in the first place. Sure, she was pretty, but not as gorgeous as some of the coeds that had wanted to ride the Stallion. Yeah, she was smart, but not a stimulating conversationalist who stunned you with sparkling intellect. What really had brought him to Gwen—it was a mundane thing—was her ability to do a proper pull-up.

In his whole life he'd never met a girl that could do a pull-up. He'd seen them on TV, mostly during episodes of *American Gladiators* and *GLOW,* but none in real life. Plenty of women could be spotted in the gym on a daily basis, busting miles on the treadmill or tightening their ass on the StairMaster, or doing something in the spirit of vanity. Girls rarely worked on their upper body, it seemed to Nash, so when he came into Common Weight Room—athletes had their own facility—to meet some of his nontrack buddies, he was amazed to see her at the pull-up station, raising her chin above the bar repeatedly. Her face was to the wall, but from the back he had no complaints. She was tight from the calves to the thighs, to the lats.

His boys were at a weight bench waving him over; he held up a halting finger to let them know he'd only be a minute. He had to meet this girl.

Weaving around lifters and equipment, he reached her just as she dropped to the floor with sweat misting her forehead. She turned around and jumped when she saw him looming. "Shit," she said loudly.

His raised his hands in a peace gesture. "I'm sorry, I didn't mean to startle you."

She took a deep breath and placed a hand over her heart. "Well, what exactly did you mean to do?"

"I wanted to tell you that your upper body strength is impressive, but your hands were spaced wrong. You're going to put unnecessary strain on your rotator cuffs."

She rolled her eyes. "Thanks for the advice. Now, if you'll excuse me . . ." She sidestepped him and tried to walk away, but he gave chase.

"Wait. What's your name?"

"Why don't you ask one of these other brothers in here?" she said over her shoulder, then faced him. "They've all given me pointers on some aspect of my workout, so you shouldn't have a problem making friends."

Nash grinned. "I'm not asking them; I'm asking you."

"Well, let me ask you something first. Why is it when any mildly attractive woman sets foot in a gym, every man in the place thinks it his duty to show her how to work the machinery? If you catch my drift." She went to the desk by the exit, retrieved her university ID, and left him there to contemplate. After a moment he decided two things. One, the answer to her question was human nature, plain and simple. And two, he had to have her.

He took her advice and asked the guy at the ID desk what her name was. After that, he started to work out in the Common Weight Room more often, hoping to run into Ms. Gwen Maguire. Sure enough, he met her at the entrance one day, and he decided to take another crack at it.

"Gwen, right?"

"Yeah."

He motioned to the door. "Technically, we're not in the gym, so if I tried to talk to you out here, you won't blow up on me again, will you?"

She shook her head. "You're a bold one; I'll give you that." Her voice was still stern, but Nash detected a bit of a smile. Another victory.

Now, in the shower, he wondered what had happened to that strong-willed girl who didn't let men interrupt her workout. These days a whole gang of men took precedence over her fitness: Uncle Ben, Duncan Hines, Ronald McDonald, Dave Thomas, and so on. It's been said that men don't think about their future until they're married, and after they're married, women stop. To that argument, Gwen was exhibit A.

He got out of the shower and found her sitting on the edge of the bed. Waiting. "*X-men* a rerun?"

"No, not today." She seemed to miss the sarcasm. "I wanted to talk; we've missed each other all week."

"I work a lot; then I hit the gym in the evenings so I don't get"—he emphasized the word—"*fat.*"

"And you're at the track in the mornings. You haven't done two-a-days since you stopped competing. You in training again, or . . ."

"Or what?" He dropped his towel, and he could feel her eyes tracing the contours of his body, focusing on his southern region. He ignored her and slid on some fresh boxers.

"Or are you running from something?" When Gwen had something to say, she never came out with it—oh, no, it was always some ambiguous soap opera bullshit.

"I'm lost, Gwen. What are you talking about?" But he knew. She wanted attention, and time, and romance, but didn't consider how she was letting herself go. Before, he didn't understand how other men could take a vow of marriage and cheat on their wives, but as her waistline grew, so did the urge to find someone new, just as a distraction. She was like a marshmallow now: soft and gooey. That ain't the shit he said "I do" to. He still loved her as a person, he supposed, but there were other things to consider.

She sighed, "I just feel like we're growing apart. I feel like . . ."

He crossed the room and kissed her hard. He pressed his weight against her until she was flat on her back. Moving his mouth to her ear, he whispered, "We're together now," and she giggled.

He slid off his clean boxers, tossed her panties on the floor beside them, and loved her long and deep, until he felt her arch beneath him. Then he gave her some more for good measure. When they were done and he was sure she'd sleep for a few hours, he got back in the shower and made sure the water was extra hot.

On Monday, Nash arrived twenty minutes before his usual running time. His ass was dragging, but he wanted to beat the Pud, assuming he showed up at all. It was an intimidation technique he'd picked up from various coaches over the years—always be one up on your runners. Everything's a race; always be first.

While he might have beaten his new student, he was still behind others who were already busy circling the track.

He looked at the descending concrete steps that led to the clay, and massaged the muscles at the small of his back. Any other morning he'd have jogged down the path, but now, still yawning and wiping sleep from his eyes, he knew it wasn't happening.

Walking slowly gave him time to reflect on the oddity of the track. It was sunken, which wasn't unusual in itself. Depending on preference and money, a lot of schools would build tracks at the base of hills and build bleachers for spectators in the hillside.

Stepton, however, had dug a hole for their track. And it was a damned deep one. Nash estimated between 70 and 100 feet. When construction began, he'd thought it was the foundation and basement of some huge new building. Then he heard that no building was in the works, and wondered if they were digging for treasure. Who knew? At the top, from a distance, you could almost miss the damned thing because of short bushes bordering the hole.

The finished product rested in a pit that tapered down to a thin, grassy border, where large light poles were mounted. Then there was the clay oval with long- and high-jump setups in the middle. The city still hadn't shored up the soft earth sides of the hole. It seemed like they would've done that before they opened it, since a strong rain could cause mud to slide down the steep incline and tarnish the field. They'd built the track with one way in and one way out. Nash never understood the dumb-asses in power, especially in Stepton—they did the craziest things.

Halfway down the steps, Nash glanced to either side and saw the usual city workers in their orange jumpsuits and high boots. Another track oddity he'd gotten used to.

They were there every morning with their bags and pikes, mostly picking up trash and debris on the slopes of the pit. But every so often, he'd seen them toss a dead squirrel or bird in their sacks. Animals seemed to think of the hole as a grave and flocked to it when they were at the end of their short-ass lives. He hoped their instincts would lead them somewhere else whenever the city decided to put the bleachers in.

At the bottom, he found a spot in the grass and started his stretching. A few moments later, Ray waddled his way.

He had a manila folder in his hand, with the paperwork Nash had requested. He looked over it while Ray did some halfhearted stretching.

"You know, I'm on the city council. I helped allocate the funds for this track."

Nash only halfway heard him; he was at the money part of the document.

"The school needed it; they really did. We had a time getting it done, though. There were so many strange accidents during construction, then the town folk bitching about their taxes. Never thought this thing would be such a hit. People are out here at all times of day and night. If we charged admission, we could make our money back."

If they charged admission to use the track, nobody would come. People would run around their neighborhood for all that. Ray was a businessman and was always thinking money, even if the idea was stupid as hell. He was right about one thing, though. The track was a hit.

Nash knew the number of users would decrease soon, but the frequency of track use was high. The clay never seemed empty. It was shortly after five-thirty in the morning, and almost a dozen people were doing laps, with the sun just creeping over the horizon, shooting purple and gold streaks in every direction. He didn't think the high school turned on the stadium lamps except during track meets, so that meant . . .

. . . people were out there walking and running in the dark. That was odd, and Nash didn't know what to call people like that, because with that type of dedication were they really resolutionists?

He laid the folder on the grass border of the track and sat his water bottle on top of it so the wind wouldn't scatter the papers across the world. "Everything looks fine. You ready to sweat?"

Ray looked unsure. "I guess so."

"Follow me."

He did a warm-up lap at a light pace. When they finished that first quarter mile, Ray's breathing became shallow pants. Nash stepped it up, intending to cover as much distance as he could in thirty minutes. He knew his trainee wasn't going to be able to keep up, and that was the point. This training thing was a joke; if Ray didn't know it, Nash did.

Before they did a half mile, Ray fell behind and eventually started walking. Nash paid him no mind and lapped him several times. He did pat him on the back whenever he passed him—you know, for encouragement.

Thirty minutes later, Nash was on the side, stretching, ready to go home, shower, and get to work. Ray lay flat on his back.

"That's it for today, Ray."

The man's face had gone a pasty color, looking more like dough than skin. He gritted his teeth like a woman trying to give birth.

"My legs are cramping," he hissed.

Nash didn't spare him another glance. "Rub them. When they stop, stretch. Eat a banana before you come out here tomorrow." He stood up and made sure to grab his disclaimer with the Pud's signature on it. "I've got to get out of here. You need help getting to your car?"

"I'm going to stay out here for a while, Stallion." It seemed he had a little pride left in him.

Suit yourself, Nash thought. He climbed the steps to the top. He didn't notice that one of those special nighttime resolutionists had stopped midlap to come over and speak to Ray.

Fat Boy lasted just under six days. Each day he'd stayed at the track after Nash left, but on the sixth day, Saturday, Nash came home to a message on the answering machine.

"Nash, good buddy, I'm going to have to break our little agreement. Your schedule's a little too rough for an old guy like me. There are some people out here that are on a plan that suits me a little better than yours. Thanks anyway."

No problem at all, he thought. That's the easiest five large I ever made in my life. He erased the message, only dimly aware that Gwen was standing behind him.

"What agreement?" she asked.

"Ray Pudletter wanted to run with me to get in shape," he said, then added, "for his wife." He hoped she'd catch the hint, but knowing Gwen, it'd probably shot right over her head.

"That's not a bad idea. Bathing suit season is around the corner."

He smiled. Maybe his wife wasn't as dim as she acted. "You could come and run with me if you wanted. I need a replacement partner."

She frowned, "I don't know, I don't really like to run. Maybe I'll get some of those tapes with that karate guy."

"You've already got tapes." He motioned toward a tall bookshelf in their living room, full of cassettes. "They've all been played once, not even all the way through."

"I just don't have the time."

"But you have time to watch cartoons?" he said, louder than he intended.

She responded carefully, "What's your problem?"

He was tired of sparing her feelings. To tell the truth, he was very unhappy. Some people may think it's a small, superficial thing, but it wasn't to him. She wasn't the same person he'd married. Physically or mentally. Every aspect of her had grown soft, and if she didn't do something to become that girl he'd met in the gym so long ago, he was going to leave her. It wasn't something he'd been planning, but it was just something he felt, like when you've run too long and you know that crippling stitch is about to tear through your side. So he told her, "You've really let yourself go in the past few years. And if you don't do something about it, it's going to get out of control."

"Out of control?"

"Right. Like those eight-hundred-pound people on the talk shows that have to have walls cut out of their homes so they can get outside." That was extreme, but it was what he'd been thinking. Now that the floodgates were open, he didn't know how much was going to come pouring out.

"I've gained maybe fifteen pounds since college." It seemed she was speaking more to herself than him.

"How long before fifteen becomes thirty? Then sixty? Come on, Gwen, what if we have kids?"

She looked up at him, her eyes bright and shiny with tears, but her voice didn't crack. "What if we do? What if I blow up like a damned air bag? Then what, Nash?"

Could he tell her what he felt? Could he let her know that if her downward spiral continued, he'd have to find some young sex pet with a tight ass and stamina for days? "I was just trying to offer some constructive criticism." No, he couldn't tell her, but that look in her eye and the way the corner of her mouth twitched told him she already knew. "I'm going to hit the showers."

He made his way to their bathroom, peeling his sweaty shirt off as he walked.

"Nash?"

"What?" He didn't face her.

"You're such a fitness expert . . ." The contempt in her voice was almost a physical thing. "What should I do, then, Stallion?"

He sighed. "Whatever it takes." Once in the bathroom, he closed and locked the door.

God rested on Sunday. Nash didn't. Apparently, he wasn't the only one. He was at the track at seven sharp, and as always he seemed to be the last one to the party. The sky lightened, and for the first time he took a second to observe the runners instead of jumping directly into his routine. The numbers had decreased; the first resolutionist downsizing had begun.

He knew many of the people from town, and he remembered that most of them had partners a week ago. Now, they were all solo. One lady who jogged past him used to bring her dog, but at the rate she was moving, in a few weeks she might have outrun the canine. An elderly woman he'd remembered walking with her husband seemed to have traded the old geezer in for a Walkman and some ankle weights. She power-walked with her hips swinging like a pendulum. Then there was a man Nash knew from work; he was a tech, but he recognized the man one morning when he was walking with his fat teenaged daughter. Now, the girl was nowhere to be found. But that guy was running pretty fast; his rolly-polly kid had probably been slowing him down.

Then something else caught his eye.

Nike spandex pants.

Fitted cotton top.

And an ass that would make *Sports Illustrated* redo their swimsuit cover.

Who the hell was she? he thought. He'd never noticed her before. She had dark, flawless skin, just enough tits, and a short Halle-looking haircut. And the absolutely best part of it, even better than her model looks, was her stride. Perfect form, measured breaths—had to be an athlete. Who did she run for? he wondered. There was only one way to find out.

Nash couldn't contain his smile; he loved to see people that were serious about the workout.

Anxious to get out there with like-minded people, he skipped some stretches, set his watch, and took the outside lane. A lap and a half later, he veered toward the cutie with the killer stroke; some old school anticipation heated his insides. Just going to strike up a little conversation, that's all. Runner to runner.

He was suddenly conscious of his wedding band. He began to work it off with his thumb and moved that hand to his pants pocket. When he removed the band, he resumed his best stride, more excited than ever.

There were only a few yards between him and her. Licking his lips, he sped up, ready to say something.

Then he heard someone coming up close on *his* heels. He saw Ray Pudletter jogging in his peripheral vision.

"Morning, Stallion."

"I thought you were through with the early running." He didn't want to waste his talk on Fat Boy, so he speeded up slightly. It wasn't noticeable, but it would wear Ray out sooner or later and leave Nash alone with her.

"I was restless this morning. Figured I'd give it a go. I've gotten my wife in on it, so it should be easier from now on," he spoke evenly, as if he were in a brisk walk instead of a light run.

Nash stepped up some more; Ray kept pace. He glanced over his shoulder, trying to spot Mrs. Pudletter. "So what, you trying to lap her?" The woman was probably in worse shape than him, if that was possible.

"No," Ray said, then laughed, "I'm trying to lap you."

Nash didn't find the joke funny. He kicked it into high gear. "You don't want to race, Ray. It might blow your ticker, old guy."

The challenge had been issued, and Ray accepted. He passed the sexy woman and decided he'd kick it with her after he handled some light work. Plus, it wouldn't hurt to show her what a real runner was about.

They started neck and neck and hit the first turn. Nash paced himself halfheartedly. He could beat this guy with one foot.

He intended to hit the next turn at a pretty good pace, then dust him on the straightaway. They hit the turn; Nash started to count his steps, loosen his hands, and focus on his form. He was shocked because Ray was still with him.

The morning air became needle pricks in his chest. His thighs felt leaden. If I feel like this, Ray must be dying, he thought. Then, some-thing else occurred to him, something odd.

Where did all the other runners and joggers go? Where was the woman?

There were no people on the straightaways. They hit the turn, and the next straightaway was barren, too. All the people stood on the side, like this spontaneous race was an official meet.

Sweat dripped into the corner of his eye like a drop of lava. He couldn't keep this up much longer. They'd done a quarter mile at a near sprint, and Nash's body wasn't used to that type of exertion anymore. Plus, his left calf muscle was getting too tight. How the hell was Ray keeping up?

Just as he asked himself that question, something spectacular hap-pened. Ray began to edge ahead of him.

Nash put on one last burst of speed to end the whole thing. And that's exactly what happened. A painful contraction shot through his leg, and he pitched forward, rolling in the clay, scraping his knees and elbows, sending bolts of pain through them.

He ended his tumbling act on his back. His entire body burned. He stared up at the sky when a shape floated over him and blocked out the sun. It was Ray, backlit. A living shadow.

"You okay, Stallion?"

He didn't respond. This wasn't a real meet. There was no need to be a good sport. Nash figured Ray would offer a helping hand next, but he didn't. He just hovered over him. Then other living shadows appeared in Nash's field of vision: the spectators.

"It's pretty amazing how a guy like me, a real fat-ass, beat you. You're probably just overdoing it, Stallion. Muscles can only take so much." The other shadows nodded. "Maybe you should stay away from here for a few days, until you're fully rested. You get what I'm saying?"

No, he didn't. He couldn't possibly be getting what Ray was saying, because it seemed almost like Ray was warning him—threatening him—to stay away from the track. Looking at the Pud's shadow, some-thing else struck him, but it had to be a trick of the light or sweat in his eyes, because Ray seemed thinner.

The shadows left his field of vision one by one. Ray was the last, and he seemed to take an extra-long time to go away. Once he did, Nash lay there awhile longer. Ashamed. Finally, he got up. He got up and left the track.

Like he'd been told.

* * *

It was nearly nine o'clock in the evening, and Gwen wasn't home yet. It was bingo night, so she must be feeling lucky. Good.

When he'd come home from his thrashing, it was a relief to have the house to himself.

Maybe she won't come back, he thought playfully. Then, not so playfully, he thought about that gorgeous thing from the track this morning. He though about how he could never face her again. He'd beaten some of the better runners in the country in his prime, which wasn't so long ago. A jumbo like Pudletter beating him was just unreal.

Unnatural, even.

Steroids?

He struck the idea almost as soon as he thought it. He'd known guys who were into that stuff. It was a performance enhancer, but you had to have the skill to enhance first. The Pud had bad form, bad stamina, and bad breath seven days ago. No drug could improve a person that fast.

Then what? Or who?

He boiled an egg and made some toast, no butter, while he mulled it over. Who were those people who seem to be at the track at all times? Ray's new buddies? Nash didn't know half of them, and didn't think he wanted to.

Over the course of the day he watched a ball game, took a nap, and looked over some paperwork from his job until it was dark. Gwen wasn't answering her cell phone. Irked by the day's events, he was kind of wishing she'd come home. A little stress relief would be nice.

The weight she'd put on was unsightly, sure, but in the dark, fat could become P-H-A-T real quick. He could pretend she was J.Lo.

Nash checked his watch again. Where the hell was she? Bingo don't last this damned long.

Shortly before midnight the phone emitted a half ring as Nash snatched it from its cradle.

"Hello?" His voice was gruff. A string of curses formed a chain in his head as he anticipated Gwen telling him something about hanging out with her girls and losing track of time, or some other disrespectful nonsense. When he heard the voice on the line, he wished it were someone—anyone—else.

"Nash, that you?"

He sighed. "What is it, Ray?"

The man began to whimper immediately. "I need help. I'm in trouble."

"I haven't heard from my wife, Ray. I need to keep the line clear."

"Your wife's at the track, Nash. We need to go get her, before it's too late."

"What the hell are you talking about? Why"—and he sincerely wanted to know—"would my wife be at the track?" That's like Saddam Hussein being in Denver.

"It's the track. They worship the track."

He had a crazy vision of men and women in athletic wear bowing before a worn Nike CrossTrainer and some Gatorade. A yuppie version of *Lord of the Flies*. Still, Ray had his attention.

"Slow down, Ray. What did you just say?"

He told him a story about how he'd been approached by a group of runners after their first training session. He was hurting really bad, and they'd said they could help him get in better shape than he ever thought possible. They spoke to Ray like he knew them, but he would've sworn he'd never seen the people before in his life. That is, until they introduced themselves. Ray recognized their names from various functions around town, but these couldn't be the same people, he'd thought then.

"When I knew them they were fat, Nash. I mean huge. Now, they're almost as small as you."

It seems the fat-people-turned-thin owed their newfound physiques to running and chanting at the track. Like a group hypnosis. But now the leader of all this wanted them to pledge their allegiance, and apparently he was making threats to those who chose to do otherwise, those like Ray.

This reminded Nash of that Eddie Murphy movie, the remake of that old Disney flick where he was a fat professor who took a Jekyll-and-Hyde formula to get thin. This fitness-cult stuff sounded too wild to be true. Then again, so did Jim Jones with his poisonous Kool-Aid.

"Why don't you call the police, Ray?"

"Because some big-time townspeople are in on this, too."

Wow. A conspiracy. "So why are you telling me?"

"I told you. Your wife is out there. You don't want her involved with these people. They're bad news. With you on my side, we can expose them."

Shit. If they could help Gwen drop a few pounds, they were all right in his book.

"I'm sorry, Ray. This sounds a little too *X-Files* for me. I appreciate your concern"—not really—"but I seriously doubt Gwen would have anything to do with fitness, let alone a cult."

There was a pause on the line; he thought Ray may have hung up, but after a moment, he responded, "You've seen those weirdos that are there all the time. I know you have. Don't you want to see what they do when nobody's looking?"

Now Nash was intrigued. "You trying to tell me they're out there right now?"

"See for yourself."

Those night resolutionists were a strange bunch—motivated, if nothing else. And Fat Boy said Gwen was out there with them. Their little talk yesterday must've really gotten to her. About damned time. Maybe this was worth a peek.

According to his watch, it was midnight. He'd missed his bedtime already, so he'd be skipping his run and sleeping in tomorrow. Another hour or two wouldn't hurt. "Come get me."

He hung up. Ten minutes later Ray was at his door. When he stepped out of the night and into Nash's brightened entryway, Nash saw what he'd thought was an illusion earlier. The man *was* thinner. The doughy skin around his jowls was tighter and firm. The radial-tire bulge that was his midsection was more like a miniature spare now.

"You all right, Ray?" Maybe the guy was sick—mono or something.

"I'll be better once someone else knows the truth."

Nash rolled his eyes. Whatever. He still wasn't buying this whole cult thing. "Let's get this over with."

They parked in the high school lot. Plenty of cars were already there. Diffuse light filtered from the track's pit, like meteor radiation seeping from a crater in old horror movies. Guess they do turn the lights on at night.

He walked to the edge of the pit slowly; Ray followed. Down below, all sorts of people—at least fifty—were running laps with their hands held high. They were all holding things. He couldn't make out what they were holding, but it could've been the Olympic torch the way their arms were stretched to the sky, as if saluting the gods.

Nash tried to spot Gwen, but from his height and vantage point, it was impossible to tell if she was down there at all. What was apparent was the chanting. Not English—he didn't know what it was, but it was one unified voice. "Well, I'll be damned." He turned. "Ray, that's cra—"

Ray's pistol was pointed at his sternum; a cool smirk appeared on his newly slim face. "I don't want to have to shoot you, Stallion. But you know what they say—old horses make new glue."

Nash didn't know they said that, but he took Ray's word for it. "Take the path down."

Careful not to make any sudden movements, he did as he was told. He wanted to scream but was afraid of a bullet in the back. What did Ray have in mind for him? They stepped onto the clay, and everyone who was running began to fall in tow with them as they cut across the lanes and onto the grass center of the quarter-mile track. They went to the single clay strip that led into the sand basin of the long-jump pit, and stopped while everyone gathered around.

Dull shock overcame Nash as he scanned the faces of the people that were a part of this cult. They were faces he knew vaguely, but just like Ray said, they used to be fat. Now they were all slender shadows of their former selves.

Ray backed off Nash; the crowd fell in behind him. Nash spun around with his back toward the long jump pit. "You're the leader, aren't you, Ray?"

"No, I'm only a servant, Nash. Only a servant."

He lowered his gun; a serene expression graced his features "We brought you here for the initiation, Nash. All new members have to be initiated with a display of loyalty. You have to give to get," he chuckled, patting his shrunken gut. "Well, I guess in this case you have to give to lose."

In his mind, Nash saw the members slicing their palms with a knife and joining hands in some sort of blood pact. "I'm not joining your crazy cult."

"You don't understand," Ray said.

The crowd split. Gwen stepped into the open in a brand-new Adidas sweat suit.

"You're not the one being initiated," Gwen said. "I am."

"What the hell's going on here? What are you doing out here with these nuts?"

"After those things you said to me, I went to Beasley's Grocery for some Maxi-Trim pills to control my appetite." She glanced Ray's way. "The Pud saw me, said he knew my hurt, and he knew a better way. Then he brought me to the track, and I understood."

Just then he smelled it. It was a stench he knew from a time when he and Gwen had gone on a week-long cruise and forgot to empty the trash, not realizing that the remains of a chicken dinner were resting at the bottom of the Glad bag. When they returned, their entire house smelled like the pocket of air Nash was now in. Rotting meat.

The group smiled simultaneously, even Gwen. He backed up a step. "You crazies stay away from me. You hear me? Stay away. Damned resolutionists."

He scanned the crowd and finally realized what they were holding to the sky as they paraded around the track. One lady's was long and white with a jagged end. Another had a short jointed one. And then another, the man who used to bring his dog to the track, held something that seemed like a mandible—not human, though. They were all bones, and that's what mattered to Nash, because things were starting to click into place, despite his reluctance to recognize the truth.

For a brief, insane moment, he had a flashback of a Slim Fast commercial where a lady, after shedding 150 pounds, proclaimed, "I lost a whole person."

Fuck this. He rushed Ray, the man with the weapon, catching him off guard. With a right haymaker he tried to break the Pud's jaw. With his left he snatched the pistol from his hand.

As the Pud collapsed, Nash wrenched Gwen's arm and prepared to shoot his way through the crowd blocking the way to the stairs leading out of this hole.

"Let us through. Now."

No one budged, or even seemed concerned.

Fine, that's how they want it.

He told his hand to squeeze the trigger, but just as he did, a line of white fire shot across his arm. He heard the shot go off, but it didn't register that the gun was on the ground.

Along with his hand.

The bloody stump of his wrist shone like onyx in the moonlight. He smacked the ground with a thump when his legs were yanked out from under him.

"I'm not the leader," he barely heard Ray say over his own screaming. "The track is."

The pain in his wrist was immense. He teetered on the edge of shock. Still, he recognized that the squeezing tentacles wrapped around his legs were actually the white lines that bordered the strip of clay leading to the long-jump pit. One tentacle—the one that lopped off his hand—was smeared red and pink from his blood. They reeled him toward the sandy pit, which had opened to expose long, rock-hard teeth that pointed to the sky like stalagmites.

"No, Gwen. Please!" he screamed, and wished for shock to set in.

She glanced at his severed hand and grimaced. Ray motioned to it. "You have to take it; it's a talisman for the change."

"You told me to do whatever it takes, honey," Gwen said as she steeled herself, bent, and scooped up his hand. Though it was dark, and despite the feeling of his sanity being uprooted, Nash knew he wasn't hallucinating. His wife lifted his hand to the sky, chanted, and transformed. It was subtle, but she became noticeably thinner.

"Please stop this, Gwen," he was blubbering like a child. He saw his wife look at the Pud, and the rest of the resolutionists. Something happened. They all nodded in agreement and faced him.

Suddenly, the paint-stripe tentacles loosened, then released him to return to the sides of the clay strip. The teeth sank into the pit. The track was a normal track again.

Two resolutionists came and helped him to his feet, using a sweatband as a tourniquet for his gushing stump.

"Gwen, thank you, baby. Thank you. I love you so much, I'm sorry about all I said. Now that you're giving me a second chance, I'm going to treat you right."

"I'm not giving you a second chance, Nash." She lifted her knee to her chest, stretching her hamstring. "I'm giving you a head start."

A female resolutionist, the same woman he'd fantasized about just yesterday, picked up the pistol and aimed at the sky. She fired.

His head jerked back and forth, watching them all begin limbering up.

Ray said, "You've got thirty seconds, Stallion."

Nash stumbled across the grass to the inside line. He hobbled up the straightaway. The exit was blocked; the slopes were too steep to climb in his weakened state. Still, he couldn't just give in and accept defeat. He would run in a race he had no hope of winning.

It seemed he wasn't going to outlast the resolutionists after all.

If the Walls Could Talk

L.A. Banks

Philadelphia. Winter

Dominique stood slowly, stretched, and allowed the chill within the three-story brick house to embrace her and dry the sweat from her skin before putting on her robe. Crimson silk slid against her and made her shudder, the robe a smooth caress that reminded her of Eric's touch. The deep valley between her legs was still sopping from the encounter, and every now and then a pleasant twinge reverberated through the soft folds of it, a slick trail of moisture beginning to creep down her inner thighs.

In the early morning darkness she looked back once at the prone, sculpted male body in her bed, her glance lingering to appreciate its magnificent structure. There was nothing like a black man—and in Grandma's house, at that.

Cold hardwood floors helped bring clarity to her mind as she left the warmth of the Oriental bedroom rug and padded barefoot down the long, narrow hall, then descended the stairs. *You know you should have left that nice young man be.* Dominique smiled. The shades didn't know the half of it. She was young; they were decrepit. Celibacy wasn't her thing—not at twenty-eight years old.

She stopped at the landing and glanced in the large, ornate mirror. What was she doing? A bad economy and no job had sent her to live in the family home once more and had taken her away from her once independent apartment life. Now she was back here with *them* again. The crazy people. All the rest of her cousins had had enough sense to get out and stay out, but four months with no job had considerably altered her circumstances. None of her friends were in a position to let her move in with them; go figure.

Dominique let out a sigh. Sooner or later she'd been bound to break down, and Eric had worked his magic on her. What was a girl to do? Turnabout was fair play; now it was time for her to work a little magic on him.

"Sorry, Nana," she whispered offhandedly. The moot apology would have to suffice. They should have gone to his place or a hotel, but then, he had fifty excuses about why that wasn't possible.

Waning moonlight cast a bluish tint to her dark walnut skin. Her thick, shoulder-length natural hair was tussled and gave the impression of a banshee rather than a woman after an all-nighter. Then again, perhaps the illusion was accurate. Her lipstick was gone; her mascara formed dark rings under her eyes. But it was so good; however, he belonged to somebody else. Maybe her curves had overcome his resistance. That wasn't her fault, though. Dominique pouted, her full mouth still swollen from the battering of his. What to do, what to do?

Tea would be the answer. She could sort this out over an herbal brew. Grandma always made herbal remedies, and stood before the stove when there was a question to be answered. Dominique closed her robe tighter, withdrew her gaze from her reflection, and made her way to what had always been referred to as Nana's laboratory—the kitchen.

Not needing to turn on the lights, she knew her way around the finite space on Girard Avenue blind. *Don't do that boy like that, Dom.* Yeah, yeah, whateva. The walls were talking again. They had some nerve offering such conservative advice when back in the day . . . shoot—anything went in here.

"All's fair in love and war," Dominique whispered, creating a soft echo in the empty room as she turned on a gas burner and watched the low blue flame under the kettle. He was already done—he'd eaten from her kitchen the night before. It was an elaborate dinner of Creole cuisine. Wine, candlelight, soft music, and wanton love . . . this was just the finishing touch. A little finesse to keep him coming back for more.

Nana had been gone for years, just as all the Jackson women had died one by one, and yet they were still trying to run her life. *Hmmmph, hmmmph, hmmmph.* Dominique took down a tea ball from the windowsill. Frost had created a wintry lace edging to the panes beyond the lemon yellow curtains. That was Nana's favorite color; the hue of sunshine was all over the house.

She considered what they'd said, and issued a soft tick of defiance with her tongue. Didn't they already know it was too late? A brother shouldn't have lied, fine as he was and all, notwithstanding. This was a matter of honor, about respect. The question she'd posed had been a simple one: Are you married? The answer had been an equally simple lie: Of course not, baby.

Closing her eyes, she let her hands travel along the length of Mason jars on the drain board, stopping when her fingertips began to tingle . . . just like she'd seen her grandmother do so many times before. Conjuring was an art merely complicated by herbal science in her family. All the women were proficient masters of the craft. Dominique's fingers deftly worked at the brittle leaves in the darkness, filling the tea ball as the kettle began to rumble quietly.

What did they want from her? This was in her nature. Her earliest memory of this skill was as a child of five, riding on the bus and feeling Nana's grip tighten on her hand when her gaze became riveted to another old lady's parcel. It was like an unspoken warning had been transmitted from adult to child, but she couldn't stop looking at the moving bag.

Clear as day, she could remember the brown sack twitching and jumping on the woman's lap. Her eyes had remained steadfast, and yet there was something in Nana's hold that cautioned her not to ask questions until there were no listeners around.

"Why was that lady's bag jumping, Nana?" she'd whispered once they got off the bus.

"Lady had a rooster in there from the farmer's market. Gonna do some work," Nana had said bluntly.

"But you do work, and I ain't never seen no roosters in your kitchen, Nana." It had been a simple question then, coming from a child.

But the response from her grandmother was oblique. "There ain't no such word as 'ain't,' baby. Learn to talk the king's English, and go to school. Don't you be worrying your mind about old women's work."

Dominique looked up from her still position before the sink when the murmur of female laughter beyond the white-painted metal cabinets greeted her thoughts.

"Am I lying?" she asked the nothingness.

No, baby . . . but . . .

Victory tugged at the edge of Dominique's mouth, creating a lopsided grin. "Uh-huh. Y'all did work like this back in the day, didn't you? Be honest. And you never really answered my question, Nana."

That's because ya need to leave sleeping dogs lie, before ya get up with fleas.

Now, this was some mess. They'd gotten her mother into this, too. Her mother's voice was always distinctive. Millicent's voice was the bossy one. She could tell it from Nana's in a second, just like her aunts Jessie, Joyce, Betty, Lena, and Maude—all had their unique ways to let her know they were in the room. This morning, she wouldn't let them get under her skin.

"Mom, you are the last one to have anything to say about this—like you can talk."

The response was immediate. Several cabinet doors opened hard, banging against the ones adjacent to them. Her mother always had the worst temper. When Dominique reached for a cup, an angry cupboard door slammed shut. Oh, so it was gonna be like this, huh?

"Need I remind you about the men in the basement?" Dominique folded her arms over her chest, losing patience. The cupboard door creaked open, and she retrieved the cup she wanted with an exasperated sigh. *That's right.* Her aunties were now in it, taking her side. Dominique went back to the sink and dropped the filled bamboo tea ball into the mug and reached for the kettle.

But as soon as the water hit the cup, dissenting murmurs filled the kitchen. The sweet scent of the tea leaves threaded through their voices until the steam from the kettle was almost a visible fusion of sound, smell, and thick vapor. What was all the fuss? It was just a man.

But his poor wife didn't have a thing to do with this, Dom.

"I'm not messing with her."

Yeah, but, we've learned the hard way, what goes around comes around.

"True, but that took years, right? And you're still here."

That's the point, baby-girl. Do you still want to be here after it's all over?

"How is that a bad thing?"

Betty, the child has a point. It's really not that bad.

"See." Dominique shook her head as she stirred her tea, listening to the debate from a very detached place in her mind.

I just don't want her to go too far . . . seeing that, it's ugly.

But, Millie, we never went that far . . .

Yes, we did. Don't lie, Jessie.

When!

Need I remind you about Zeek?

Hush—and he deserved it.

Dominique set down her cup, covered her mouth, and spoke though her fingers. "Y'all did Uncle Zeek?"

Had it coming.

Was no way 'round it, right, Lena?

Joyce would know . . . Wouldn't leave that heifer alone. So Maude got him good.

Made a baby, he did.

That's why the lady workin' for her had that bag, baby-girl. Don't test your Nana; I know what I'm talking about.

"What!" Now Dominique was moving through the kitchen, rounding the table as though she were floating with their voices. "Nana, you knew that lady on the bus?"

Yeah, I did. We all know each other. Bitch.

Silence. Nana had cussed?

She was gonna find out sooner or later, Millie.

A deep sigh echoed through the kitchen.

Comes by it natural.

Dominique picked up her cup and took a very slow sip. Her eyes studied every surface in the room. She watched a mouse nervously edge along the baseboards, and she surveyed the peeling linoleum—waiting.

We used to just help folks straighten out entanglements, baby-girl.

Or would block negative energy—we never blocked blessings.

Your momma's right. We didn't generally do revenge work, or pull a man from where he was supposed to be.

We helped women get rid of problems. That's all, child.

But you fixin' to take somebody's husband just 'cause you want him, and that's not allowed.

"No, I'm not," Dominique said fast, her voice becoming shrill as it bounced off the cabinets and the walls. "I'm getting ready to help this woman get rid of a problem."

All right.

If you say so.

But seemed like to us that you kinda getting yourself pretty attached . . .

"I thought we had an agreement about what goes on in my room." Hands went to her hips as she quickly set down her tea.

We ain't hafta go in your room. Your ass was loud enough—

Jessie, please!

"Then tell me, who are all the men in the basement—all the young voices? Especially which one is Uncle Zeek's?"

Well, now, that's a long story.

A cabinet slammed open, then shut, and the house went still again. She could hear the kitchen clock tick, and the faint drip of water as a drop exited the faucet and splattered against porcelain.

Dominique sipped her tea, her nonchalance a thin veil for her threat. They were truly getting on her last nerve. "I might have to go down there and ask them one day, if—"

Don't you dare!

All four burners on the stove lit, flamed high, and then went out.

"Then stay out of my bedroom," she challenged. "You all swear you weren't in there when—"

Of course not! That's the last thing we wanted to see—and you shouldn't have been so nasty in Nana's house!

Dominique chuckled, her senses getting keener with each sip of tea. That had always been the compromise—she would not talk to the male voices in the dusty old basement if the women in her family would stay out of her bedroom. Cool.

She glanced up at the ceiling, wondering if their warnings had merit.

Finishing her tea, she could feel her strides out of the kitchen become as agile as a cat's. She took the steps two at a time without effort and slunk along the narrow corridors to her third-floor bedroom—hunting. From the corner of her eye she could see shadows moving along the paint with her, trying to be inconspicuous. She focused on her houseguest, ignoring her family's intrusion. She scowled at the hallway picture as she passed it, and waited a moment before approaching the bedroom door, telling them without words that they'd better stay out of *her* room.

And there he was . . . still lying in the same position she'd left him in. On his back, a gentle smile on his face, his eyes closed, breathing the heavy inhales and exhales of the extremely contented. Such a shame. But he shouldn't have lied. There was nothing like a black man, though . . . especially a tall, six-foot-four one made out of onyx steel.

"Hey, baby," she whispered low in her throat like a purr when she came to the side of the bed. "It's almost daylight. You better get home to your wife before you get into trouble."

His laugh was a low rumble that came up from the center of his chest. She covered the sound with the flat of her palm, enjoying the vibration it sent through her hand.

"She's cool," he said in a sleepy voice with his eyes still closed. "It's all good."

Dominique cocked her head to the side, muscles beneath her butter soft skin twitching. *Thought your ass wasn't married.* Rage began to consume her, starting a low rumble within her just like the teakettle had slowly boiled.

"You love her?"

"Aw, baby . . . don't get deep on me. We had a great night. I'll be back."

"I know you will," she said ever so sweetly. "You sure you wanna leave?"

"Naw," he murmured, pulling her down on top of him. "I could stay here forever, baby."

"I thought you weren't married." She'd asked the question as she found his mouth, her tongue tangling with his.

His deep, rich moan traveled up the length of her, just ran all through her.

"A technicality," he murmured when their mouths parted.

"You got any kids?" Her question was hard to ask as his hands found her bottom and began making slow circles against the silk fabric of her robe. But none of that changed how angry she was at him. The more he touched her and the hotter he made her, the madder she got. *Liar!*

"Naw . . . I mean, not with my wife. Why, you want one?"

Total, unmitigated gall. She smiled as she stared at him. His sleepy eyes looked so sexy and lazy, like they could just drink her in. Now, see, this kinda brother was problematic. "You sure you wanna stay, or—"

"Yeah, I'm sure, baby. Shit, after last night, I'm not trying to go home."

"Okay," she replied in a throaty whisper. "Have it your way, but don't say I didn't warn you."

It was *very* hard to get up. The rock-hard length of him was pulsing against the slickness of her damp thigh. But the sun was almost up, too. So she needed to make a decision. This brother had no conscience.

"I think you should leave," she said fast, and gathered her robe around her, then stood.

"What? You mad all because I'm married, and gonna leave me hanging like this?" He sat up and threw his legs over the side of the bed and stood, a scowl now replacing what had been such a handsome smile. He began searching for his underwear.

She studied him with one hand on her hip, looking him up and down. Didn't make no sense. Brother had no remorse, no shame. But as he paced toward her, his energy wasn't right.

"Look, you probably knew the deal before we even went here. You were game, I was game, and wasn't nobody in the mood to get deep— feel me? So don't play this wounded-woman thing. What good-looking brother with a good job doesn't have a wife or a woman stashed some- where?"

"All I asked was for you to tell me, so I could decide," she said in a quiet voice, glancing at the walls when the lotion slid along the dresser two inches. This man was towering over her, looking like he wanted to slap her. All of a sudden being five-six felt *very* short next to him.

"I'm out," he said abruptly, and began hunting for his pants. "I don't need this bullshit."

Dominique shook her head. "Too late, baby."

"What the fuck are you talking about, 'too late'?" He glared at her with such disdain that she almost turned away.

"You ever hit a woman?"

"Don't play with me. I'll kick your ass if you come at me. Where's my damned shoes! That's all I need is some psycho bitch trippin' and send- ing me home to my wife with—"

"See, that's just the thing. You're not going home," she murmured. "You're the problematic kinda brother. . . . She doesn't even know it, but she's better off without you."

"What! You threatening me? Threatening to call my wife?"

The girl was right.

Yup.

Good instincts.

Baby-girl, put that fool in the basement.

"What the hell is going on?" He turned first one direction, then the other, trying to get a bead on the voices that seemed to emanate from the walls. "You'd better stop playing games, and tell your girls to stop playing games! I'll sue your ass and kick it, too, if you have some video- tape bullshit going on—trust me." Whipping on his briefs and jeans, he yanked his zipper up, snatched his fleece and T-shirt, and reached under the bed for his socks and shoes.

That's when the words that she knew by heart began to tumble from her lips. That's when time stood still and the room got very, very cold. That's when the door slammed shut and something held his hand under the bed, making him thrash about like a jackrabbit caught in a snare. That's when pure panic slapped the arrogance off his face. That's when tears welled up in his eyes. That's when he opened his mouth to yell, but no sound came out. That's when the furniture began to shake and the panes in the windows rattled like a trolley was going by. And as her mouth continued to move, the sweet taste of Nana's tea made her lips sticky, and her breaths slow and controlled, and made her fingertips tingle until, inch by inch, that tall fine man got drawn into a dark place under the bed.

She could hear an extended holler reverberate through the house. Sounded like he was in the pipes on his way to the basement. With care, she made the bed and straightened the bureau, taking her time to fluff the edge of the rug and restore order. Too bad, so sad . . . and the brother was *excellent* in bed.

"Y'all came in my room," she said quietly, not angry, just weary as she went downstairs.

Well . . . under the circumstances . . .

"I hear you," she replied without emotion.

He deserved to go in the basement, baby.

"Yeah. He did."

"Is that how the other men got there?"

More or less.

"That's all y'all had to say," Dominique mumbled as she went to the kitchen to fix herself breakfast.

It would have been unseemly for us to tell you about all the ex-lovers in our lives.

Isn't proper.

No real lady tells her business like that—not even to family.

You were too young.

Dominique sighed as she found the egg carton in the refrigerator and broke open an egg in a bowl and began beating it. "I hate to tell you ladies, but this is the new millennium."

See, that's the problem—you young girls have no couth.

"Nana, please."

That's why we didn't want your fast behind to go down in the basement.

Would shame us all.

"How many men are down there?"

Silence.

Dominique chuckled. "Okaaay. Then, how long do they stay down there?"

Until you're not mad at them anymore.

"Then what happens to them?"

More silence.

She didn't care. At least she could eat her French toast in peace.

Rather than speak into the nothingness, Dominique took her time, leisurely preparing a full breakfast. She would spare no detail on herself this morning, even pulling out the nice ivory linen napkins she kept in the dining room breakfront, folding one carefully to set it beside the good china plate rimmed in gold. All women needed pampering after an ordeal. But all the fussing about, and despite her steadfast determination not to think about what her mother, Nana, and five aunties could have done—with who knows how many men—in the family house basement what happened would not go away.

She was quite sure that she'd heard a titter of laughter coming from behind the china closet. They were definitely getting on her nerves. Sometimes she wished they'd all just go away, would just follow the white light and vanish over onto the other side like normal folks did.

You don't mean that. Her mother's voice was like a smooth balm as it caressed her awareness.

The child is so sad, and all by herself. Millie, let us tell her.

Sudden tears formed in Dominique's eyes, and she took a healthy slurp of her orange juice, feigning indifference. "If you all have some old, deep dark secrets down there and don't want to tell me, fine. I'll just sell the house and move out and live like a normal person."

A scattered gasp rippled past the hung pictures, down the molding, and under the rug. Why she hadn't thought of that before gave her pause. But even to her own ears it sounded like an idle threat. This house had been in the family for generations, and she was the only one left with inheritance papers to claim it.

"No normal man would stay in here with me," she told the large, vacant parlor. She looked down at her plate, having lost all interest in the elaborate meal she'd prepared. "And if I ever did find someone who wanted to marry me . . . What if he wanted to do what regular people do—fix up the basement and call it a rec room, huh? Would you all be down there scaring him to death, or my kids? Then, what if I got a really good job in another city, or married a man whose job required that we move? See, you all never thought beyond the four walls of this house. In your day, people moved somewhere, planted roots, and stayed put!"

She stood and collected her plate, fighting back the tears as she yelled all her deferred hopes and dreams into the empty room. Silence greeted her as a response, and for that she was thankful. She wanted to boo-hoo wail. They just didn't know.

Standing before the garbage pail, she scraped her plate, watching good food go to waste and not caring. She was going to waste in this house, becoming something tainted and rotten, and it was time to go.

Baby, a soft voice whispered, *you're right.*

We were just having so much fun for a while.

"What's in the basement, Nana?" Dominique's voice was brittle, but the weariness within her had taken much of the attitude out of her tone.

Aw, baby-girl, her aunt murmured from near the refrigerator, *every lover that did us or one of our girlfriends wrong is down there with his dick hard.*

"What!" It was all Dominique could do not to drop her mother's best plate.

Lord have mercy, Jessie. Did you have to say it to the child like that?

Well, it's the truth, Mom. The child is of age.

That's not the point!

When a chair slid across the room, Dominique jumped back to get out of the way.

I'm just saying, we take turns, niecie.

"Aunt Joyce?" Dominique set the plate down very slowly on the counter. "But . . . but, you were *saved.*"

I am saved—every Wednesday night, a shrill voice giggled. *Your Mom has Tuesdays; your aunt J. has Thursdays—*

That's grown folks' business!

She couldn't help but laugh as a raucous argument ensued. "Hold on . . . you mean to tell me those men—however many we won't even discuss—are down in the basement as a permanent part of *this* house, ready to . . ." Dominique couldn't even finish the thought, much less verbalize it out loud; it was too wild.

That's why your Nana didn't want you down there. They was left in the last state they had been in before things got . . . well, ugly. The way we liked them best, when they was being nice—and useful.

Truth, niecie. Before we all passed . . . remember them cabarets we used to throw in the house?

"Oh . . . my . . . God . . ." Dominique just blinked, and she could feel the muscles in her jaw go slack.

Your Nana read cards, did potions, and helped women with their troubles. Sometimes she'd have a client that needed to . . . uh, address her loneliness. Especially during the war years. Wasn't no harm in it all. They was all dogs, like that one you just sent down there.

A thousand questions slammed into her brain at once. Her Nana was running a ghostly male brothel in the basement? Words were slow to form, and those that did came out in disjointed fits and starts.

"Let me get this straight . . . Your spells have made these men a permanent part of this house, like you all . . . and if a woman goes down there . . ."

All she has to do is call one by name. It's fixed up real nice down there.

Not musty and damp and scary at all.

Very pleasant, with feminine touches.

"And what about the ones you don't call? What are they doing? Hanging from the freakin' rafters?" She was incredulous. A series of high-pitched giggles surrounded her.

No, they wait their turn, and behave themselves—or it can be years before a woman might have a mind to call on them.

Best thing is when the wives come and call a different name. Almost had the hot water heater overturned a coupla times, and my pipes busted, chile. And all they can do is fuss and watch.

"But you killed them!" Dominique felt a queasy knot developing in her stomach as she thought about the brother who'd just been sucked out of her bedroom.

Now, now . . . they ain't dead. Didn't nobody kill nobody.

A chorus of agreement zinged through the kitchen, making the curtains flutter at the window.

Young people. Too dramatic. They's just trapped—in stasis. We turn some back out of doors, when we have a mind to do so.

Dominique's gaze went toward the pantry and out the small window in the back door. Ice had covered the bushes and the trees, forming a thick crust on everything in the yard and alley, even the trash cans. She could only pray that those men were like that—frozen, trapped, their spirits in some netherworld state, but still alive. They were skilled professionals, herbal artists, not murderers! Weren't they?

"Nana, I'm going to ask you this one time, and I expect a straight answer."

Don't you take that tone with me, girl. I—

"Nana," Dominique repeated, "I'm serious."

Silence. Not even the faucet dripped. Good. They were listening.

"If I sell this house, rent it, or leave for any reason, what happens to all those men in the basement?"

Silence. Then a murmur of dissent.

Aw, them old buzzards would just go on home.

"How long some of them men been gone, Nana?"

Fifty years, give or take. Why?

"Why? Why!"

What's the difference, daughter of mine? Their normal age would catch up to 'em, once they leave this house. They'd go back talking some crazy mess about being abducted by witches that would sound like a pack of lies, or like they were nuts or having senior delusions. Men lie all the time, and tell long stories. Their families would probably take 'em back when they wandered on home. No harm done. We just got them out of some poor woman's hair for several years, without any legal drama.

One thing's for sure, though—they'd be cured of chasing stray tail.

Old as their asses are now, shoot . . . they can't chase nothin' but some Geritol.

Completely speechless, Dominique closed her eyes. These old dolls were crazy!

Now, the young ones would just go on home a few years or days late, if you thinkin' on that young boy you just sent to the doghouse. He'd have to explain his whereabouts, but another thing for sure—he most likely won't be messing with nobody but his wife till the end of time.

"Y'all . . . what do I have to do to clean this house out?"

Aw, baby-girl, you gonna shoo all the menfolk away? They do have their purposes.

"Yes, I am."

Not Zeek, though, suga. I ain't done being mad at his rusty behind.

"How long you had my uncle down there, Auntie? I thought the poor man died sixty years ago from mustard gas complications he got in World War II."

Well . . . not exactly. Been mad at him since then, but didn't consign him to the basement till he lost his damned mind in 1983 and made a baby by some club hoochie. You was only eight, and that chile he made a baby with wasn't all that much older than you—still in her teens! So, on my nights I pick everybody but him, and my sisters ain't having him. His ass been strung out watching since—

"Uh-huh . . . I understand, and that was more than I needed to know . . . but enough is enough, ladies."

A collective groan swept through the kitchen. She could just imagine her mother and aunties manifesting in their club finery from the forties era, hair all done up, nails painted, figures svelte, or even her Nana serving pure roaring twenties, and macking the basement as though it were a Harlem supper club. Selecting men from the menu to take a stroll in the back room—only the lucky ones allowed to manifest in the twilight hours, while the others waited and hankered for attention. Not under her roof. It was like reigning in a houseful of out-of-control teenagers. They'd run amock. Totally outrageous.

"Weren't you ever afraid that one of them would become violent and wring your necks from all this yang you did to them?"

Pullease, her mother's voice sniffed. *This is a black woman's house; we run this joint.*

That's right, one auntie chimed in. *We just wave our hand and they're wood.*

They start complaining and we snap our fingers and drown out the la-la with some Billie Holiday.

You know, you could stop worrying about finding a regular job and do some real work, another aunt offered. *The pay is way better.*

All you have to do is read the cards down in the basement, and have your client lie down on the sofa, get a description of her dream man, and come upstairs, shut the door, and have some tea for an hour.

During the lean years, her Nana agreed, *we made a bundle—the Great Depression didn't have nothing on us. And when the Italians tried to take our after-hours club . . .*

"You *do not* have Italian men down in this basement, Nana!"

Men is men, baby.

Dominique covered her face with her hands.

Didn't they teach you anything in business school? Gotta diversify your portfolio.

"I'm cleaning out this house, y'all," she whispered on a heavy sigh. "I love you all, but you're gonna have to go into the light."

Fat chance! her Nana chuckled. *We gonna hafta have a long conversation with the Almighty to get into the light after all this.*

It was a nice run while it lasted, though, Mom.

Yeah, girl, I'ma miss the ones stashed over by the double sink.

Uhmmm-hmmm . . . see, young people have no appreciation for the finer things in life.

"Tell me how to do it, so we can just be done." Dominique sat heavily in a yellow plastic-covered kitchen chair.

Nope.

"C'mon. Stop playing, now."

Nope. You have to stop being mad. That's the only way the reverse spell will take.

"All of this is pissing me off, truly."

See . . . now you understand why we could never do it.

That's right. Every one of us had just cause to be mad for years.

Uh-huh. How a sister gonna get rid of an attitude, when she came by it with righteous conviction?

You know what? Maybe she do need to go on down that basement and listen to all them sorry-ass excuses we've collected from menfolk over the years. Maybe she needs to hear why they was running on wives, doing heartbreak and mayhem . . . and if they don't make her mad, then she can let 'em go.

Silence. But this time it was a standoff. Dominique could feel their challenge throb in her temples like a pulse.

She wouldn't dare.

She ain't lived long enough to know how hurtful they can be.

Let her go 'head on.

Now they were talking smack. Okay.

She took her time to collect herself and walked to the basement door, cracking it open ever so slowly. The intellectual side of her mind told her this was nuts. A reasonable person would just sell the house, but then, she had no idea if a real estate agent would even be allowed enough peace to do a walk-through. These murmurs and whispers had been with her as a child, had always been a part of the family—just like stirring bubbling pots, cutting cards, and selling bootleg liquor amid love-drunk adults stumbling from the under-radar club her family ran. All of it had been just a part of growing up in Nana's house.

For as long as she remembered, multiple family members lived in this one huge house. Cousins and aunties, husbands came and went and disappeared . . . The neighbors gossiped, but all still returned for specialized services or a pack of undisclosed herbal remedies that could fix what ailed you—all unregulated, non–FDA-approved medicinals provided by her grandmother, then her mother and aunts. This house was a warm, vibrant, crazy home filled with life, history, voices, and energy—a neighborhood institution, a treasure, really. Things that were grown folks' business were about to be revealed, and a part of her was sad that she'd have to let it go.

"Daddy isn't down here, is he?"

No, chile, pullease. He died before me of natural causes.

"You sure?"

A long sigh whistled through the kitchen as her mother's answer.

Without much room to stall, Dominique flipped on the light and gazed down into the space that she'd been forbidden to enter as a child. It was so clear now why the washer and dryer were out in the pantry instead of in the basement. She almost laughed as she carefully picked her way down the carpeted steps.

There was nothing scary about the space, truthfully. It was well lit, with pretty Tiffany lamps on either side of an impressive, top-shelf-liquor–stocked mahogany bar, complete with a brass foot rail and red velvet cushioned stools. Small round tables were scattered about the wood-paneled space, and an old jukebox stood alone in the corner. The odd thing was, nothing was dusty when she went down into the place that had been uninhabited by the living for years. Then again, everything about all this was odd.

There was a steel door that led to the street, which was bolted, and as she made her way deeper into the unfamiliar terrain, there was a back room separated by a curtain of beads, with a love seat, a chaise lounge, and a queen-size bed. Hmmm . . . a play room, no doubt. Dominique shook her head.

Yet, she marveled at how the white satin duvet and pillowcases looked fresh, and there wasn't a thin film of dust on any surface. Above a cherry dresser was a large gold-framed mirror . . . the one that had been in her mother's bedroom.

Pick me, a deep, baritone voice whispered, making her start and turn around.

Call me by name, baby. I'm Tony.

She got me all wrong, sweetness. I'm Duce. Let me buy you a drink and I'll explain everything.

Hey, gorgeous . . . got a minute? They call me Ice; let's just talk for a few and we can work this out.

Rich-timbered, wonderful, sexy male voices all whispered pleas, layering their murmurs, their sounds, their complaints upon the next until she could no longer make out what any one voice in particular was saying. They all had a story—a long, convoluted story about how their dilemma wasn't what it seemed, and what had transpired to land them in the basement.

Soon she became aware of the scent of the men's cologne—different flavors, fragrances, almost as if the different hues were battling and competing for her attention, for a little release from wherever Nana had banished them. She could almost feel the warmth of their breath against her face. Then she heard a record drop in the other room. It made her freeze and then hasten her steps into the main bar area. She watched the lights on the jukebox blaze on, and the scratchy vocal from Billie Holiday filled the room: "God bless the child who's got his own."

"So, true, Nana."

She took a seat at the bar and listened to the sultry lament coming from the jukebox, trying to decide. It was so early in the morning, but she could definitely use a drink. As she stood to round the bar and pour herself a stiff one, that's when she saw them. Her mother, her grandmother, and five aunties sashayed in, manifesting from behind a column, a doorway, from behind a picture hanging on the walls, and they were each so beautiful, just as she'd remembered them but better, more radiant, younger. Hair up-twisted and rolled, ball gowns that hugged every curve, deep-plunge V necklines, slits up the sides of satin, seam-up-the-back stockings, rhinestone earrings, small beaded clutch bags, and icy pastels in blues, white, aqua, mauve, lavender, pink, and of course, yellow . . . each unique, each holding her own against time.

But the vision of her mother took her breath away. Seed pearls scattered a sexy pattern over her mother's ivory dress, and it was the same one in an old photo album from years gone by. The sight of her mother's smile made tears fall in earnest this time, and as the apparition drew near her, a kiss swept her face like a gentle breeze.

We are all so proud of you, baby-girl. We been misbehaving, we know.

We were just having fun, her grandmother said, chuckling. *We know we've gotta go.*

Her aunts nodded and all conceded on a weary chorus, *All right, Mom.*

Gentle breezes, kisses, and hugs petted her face, and she watched in awe as the women in her family stood side by side, hands on hips, and began a lengthy roll call that could have belonged to the armed services. Fine men, short men, tall men, men in uniform, men in suits, men in work duds, stocky men, slim goodies, pudgy men, brick-house-built men, all flavors, all colors, began filling the room, all talking at once, all confused, all competing for the attention of the woman who'd claimed him.

Open the door, suga, her aunt Jessie called out. *It's standing room only in here, baby.*

Dominique's motions were jerky as she walked to the door, opened the bolt, and let the light in, still watching the scene as though from a remote place in her mind. The surreal had been her life.

Your grandma and I never wanted you to see how much fun we'd had in our day.

Might taint ya, make ya loose . . . hafta keep a little discretion about yourself as a lady.

Millie, we told you the child would find out sooner or later—the truth will always out.

Her other aunts simply nodded and sighed but flashed wide grins, their eyes gazing tenderly at each suitor as they said a few simple words: *I ain't mad no mo', honey.*

Then she watched each man take his leave of the house, going through the basement door and out into the light. Some young ones grew old as soon they crossed the threshold; some glanced around and ran like a shot out of a pistol; some just wiped their eyes and rubbed their faces as though shaking off an all-night drunk. But the one that hurt her heart most was watching her Uncle Zeek cross the threshold, look back at the house, and begin crying.

His words tore at her soul when he murmured, "I didn't wanna go, baby. Ain't no life out here on the outside without your aunt. They's all gone. I'da stayed with that woman forever—no matter what."

"I know," Dominique said quietly. "I'ma miss 'em, too. Crazy, outrageous Jackson women. Come on home, Uncle Zeek. I'll make you some breakfast. You can stay in this house."

All the women stood in awe as the hunchbacked old man walked back through the basement door of his own accord. Dominique's aunt Jessie covered her mouth, and quiet tears streamed down her face. A mother's arms embraced her, and they all welcomed Zeek back into the fold. He peered around the now dusty basement and glanced at the cobwebs that now covered the liquor bottles. All Dominique could do was stare.

"We used to have us some times up in here, ladies."

Won't be long, Nana admitted, tears glistening in her eyes. *We ain't do that man right. We sorry, Zeek.*

Time sorta flew by us, you know? Dominique's mother said with a nervous shrug. *We all had a lotta good years before my sister got mad at ya, though.*

He nodded and smiled. "I know. I'ma just eat me a big breakfast. Might catch up to y'all later on today, if that's all right."

We'll be pleased to see you on this side, Zeek, Nana murmured. *You good people.*

You ain't mad? Jessie whispered from beside the jukebox.

"Naw, had it coming," he said in a resigned tone. "Shouldn'ta been messing with that young thang. But would like to spend some time with ya when I cross over—you at least owe me that much, woman."

The two old lovers looked at each other and laughed, making the others around them chuckle. Then, one by one, the women's voices faded, becoming as transparent as their forms. Dominique's mother blew her a kiss, and her Nana waved good-bye, her aunt Jessie gave her a sly wink, and as quickly as it had all begun years ago, they were gone.

A heaviness filled Dominique's chest, and all she could do as she watched them depart was accept the hug from the old man she'd loved all her life.

"I know jes' how you feel, baby."

Those words were enough to make her cry in earnest. There was something so true and so final to seeing them go this time. Uncle Zeek was probably the only living soul who could vouch that she wasn't crazy, and had seen it all up on Girard Avenue.

He held her away from him, his tall form now bent with age, his once caramel skin puckered and wrinkled and lackluster, the whites of his eyes now yellowing. But his dark brown eyes held no anger, no remorse, nothing but love. His hands were still strong for all their years. Dominique let her gaze rove over him, remembering how fine that man was back in his day.

"You forgot one still trapped. Just sent him down here this morning. Let him go, baby. If he ain't no good, best thang you kin do is send him out that back door."

She sniffed and chuckled, nodding her agreement as she called a name she would soon forget. It took everything within her to keep from laughing as Eric fell to the floor from an overhead water pipe.

"Oh, shit, oh, shit—oh—*man* . . ."

Her lover was on his feet in seconds, spinning in circles, patting his body down as though a part of it might have gotten left behind.

"I know, son. Take it from an old dog. Bring your ass home when you supposed to. Don't be messing with no woman in the streets. It's a lotta things out here that can change a man's life. Dig it?"

With a nod and a scared glance around the room, the last man standing was out of the Jackson house like a bullet. Uncle Zeek clasped her hand and led her up the stairs toward the kitchen.

"What would you like for breakfast, Uncle Zeek? You name it."

He just chuckled, taking his time to climb the steps one by one.

"If you can cook like your Nana say you can, how about a lil' somethin' to take fifty years off a man's life?"

The Fourth Floor

Ahmad Wright

"Good night, sir," Treadmont Lebovier said, with his head down almost to the floor. He stirred his cleaning solution as the boy exited his office door and stepped into the hallway.

"I'm not a *sir*. You don't have to call me that."

"You're a doctor, ain't you?" Treadmont flipped up the bill of his cap to check the boy eye to eye. "Doctors is sirs."

"I'm only twenty," said the boy. "We've been over this."

Treadmont pushed the pail to the center of the floor.

"You're a sir to me, sir. Every doctor is a sir at Walter Reed Hospital."

"Whatever."

The boy, still adorned in his suit and lab coat, pulled a shoulder bag to his collarbone and raced to the stairway exit. Treadmont waved.

"Good night, sir."

Treadmont had never seen or known what a prodigy was until he heard about the boy, Francis "Baby Doc" Harris. Wonder boy. College at fourteen. Medical school at eighteen. His rotations as a resident were a savvy blip on his résumé, and he came here like his grandfather, Martin "Daddy Doc" Harris to begin his surgical rotation of choice.

Treadmont owed the old man his life—literally. The nineteen-fifties were the silver age for black Washington, D.C. Doo-wop was still king. We kicked Korea's butt, and vets could get jobs. A young Treadmont even won his current job during a bet with a fellow navy cook who hated to lose. The man double-dared Treadmont that he couldn't name the fifty states—in any order. At around Montana, having already hit the eastern seaboard and the southern bible belt, he stumbled, not knowing the position of Utah and New Mexico from Nevada and Idaho.

The man would have gutted him like an eel if not for Doc Harris's say-so. Daddy Doc was big then, a rugged navy boxer who'd trumped his way into Howard University Medical School with the same fire he attacked his opponents' heads. He paid for school by managing Walter Reed Hospital's maintenance crew. He'd put in a good word for Treadmont. Gave him his first check. He'd even picked out Treadmont's new silver pail and metal-hinged mop, the one he used to this day.

The family resemblance between Daddy Doc and Baby Doc was uncanny. Same cinnamon-stick legs, bullet head, and squashed disposition. The eyes clinched it, though. Both men had eyes so clear that light shined right in and through to the brain. Knowledge filled them like puddles of rain.

The twenty doorknobs of the fourth floor were Daddy Doc Harris's last remaining legacy. The Doc had ordered them steel, but Treadmont had replaced them with brass out of an advance from his own pension; he shined them out of respect with the same due diligence he showed the floors. The ritual eased his memories to his old departed friend and provided him with the spark he needed to get through the night. It was comforting to know that every door was secure. He was *safe*. At least that is what he told himself every night.

Treadmont looked to the right of the dim hallway, where the sour gray decor was meticulous and commanding as still water. To the left, the emergency exit sign added a hint of red, bringing color relief to the sullen sight. *Shined brass would be good. Brass under the red light look just like Christmas!*

He turned the mop again, dipped and twisted the sucker three more times before placing it into the wringer, and cast it across the floor.

At sixty years old, Treadmont could still glide-mop the length of the hallway floor with a speed skater's gait. He traced the instrument from waist level and twisted from the torso, side to side. Finishing the job was a given. *Can't no one say Treadmont Lebovier can't finish a job.* It was the timing he was worried about. Timing over distance. Eighty strokes and three pail dips per floor had turned his life into a seven-hour-a-night calculation of sweat and muscle. Wearing his trademark gator-blend jumpsuit and leather work boots, he was blessed with the heart of a rhino and invigorated by the wheat germ and raw egg pulsing through his bloodstream. Over the years (by enduring his wife's bad cooking) he had developed a cool stamina for his work. His movements were furious, choreographed, and succinct to compulsive perfection. *Can't nobody say I don't work . . . can't nobody say I don't work.*

And nobody had. Nobody could. Yet each time he finished the fourth floor, Treadmont worked his way backward to the top of the hallway, to the supply closet all over again. Each time, he changed his pail water and mopped again. Daddy Doc Harris's old floor was never clean enough.

But that wasn't the problem.

The inevitable would soon occur, and Treadmont could only blame himself. He would concentrate on his own shining reflection on the floor. When it really got bad, he'd dig into his back pocket and pop the pills that Baby Doc Harris gave him to keep calm. Come hell or consequence, Treadmont Lebovier would bear the episode to come. He wrung the mop again and entered the supply closet to change the water.

The rusted sink had seen better times, but old as it was—corroded from years of fancy cleaning chemicals—it was still just what he needed. He hefted the full pail to the lip of the basin as the dirty water found its mark. The sink's knobs were rusted, but they agreed to his touch. He gripped them like a tired old friend and let the clear hot water run its course.

Starting the entire cleaning process over, Treadmont arched both arms high above his shoulders and emptied two bottles of industrial-strength disinfectant onto the mop head. Once the liquids turned the cloth tendrils from gray to green, he dunked them into the steel pail of hot water and stirred the solution into a fine syrup. This was the "twist and jerk" method he'd learned from Daddy Doc Harris. *Saturate the mop but not the water, and the shinier your floor will be,* he had said, flashing a buckled half-grin. Doc must have used the same grin on employees way before him while working his way through school. Treadmont hunched over his mop and reminisced on his deceased mentor's old-time cleaning method. It was sloppy and antiquated, but it beat the fancy machines ten to one, and he never once was forced to stay late to redo a job. Treadmont mopped all sixteen floors of Walter Reed Hospital from five until midnight.

Every night.

Never had a complaint.

They couldn't see like he did.

Dust. Lint. The rise of overrun cement in the corners where the floor tile lay uneven. Cigarette stains. Smudges. Treadmont caught it all. Footprints were the worst proof of the human comings and goings. They were distinct in their damage to his tasks, but that came with the job. It was all there, prime and naked under the faint fluorescent light.

Treadmont would set things right.

He did it without intrusion or supervision. The new manager had just got cancer of the guts. The assistant manager was married two Fridays ago and disappeared on what was described as a *permanent* honeymoon. Treadmont didn't need either of them, though. The lone practitioner of hallways, he had mopped them to a shine for two thirds of his life.

Three more floors, he thought. The pail burned to the touch, soothing the calluses on his worn, dark, ungloved hands.

They shook as he set the pail in the hallway.

It was this moment that had defined his terror for years.

To his pharmacist every week: *Phillip, my own insides jump. Swear to Christ! And my neck ... I can feel ...*

It's all in your head, Treadmont.

You ain't a doctor.

Then go back to Baby Doc, man. He gonna tell you like I did. It's all in your head.

Phillip would put in Baby Doc Harris's prescription, and that was that.

Always.

The pressure at his shoulders, the impalpable feeling of a human touch, would persist each night at this time. He quit the job once, and the occurrences intensified. It followed him to the supermarket, to his football game chair, and to the marriage bed.

Honey, was that you?

He reinstated himself pronto, and the invasion of privacy stopped outside the job. But here, in the waning hours on the fourth floor, Treadmont was never alone. Ever.

He dipped the mop in the water, and the clang of the steel catch hit the pail and echoed with the force of a gunshot. The pressure and equilibrium of the touch was still there, the squeeze at his neck and shoulder, without breath or body to accommodate the sensation. The mop water got cold. Always did. Treadmont never turned around. For twenty years he never once checked behind him.

He never told Baby Doc Harris. The boy was to be left to his own genius. The last thing he needed was some janitor spooking him with some old spook talk. Treadmont said his good-byes to the boy every night and went about his work.

Tonight, the time lapse was less than a minute, but between contact and release it could have been ten minutes. Felt like an hour. Tread-mont opened his eyes and stared down at the floor, the ritual nearing completion. His reflection was drawn and rigid. The shape behind him loomed like a shadow, a shade in a lab coat. The weighted hands patted him gently for the night, and Daddy Doc Harris disappeared.

Empty Vessel

Lawana Holland-Moore

St. Francisville, Louisiana, 1821

This is one of my favorite places. It's where I'd like to stay. Sometimes you'll find me walking along the long front porch, trailing my hand along the verandah's grillwork with its iron clusters of grapes and leaves. Often I wander in the gardens or watch folks coming in through the gates. This place suits me just fine.

I wonder where the children are, but I think they're scared of me. There are many others who live here, too, but we are all preoccupied in our own worlds and playing an elaborate game of hide-and-seek.

There was no question that working in the house was easier than having to be out in those fields with their hard life of toil, sweat, and beatings. House life was better, but brought its own trouble. All I could comfort myself with sometimes was being able to get out of that sun.

My momma was a mulatto woman, and they used to tell me I took after her with the dark, wavy hair and dusky-brown skin. After me, she became barren—a useless slave woman with an empty womb—so they sold her. They said her master was a Frenchman and my papa, but the only papa I knew was a strong field hand named Aaron, who loved her. It was that very strength that made the owners keep him, and I could only hope it sustained him when I was sold away from him, too.

I missed my papa's stories, his smell, and the way he hugged me with his laughter. In my dreams I saw his face.

I wondered if he could see mine.

* * *

I was raised by Nana 'Tima, who told me about the villages and places where she had lived as a free young woman before she was caught and brought over on the ships. Her stories of her home, where peach sands covered the ground and trees grew with trunks so wide people could live in them, sounded like heaven on earth.

She taught me about herbs and things that could heal or harm. "Don't go around here puttin' roots and goophers on folks," Nana 'Tima once told me as I went with her on her rounds.

"Yes, ma'am," I said, adjusting my white oak basket that was filled with little jars of poultices and salves and other things. How many times had I gone into the woods with her to help collect the ingredients?

"I am teaching you this to help and heal, not to do bad with it," she said. I paid close attention and soon was able to remove hexes, make mojos and protection talismans, and help heal sick folks. Everyone respected my knowledge and came to me often.

Years later, I held Nana 'Tima's hand as she passed on, and as I looked into her eyes, I felt so lost and alone in the world yet again. There had always been a void in my very being, my deepest soul, which could never be comforted just by the thoughts and hopes of my parents somewhere thinking of me. With Nana 'Tima gone from me, too, that hollow space only opened wider.

How much more loss could I take, and how much more pain did I need to reap before I fell into it?

My days were spent cleaning and cooking, and Lord, those folks had so many fine, fine things. For Christmas, Missus gave all us slaves presents, whether it was foodstuffs or, for us house slaves, hand-me-down clothes from her and Judge. When Missus gave me mine, I just cried out at the sight of the satin dress. I had never owned anything so wonderful, and its color reminded me of the green glass bottles on the tree near Nana 'Tima's. I held it against my skin, and it felt so good, I felt like a rich lady myself. I thanked her, and she told me to try it on, since it was Christmas after all. I did as I was told and turned shyly in it for her. She told me how pretty it was on me, and as I turned toward the doorway, I noticed Judge staring. We caught eyes, and he looked nervous and hurried away. I ain't think much of it. I took that beautiful dress and folded it up in my cabin.

Their things were so nice that sometimes I'd just run my hands over the fine linen or the shiny fabrics of the Missus's dresses and close my eyes. Liza, who was about the same age as me, sometimes did the same thing.

"Chloe," she'd say, "you cain't let 'em catch ya touchin' they things like that!"

"Liza," I'd say to her, "I ain't! You do it, too! If they ain't caught us by now, they ain't gonna, so shush!"

Liza's tan face would frown up, and she'd continue with her dusting, sweeping, folding, or whatever task she had at the moment.

One of my favorite things to do was to watch over the children. I loved their bright little faces and small clothes. What a shame that the little ones like me couldn't have those nice clothes, too. It just wasn't right. I would see the little slave children in their tattered rags, and it tore at my heart.

Judge was known for being with the ladies—white ones like him or slave ones like me. Didn't matter to him, so I wasn't surprised when he started making eyes at me. One day he touched my hair, and I jumped back when he did. I didn't know what to think, and was shocked the night he came to my cabin and asked me to put on that green dress.

What was I to do? I did what my massa told me to do. I put on that green dress.

When he took me to bed, I wasn't Chloe anymore. I wasn't anyone anymore. I was nothing but just maybe, just maybe, just *maybe* an empty vessel to be filled up so my life could be different.

When he wanted me, I went. When he summoned me, I followed. I realized I needed him if my life was going to stay the same. I couldn't go out in the fields! I've seen those scars from the lash of the whips! I've tended to those poor souls who got beat down by the overseers or Judge himself. Put my poultices on and fixed up brews to make 'em better. It just was not a future I wanted for myself. Over and over and over I went to him, and each time I prayed in my heart for his seed not to take root, while a piece of me died inside with every caress. I cringed inside from his touch. His fingers on me, his being in me.

Then, one day, he didn't call for me. That day turned into many, and then the days into weeks. I was frantic. He would look at me, then turn away. Was he sending me to the fields now that he didn't seem to want me anymore? The very person I wanted to see the least I felt I needed to recognize me the most. I was devastated. Then obsessed.

"Chloe," Liza said to me one day. "You all right?"

"What do you mean?" I asked her.

"I know, Chloe," she said. "All of us know 'bout you and Judge. Even the missus knows, but what can she do? Judge got the money. It's a wonder she ain't done nothin' to ya herself. I've heard some stories about them gettin' payback on the slave womens they mens lay down with . . ."

Her voice seemed to chatter on and on to me as she continued. I felt as if I was falling inside. She leaned over to pick up a basket. "Watch yo'self girl. Watch yo'self."

I sniffed at her. Watch *what*? What's to watch? *At least not anymore*. What had I *done*?

I started listening at doorways, stopping outside rooms when I heard his voice. I wanted an inkling of news, something, *anything* to explain his rejection. To hear if I'd be sent out into the sun and headed for backbreaking work. I may have been a slave, but I was a woman first—I also needed to know why I wasn't wanted anymore.

Turning to the children for diversion, I found they mostly happily played and laughed—oblivious to us slaves except to tell us what to do. It was truly their world, and sometimes it was nice to escape within it. Often I played tea party and wood blocks with them, but inside me there was this empty, gnawing, hurting ache in my soul at knowing that perhaps I'd failed.

Then one day, I'd gathered up some laundry and walked down the hallway. Passing Judge's room, I thought about being out in those fields. Hearing a noise, then his voice, I stopped and stood there quietly listening to what I realized were muffled moans and grunts. The noises stopped, and I felt my face go hot from what I'd heard. Before I could recover, the door was snatched open, and I was horrified to find myself staring straight into Judge's face. Liza was in the background, hurriedly trying to get back into her clothes as I stood there frozen in terror.

He glowered at me, his face red, his mouth set, his eyes full of fury. No matter what I knew to do, I just couldn't move out of that spot. Where was I going to go? Nothing could help me. My mouth was open, and a gurgled sound came out from my throat. Before I knew it, he struck me so hard across my face that I fell to the floor, stunned. He slapped me again in the face, and I started screaming. My basket of clothing fell from my hands and rolled away from me, its contents spilled across the floor.

"You nigga bitch!" he yelled at me. I winced and cried, and the tears flowed hot from my face. I was curled up in a ball with my skirts mussed about my legs as his blows flew furiously around me. Liza slipped from behind him with tears in her eyes and a stricken look on her face.

Liza?! Her too? Was she why he didn't want me anymore? How long? He had made her next! Oh no.

I didn't know if my next cry was from that knowledge or from the pain of his grabbing me by the arm and dragging me down the hall. My squirming and screaming only made Judge yank me harder.

"Stop this struggling or I *will* kill you! As it is now, I just intend on giving you and the others a little to think about instead," he snarled.

My eyes widened even more as I was dragged down the steps one by one and out the front door.

"Simeon," Judge said. "Go call the others to the front of the house." Simeon's kind older face was confused and concerned, but out of his fear of Judge, he quickly headed down toward the quarters. It seemed like I was on that porch forever. Through my tears I saw groups of brown faces coming toward me. My face was stinging and starting to swell from the pain, and my head hurt so badly from bumping it on the floor and the stairs that my ears were ringing.

"Get me some rope or twine," Judge said to Brooks, one of the overseers who accompanied the slaves up to the house. Brooks came back shortly, and Judge tied my hands behind my back. I had stopped struggling, and all I could do was lie there on that porch. One of the little girls started to come out of the house and she screamed, "Chloe! Chloe!"

"Take her back in!" Judge yelled to no one in particular. I saw out of the corner of my eyes that the someone who did was Liza. Her eyes were so sad and full of pity as she hushed the children and slowly closed the door behind them.

"Now," Massa said. "I'm gonna show you all what happens when one of you gets uppity enough to ever so much as *think* you have a right to listen in on my conversations or business."

Looking out into the crowd, I saw young, old, short, and tall. All looked at me blankly, yet some did so with fear and others with anger. What surprised me is that I saw some looking on with expectation.

As I was watching them, I didn't see Judge grab a long, sharp knife. "Help me hold her head, Brooks!" he shouted. Everything happened so quickly that it didn't seem real at first. Brooks held my head, and next thing I knew, I felt an excruciating, searing pain as my ear fell beside me. Despite my howling and shrieking both from the pain and seeing my flesh lying on the porch stair next to me, I heard a collective gasp and felt warmth running down my head and neck. What was once my ear was now just a piece of me there—separate, separated. Judge said, "Let this be a lesson . . ." and everything went black.

When I woke up, I was in someone's cabin lying on a corn-husk pallet, feverish and feeling as if I'd been blinded. There were shapes above me and a soothing voice I recognized as Auntie's. My throat was dry and parched as visions ran in and out of my mind.

My father was standing there crying and getting farther and farther away from me, and I could hear the creak of the wheels as the cart I was loaded into lumbered off down the dusty road. My cries were like echoes in my mind.

Nana 'Tima came to me, I know, and told me, "Hold on, chile, hold on. Ev'rything'll be all right. It will . . ." I saw her and wanted to be with her, and I reached for her. As I did, my hand somehow brushed my head. Where my ear should've been was only a bandage of some sort now. I shrieked and flailed around until Auntie and another slave woman named Ona had to hold me down. Ona's dark-chocolate skin gleamed in the heat of the cabin as she squeezed out a wet rag over a cracked bowl of water.

"Poor thing, poor thing," she muttered as she laid it across my forehead. She then prayed over me in some language I'd never heard before, but its tones were calming and melodic. I faded away.

I drifted in and out as I heard voices speaking. "That girl been showing off her fancy clothes hand-me-downs and look where it got her. Judge ain't want her and then went and did this to her!" a woman said.

"That's what happens when Massa Judge just takes a woman like that. Just wrong 'er and spit 'er out. 'Member how he did that other girl?" a male voice said.

"Hmph," another female voice said. "Look who takin' care of 'er now. I'm sure Massa Judge don't think she so pretty now."

"Hush that talk," I heard Auntie say. "Hush that talk."

What was once my ear was now scar and bumps—a hole that was just there. I didn't want people to look at it and see my shame—even though everyone knew, so what difference did it really make? It made one to me because I was a freak. A freak who was beautiful to no one anymore.

I went down to the water to wash myself once I was up again. Looking into the water, I saw myself looking back and screamed and screamed, tearing at the image in the water until it dispersed and was at odd angles and curves—much like the real thing. I dropped to my knees as I cried and cried. I ran my fingers along the ridges of my former ear. I was disfigured. I was ugly. I was not me. I ran back to my cabin and went straight to that green satin dress. I ripped it up in a frenzy and tied the fabric around my head like a headdress. The most beautiful thing I've ever owned will now cover the ugliest.

I think that they considered sending me to the fields, but the children wanted me near. Judge wasn't too keen on having me around, but the missus seemed to take some sort of pleasure in seeing my misery. I was given more kitchen work and had to help Nellie, the cook, with preparing the meals. Cakes I made became a family favorite.

For Li'l Miss Birthday, they asked me to make a cake. I went out into the woods and got some oleander and crushed 'em up real good and stirred them into the batter. I had such a smile on my face as I stirred and stirred. The pale batter folded over my spoon in thick, viscous swirls as my smile got even larger. This, I thought, would work.

The other slaves came and dragged me out of my cabin themselves upon hearing the news. The night was hot and muggy, and I had been sleeping fitfully anyway since I knew the worst was coming. For hours and hours, I had been up there at the house trying to help. I never thought this would happen. When they came to me as a group, I went willingly. Once again, my hands were tied behind me, but this time by my own people.

"Those two chilluns and the missus died afta eatin' your cake!" they cried. "We know you cooked it and we know you got the knowledge. We know what you did! We can't hide you down here no more or Massa Judge might come down real hard on *us* off of you! To save ourselves, we will have to take care of *you*."

I didn't struggle—just as always, it seemed. I felt so dazed and numb. I saw Auntie in the crowd with Ona, and they were weeping. Originally, I just wanted to make the children sick a little so I could help nurse them back to health and be back in good graces. But the more I stirred that batter, the more I thought about how I was used—

how he used my body. How I really *was* an empty vessel—not to be filled up but to be drained of my soul. Drained it right out of me along with my blood when he cut off my ear. I stirred myself revenge, which is sweet. So sweet, like an oleander cake.

They threw me in the river after they hanged me. That's the snatches of the story I've heard folks say as I still roam these hallways, walk along that long front verandah, and wander in the gardens. Sometimes I have my candlestick with me as I look in on folk, hoping for a familiar face. All I see instead is their fear when they look at me, and once again I am alone.

This place is a favorite haunt of mine, but it's where I'd like to stay.

I, Ghoul

Christopher Chambers

> BODY SNATCHER, n. *One who supplies the young physicians with that which the old physicians have supplied the undertaker. Or a demon with the reprehensible habit of devouring the dead.*
>
> —Ambrose Bierce, *The Devil's Dictionary*

"*D*r. Ombre . . . paging Dr. Affamé Ombre, line two."

I'm stretching for the paging phone handset while a female Baltimore City cop named Matthews mewls to one of the janitors about the "desecration" of the body found in the Dumpster behind the Giant Supermarket on West Pratt Street. A staffwide e-mail I'd read when I got on shift said the dead woman was a third-year U of M student named Mindy Shulman, missing since Tuesday.

Matthews is a squat sister whose permed hair is twisted into a severe knot; she's been jocking me since her gum-snapping self waddled off the elevator to check on a multiple-stabbing victim I'd treated. Now she's all teary-eyed when she says this Mindy Shulman's toes were bitten off by stray dogs. Yeah, right. Well, the dutiful robots on my team couldn't give a shit about that or those nine med school cadavers missing since Thanksgiving, or the blizzard winds howling like werewolves, or whatever Matthews is sniffling over. No, the nurses and techies in these ugly-ass pale pink Shock Trauma scrubs we wear as our little badge of superiority over the green of the regular staff are frowning at me because I'm on a personal call.

"Yes, this is Dr. Ombre," I answer. It trips folks out that I don't have an accent like the cheesy one Eddie Murphy had in *Coming to America*.

Shit, it's Cliff. Aw, man. I swear I can hear the *boosh-boosh-boosh* of his heartbeat over the phone. My boy Dr. Clifton Lemieux's usually booming bass voice is wet, whispery. Pretty soon, I'm hearing the thumping of my own heart against my sternum as I listen.

". . . and Mindy, she had the CDs in this Lands' End satchel she always carried."

"Damn, Cliff—you knew her, the dead med student?"

"Listen . . . I gave them to her because she said she knew an anthropologist down in College Park who might have some background on this . . . phenomenon. I went home. She stuck around the Med Center until maybe midnight. She lived in a condo on West Portland, down near Camden Yards, so she could walk . . . I was talking to her on her cell. She did that sometimes—talk on the cell—at night, alone. The streets are well lit. And you know the brothers won't try shit in a gentrified area or the cops will kill them."

I'm trying to look nonchalant as staffers brush past me in the corridor. Goddamn hard when Cliff's scaring me shitless.

"Still . . . she said she heard footsteps behind her. She'd turn, see nothing. Disembodied steps. Then, other times, she'd take a look, just to be sure. No footsteps, but . . . only a shadow. Moving up on her. Like an echo of a person, ya feel me? Twice it happened. She started running, all the way to that Mobil Station off Russell. Ducked in there . . . The clerk, the people pumping gas, the homeless assholes offering to pump gas—not a soul was bothered, acted weird, saw anything unusual. She chilled there a few minutes, felt okay, I suppose—giggled, bought a Krispy Kreme and a milk. Told me she'd call me the next day.

"She called an hour later, caller ID on my cell listed her cell number, not her home phone. Voice was . . . choppy, weepy. She was in her robe, locked herself in her bathroom. Said her landline didn't work, so she couldn't call nine-one-one, and she had no idea how do so on a goddamn cell phone. The girl was terrified . . . said there was someone on her fire escape, man. Her damn fire escape! Scratching the glass of her bedroom window. Not a shadow this time. Naw, she saw fingers . . . yellow nails, knuckles covered with dense, matted hair. And then the signal died. I called back, got the usual cellular message 'subscriber unavailable.' I—I didn't call the police . . ."

Laboring to inject some calm or some sense, I say, "Listen, go home before the streets are so bad you're stuck at the Med Center. I'll call you when—"

"It tore up my locker! A metal locker, shredded like Styrofoam. And my desk . . . top drawer where I kept the CDs I burned on my laptop—smashed to splinters! Police and University Security aren't gonna buy what I gotta tell them. Hell, no."

Huh? Did he say "it" tore up his locker? *"Mon frere,"* I say, "plan B:

Go to the Student Union. I heard they have hot food, cots for staff and visitors stranded by this storm. My team breaks at two a.m. I'll roll down there and we'll talk over some oatmeal or something, cool?"

I cup the phone when my co–chief resident, Dr. Paula Zirelli— gawky, meatless, hook nose—invades my space. Paula's got a mannish voice like Bea Arthur.

"Doctor, a moment?" she presses, bony arms folded across a flat chest.

"Whatchew need?"

"There's a medevac inbound, ETA twenty minutes, from the tractor- trailer jackknife and collision on I-ninety-five. After that, nothing— maybe everyone's shut in from the weather. With the lull, my Alpha Team will take the inbound."

I'm nodding at Paula while Cliff mutters, "Notes and photos are on the CDs. The University of Maryland Medical System would've been kissing my black ass over what I've compiled. But now . . . bruh, I just wanna live to see the sun come up!"

"Accordingly, Dr. Ombre, your Beta Team can take its break now if—"

"*Fine*, Paula." I spin away from her and whisper, "Where are you?"

"Place off Paca and Lexington Streets, 'cross from the Market— Marvin's Deluxe? Hurry, man. Godsakes, hurry."

Cliff's a Fellow in the Pathology Department at our home, the University of Maryland Medical Center. Before he hangs up, he comes clean and confirms for me that he was a tutor for this white girl Mindy Shulman during her pathology rotation, right before she vanished. The way he's blubbering, I think they hooked up. He won't say. You know, he'll dump-truck this *Kolchak: The Night Stalker* shit on me, but he won't tell me if he's been boning a med student! Well, now the brother's made himself a material witness in a kidnapping and homicide, and I'm musing over how much shit the cops are going to put him through once they find out. Right now, yeah, I'm stomping into the residents' lounge to grab my pea coat, ski cap, and Yukon Cornelius snow boots. Listen, Cliff and I are only two of a handful of black male MDs at this place. He's an Ivy Leaguer and New Orleans redbone: the kind with good hair and light eyes who grabs the choice sisters (despite their stated penchant for the tall, dark, and bald, like *moi*). I'm not hating. He and I are tight and joke each other all the time as if we're siblings, okay? So I'm being honest when I say that Cliff's only deal-breaking flaw was al- ways playing up the Creole-voodoo rap with ladies and colleagues.

Couple that with his specialty, and you know why the nurses nick-named the niggah "Gomez," as in the daddy in *The Addams Family.*

Cliff got twisted when the med school cadavers vanished—along with three bodies recently deposited with the Pathology Department by its steady suppliers, the oncologists and cardiologists. Cliff's trips to the Health Science archives and Enoch Pratt Library began then. By January the motherfucker's gushing about a "discovery" at the same time he's jabbering about "somebody having more than turkey and ham for Thanksgiving and Christmas dinners."

I'm trudging down Lombard to Greene Street now; city snowfall isn't pretty. It's jaundiced as an old corpse, from the hue of the halogen street lamps. My scrubs feel like mere pajamas under my coat. I don't see a single city plow or salt truck, so unh-unh, no warm taxi ride for me! I glance over at the hundred-ninety-year-old dome of Davidge Hall, our own little copy of Jefferson's Monticello, I suppose. Its self-indulgent floodlights paint it as such a stately fucking spot, with its frosting of snow. It's a monument to long-dead, rich crackers, and I don't give it a second thought. Hey, I don't see another soul until I get up to Westminster Church Cemetery. It's a guy on cross-country skis, toting a backpack. Only white folks! When he merrily swishes by, I'm all alone again.

Instead of crossing Fayette Street, I turn to watch my shadow play on the old churchyard's crumbling brick wall. Hey, even a shadow can be a companion. Besides, through an iron gate I spy the pitted gray headstones of even more moldering crackers. Fuck 'em. Edgar Allen Poe's buried in there, though. Now, he was cool, and I'm being a Poindexter and reciting "Annabel Lee" in my head. . . .

Until I see another shadow on that wall.

No footsteps are crunching in the snow. Yet this shadow's moving. Only dope fiends, cops, and fools like me are out on nights like this, and none cast shadows without bodies.

I suck in an icy breath and slosh across Fayette. I stop, panting. I turn. I see a figure with a billowy coat, tiny head, skulking out of the streetlight's reach. I holler, "Yo, you need something, cuz?" No reply. "Asshole," I grunt. In some neighborhoods in Crab Town, those excla-mations would get you a 9-mm round in your ass and a trip to Shock Trauma. I don't care. I struggle through a drift on the sidewalk. Turn again.

Motherfucker's still there, but now he's crouched over. He rises. I hear the echo of a nasty cough. What the fuck? He's winding up like

he's a starter for the Orioles. It's flying toward me . . . like slow motion.
A damn snowball . . .

I cry out because the impact's more like an ice spike than a soft
slush. Right on my chin. I reach up with a gloveless hand to check the
damage. I feel something clammy, not cold. Viscous, then tacky. I'm not
injured, but . . . I'm holding my hand up . . . blood on my fingers. My
knees buckle. One drops to the snow. I peer down by my wet knee.
There, a remnant of the snowball. Pink, like a cherry snow cone. Aw,
God—more blood? I flick the snow away. Even a trauma surgeon
would've retched.

It's a piece of someone's gum and jaw, two molars still attached. It's
ripe. Wet. And it smells of hydrochloric acid and bile . . .

I'm sprinting like an arctic fox, and I don't stop until I see the glow
from the fogged, grimy plate glass of Marvin's Deluxe Home Cooking
& Carryout. . . .

My hands are shaking as I gulp down tepid coffee. Under his
glasses, Cliff's green eyes are hooded, tinged as pink as that snowball.

"Interesting," he says. "Did you pick up the jaw fragment?"

I almost choke on the last swallow. "You outcha' mind?"

"It's evidence, man. Could have been helpful. I could have matched
it to *missing items*." He leans under my gaze. "No going back now. No
reprieve." This next look Cliff shoots me has truly got me tripping.
He's grinning, okay? *Grinning!* "Going to the cops," he says, "is what *it*
wants. Paint me to be a lunatic. Disgrace me. Finish me at its leisure."

"Lemme tell you," I hiss. "For the past three days you've been
jumpy, bleary-eyed, and, according to the chief of Pathology, damn near
AWOL. On the phone you sounded crazy. In person you're worse. Tell
me what's up, or I will go to the cops and University Security myself—
after I knock you out."

Cliff just lolls in his goddamn chair.

"You listening to me, man? *Stop* this bullshit." I'm still trying to
keep my voice down because there are still a bunch of people in there
grubbing on hypertension food. "Yeah, I'm a true believer in something
haunting this hospital, all right. He's a fetishist—med school reject
maybe? Jeffrey Dahmer type, just discovering that sex with a live person's better than that with stolen corpses."

"Bushrod Mingo," Cliff says softly.

"Huh?" I'm squinting because the harsh fluorescent lights in that
greasy spot are splitting my already throbbing skull.

Cliff leans close. His breath stinks worse than mine at this hour. "Mingo's old name was Hercule. He was a house slave to a Dr. Etienne D'Orsay. D'Orsay was in a group of refugee French planters, escaping from Toussaint L'Overture's slave revolt in Haiti."

"You're gonna throw away your career on this bullshit."

"There's more at stake than that, bruh. Hear me out. See, Hercule petitioned D'Orsay for freedom. D'Orsay agreed, inexplicably, upon becoming an American citizen. He did keep Hercule on as a salaried secretary, valet, handyman. I have a copy of the manumission documents from the circuit court archives. Well, *had* a copy, on the CDs Mindy kept. Hercule changed his name to 'Bushrod Mingo,' because, according to the diary of a Quaker merchant who paid for Mingo's schooling here, he wanted to sound like a real American 'frontiersman.' A fresh start, hope, grace. There're worse things to escape than slavery, poverty."

"Uh-huh. Such as?"

"Mingo could trace his ancestry to the *odujinja* Odumare in West Africa. How's your Dahomey or Swahili these days?"

"Rusty. I think it means . . . 'abomination to Odumare.'"

He nods. "Odumare is the Great Wise Spirit. But these guys were sorcerers who could commune with demons to see the future. Apparently, they didn't see white men nabbing them and shipping them off to Haiti. Survivors masqueraded as the more benign *jou jou* shaman. Mix the slaves' traditional spirituality, folk religion, with French Catholicism, *et voila, maintenant,* you've planted the seeds of *vodou.* Moreover, I excerpted Haitian slave narratives commissioned by L'Ouverture himself, that accuse D'Orsay of whipping knowledge of *odujinja* rituals out of a young slave named Hercule. Check this out: D'Orsay was a quack who fled France one step ahead of a fraud conviction . . . but more so, under suspicion of necromancy. Witchcraft."

"Cliff . . ."

"Wait, he remakes himself in Haiti as a gentleman sugarcane planter and country doctor, and how better to control your niggers than to use something that scared them even more than the dark side of voodoo, huh? The rituals involved eating human flesh, Affamé. *Meat*—both living and dead."

"Goddamn it!"

He just shoves on. "And Mingo was adept at procuring both for his master's hobby, as well as supposedly legitimate medical studies. He could slow or suspend a victim's vital signs. Biochemists figured out barely twenty years ago that voodoo *bocurs*—witch doctors—were using blowfish nerve toxin to make zombies. As you can imagine, D'Orsay wants to put that shit behind him and become a fixture in Maryland's gentry. Schmoozing pays off when he's invited to a ball at the Talbot County plantation of Dr. Enalls Martin. He bullshits the guests about all the exotic drugs he's synthesized from Caribbean flora.

"D'Orsay returns to Baltimore with an introduction to fellow expatriate Frenchman Maximilian Godefroy, who's an architect married to the former Eliza Crawford. Eliza's father is Dr. John Crawford. Dr. Crawford and Dr. Enalls Martin run the Medical & Chirugical Faculty of Maryland—'the Med-Chi'—with their pal, Dr. John Davidge, of our illustrious Davidge Hall."

"That shit's in the U of M tourist pamphlet."

"Think so? See, the Med-Chi wants to build the first self-contained, modern medical college in the United States. Take medicine out of the world of leeches and sawbones. Godefroy and another guy named Robert Long design and build the domed edifice down there on Lombard Street. Eager pupils are ready to enroll. All they need are raw materials. That's how they learned their craft back then, dawg— hunched over a balcony in a tiered, gas-lit theater as they watch older docs dissect a fresh corpse. Maybe a dead convict, or even a runaway slave? The bigger the student body, the more meat they needed. But the school was broke despite the high tuition. Wild rumors flew around Baltimore about spiritual desecration, grave-robbing. Mobs ransacked the place. Crisis. To the rescue comes Etienne D'Orsay, who claims he can invest capital. And, he's got a plan for equipping the school."

With a grimace I say, "Access to fresh bodies?"

"No. Access to Mingo. Thing is, Mingo's a free man of color now, and he refuses to snatch bodies. D'Orsay frames him on a larceny charge. By law in 1810, a manumitted Negro found guilty of a felony could be sold back into slavery. Mingo's no fool. By 1812, the Medical College of Maryland is *the* preeminent school of medicine in America." Cliff's easing back now. "All thanks to Bushrod Mingo, because the school *also* becomes the biggest cadaver wholesaler to physicians and med schools from Boston to the Carolinas. It was Mingo who figured out the best way to transport the raw parts. Barrels of whiskey. Then they'd turn around and sell the booze to the med students, rednecks, and Irish immigrants. Hence the term 'rotgut' liquor."

There's a horrible ringing in my ears now. I slam both fists on the stained Formica tabletop to arrest the shit. It doesn't work, and the eatery's owner, a Korean, fidgets behind a Plexiglas barrier. I'm mumbling something like, "Mindy Shulman's dead, and all you do is *rehash* this shit for me? A slave named Mingo? Do you hear yourself? You get that name outta a Mark Twain novel? Dude fucked over by his ex-master and he's roaming the streets of B-more almost two hundred years later, robbing graves, making cadaver burritos?"

Cliff exhales so, so slowly. His unshaven face . . . I don't know, is that dismay on it? Despair? Yet I'm the one shaking again.

"Yeah, maybe I should go to the cops," he whispers with this weird calm. But he's gripping the corners of the table until his knuckles blanch. I can barely hear him, and it's not because of the low tone. His voice is garbled, distorted in my head. A single tear escapes my twitching left eye, and I don't fucking know why.

We leave the diner. Not a word passes between us until we're well down Greene Street. And then Cliff blurts out the name.

"Stephen Dorsey."

I stop dead. "Who? Niggah, no more ghostly shit."

He moves ahead of me, but he can't keep his mouth shut. "The Army caught him in September 1814, after the Battle of North Point and the siege of Fort McHenry. A spy for the British when they marched into D.C. and burned shit down a couple of weeks prior. Made a tidy profit. No matter, because he was tried, hung, and buried in a potter's field. He insisted he was Canadian, but he was shrieking in French before the rope snapped his neck. One of the soldiers translated it as 'You reap what you sow.' Or, possibly, 'You are what you eat'?"

The ringing is like spikes through my skull now; we're at the corner of Lombard and Greene. I'm in pain and I'm motioning Cliff to head down to West Pratt Street, where BCPD has its University mini-precinct. The motherfucker just heads toward Davidge Hall instead. My break ends in ten minutes. I feel my stomach down in my knees. I don't need this. I can't follow . . . Cliff plows ahead of me, intent on some demented mission.

Dragging, I follow from a distance. Now I'm beneath the southwest wing of Davidge, emerging from a metal stairwell encaged in steel mesh. Looks like it was installed in the 1950s or something, like during the Cold War. Yeah, there's that old radiation-fallout shelter decal. It stinks down here: must, mold. I step through a steel door, and all of a sudden I hear footsteps down a concrete-lined corridor—more like a narrow tunnel, I guess. This tunnel's lit by sputtering tubes. I'm limping because my head feels like an ax has cleaved it. I look up, and the concrete lining the walls is giving way to crumbling, damp masonry.

I'm shouting, "Cliff, how long you think before Security rolls up in here? We ain't frat boys on a prank, man! Cliff?"

"In here, man," I hear him say from somewhere ahead. "It's almost over."

I push open a heavy plywood door to find him sitting on a rusty folding chair. This room's lit only by a single hanging fixture. Damn . . . the place looks like a crypt but for the empty cardboard boxes and wooden warehouse pallets strewn around. What the fuck would they use this for now? I can smell cold, wet air coming in from somewhere, but Cliff's pointing opposite the draft, to what looks like a small, bricked-up arch.

"That's where the bodies would arrive, via dumbwaiter," he explains. "Tumors excised, organs removed for pathological study."

In the meager swinging light, I see he's got a black iron spike in his other hand. I mean, this thing's thick and maybe a foot long, like ones you see holding old railroad tracks to wooden ties. *Oh, my God . . .*

"Wha-what's that's for, man?"

He just shrugs.

"Um, look, let's get outta here," I say. "Fuck my shift. You can crash at my crib . . ." I hear the steel door at the head of that metal stairwell slam. "We're busted. They're gonna think we're down here smoking blunts."

My boy's tone was serene, easy. "Before the British invade, Mingo tells the trustees of the medical college he refuses to rob graves, invade folks' homes for their dead relatives, anymore. Of course, the bigwigs didn't want to acknowledge this had been going on, so they just send him to Dr. D'Orsay. Music to Mingo's ears, because he knew his old master was endorsing worthless bonds over to the college, as well as embezzling from the Med-Chi itself. Enough leverage, even for a black man at the time, to trump the fake larceny charge D'Orsay'd hung on him."

I'm sensing movement down the corridor. "Hurry this up."

I know he's watching my eyes dart, my hands tremble, just a little. "Look at me, Affamé," he says with such weird calm. "Imagine the horror. Tossed in a quarry, sealed up with dead and dying . . ."

Now our gazes lock.

". . . nothing more than meat, I suppose. Putrefied, then petrified meat."

Christ, his voice sounds garbled and grotesque to me. It grates. Slices. Sears. Yet all he's doing is whispering. Shut up! Just shut the fuck up! But I can't shout, like my trachea's crushed.

"I—I don't know what you're mumbling about, Cliff. But you gotta stop this crazy shit, man . . ."

"They didn't have EKGs, EEGs, defibrillators, respirators, epinephrine, back then, Affamé. Who was really dead? Who could be resuscitated? The old vampire legends probably came about because poor saps were buried alive. When they regained consciousness, they found themselves in a pine box, in pitch blackness, suffocated by six feet of dirt. Dig yourself out and you tend to look a bit scary."

"Stop . . . Cliff, please . . ."

"More than your physiology changes after that horror. Your soul, too. Corroded. Isn't that right?"

I wheeze, *"Shut . . . the fuck . . . up . . ."*

Cliff's standing. He's barely an inch from my face, and I see . . . he's weeping. Tears? Why? Because . . . oh, God . . . *I'm* weeping . . .

"Mingo threatens to expose D'Orsay," Cliff recounts. "D'Orsay skips town, but not before he sends a letter on Med-Chi stationery to a German immigrant woman named Ada Schuldice. The note, written in German, tells Mrs. Schuldice that a free Negro named Bushrod Mingo kidnapped her twelve-year-old daughter, already suffering from pneumonia. That he brought the girl's body down to this room. Stung her with his old nerve-paralyzing voodoo cocktail, though she was already near death. And a group of unnamed, rogue med students unknowingly vivisected her . . . after this nigger defiled her. A copy of the letter and an English translation ended up on the Baltimore state attorney's desk."

I'm doubling over, but not before I see Cliff wave that spike in his hand like a baton as he says, "It was a lie—all except the kidnapping part, right? Mingo was trying to help the girl."

"H-help her?"

"He lived next door to the family. Broke his heart to see her dying . . ."

I nod, bawling.

"So he secreted her away one night, kept her in this room in the hopes that the students could treat her, not cut her up alive. The Schuldices didn't have any money, nor could they barter for medical services. And Mingo even tried Haitian folk remedies. But she died. Now what was he to do? He'd kidnapped a white girl, no matter the motive. He panicked. He left the body for the morning's anatomy lecture. I'm trying to recall the girl's name, from the court records."

"Fr-Frieda. Frieda Schuldice."

And I feel the point of the spike pressed to my forehead as I clutch at Cliff's sleeves. I hear his voice right in my ear. "Yes, that was her name. Mingo gets a summary trial. Offers nothing in his defense. The medical establishment won't speak up for him because of the body-snatching scandal, and do they really want it known that a French quack and grifter has ripped them all off? So Bushrod Mingo awaits execution in the old jail on Calvert Street. While the War of 1812 rages, a cholera epidemic hits the city. Hardest hit: free Negroes, poor immigrants. And prisoners in the jail. Bailiffs find Mingo in his cell—limp, damp from fever, no heartbeat. They took him to where the city dumped some of the victims during that hot summer of 1814. A small limestone quarry off Hempstead Hill. But he wasn't dead."

No, he wasn't. And now his soul's naked before his only friend.

"You slaughtered Mindy." This time, Cliff's voice is raspy, bereft of empathy. Or fear. His swollen eyes widen with my plea.

"Kill me."

He mashes the spike harder. He's grunting, stammering as he speaks. Like he's battling himself. Oh, I know that pain so well. "I lied to you. Mindy Shulman wasn't taking the CDs to an anthropologist in College Park. I'd already consulted with the guy. And a historian. And a genealogist. And even ... a priest. Mindy ... Mindy was supposed to share the info on the disks with a private detective I'd hired." To my shock, he sloughs my arms, withdraws the spike. His voice softens. "To check on *you*, bruh. I—I'm ... a doctor, a scientist—and your friend. All you ever wanted was an escape, hope, right? But tell me ... why ... why hurt Mindy?"

"You have no idea," I croak.

"*Affamé Ombre?*" Now he's snickering tearfully. "It's French for 'hungry shadow.' Somehow, you've gotten over on countless dumb-asses, and I won't ask how you did it in this age of digital info. But I'm from Louisiana—how could you think I wouldn't question that name? Hound out the truth?"

He already knows the answer. My boy must've read the dusty old books about what I'd become. One piece of iron, just for me. In my brain. To kill the hunger. To give me peace. And a voice inside me had been hoping for that end, by a friend's hand, for a long time. Humans call it conscience. Atonement. I don't know—I gave up on humanity as I gnawed on an old man's thigh bone to get at the pulpy marrow ... there, in the dark ... under slabs of cracked limestone ... where all I heard were the moans of the people not yet dead. And my chewing.

I mutter to Cliff, "I—I've worked at the hospital . . . for decades, under different names. Joining Shock Trauma . . . my chance to mend people. Maybe stay out of hell." I gulp air. "So are you going to send me there anyway?"

"I have to."

The lights in the corridor flicker, wink out. University Security wouldn't do that. Wouldn't we hear their voices, or two-way feedback? That single bulb's now swinging madly, playing weird flashes and shadows on the brick walls.

Shadows . . . on the walls.

Foom!

Door planks explode into splinters. Cliff's stunned, on the floor. In a swath of light, I see a hand. Yellow fingernails. Matted hair on the top, on the palm. Just like mine, when my stomach growls. There, a hairless, oblong head. Ears feathered and pointed like a hobgoblin's. And a face. Familiar. Smiling with a crooked mouth full of rotted, pointed teeth.

The motherfucker chortles, "Did you enjoy the morsel I spit up and heaved at you in the snow, Hercule? You, who are fit only for my leavings?"

Now he's hovering over Cliff. Salivating, slathering. D'Orsay. My old master. Dogging me long after we both should have died. My purgatory. His hell. He taunts, "You're a *hyena*, Hercule. Cleaning up the detritus, then washing it out of your ignorant nigger memory after you feast. But this is *fresh* meat. With him gone, I am safe. *Vous, aussi. Bon, d'accord*—and where are his tenderest bits?" He reaches into the moldy pocket of the ragged mackintosh he wore the day the Army hanged him. He pulls out a human toe. Nail painted red, a silver toe ring still encircling the joint. "Saved an hors d'oeuvre for you. This nigger's white bitch. Hunting is more fun than scavenging. Just ask a lion."

No, we really can't see as well in the dark as you'd think. He's strong, though. Inhuman. But so am I. Fury, heartache, shame . . . so much pent up for so long. I won't follow him to hell. I bash the light. He chomps a hunk of flesh from my neck when I throw my shoulder into his chest. I slam him into the wall. There, in the sliver of light from the tunnel. The spike. I dive for it. He pounces onto my back like a wolf spider and digs his nails into my skin. The sound is like fabric tearing, and I shriek in agony. I buck him. He leaps again. I see his beady red eyes blink that instant, because he knows I have the spike. I pivot and rip the iron through his flank. He howls. I pull the spike out. His sticky, black blood pollutes my hand. We grapple, and his hairy paws seize my throat. He's going to pinch my head off, like a child with a dandelion. I'm going dizzy . . . one uppercut . . . one arch. All I have left . . .

I'm falling away . . . tumbling to the floor. Yet it feels like a cloud when I hit, and everything around me melts. Dreamy, gauzy. My master's spinning, whirling . . . hands on his face . . . a spike skewering his jaw and palate . . . pieces of teeth and bone cracked onto the spike's point. I hear gurgling. He runs. The screams fade down the tunnel.

I don't dream when I sleep. Otherwise, I'll remember. So I don't know how much time has passed when I open my eyes and see Cliff. I feel his hands cradle my head.

"Your blood . . . it's red, oxygenated."

I'm coughing through my words. "It . . . won't be for long. It comes and goes. I'll look and smell like him soon. Dorsey's curse isn't as bad as mine, ya know. At least there're no lies in him." Cliff's taking my hand, but I exhort, "You got to finish me."

He sighs. "Can't, bruh. The spike's gone with . . . that thing, Dorsey. I am so sorry, man. I wanted you to suffer for Mindy. I had to lure you here. . . ."

Now I'm hearing radio feedback, voices. University Security, for real. "I'll turn soon, when the hunger hits. I'll break into the morgue . . . the cemetery. Maybe I'll hunt, too."

"No . . . no. The only thing standing between Dorsey—D'Orsay— and innocent folks out on the street is *you.*" I'm sure Cliff hears the guards coming, too, because he's jerking his head around and says, "You'll have to disappear. There's got to be another way outta this room—you were here when they built the place, right? I'll tell the guards, the cops, we were jumped, kidnapped, whatever. Say it's the same stalker who killed Mindy. Get them cronked and thus keep D'Orsay off balance. It might work, Bushrod."

I force a bloody smile because no one's called me that name, Bushrod, with affection, for almost a hundred ninety years. But then the smile evaporates when I whisper, "I have nowhere else to go."

Actually, that's not true. I can go where I please. Be who I want. You'll sit next to me on the B train from Brooklyn to Manhattan. I'll play pickup half-court with you at that new gym opening in Buckhead. Your girlfriends will whisper and cackle about who that fine new brother is, sitting in the club on Sunset Boulevard, sipping Haitian rum. Or a colleague at a hospital in Houston will say, "He started in the

ER on Monday—trauma surgeon, from Boston, I think . . ." Yes, if your
body's broken and battered, absolutely, I'll fix you. But if you die on me,
it'll take a lot of willpower on my part not to come dig your ass up later.
Luckily, I'm a brother with discipline.

For real, though—I implore you to watch your back if you're walking with your honey to your car in a mall parking garage, or you're
putting the trash cans to the curb on a crisp night, or even rolling out
for the evening, all primped and smelling delicious. For godsakes, take
a *long* look over your shoulder before you open your car door, or take
another step, or enter that stairwell or empty elevator. If you see an
extra moving shadow but don't hear any footsteps, *well* . . . my master's always hungry.

Dreads

D. S. Foxx

I always have a comb in my pocket. There's at least one in every room of my house. Spares in the trunk of my car, in purses, stuck into the bookshelf, in drawers. My friends call me vain, a peacock. I just smile. My family says nothing; they understand. They *know*.

I grew up in a vanilla town, the darkest child in my school. It didn't matter much; I had friends. A few of the parents might have been uncomfortable with me, but the kids judged me on who I was, not what, like I did them. My best friend, Mary, had the greatest hair—blond and shiny, it curled around the top of her ears like a cap.

My hair fell to my knees, black as night, always in braids, never loose except to be washed. Every Sunday afternoon, when all my friends were playing, I'd be trapped between Mama's knees while she pulled and wove. Hours and hours, and I had to sit still, and wait.

Mama'd bead them, too, some braids tipped with one, others with three, some pattern only she understood, hundreds of carved and stained and painted wooden bits for me to roll on in my sleep. The only part I liked was the singing. For each braid a different line, a hundred in all. The words meant nothing to me, but I liked the sound. She spoke in that tongue sometimes, to Grandma, to visitors, but I never thought to learn it, and Mama let it be. But even if I didn't know what they meant, I learned the songs, could sing them myself if I wanted, brushing my fingers along the beads. Feeling the pattern she had made.

Mary and a few other close friends learned to eat curry and haystacks and drink sorrel, but mostly we'd go to their houses, watch TV. Have slumber parties with little footie pajamas, giggle about kiss-

ing boys, pretend to drink tea. Normal stuff, for normal children.
Normal white kids, and me.

Mary had a brother, and I thought he was fine. Hair as blond as his
sister's, curled over his collar most times. Sometimes cut short, so his
neck would show paler than the rest. The family all went to the salon
every six weeks. It was like a ritual. I wanted to be a part of it. But
Mama wouldn't let me do anything with my hair. It was braided always,
tipped in wooden beads. Never loose except when under her hands.

"No, chile," she'd say in her voice like the ocean, "yo' hair too good
fo' dat." *Good.* A word the white folks don't understand. Neither did I
then; not really. But Mama'd spoken; arguing would do no good. I grew,
as did my hair, and Mama kept braiding, and singing as she slid the
beads along.

Sometimes, if I was very still, I could hear drumbeats in the air,
faint echoes of Mama's fingers on the wood. And sometimes I'd fall
asleep still sitting upright, held between her knees, and dream I could
hear the meaning of her songs. Mostly, though, I fidgeted and whim-
pered, begged to be let loose, to go and play.

"No, chile," I'd hear, soft and warm but unyielding. "Yo' hair not did
yet. Sit yo'self down, now. Listen." She never told me what she thought
I might hear. And I never asked, too busy wishing to be someplace else.
Wishing for hair short as Mary's, which wouldn't hold a braid. Hair that
fluttered in every passing breeze, light as a cloud.

I had just turned twelve the day Mary bet I wouldn't undo my
braids. Seems funny now, that it took so long. She dared me, and I
shook my head, beads clattering, and then she bet me, in money. What's
more, she told me she'd tell her brother I was chicken if I refused. I
couldn't have that, so I shook my braids forward, over my shoulder,
where I could reach. The beads felt hot beneath my fingers—rough,
catching my skin.

Mama? But she wasn't near. She was at work, wouldn't be home for
hours. I'd have to deal with this, whatever it was, alone. I told myself I
was imagining things, sucked my fingertips to soothe them, took a deep
breath. Chose a braid near the back, thinking I could hide my crime.
Knowing I wasn't allowed, choosing to do it anyway. I slid the beads
off—one, two, three—clutched them in my fist. Tried to pretend I wasn't
shaking, and began to unweave. Unravel. Unbraid. Undo. Hummed beneath my breath, the song to go with the braid. It reversed itself in my
mind.

"What are you saying? God, are you in pain?" Mary was almost sneering as she heard the song. It wasn't much like the boy-band stuff she—we—listened to; probably didn't sound like music to her at all. But to me it sounded like a sudden storm, power and motion with no control. I liked it a lot, the way it sounded, the way it felt, song running through my blood, making my hair stand on end. My eyes went wide, looking for something I was sure I'd know when I saw, and I sang louder as I reached the end of the braid.

A storm came to my song. To my call. My spell. One second the sun was bright in the sky; the next it might have been night, clouds so low and thick you couldn't see. Wind whipping, not moving the darkness away so much as stirring it. An odor like nothing I had ever smelled. Salt, and sweet. Almost metallic, as much taste as scent. Mary made some *ew* sound and ran inside. I stood in the street, in the crossroads, and tossed back my head, braids lighter than they'd ever been in this wild wind, deliciously different. It rubbed against me, smooth and warm; I threw my hands wide to hug it tight.

Three small wooden beads bounced free.

There were drumbeats in the air, loud enough for me to hear them, and voices like Mama's songs sung in reverse. The bit of my hair I'd freed flew wild, dancing, and I felt like I could fly, if I just knew the right words. Still coiled from its long braiding, it was like three soft ropes as it brushed my face, tugged by the unnatural, welcoming, singing weather. First one bit and then another ran over my lips, and words came to me, and I sang them, words I didn't know but understood. Names. Kin names. And then each strand fell away behind me, wrapped around something, gripped it tight, and I felt . . . I felt like I'd just been given a gift.

Three gifts. One each for the beads I'd tossed away, for the strands of the braid. To the salt and the sweet in the air came another scent, tart, like citrus, only not lemon, not orange—no fruit I knew. Three scents for three names? I tried to touch the fruit-wind, sang a name. *No*, not that one. I tried the second, but that didn't feel right, either. Smiling, I took a deep breath, prepared to sing the third, the right name for the wind. Wondered what would happen, what new gift would come, what reward. The winds ceased to blow, still there, but waiting. For me, I knew.

And then Grandma came. From wherever she had been. Smell like hot peppers and wrinkles and kinky hair. Age-creaked voice, raised to outshout the wind. "No, chile. Dis one not fo' you." Her accent was thicker than usual, almost too much to understand. I frowned, confused, as she turned away from me, looked up at the lowering sky.

I had thought she was talking to me, you see. But then came other words, in a language I didn't speak, and a laugh with no throat to come from, and the wind whipped up, and keened, and stilled. Grandma shook out a piece of fabric she took from her pocket, told me to look at the patterns. Kente cloth. It was pretty enough, I guessed, in its way, but that's not what she wanted me to see. I got it after a moment: The patterns were like my beads. "Protection," she told me, speaking careful, proper English to be sure I'd understand, "to keep you safe."

"Safe from what?" I asked her, my mind still with the winds. I thought they were still near, waiting for me to call them. I could almost hear them, almost feel them, but not quite. Grandma was in my way. My head was heavy, pulled down by the beads, bound by the braids. The names were solid in my mouth, pebbles, jewels. It was hard to speak around them.

"Chile," she sighed, then frowned. Slowly, carefully, as if to an idiot, she formed her words, set them out into the air. "Haven't you ever thought? Do you wonder why we live so far from our kin? You must know it's not natural to be alone." Her face sagged like she was tired, and I felt a vague flush of guilt. I hadn't ever wondered, really. Kids don't. But Grandma was never so happy as come reunion time.

"Why?" The word had to creep around the names, slither like a snake. My head bent back, pulled by the braids, the three tangles burning against my back. I was beginning to be scared, not by the winds—my friends, my kin—but by my grandmother as she looked at me, disappointment plain in her eyes. I didn't want to be punished, but it was more than that. I didn't want her to be displeased with me. The words seemed to grow; I thought I might choke on them, longed to spit them out, but she was speaking. I couldn't interrupt.

"To keep you safe, and them. They don't belong here, but they don't understand that. They can't. It's our task to keep them safe, at home. They'll only do harm here, and be harmed, and bring harm to us and all of ours. Send them back now, child. It's not the right time, or place." She put her hand on my shoulder, gathered up my hair, all the braids surrounding the loose section, tied the kente cloth in a bow. A ponytail, a makeshift binding.

I felt the winds sigh, like a sob, and I joined them, and the words dissolved on my tongue, their bitter taste making me gag. I'd never felt so alone before, and part of me longed to call them back. But Grandma was in charge, so I sent them away, and if her smile was sad, at least it wasn't disapproving. We went inside as the sky cleared, to drink sorrel and talk. Grandma cried as she undid my braids. It only works for the innocent, you see, to bind them safe from harm. And I wasn't a child anymore. I'd made my choice.

I cried a little, too, as she cut out the tangled parts and showed them to me. The hair looked different: paler, thicker. Like the dreadlocks my cousins wore. I wanted to touch them, to feel the textures, to see what was inside, the gifts I'd been given by my winds, but Grandma said no, and I cried over that, too. More when she burned them and made me watch, and sing to drown out the drumbeats in the air. But it wasn't all bad; she started teaching me that day. Herbs and potions and stories, songs and spells and rituals, all the parts of my heritage I'd never known. Gods and spirits and kin who were never flesh, and those gone beyond the grave, who still heed our call.

I'm grown now, and living in a chocolate city; my kids are surrounded by all their kin. They speak with the islands in their voice, grammar as different from mine as my mama's and grandma's, much the same as the tongue I speak sometimes now. I hear drumbeats in their footsteps, and my heart lifts. I hope it will be some protection when the winds come to their call, when other things try to answer, misguided spirits come to visit, knowing ones to join them or bind them or steal their souls. And, yes, I do braid their hair, the boys and the girls, and I bead it, and sing the songs as I do. But for myself, I keep a comb in every room, and one in my pocket, and spares stuck everywhere, inside and out.

I have a horror of catching something in a tangle. An absolute dread.

Plaything

Terence Taylor

The girl was perfect.

Her hair was silken, long, hung down to her shoulders in pigtails, blond, shiny as a newly minted gold coin. Her eyes were beyond blue. They were the color you saw offshore at Caribbean beaches, that impossibly heavenly hue that made your throat catch, brought a tear to your eyes. Her skin was pink, soft, warm, covered with a baby-fine down that reminded Elliot of a field of dandelions ready to release their seeds to the wind, of newborn kittens, of flannel sheets in winter.

It was the lips that sold her, not just the pout—the round fullness of them—but the pliant willingness to give when touched, the way they molded to your lips when you kissed her, wrapped wetly around your finger when you slipped it into her mouth.

"She's perfect."

Elliot said aloud what he'd been thinking, saw Roger grin in proud agreement, as if he himself had somehow been responsible.

"Yeah. I ordered her brother yesterday. I was going to wait until I saw how well this one worked out, but after my first night, I put in an order. Takes a few weeks, but worth the wait!" He gulped at his beer. "I was thinking of throwing a little party when he gets here. You should come back down for another visit."

"No, thanks."

"That's right. You're just one for the girls."

"Do you mind if I . . . ?" Elliot faltered, his heart pounding.

"Go ahead. Help yourself," said Roger. "Mind if I watch, or would you rather go it alone?"

When Elliot didn't answer, Roger finished his beer, laughed as he went to the fridge for another one.

Elliot stared at the girl, silent, his eyes trapped in hers. He couldn't look away, not even when the police smashed open the front door and officers swarmed in with guns to arrest them, followed by neighbors, pointing, accusing. He watched the girl as the cops led her outside the house and packed her into a body bag to be taken back to the station as evidence. She smiled shyly as they zipped her up, waved at him as if she really regretted that their date had been interrupted.

He sighed as they handcuffed him and took him away.

Perfect.

Cole woke up from a nightmare of living machines, big wheels and oversize gears that ground his flesh and took him apart. Punished him. He got out of bed without waking Neal, went to the bathroom, then made coffee while he checked the morning headlines on the living room HDTV. He ignored most of the e-mail displayed next to the news feed on the four-foot-long flat screen—hate letters from around the world, thanks to an Internet that made him accessible to every psycho on the planet. How long would it be before they could just target him with personal missiles tuned to his height, weight, appearance, and genetic code? Push a button in Paris and take him out wherever he was with a limited-range neutron bomb, without mussing anyone else in the room.

If they could, they would. To read the headlines, he was the most hated man on the planet. Roger and Elliot had only exercised unnatural desires. Cole was the one trying to convince a court to say it was legal.

His husband lumbered in while Cole dug the last work-related mail from the pile and answered it. Neal started making them breakfast, said nothing. He'd had enough to say last night. This case had put more strain on their relationship than any Cole had taken before. He'd defended drug dealers, abortion doctors, even gay pornographers, which is how he'd met Neal, but this case was too much even for the man who had produced and directed *Hung Jury* and *Spurts Illustrated*. At least those were films with grown men going at each other. There were no children involved. No matter how liberal they'd all become, there were still limits. In a world that finally accepted gay marriage and had decriminalized marijuana and voluntary euthanasia, sex with children was still where everyone drew the line.

Even if the children were artificial.

"I still love you, you know. How I feel about this case doesn't affect that." Neal didn't look at Cole from the kitchen when he finally spoke—kept his back to him.

"I know. I love you, too. I can't blame you for leaving the country until it's over." Cole sent his last letter off with a click, joined Neal at the table. Breakfast was healthy and nutritious, as usual. Sometimes Cole wished he could just have a plate of good old-fashioned bacon and eggs with grits drowned in butter, like his momma used to make, instead of one of Neal's vegan delights.

"It's not you; it's the shoot. I can't put it off any longer." He wasn't mad anymore, but Cole could tell he wasn't being entirely honest. Neal didn't want to distance himself from Cole, but he did want to avoid their usual late-night rehashes of Cole's day in court.

Cole knew Neal's uncle had molested him for years when he was a kid. He'd never been able to convince anyone it was happening, and had finally run away at fifteen—ended up peddling his ass on Santa Monica Boulevard in L.A. for a year just to eat. That didn't make Neal sympathetic to Cole's clients or his efforts to save them from jail time.

"They didn't hurt anyone, Neal. I understand how you feel, how everyone feels. I don't like most of my clients, but I'm a civil rights lawyer. We can't arrest people for thought crime. You'd be serving a life sentence." He tried to smile, tried to lighten the mood. "So would I."

"It's not just thought, Cole! Christ! They're doing it! They're fucking this little girl and using the excuse that she's synthetic to say that it doesn't matter! I don't care if she can't speak up for herself; I don't even care if she's programmed to like it. It's wrong. She's real, even if she's manufactured. If it looks like a duck, walks like a duck and quacks like a duck . . . it's a fucking duck, Cole. It's just wrong."

The meal was eaten without continuing the conversation.

The argument.

They didn't have much time to be together before Neal left for Spain. Neither of them wanted to waste it fighting. Cole had to spend enough of that time in court, defending two men's right to have sex with an animated Living Doll that looked, sounded, acted, felt, tasted, and smelled like an eight-year-old girl. There was no reason to let that keep him from holding the man he loved for as long as he could, from drawing strength from Neal, from their relationship, their reality, before plunging back into the mad world of his clients and their supporters.

There were supporters, hard as it was to believe. Free-speech advocates who saw Roger and Elliot's conviction as the first step on a slippery slope to censorship and curtailed liberties. Sex industry supporters who saw the new technology as a legal way to satisfy all urges, no matter how aberrant, without harm to anyone. And of course, organizations like NAMBLA that had advocated child love for decades, still trying to convince the public that children had a right to choose their sexual partners, no matter what age.

Choice wasn't the issue here. A machine had no choice. It was a possession, and humanity had finally entered an age when our machines were indistinguishable from us.

Except for their rights.

The prosecuting attorney, Rosa Goldberg-Gonzales, stopped by Cole's table at lunch. "G. G.", an old friend from college, was a large, deceptively maternal-looking woman. She'd tried for years to get him to join her in the DA's office, to be one of the good guys.

"I *am* the good guy, G. G.—black skin, white hat," he'd always answered, but after this morning in court, after seeing Neal off on a plane, he wasn't sure anymore.

"How are you doing, kiddo?" G. G. sat down without asking, waved her glass at the waiter to bring her another drink. "I know this can't be easy for you."

"Do you think I'm wrong? Off the record."

She paused, stirred the fresh drink the waiter brought her, and downed half of it before answering. "There's no easy answer, or we wouldn't be butting heads in court. We're spending millions of the state's money to figure out if what they did is right or wrong."

"It's a sex doll, G. G., a robot, even if it's organic. It's still not human. At worst they're guilty of masturbation. I can't let them serve time for that."

"Have you seen it, Cole? I mean, really taken a good close look at it? Spent any time with it? There's no Off switch. You can't shut it down. It's more than a doll, Cole. I went to the evidence room. They set up a goddamned nursery for it. It sits there all day playing with toys, watching cartoons. It even eats cookies. For all intents and purposes, it's a kid."

"If it walks like a duck and quacks like a duck?" G. G. looked puzzled. "Something Neal said. He says it's a duck, and if it's against the law to fuck a duck—even if it's a rubber duck—it's against the law."

"I'd expect him to feel that way. Didn't Neal have some history with a neighbor when he was a kid?"

"An uncle. Yeah. Neal left this morning, for a month in Spain. Says the shoot was planned ages ago, but I know it wasn't."

"Sorry. I know he's usually behind you. Can't make it any easier to work on this case. I'd offer you a shoulder to cry on, but I think that violates several statutes."

"I'll manage. I wish I wasn't up against you on this, though."

"Afraid it will affect our friendship? Or that I'll win?"

"Both."

She pretended to laugh.

"We're in a dangerous place, Cole. When the Supreme Court said virtual kiddie porn wasn't against the law thirty years ago, we didn't have biocybertechnology. No one thought we'd be making artificial people, or . . ."

"What? That we'd want them to be anatomically correct? Come on, G. G. Rich housewives across the country are doing their robot butlers; the husbands are diddling robot secretaries. Do you have any doubt that the first color picture sent over the Internet was of a naked woman? The first thing that happens to any new technology is that people find a way to steal with it and a way to have sex with it."

"Not everybody."

"Exceptions don't number enough to matter. Everyone said porn was just for dirty old men in raincoats until it hit home video and became a billion-dollar industry in the Bible Belt. Why should using a Living Doll be treated differently than using a videotape or an inflatable sex toy to get off? What if it contains their impulses well enough to make them harmless?"

"Don't kid yourself. Let them do the Dolls long enough, they'll get bored and start looking for the real thing. Even if they stick to the Dolls, what happens when sex isn't enough, when surrogate pedophiles turn into surrogate child murderers? If it's not wrong to screw a Living Doll, is it wrong to rape and torture it for a few weeks, cut it up and send it back to the shop for repairs so you can do it over and over again? How alive does something have to be before we give it the same respect that we give each other? Does not having biological parents mean you have no rights?"

"Practicing your closing statement?"

G. G. laughed. "You always bring out the best in me. I should have taken notes." She pushed herself away from the table, kissed him on top of his head before she left. "See you in court."

Cole finished lunch and found out she'd paid his bill and left a note for him with the waiter: *Good luck, kiddo. You'll need it.*

Elliot was asleep when his lawyer came to see him. He slept a lot these days. It was the only way to escape solitary confinement. For his protection, they said, but it was still a horrible aloneness. He was locked up in a closet-sized room, the way he had been as a kid when his stepfather decided he had been bad.

He had dreamed of her. They were under an apple tree, in the country. It rained around them, but they were safe and dry under the wide, leafy green branches.

"It's okay," she'd said. "We'll be together soon." Then she kissed him, slow, loving, her hand in his pants, until the guard woke him up.

While he waited for his first client, Cole arranged his things on the table, organized objects around him in an attempt to have some feeling of control over the world.

He had time to think before his first appointment arrived, not always a good thing. The case had made him look back into history for precedents. They had abandoned so many of the old taboos by the twenty-first century, it was hard for most people to remember the past. Taboos against sex, drugs, and religion, anything that impinged on personal freedoms, were gone—everything except laws against harming children.

Cole thought it had less to do with awareness of the issues than collective guilt once we realized how little we'd cared for so long. Child abuse went back to the Stone Age. It was only in the last few hundred years that anyone had done anything to stop it. The mistreatment of child factory workers in Dickens's time led to strict child labor laws; sexual abuse of boys by priests purged the priesthood's ranks and helped end the celibacy ban under the current pope; a PBS series on child brothels in Bangkok finally reformed Thailand's penal system.

Cole was sure his case was strong enough on legal grounds to set his clients free, but he knew winning would unleash a precedent that would reshape his world. He tried to imagine a society where every whim, every desire against children, against each other, could be enacted as long as it was with a synthetic human. How long would it take before the technology dropped in price enough for anyone to own one or lease one for a night, a weekend, insured like a rental car against possible damage?

That was what convinced Cole that G. G. was right about seeing the Doll for himself. Interviews with his clients, the police reports, depositions of witnesses—they didn't hold the whole picture. He hadn't talked to the "victim." Cole had deliberately avoided thinking about the Doll that way. It was a toy, not a living thing. An animated blowup doll, a service, more like a realistic flesh-molded dildo than a prostitute. He'd thought there was no more need to hear its side than to interview a porno tape.

He'd been wrong. As he kept defending his clients to the court, to his husband, the press, his friends, and now himself, the only way to convince himself that he was right was to talk to the girl herself. Itself.

He made a note on his PDA to make an appointment later that afternoon and e-mailed it to his office as Elliot entered.

"Hello, Elliot. There's not much news. We really won't know anything until after the closing arguments. I just wanted to check in on you, make sure you have everything you need. That you're all right."

That you're not being beaten, Cole thought but didn't say. That no one's tried to kill you. Yet. Cole had learned not to alarm clients with the grim realities of life behind bars any more than he had to for their own protection. He had to trust in an increasingly privatized system to remain true to its word, to live up to "innocent until proven guilty" when handling prisoners held for trial. It was the law, but Cole knew how little weight that carried on the ground. Who knew who watched the watchmen these days, besides accountants and auditors?

"I'm lonely, but I've always been that, I guess."

Elliot was a mouse of a man: soft features, soft body, a soft, fluffy halo of hair around his soft, round face. He kept his eyes down, played with the edge of the table. His hands were in constant motion, touched, felt, traveled across surfaces like spiders, described the world to him as if he were blind or a child. Cole couldn't help imagining himself as a kid, with those hands crawling over him. He quickly brushed the thought from his mind.

"I guess there's not much I can do about that. They just want to keep you and Roger away from the other prisoners." And the guards. And themselves. "So they don't hurt you."

"I know. I know it's for my own good. I was bad."

Cole listened patiently. Elliot wasn't mentally challenged. According to the records he had a normal, if slightly high, IQ. He just spoke like a slow child. At first Cole assumed it had something to do with growing up tortured by a psychotic, abusive stepfather, but it was more than that.

Simplicity, slow deliberation, was an integral part of Elliot's nature. Despite his almost moronic demeanor, he was someone who got things done. Slowly, methodically, eventually, Elliot always seemed to have gotten his way in the past. It was what Cole would have pointed out made him so dangerous, if he were the prosecution. Instead he was arguing that it was a quality Elliot would channel into his rehabilitation, a guarantee of success.

"I'd like some cake, or cookies," said Elliot. "Cookies." He was only twenty-six, but there was a quality about him that made him seem used up, as if he had been emptied, discarded like a soda can for scavengers like Roger to find.

"Did you ask the guards?"

"Yes . . . no. I was afraid." He raised his eyes from his devotion to feeling up the tabletop. "It would be better if it came from you. They wouldn't blame me, then."

Cole made a note to his assistant, e-mailed it out as he saw confirmation of his appointment to see the Doll come in on the PDA screen. "Okay, it's on the menu. Let me know if there's anything else you need."

Elliot nodded, eyes half closed, sleepy again. Cole signaled the guard, let him lead Elliot out. A few quick minutes with Roger, and he would be free to interview the evidence.

A female officer let him into the evidence lockup, led him down the hall to the room where they kept the Doll. The officer didn't talk to him on the way, didn't volunteer any information. Cole was used to being snubbed by the lower echelon of the justice system. They were more passionate in their feelings and weren't required by protocol to be civil in their dealings with him, as his peers in opposition were. Cole remarked that he'd seen only policewomen since he'd arrived. "Did you all request this assignment?"

"Is she bringing out our maternal instincts? Is that what you want to know?" She snorted. "Naw. The guys just have trouble handling her. You'll see why. She's different with them than she is with us."

"What do you mean?" asked Cole.

"You'll see," she said with a look between pity and a sneer. They stopped at the door. She pulled out her keycard and swiped it, pressed a thumb to the panel above the lock. "Visitor."

The password opened the door with a click. A cartoon danced on a TV screen in the corner, sound turned down. The Doll was seated on the floor, playing with toy dolls, as she had patiently done since being installed there.

Everyone who'd seen the Doll referred to it as "her." At first Cole thought it was because of the case, to remind them that his clients had violated a little girl, not a thing. After he saw her, he understood. She—or it—was remarkably human. No.

The girl was perfect.

Cole knew actors, drag queens and movie effects artists, friends who'd taught him to find the flaw in any illusion, no matter how well done. Whatever technicians had created this fantasy deserved praise over them all. Her bluer-than-blue eyes flew up to his from her dolls; her pupils widened as she prepared to read his reactions to gauge hers. She wasn't just a little girl; she was every little girl rolled into one—the shy kid, the tomboy, the coquette, the scamp, all programmed into the body of a flawless All-American Junior Miss winner. Cole couldn't help wondering if the public outcry would be as loud if she looked like a nappy-headed little black girl instead of a pink-cheeked blonde.

The Doll's programmed range of personalities flicked across her face like a menu, waited for him to make a selection to decide which she would use to respond.

"Hello, Carol." His clients had told Cole it was the name she was programmed to respond to, at Roger's request. It was his little literary joke; he had planned on naming the male Doll "Lewis."

"My name is Cole. I'm a friend of Roger and Elliot."

The pupils snapped back down to accommodate the room's light levels. Thousands of relays and subroutines stopped, not needed to establish this subject's character. "Friend of Roger and Elliot" was enough of a cue for her to go into coquette.

"Hi, Cole. Want a cookie?"

She held out a plate containing a few stale cookies, one half-eaten, and the crumbs of others.

"No, thanks."

Cole sat on the floor across from her, watched her bite into the half-eaten cookie. He was involuntarily fascinated by the way she finished it off. Getting it from the plate to her mouth was done with such choreographed deliberation that it had the feel of a classic burlesque striptease.

Her lips crumbled the cookie between them, curled to catch the chunk that fell into her mouth; her tongue darted out to catch falling crumbs in a manner that suggested adeptness and extensive experience with its use.

She swallowed, sighed with satisfaction, ran her tongue across her lips.

"Yum." Carol's eyes rolled back up from the plate and met Cole's with a calculated sparkle that increased as her pupils dilated again, this time with desire, twin pools inviting him to dive in. Cole nearly swooned, swore the heat in the room had increased significantly since he'd come in. He understood now why none of the men were comfortable with assignment here.

The thing was programmed for complete compliance—whether to make the molester's job easier or to lessen guilt by providing a willing partner, Cole didn't know. He supposed it was possible to set it for any response, from complicit partner to reluctant, resisting virgin, ready to be raped.

"Will you play with me?" The words were innocent enough, but the Doll played them with all the innuendo intact. "I'm so lonely. Can I have more cookies?"

She sounded as simple as Elliot, down to the damned cookies. Cole considered what else there was to learn here, and decided he was done when she coyly started to toy with the sleeve of his jacket and reached for his thigh, pouting when he pulled away instead of responding with a hug or kiss.

"You don't like me."

"I do."

"Then why won't you play?"

"I have to go back to work."

"Why?" She had just the right amount of wheedle, the perfect plaintive plea, modulated to melt the hardest heart. "No one plays with me here." The damn thing was a seduction machine. He'd seen kids like this in bad foster care cases, kids so conditioned to abuse that sex became a survival skill, their natural defense against attack.

Cole tore himself away and pressed the call button by the door. The officer opened it so quickly, she must have been waiting outside in the hall. There was a knowing smirk on her face. She must have seen the same mussed and distressed look on many others.

"How far did she get before you figured it out?" she asked as they walked back down the hall to the exit.

"Not very. I don't suppose anyone stays long."

"You'd be surprised." She didn't elaborate, and Cole didn't press for details. That was a job for Internal Affairs, if anyone.

He took a car service back to the office, sent by his office to pick him up in the underground garage. Cole finished cleaning up his notes on the way, tried to lose the desire to go home and wash.

Whatever Carol was, she wasn't a witness for the defense.

"You bastard!"

An egg hit Cole in the chest when he turned to see who had shouted. A woman dropped the rest of the carton on the floor, grabbed her child's hand, and shoved her cart ahead of her as she fled the dairy section of the supermarket.

Cole could hear the hysterical cries of the child as she dragged it away; it probably fell in its mother's rush to get it away from the big bad defense attorney. He put a milk carton in his cart and headed for the checkout line, hoped he could get through it before the rest of the customers recognized him.

It was too late. By the time he got to the register, the whole front of the store buzzed like an angry hive. Cole put his groceries on the conveyor belt and pulled out his debit card to pay his bill as fast as he could. It didn't work when he swiped it. The clerk glared at him, dubious, as he keyed in the numbers.

"Do you have ID?" he asked.

Cole jerked a thumb at the staring customers on other lines. "Just ask them," he said. They all looked away as the clerk looked at them, then back at Cole's card, recognized the name and then the face.

"Oh, yeah. Right." He bagged the groceries and tossed the bag to the end of the counter. "Next!"

Cole picked up his bag, felt them all watch him leave, heard them start to buzz again as soon as the doors closed.

There was a message from Neal blinking on the wall screen when Cole got home. He played it while he put down the groceries, tried to wipe what was left of the raw egg off his jacket.

"Hey, babe. It's going okay. Scotty is a bitch as usual, and if it weren't for that new Viagra, Ken would be useless. He's back on crys-

tal, I'll be damned if I know how. I cut him down to one scene, and I'm
sending him back into rehab as fast as I can. Jesus . . . what now?"

There was a sound from off camera. Cole looked up from his cleaning
to see Neal glaring with the mute on, talking to someone at the door of his
room, probably his assistant Joey, another ex-porn star, turned produc-
tion manager. Neal took his finger off the mute and turned back to Cole.

"Gotta run. The boys have started a hair-pulling match on the set.
Talk to you later. Call me."

His face faded from the screen.

He didn't say, "I love you."

He'd ended every call but this one since their marriage with those
words. Cole started pulling groceries out to make dinner, to keep his
promise to Neal to eat right while he was gone, then put the food away
and, instead of cooking, called for a pizza loaded with as much pork as
they could carry. He opened a beer and pulled out his briefcase,
dropped into the armchair in front of the HDTV with his laptop and
started work.

The pizza came; Cole picked at it, drank more beer and came up
with excuses not to call Neal. When he couldn't work anymore, he lit a
pipe of Neal's California weed and put one of his old porno disks into
the DVD player.

Neal was called Jack in this one, when he was barely twenty, before
he changed his professional name to Chance and turned himself into a
gay-porn legend. To diehard fans he would always be the lean, muscled
big-dick boy he was here, always smiling, always ready and willing for
action. Watching Neal on camera usually gave Cole the guilty pleasure
of having him near, despite Neal's stories about that kid, the things
he'd done, drugged up and drunk enough not to feel anything, hustling
on the side for enough bucks to quit. Tonight, watching young "Jack"
gasp and moan with faked passion in a three-way with two skinny
teenagers only made Cole feel guilty of the same offense as his clients:
using an artificial image of desire to satisfy himself in secret. It didn't
help to know that Neal found it funny and cute. Tonight it felt cheap
and dirty, but not in a good way.

The screen beeped. A call was coming in. It was one a.m., seven in
the morning Barcelona time. Cole froze the HDVD picture in
midthrust while Neal's face popped up in a window over it. His face
was puffy from lack of sleep, his clothes the same he'd worn in the earlier message.

"Hey, babe. Glad you're still up."

"Yeah. Just watching some TV to unwind."

Neal grinned, halfheartedly but still amused. "I'll bet you were. Hope the real thing doesn't pale by comparison."

"I'd prefer the real thing. Wish you were here instead."

"Maybe I'll send you a Living Doll to keep you company. At least that way you won't be cheating on me. Technically."

Cole winced. "Let's not."

"How's it going?"

"It goes. I close tomorrow. Then we wait."

"I wish I could wish you luck and mean it."

"Me, too."

They stared at each other across thousands of miles. Ordinarily they would have given in to videophone sex as some kind of contact, no matter how small, just for the fun of it. The mood wasn't there tonight, and not because they were both so exhausted.

"I love you, Neal."

"I love you, too, babe. I was in a hurry when I signed off earlier; I didn't mean . . ."

"I know. I just had to make sure."

"My feelings haven't changed, not about you or the case."

"I didn't think they had. I want this over with so you can see me and not them."

"I don't see them. I see me, a long time ago. I see the kids I work with."

"It was a Doll, Neal. Not one of them. Not you. Some kid got saved from that because they had the Doll to play with. Maybe there's some kind of treatment in that. I don't know."

"You always want something noble to come out of the work you do. Sometimes it does, but sometimes it's just not enough to make up for the bad. I can't forgive or forget what they were doing. Even if it was a robot, in their heads it was a kid. That's what turned them on, not hardware. That's what makes it wrong."

"But not illegal."

"It . . ." Cole could see Neal stop himself from going into a rant. "Justice isn't always about the letter of the law, babe. Right and wrong don't always matter in court, but they matter to people. I know you can cite a hundred cases to let these guys walk, but in the end it's just sleight of hand, smoke and mirrors."

"That's not what you thought when I got you off on obscenity charges six years ago."

"I knew it then, but I didn't care and I'd be a hypocrite to deny it. But I didn't do what they did. I paid adults to do adult films. My professional and personal life has been spent trying to undo what men like your clients did to kids like me."

"How many guys watch your college jock videos and pretend they're watching high school kids?"

"And I take their money and support clinics to help boys who lived through the reality. I call that justice of a kind."

"What I do keeps you in business. If my clients go down, the First Amendment goes down with them."

"Poor choice of words, babe. Puts us back where we started, which is why we shouldn't talk about this. I have to get some sleep before I get back to the set. You get some sleep, too. Wouldn't want you to miss your big day."

Neil's image vanished, left young Jack frozen on the screen. He grinned down at the two stoned teenagers who polished his crotch and ass with wet tongues. Cole turned it off and went to bed, worried that this call, too, had ended without "I love you," no matter what Neal had said about his feelings not changing.

Cole didn't sleep that night. He lay awake in their bed; his conversation with Neal rolled around in his spinning head like a marble on a roulette wheel.

The law had always been how he defended what he thought was right. Classmates had made millions helping big business crush consumers, avoid taxes, lie to the government and get away with it. Cole had always prided himself on manipulating legal language to protect the freedom his great-grandparents had moved here from Jamaica to enjoy. When he'd been seduced into his field of law by an enthusiastic law professor who later became his mentor, he'd seen himself carrying on the good fight started by America's founding fathers.

Now he had doubts. He'd always had clients who tested the limits of his belief in the larger principles he defended, but this case was turning into the last straw. The more he justified himself to Neal, the less he believed in himself. He knew he was on solid legal ground, but his moral footing was starting to slip out from under him.

He started falling asleep after hours of playing old blues CDs on his antique player; Billie Holiday's "Strange Fruit" rang in his ears as the sun rose on the dawn of the day he would win or lose his case.

If only he knew which it was he really wanted.

* * *

Cole spent the days after the trial in hotel rooms while the jury deliberated, unwilling to go home to Neal's, where the mob could find him. The protests outside their building had brought the wrath of the co-op board down on him. Their neighbors, corporate lawyers, rap producers, and movie stars, millionaires all, had made it clear that until this case blew over, he was no longer welcome.

He didn't care. It was Neal's place, not his. Cole made a good living in law, but not enough to support the penthouse lifestyle of a world-renowned pornographer. If he found it funny that his neighbors preferred Neal's profession to his, he got no joy from it. There was very little to laugh about in a sterile hotel room, living under assumed names, staying only until maids or bellboys figured out who he was and sold his location to the tabloids, or worse. Cole had moved four times in five days, felt like Salman Rushdie the first year of his death sentence from the ayatollah.

The jury came back with a verdict faster than expected.

Cole got the call less than a week after closing arguments. He knew what it was before his legal assistant buzzed, told him they had to be in court the next morning. He'd dreaded the call, even though he was fairly sure the verdict would go his way.

That was the reason he was so nervous the next morning.

Cole left without calling a car, stepped off the curb, and raised a hand to flag down a cab to the courthouse. A man shoved him into the street from behind; cars sped past Cole, too close for comfort, honked, swerved to avoid hitting him.

"Sorry," said the man as he climbed into the cab that had barely missed Cole, "Counselor." He spit the word out as he slammed the door and the cab took off. Cole trembled with rage and relief that the car hadn't hit him. Another cab slowed, passed him when the driver got a good look at his face. Cole walked back to the curb and called the office to send him a car. There was still no way for him to stand on the street long enough to get a taxi without being spotted and struck or spit on. If anyone had done that to any other black man on the street, they would be up on hate crime charges, but that there was no one to defend the defender was another irony Cole was too tired, too disheartened, to laugh off.

As usual, the police had to get Cole into the building. Protestors lined the barriers along the sidewalk, waved protest signs like villagers brandishing torches outside Castle Frankenstein. The courthouse had been surrounded since the trial began, but angry demonstrators soon outnumbered the few supporters by so many that they'd fled, unwilling to risk their lives for their causes. Random objects flew at Cole from the crowd: eggs, rotten fruit, cans, bottles—all bounced off the bullet-proof clear Plexiglas shields the officers held up around him.

The jury filed in without meeting even one another's eyes. The foreperson handed their verdict to the bailiff when asked, as if she were handing off an accursed artifact, relieved to be rid of its evil influence. The judge unfolded the slip of paper, the only procedure still not computerized in the modern court system—one last small touch of humanity in the legal process.

Cole felt Elliot shudder beside him, as if he'd just realized what was really happening here and what it meant. Roger grinned at Cole and winked. Either way would be fine with him, he seemed to say. He'd had his fun. The ride was worth the fare.

"Will the defendants rise?"

The judge waited for them to stand. Cole listened to the drone of the usual formalities as if in a trance, felt the hot air in the room tighten around his face, his throat, like a moist velvet glove. The words were a dull buzz, like flies on dead meat as they consumed young flesh left to rot in the woods.

"Not guilty."

It was all that cut through the haze of his thoughts. Cole thought he'd heard it wrong in the stunned silence that followed, until the room exploded in protest.

The judge pounded his gavel, called for silence.

"Clear the courtroom!"

He shouted; no one cared; he couldn't cite them all for contempt, and that was what filled the room.

Officers surrounded Cole, his clients, and his legal assistant, moved them toward the side doors that led out to the holding rooms and exits. The room surged forward, then exploded again, literally, as an outer wall fell, smoked. Brick and plaster blew in with the flames as Cole realized it had to be a bomb or missile, how or from where, he couldn't tell. Word of the verdict must have already made it out of the room, despite all precautions.

Roger was being hustled out when it exploded, far enough in front to be almost out the door, but Cole was flung to the floor by the blast. He lifted his head to see the officer escorting Elliot downed by a brick in the back of his head, face frozen in surprise. Elliot was nowhere to be seen.

Cole got to his feet, left his briefcase on the floor. His assistant was screaming but unhurt. Cole tried to pull him to his feet, but the experience had been too much. The door to reality had slammed shut, and he wasn't coming out soon. Cole left him to the cops, ran out the door before the crowd realized they weren't too hurt to kick his ass.

On the other side of the door was a maze of halls to holding cells, the judge's chambers, evidence rooms . . . Cole ran in panic. If a bomb was the first strike, he didn't want to be around for the follow-up.

Elliot ran through the door when the explosion hit, and kept running; he didn't know if he was being followed or not. When no one stopped him, he kept going, moved instinctively toward the room he knew was down here somewhere, the room where they kept her. He would find it, and when he did, he would take her away, far from here, where they could finally be together.

Cole heard the distant sound of many feet pounding behind him, moving like a great beast through the corridors, sniffing him out. He saw Roger through a hall window as he was bundled into a van that tried to push its way through a crush of spectators outside. One of them saw Cole's face at the window, pointed at him, and he ducked down, ran farther down the hall, away from the sounds of pursuit. Alarms rang on the upper floors. Someone must have started a fire. Sweating, Cole stumbled down a smoky stairwell, opened a door into another corridor, and ran again, lost in the maze. Before he reached the end of the hall, he passed a half-open door and stopped. In the stillness of the lower floor he heard a velvet gasp, a moan and a wet sound, a soft, persistent suckling.

The door was just behind him. Cole walked back, almost knowing what he would see, but still unbelieving, even after he stood in the doorway and pushed the door open all the way.

It was Elliot, on his feet against the wall, his pants around his knees. His head was back, his eyes closed, lips parted. His breath came in soft, short gasps; his lower lip was wet with spit. His hands, wrists still cuffed, rested on top of a head of blond hair, hung onto Carol's perfect pigtails like handlebars, as if riding for his life, while the Doll pleasured him with its all-too-real, all-too-willing mouth.

They ignored the chaos outside to have their moment together, de-

layed for so long by the court system and the trial. Cole didn't know
how Elliot had found her, but knew it would have been easy to get her
to follow him anywhere, especially with the cookies that sat on the
table next to them, obviously smuggled out from his cell to here, concealed in his clothing. The cookies Cole had ordered for him. Until now,
the idea of what his clients wanted, what they did, had been abstract,
intellectually wrong but bearable. Now, seeing the Doll on its knees in
front of Elliot, panties down, dress pulled up, its mouth pumping, it
wasn't intellectual at all. It was everything Cole had feared it was,
deep down inside, late at night.

And it sickened him.

There were shouts from the stairwell; feet ran in the wrong direction, gave them time to escape. Elliot's eyes flicked open, panicked for a
moment as he saw he was not alone. Then he saw it was Cole, and his
face broke into the same idiot grin he'd worn when Cole visited him in
jail and promised to send him the damned cookies.

You're my friend, it said. You're here to help me.

Cole had seen many horrors in his life, but none equaled this—to
witness this scene and be befriended by the monster committing it.
Without thinking, with a single syllable, he erased his past, threw away
everything he believed in and had defended all his life.

"Here!"

He shouted before he knew what he was doing, aware only that if
Elliot got away with his victim, his crime would continue in hiding,
night after night, the lifelike velvet lips and thighs scrubbed down
daily to be soiled anew.

Cole knew the mob was running in the wrong direction, knew he
had to stop them, to bring down the Furies and let fate take its course.
He used his only weapon, words, even though killing Elliot's chance of
escape killed a part of himself, his connection to who he was and what
he believed.

"He's in here! This way!"

Then he ran the other way, as far and fast as he could, put Elliot's
shocked and betrayed face out of his mind. Extra police officers
brought in to control the situation found him as he burst out of the fire
exit, too late to save Elliot but soon enough to get Cole away from the
building and to the airport.

A friend brought his passport and extra clothes, and Cole bought a
first-class seat to Barcelona. He had plenty of time to think about what

he'd done on his flight, but slept instead. When Neal met him at the other end and made sure he got through customs and away from the press, he spared Cole the details of what had happened at the courthouse after his escape. Neal had copies of the newspapers stacked in their hotel suite, but didn't let Cole read them or watch the news until he was rested.

When he did, there were few surprises. The news crews had poured into Elliot's love nest with the mob, recorded everything that happened, everything Cole had been spared. The police confiscated the disks as evidence; carefully edited clips were aired on the news. It had taken Neal less than an hour to find the unedited video on the Internet.

At first Neal wouldn't let Cole see it. When he finally gave in, he brought Cole a glass and a bottle of Scotch and left him alone in the computer-filled room he used to edit. Cole watched without emotion, still unsure how to react. He'd read the news stories, seen edited TV coverage, but seeing raw footage was different.

When the mob found him, Elliot was torn apart, along with the Doll. She surprised the mob as much with her lack of resistance as with the milky fluids and abstract-impressionistic organs they found inside, not that it stopped them. What was left of Elliot was taken away in a body bag. The Doll went back to evidence, this time as parts.

Cole e-mailed his resignation from Neal's computer when he was done watching, poured the last of the Scotch into his empty glass, and left any other decisions about his future to whenever he felt fit to go home after letting his client be lynched. There were still questions about his actions, from the authorities and himself. He would stay here, learn who he'd become that day and how he felt about himself, before he went home to a changed country, a changed man.

Images of Elliot's public execution repeated on the computer screen in slow motion, over and over from different angles, as Cole left the room to rejoin the man he loved, someone who still loved him until he could find a way to love himself again.

The Power

Linda Addison

The first time Brenda saw her cousin Angelique, she looked like a black angel. Dark as sweet chocolate, dressed in shades of cinnamon chiffon. As Angelique stood at the top of the Amtrak train stairs, Brenda took one look at her and knew she had the Power. It glimmered around her. She glanced at her father. He obviously didn't see how special Angelique was; even Angelique seemed unaware of the strength of the sparkling light she threw out that Saturday morning.

"Angelique, is that you?" Brenda's father lifted the girl from the train to the ground. The layers of her dress floated in the air like wings. "Look how you've grown. Last time I saw you, you were only as tall as a dream, and now you and your cousin Brenda are growing like rainbows into the sky."

Brenda was used to her father talking like poetry every now and then. Grandmom said he was one of those people who'd been born in a moment of luminosity and had no choice. He was an artist who made things out of anything he found on the street, and he taught elementary school. Fortunately, Brenda was never in his classes, but Grandmom said that was just the way it should be, plain and simple, and Brenda should thank her mother in heaven for looking after her.

A porter carried Angelique's suitcases to the platform.

"Girl, your mother sent you with enough clothes for a year, and you're only here for the summer. That's just like Julia." He laughed. "This is a beautiful dress, but I hope you got some playing-around clothes."

"Yes, sir," Angelique said.

"In North Carolina that's the polite thing to say, but there are no 'sirs' here in Philly. Uncle Larry will do. Okay?"

"Yes, Uncle Larry," she said slowly.

"How's your parents doing?" he asked.

"Mother is busy with her charity work, and Father's business is doing very well." Angelique smoothed her dress.

"Good. Now, let's get you home so your grandmother can take a look at you. She's cooked quite a feast in your honor."

Larry picked up as many suitcases as he could carry; the porter trailed behind with the rest.

Brenda took Angelique's hand and pulled her along with them. "I'm so happy you're here. You're staying in my room. I've got two beds. We can be like twin sisters, just like our moms really were."

"I'd like that." Angelique squeezed Brenda's hand.

When they reached the parking lot, Larry paid the porter and packed the suitcases in the car. Angelique whispered in Brenda's ear, "Do you know that old woman following us?"

"Where?" Brenda asked.

"Behind me, across the street." Angelique turned around. "She's gone now, but she was staring at us on the train platform."

"I didn't notice her." Brenda shrugged. "Could've been anybody."

As they drove to west Philadelphia, Brenda talked about all the fun they would have over the summer. They pulled into a driveway next to a three-floor wood house off Lancaster Avenue. As they stepped out of the car, their grandmother waved to them from the porch.

She gathered Angelique into her strong arms and gave her a huge hug. Her deep laugh echoed on the porch as she held Angelique at arm's length.

"Girl, look at you. Grown up enough at twelve to travel by yourself." She shook her head while smiling.

Larry carried some suitcases to the porch and went back to the car for the rest.

"Everyone grab a bag," Grandmom said.

The house was filled with the smell of roasted chicken and apple pie. Grandmom settled in the green velvet couch and made Angelique sit next to her. "Now, let's give your mother a call."

"I'll do it." Angelique picked up the phone.

"Hello, Mother."

"Yes, the train ride was fine."

"No, I won't forget.

"Yes, Mother," Angelique said several times as she chewed the corner of her right thumb.

"Good-bye." She handed the phone to her grandmother.

"Hi, honey.

"Oh, you worry too much. Nobody is running wild here. Her and Brenda will have a great summer." She winked at Angelique.

"We'll give you a call next week. Bye, sweetie."

She patted Angelique's hand. "That daughter of mine always did worry too much. You know, I think it'll be good for both of you to have a little space. Now, let's eat some of this food I've been cooking."

The dining room table was set up with the good china and silverware on a white lace tablecloth. White candles stood in crystal candleholders, and a crystal bowl filled with daisies decorated the center of the table.

"It looks like Thanksgiving," Angelique said.

"And that's just what it is, child, because we're thankful to have you here." She hugged Angelique. "You girls wash your hands and help me bring out the vegetables."

The doorbell rang. Larry answered it, and the house filled with the sounds of children and adults as his two brothers and their families came in.

The evening went like a family reunion, everyone talking and eating. Angelique answered everyone's questions politely, smiled shyly and stayed near Brenda or her grandmother. After dessert, the adults sat in the living room drinking and smoking while the children played checkers in the dining room.

Everyone left around nine, and their grandmother sent the girls to bed, saying Angelique was tired from all that traveling, and Brenda from being so excited.

The next morning, after breakfast Brenda asked, "Can we go to the video store, Grandmom? I want to show Angelique around the neighborhood."

"That's fine, just be back home by lunchtime."

"We will," Brenda said.

They walked to the corner of the block. They passed a couple of neighbors working in their yards, but once they turned onto Lancaster Avenue, the sidewalk was full of people. Brenda and Angelique looked in the windows of the shoe store and clothes store and ran into some of

Brenda's friends on the way to the video rental store. They spent a long time looking at the new movie and game releases before picking an action movie to rent.

On the way home they heard a shuffling behind them. Brenda looked back quickly. "It's that crazy old lady from across the street."

Angelique glanced at the woman. "That's the woman I saw at the train station."

Brenda frowned. "Just ignore her." She pointed at a small deli on the corner. "Let's get some sodas."

When they came out of the store, the woman was not in sight. They turned the next corner onto the block of their house. The old woman limped out from behind a large oak tree. She was dressed in layers: torn red pants under a gray dress and dirty beige sweater.

She gestured with a bent finger at them. "You shoulda been my sweet girl. I be teaching you right stuff—make good use of all that sweet sparkly breathing out of your skin. She won't show you all the light-dark makings." She spit in the direction of their house.

"Mrs. Johnston, we need to get home," Brenda said, pulling Angelique around the woman.

"Don't you worry, it ain't you I got the problem with. Keep up your learning. Yeah, that's what you do, my shiny diamonds. I follow your light. You my pretty key." She laughed through a mouth of missing teeth.

They heard her shrill laughter as they rushed down the street. When they turned around, she was gone. They sat on the porch to get their breath.

"What was she talking about?" Angelique asked.

"Don't pay any attention to her. She's been strange ever since I can remember. People say she lost her mind when her husband and son died in a car accident." Brenda pointed to a broken-down house across the street. "That's her place."

The yard was overgrown with weeds and a wild rosebush covering the front porch. A couple of windows were broken, and paint peeled from the wood frame.

"That house doesn't look like anyone lives in it," Angelique said. "Are you sure she's not dangerous?"

"She can't hurt us; we're protected."

"What do you mean?"

"I'll explain later; let's get lunch." Brenda unlocked the front door.

* * *

After lunch Brenda asked, "Grandmom, can we go to the attic?"

"Okay, honey. Be careful up there." She spread fresh herbs from the garden on the kitchen table.

"We will," Brenda said.

They went up to the second floor. Brenda pulled the attic cord, lowered the stair ladder, and scampered up into the dark opening. Angelique took one step and stood at the bottom.

"It's kind of dark," she said.

"Just a minute." Brenda disappeared into the attic, and a light came on. After a few seconds she popped her head out of the opening. Angelique was still on the first step. "You coming? There's lots of cool stuff up here."

Angelique stepped up and tottered forward to hold on to the upper steps. "I-I—"

"You've never been on a ladder before?" Brenda asked.

"Ladies don't climb ladders." She held on to the step.

"I don't know about that, but if you want to get to the attic, you're going to have to climb this ladder. Here, back off." Brenda climbed back down. "You go up first. Take one step at a time; hold on to the step above if you need, but don't look up or down—just go for the next step until you're at the top. I'll be right behind you. I won't let you fall. I promise."

"Okay." Angelique took each step like a baby learning to climb stairs for the first time, but finally got to the top and pulled herself into the attic.

Boxes, trunks, and old furniture crowded the floor. It smelled musty, and a fine layer of dust had settled on all the surfaces.

"It's not very clean up here." Angelique touched a carton. She wiped her fingers on her jeans.

"Don't say that too loud. Grandmom will have us up here with a bucket and rags, cleaning." Brenda took a couple of old towels from a box in the corner, threw one at Angelique, and used the other to wipe off the top of a wooden box. "Some of these things are from when Grandmom moved here to help take care of me after Mommy died."

"Let's see what's in here." She read the label. " 'Brenda baby toys'— not very interesting. What's that trunk near you say, Angelique?"

She wiped off the dust. "It's my mother's toys."

"Now that's more like it." Brenda unbuckled the leather straps and flipped open the trunk. The acrid scent of mothballs drifted into the air.

There were baby blankets on top, inside plastic bags. Underneath were baby clothes in shades of pink, yellow, and white. They stacked them on the floor. At the bottom they found a rag doll and other toys. The material of its body was made from worn blue flannel, with brown yarn hair, button eyes, red felt lips, and a faded red flannel dress.

"I've never imagined my mother playing with dolls," Angelique said.

"Well, Aunt Julia definitely played with this doll." Brenda handed the doll to Angelique. "There's more toys in here." She pulled out stuffed animals, a wooden pull car with a frayed cord, a metal tobacco tin filled with marbles and ribbons.

Angelique touched each toy but kept the doll in her lap. She carried it tucked under her arm as they investigated other boxes, finding old clothes and dish sets. Brenda went through the drawers of a dresser and discovered a small red bag tied with white cord. She brought it to the light and sniffed it.

"What's that?" Angelique asked.

Brenda carefully untied the bag and emptied its contents in a teacup. It was a ball of white wax with little bits of what looked like sticks lodged in it.

"It's a conjure ball. Looks like a spell of protection."

"How do you know that?" Angelique said.

"Don't you know the power runs strong in our family. That's what Grandmom says."

"Magic isn't real."

"It's real enough. Grandmom says I'm too young, but I've learned a lot about magic online." She dropped the ball back into the bag and tied it closed. "Can't you feel the light around this charm? It's been up here for years and it's still glowing." Brenda held the bag up by its cord.

"I don't see anything but an old bag," Angelique said. "Mother says voodoo is uneducated superstition."

"Voodoo isn't the same thing. Anyway, magic is just people using their power, mostly to help others," Brenda said. She took Angelique's hands in hers. "It's inside everybody and everything; some people have it stronger than others. Can't you feel it?"

Brenda put Angelique's hands on her chest and closed her eyes. She took a slow breath. White light flickered behind her closed eyes. Tingling began below her belly button and pulled up through her chest, gathered in her next breath. She pushed out and opened her eyes.

Angelique stood with her eyes closed, smiling. Her mother's doll rolled out of her lap to the floor. Brenda could feel her light mix with Angelique's and drift into the air around them.

"You see," Brenda said.

Angelique opened her eyes and took a deep breath. "What was that?"

"Me reaching out to you. What did it feel like?"

"Like electricity and light and warmth, like a dream." Angelique held her hands up, looked at each finger.

Brenda saw the warm glow of gold light outline Angelique's hands, and it was clear that Angelique finally saw it, also.

"This is no more of a dream than any of us see when awake. Grandmom says God is dreaming us all the time."

"That was just a trick." Angelique stepped backward, away from Brenda.

"You know that's not true. You can feel it inside, whether you believe it or not."

"Well, I did feel something. And that glowing ..." Angelique sat down on a trunk and folded her arms across her chest. "Even if I have this power, what good is it?"

"What do you wish for more than anything?" Brenda tossed the rag doll to her.

Angelique picked up her mother's doll, smoothed its hair, and held it close to her face. She closed her eyes. "I wish—I wish my mother would love me."

"We could do that, Angelique. You and I together could do it."

"You think so. Really?"

Brenda nodded. "She's your mother, so she already loves you. It's just locked away inside of her. We can make a gris-gris to open her to you."

"Even though we're here and she's in North Carolina?"

"Distance don't mean a thing. We'll need something that's been close to her."

They both looked at the doll.

"And I have a handkerchief of hers in my suitcase," Angelique said, hugging her mother's doll.

Brenda rubbed the silver key on the chain around her neck. "Good, then we'll make the charm tonight. I think some of my mother's toys are over there. Let's check it out."

Brenda put the conjure ball back in the dresser. They spent the next two hours going though the trunks, trying on clothes, and setting up old dishes and glasses for pretend meals, until their grandmother called them for dinner.

That night they sat on the back porch eating ice cream while Brenda's father had some friends over after dinner. Jazz played in the background as the adults talked and laughed in the living room. The lightning bugs drifted above the grass and the herb garden like stars while the girls ate their ice cream. Crickets sang from the bushes along the back of the yard.

"Make a wish on the next lightning bug and it'll come true," Brenda said.

"Is that more magic?" Angelique asked.

"Naw, just a saying. But it couldn't hurt."

They both whispered wishes and laughed.

Brenda stood up from the wicker chair and peeked into the kitchen window. No one was there.

"Want to make that gris-gris for your mother now?" she asked Angelique.

"Tonight?"

"Why not? It's as good a time as any."

"What if something goes wrong?" Angelique asked.

"First lesson in using the power: your intent makes the magic. It's not a complicated spell anyway."

"I don't know about this. . . ."

"Of course you don't. That's why I'm going to teach you. Come on."

They entered the empty kitchen through the back door. Brenda found a small brown paper bag in the cabinet and sprinkled sugar in it.

"We'll put it together in our bedroom," she whispered.

They walked quickly through the dining room. Larry and his friends were in the living room, laughing and talking over the music. The girls dashed up the stairs. They tiptoed past their grandmother's room, where they could hear her talking on the phone.

In the bedroom, Brenda put a bracelet with little bells on the door-knob. "So we can hear if someone opens the door," she said.

She put the desk lamp on the floor and used the two bedposts to make a tent out of a sheet. They crouched under the sheet.

"Spread the handkerchief on the floor," Brenda said.

Angelique laid the delicate square on the floor. It was white with white lace roses along the edge and her mother's initials sewn in yellow on a corner.

Brenda pulled a light wooden box from under the bed; it had a sun painted on it. She took the silver chain with a heart and key from around her neck and unlocked the box.

"I thought that was just a charm necklace," Angelique said.

Brenda winked at her and opened the box. It was filled with yarn, bits of material, and things that jangled at the bottom. Brenda took out a ball of red yarn, pulled about twelve inches off, and cut it with a small pair of scissors from the box. She took a little pad of paper and a pen out of the box and handed it to Angelique.

"Write your mother's first name nine times, real small."

Angelique wrote her mother's name in careful strokes.

"Now fold the paper up as tight as you can and put it in the middle of the handkerchief," Brenda said. She held the paper bag open. "Take a little sugar and sprinkle it in the handkerchief, to sweeten her to you."

"You have the doll?" Brenda asked.

"Yes." Angelique got the doll from her dresser drawer.

Brenda handed her the scissors. "Cut a tiny piece of the dress and put it in the handkerchief."

Angelique looked at the scissors and the doll.

"Come on, Angelique. Think of it as an experiment—we just need a little bit."

"Okay," she said slowly. She cut a teeny piece of material from the inside hem of the doll's dress and put the threads into the handkerchief. "Just as long as we don't have to sacrifice an animal or cut ourselves for this."

Brenda laughed. "You don't know anything, do you? You don't use blood for a love spell. Fold the handkerchief up.

"Now wrap this yarn around it nine times and put nine knots in it— to hold it forever."

When she was done, Angelique stared at the small package they had made.

"You've made your first gris-gris." Brenda tapped it. "The last step is to sleep with it under your mattress."

Angelique slid it under the mattress. "Will it work?"

"Of course, between your power and a perfect gris-gris, it'll work."

Angelique laid the doll on her bed. "How long will it take?"

"You can't put a time on something like this."

The doorknob jangled, and they both jumped.

"Brenda?" Her father knocked on the door.

They took a deep breath in relief. Brenda locked the box and slid it back under her bed. "Come in."

"What's this, camping out?" he asked.

"No, Daddy, just swapping secrets."

He smiled, a little too wide, as he leaned against the door. "That's good." He turned to leave and swung in a circle. "Oh, your grandmother wants you two to help her in the kitchen."

"Okay." Brenda put the lamp back on the nightstand.

Larry turned and walked away.

Brenda made a sign like drinking with her hand. They both giggled.

"He's funny when he drinks. It doesn't take much. That's why he doesn't drink the hard stuff. Does your dad drink?" Brenda asked.

Angelique nodded. "He likes Scotch and soda, two ice cubes. I make it for him when he comes home from work."

"Really? You ever tasted it?"

She made a face. "Yes. I like white wine better. That's what my mother drinks."

"Your mom lets you drink?"

"She gives me a little wine on special occasions, so I can develop my tastes."

Brenda threw the sheet back on the bed. "I've tasted beer. It's all right, but I like cherry soda better."

On their way down the stairs, Angelique said, "Shouldn't we check with Grandmom about what we just did?"

"No," Brenda said quickly. "We don't want to bother her about something this small. Okay?"

"Grandmom doesn't know you're doing magic, does she?" Angelique asked slowly.

"Shhhh—do you want it to work or not?"

Angelique nodded.

"Then let's go."

They helped clear the table and wash the dishes. Most of the time one of Larry's friends sat in the kitchen talking to their grandmother about problems with her husband. After they finished drying the dishes, the girls went to bed.

In the bedroom, with the lights out, Angelique asked, "Is it going to work?"

"Don't have any doubt. It's important to be confident."

"Okay. Good night."

*   *   *

The rest of the week Angelique tried not to ask Brenda about the gris-gris for her mother. Every night she checked under her mattress to make sure the little white bundle wrapped in red yarn was still there. They played video games during the day and met with Brenda's friends to jump rope and window-shop. At night Brenda showed Angelique her favorite Web sites on spells.

Friday evening the phone rang. Their grandmother called Angelique from the yard.

"It's for you," she said, handing the phone to Angelique.

"Hello, Mother." She told her about the fun things they did, leaving out the magic discussions. Her mother sounded about the same. Angelique gave up all hope.

"Talk to you next week," she said, ready to hang up.

"What?

"Oh. I love you, too." She stared at the phone after her mother hung up.

"She said she loves me," she said, hugging her grandmother.

"Well, of course she loves you, honey."

"But she's never said it before. Never." She ran out of the room to the yard, grabbed Brenda, and swung her around. "She loves me. She said she loves me."

They danced in a circle until they collapsed on the grass, out of breath.

"It worked, Brenda; it worked."

"Of course. I had no doubt."

The first half of the summer went fast. Between playing, Brenda taught Angelique what she knew about magic. They found spells online for making someone leave, to cure different kinds of sickness. They made a list of the kinds of objects carried in a nation sack. As they played and shopped, they collected unusual rocks from the park, or feathers. Every now and then, they would find some interesting piece of metal or glass on the ground and added it to their box of magical material.

They gathered ingredients for small spells but never put the whole spell together. They saw Mrs. Johnston every couple of weeks; she stared at them from across the street and whispered to herself, but she didn't talk to them again.

Angelique never saw their grandmother doing magic, but every now and then someone came by the house, and Grandmom gave them a package wrapped in brown paper. She once saw her grandmother take a small pale blue bag out of her blouse, rub it, and put it back. Brenda said that was her nation sack, where she carried special things for protection.

Every time Angelique's mother called, she told Angelique she loved her, and even said she missed her.

One hot July day, Brenda and Angelique came in the house laughing after a day at the park and found their grandmother in the hallway, on the floor. Her chest was covered with a dark cloud of squirming snakes. The girls screamed, and the snakes melted away.

Brenda ran to her grandmother's unconscious body and shook her, yelling, "Grandmom!"

Angelique ran to the living room and called 911. The ambulance came quickly. Grandmom's friend from next door rushed in when the medics arrived. She called Larry's school and left a message. Brenda stayed by her grandmother's side as they carried her into the ambulance.

"I need to go with Brenda," Angelique said.

"Go ahead," the neighbor said. "I'll watch the house. Larry will be there as soon as he can. I'll be praying here."

Angelique glanced across the street before getting in the ambulance and saw Mrs. Johnston standing in the shade of a tree, pointing and smiling. When she looked out the back window of the ambulance, the old woman was gone. Nausea gripped her stomach. Could that woman have had something to do with this?

The medics had an oxygen mask on the girls' grandmother, but she was still unconscious. Brenda crouched on the floor, held her grandmother's hand, and cried softly. Angelique tried to talk to Brenda, but she pulled away.

At the hospital the doctor made them stay in the waiting room. Brenda held Angelique's hand but still wouldn't talk. The waiting room was filled with men, women, and children clutched in little groups. Most stared at magazines or the droning television hanging from the ceiling. The sound of wheels rolling through the corridor broke through the whispers of people comforting each other.

Angelique stared at the door, waiting for someone—anyone—to come in and tell them how their grandmother was doing. Brenda stared at the floor.

Larry walked in, out of breath, as if he had run to the hospital.

"Are you girls all right?" He hugged them both.

"Is Grandmom going to die?" Brenda whispered.

"No, your grandmother is the strongest person on this planet. I have to talk to her doctor. I wanted to make sure you two were okay first."

"We'll be fine, Uncle Larry," Angelique said.

"I'll be back as soon as I can." He dropped his backpack and rushed out of the room.

Brenda wrapped her arms around herself and started rocking back and forth. "She's going to die. I can feel her . . . slipping away."

Angelique could also feel the wrongness, like air being sucked out of the room. "Somebody is doing something bad to her. You saw those snakes back at the house, right?"

Brenda nodded, her eyes puffy and red from crying.

"Somebody—I think the old woman from across the street—did bad magic against Grandmom. I saw Mrs. Johnston when the ambulance drove away. She was smiling."

"But—but Grandmom's protection should have kept her safe," Brenda whispered.

"I know, but somehow it didn't. Those snakes weren't real, but we saw them. Do you remember reading that sometimes you can see spells working through animal spirits?"

Brenda nodded.

"We can do something about this. We have to do a spell to stop it."

"Maybe," Brenda said. "Maybe we can."

"We'll pray now, and later we'll do more." Angelique put her arm around Brenda and closed her eyes.

Someone tapped Angelique on her shoulder.

"Uncle Larry, how is she?"

"They think she had a stroke. We have to wait and see. The next twenty-four hours are very important." He took a deep breath. "I'll take you girls home, then come back here."

"I need to see her," Brenda said.

"We can't right now. She's in intensive care," Larry said.

"I've got to see with my own eyes that she's not dead," Brenda said loudly.

"But, Brenda—"

"I'm not leaving until I see her." Brenda crossed her arms and sat back in the chair.

A doctor pulled Larry aside. After they talked, Larry waved the girls over. "The doctor said you can see her for one minute. That's all. Even though she's unconscious, she can still hear us, so no tears. Okay?"

"Okay," they both said at the same time.

All three followed a nurse to the intensive care ward. "Only two at a time," she said.

"You girls go ahead. I'll wait here," Larry said.

After they put on a gown and mask, the nurse took them to their grandmother's bed. "Just one minute," she said, pulling the curtain around the bed.

"Grandmom?" Brenda whispered.

She was hooked up to all kinds of tubes and monitors. A wall of machines blinked and beeped on the other side of the bed. The air was a suffocating blanket of pine cleaner and ammonia.

Brenda reached through the wires and tubes to touch her face. "I love you, Grandmom."

"Me, too," Angelique said, caressing the back of her hand. "We saw the snakes. We're going to make a special gris-gris for you. To help you get better."

Brenda looked at Angelique, then back at her grandmother. "We'll make the best healing gris-gris ever when we get back to the house."

Her eyelids fluttered, but her eyes didn't open.

"Stay with us, Grandmom," Brenda said.

The nurse pulled the curtain open. "We have to let her rest now, girls."

Outside the room, Larry said, "Let's get you two home."

Once they were back at the house, Larry said, "Call me on my cell phone if you need anything. I'll be back in a few hours. Will you be all right by yourselves? I can have someone look in on you."

"Daddy, we'll be fine. Go ahead." Brenda gave him a hug and kiss.

"We'll take care of each other," Angelique said, hugging him.

After he got in the car and drove away, the girls ran to their bedroom. Brenda emptied her box onto the bed.

"Do you think it's Mrs. Johnston doing bad magic against Grandmom?" Angelique asked.

"Maybe, if somewhere in her crazy mind she decided Grandmom had done something against her. I can't imagine anyone else wanting to hurt her." Brenda spread out the ribbons, rocks, and pieces of glass and metal from the box.

"This is all junk." She took a handful and threw it onto her pillow. "Nothing good enough to help her."

"Then we've got to find better things. Grandmom must have good stuff in her room, don't you think?" Angelique asked.

"Yes, but—"

"We're doing this for her." Angelique grabbed Brenda's arm. "Come on."

They entered her bedroom. A sweet scent, like roses, filled the air. Brenda pulled the thick, white curtains closed and turned on the light. Angelique stood near the dark wood bed. There was a hot ripple in the air, like the wake of a boat in water. "Do you feel that?"

Brenda lifted her hand to the air. "Yes." An edge of blue suede peeked out from under the bed. "What is this?" Brenda picked up the small bag. "Grandmom's nation bag. She always carries it. Why would she leave it here?"

"I don't know." Angelique laid the bag on the middle of the bed. "But maybe we can use it."

Angelique opened the closet, and a mix of earthy scents floated into the air. They found a wood cabinet in the closet, with jars and boxes of herbs, roots, and powder.

"This is strong magic stuff," Brenda said.

"Good. That's what we need."

"This is too much for us." Brenda backed out of the closet.

Angelique grabbed Brenda's arm. "We can't have any doubt. You taught me that." Angelique slowly moved her open hands over the containers, letting her light guide her. She kept the image of her grandmother healthy in her mind. When the center of her palm tingled intensely, she picked up a jar. She handed three jars to Brenda.

One had "John root" written on its label. The other two had designs drawn on their labels.

"We'll do it here," Angelique said.

"How do you know those are the right things?" Brenda said.

Angelique took her hand; they touched each item together. "You see. They feel right."

Brenda nodded.

"We need to do a spell of protection, then make the gris-gris. I'll be right back." Brenda rushed out of the room.

Angelique waited in the middle of the room. There was a quick movement in the corner. When she turned her head, there was nothing there. Each time she blinked, something fluttered in the air, just out of her vision. Her heart beat faster. It took all her strength not to run out of the room. She opened her mouth to call Brenda but closed her eyes instead. Whatever it was, it couldn't or wouldn't touch her.

She stood still until Brenda returned with a paper bag. Brenda emptied the bag on the floor. There were five different-colored candles, matches, chalk, a pair of scissors, and a can of beer. She pulled a piece of red flannel and a ribbon from her pocket.

"For the spell of protection," Brenda said. "Do you remember how it's made?"

Angelique nodded, took a pillow off the bed, placed it on the floor, and put her grandmother's nation bag on the pillow. "This is Grandmom."

They drew a chalk circle around the pillow and placed the candles on the edge of the circle. Angelique opened one of the jars with a pattern on it and sprinkled a few grains of the black powder in between the candles.

"To keep her safe," Angelique said.

Brenda laid the six-inch square of red flannel on the floor. Angelique held a pen over the material without touching it, then after a few seconds drew a pattern on the material. Brenda wrote their grandmother's name nine times on a piece of paper. Angelique laid a piece of John root in the paper, sprinkled the brown powder from the other jar on it, and folded the paper up. They tied it closed; each took turns tying a knot in the ribbon.

Brenda opened the beer. Angelique dipped her finger in the can and dripped beer on the gris-gris to feed it. They placed it on the pillow next to the nation bag. Brenda lit the candles while her cousin dribbled a little beer in her hands and threw it in each corner of the room. They sat on the floor, held hands, and watched the candles burn. Shadows slid and jumped in the corners like trapped animals.

"Whatever you are, you have to leave this house," Angelique said.

Shadows crawled up the walls. The candles' flames jerked back and forth. A crunching sound, like mice chewing paper, came from under the bed. Brenda peeked under the bed but saw nothing.

"It's time to go away and leave our grandmother alone." Brenda pushed light from deep inside. Warm yellow light like melted butter dripped from her hands and feet.

Angelique saw Brenda's light and gathered stillness inside and pushed out. Gold light from her hands and feet mixed with Brenda's light and pooled on the floor around them. They stared at the candles.

Their light streamed to the dark corners. Obscure shapes twisted up the wall, away from the girls' light.

A giggle snapped in the air above them. They looked up for one second, into each other's eyes. In a blink, they were sitting in a field of daisies. A warm summer breeze bounced over the flowers and caressed their faces. The setting sun filled the sky with streaks of blue, purple, and white.

They were two other girls, holding one flower. They took turns pulling petals off.

"He loves me," one girl sang.

"He loves me," the other girl chanted back.

When the last petal was pulled, the girls fell into each other's arms laughing.

Angelique and Brenda plummeted through a dark tunnel and were back in their grandmother's bedroom.

"What—what was that?" Angelique asked, gulping for air.

"I think that was Grandmom and"—Brenda shuddered—"and Mrs. Johnston."

"How could that be?" Angelique asked.

"I don't know. Grandmom never said anything about them knowing each other when they were younger. Maybe it's a trick."

Angelique shook her head. "That felt true. Something happened between them, something that made her hate Grandmom."

"I don't care what happened. I won't lose Grandmom," Brenda said. "Look—they're coming back. This was just something to stop us."

The shadow things had leaked back down the walls as the girls' light dissipated.

"No more tricks, true or not." Brenda concentrated on the candles again. She took deep, slow breaths to calm down.

Angelique held Brenda's hands and did the same. The light flowed again from them, at first in a steady stream and then a rushing torrent as they kept one purpose in mind: to rescue their grandmother. Sounds echoed above them: giggles, singing, small feet jumping up and down. No matter what they heard, they kept their eyes on the dancing flames. Gold light filled the floor and lapped up the walls. They didn't even look up when the crying started—a little girl wailing deeply.

The shadows on the ceiling curled in on themselves, wept down the walls to the floor, and faded away. The girls watched the candles burn until they were so tired they couldn't keep their eyes open. The shadows and sounds didn't return.

"It's gone." Angelique put out the candles. "We'll take the gris-gris and nation bag to her tomorrow."

Calm quiet surrounded them. Brenda nodded.

They put the pillow back, picked up the candles, swept the powder and chalk into the paper bag, and went back to their room. Too tired to eat, they fell asleep and didn't hear Larry come in.

He woke them in the morning to take them to the hospital.

Once they arrived, the doctor told them that their grandmother was out of intensive care but still being watched. She hadn't regained consciousness, but her vital signs were stable. The girls looked at each other, smiling.

The nurse took the girls to their grandmother's room while Larry talked to the doctor.

She wasn't hooked up to as many machines as the day before. Brenda kissed her hand.

"We made a gris-gris for you, Grandmom. Angelique and I did it together."

Angelique took the charm out of her pocket, placed it in her grandmother's left hand, and held it.

"And we found your nation bag." Brenda placed the bag in her grandmother's right hand. "We did the biggest magic we knew, Grandmom."

"We did it because we love you and want you back," Angelique said.

Brenda jumped. "She squeezed my hand."

Their grandmother's eyes opened, and she smiled.

Brenda leaned forward to hug her, but stopped as another face floated over their grandmother's face.

"You my girls, my shiny light," a familiar voice said.

The face smiled with broken teeth.

"Get out!" Brenda said, trying to pull away from her tight grip.

Mrs. Johnston laughed. "Why should I? You play, let me in. I'm staying now. You mine."

"Oh, no," Angelique said. She finally saw how this had happened. The magic they'd practiced in the house must have made an opening in Grandmom's protection. "It was us. We let her in."

Horror flashed on Brenda's face.

"No!" Brenda said. Light shot out of her free hand and poured over Grandmom.

"That's right, give me your light, my shiny key."

Angelique pushed light out of her hands, but none came out.

"Not yet, my sweet. Later, there'll be time for you and me later," the face over Grandmom's said.

Angelique's light and voice were locked inside. She could do nothing except watch Mrs. Johnston absorb Brenda's light. The old woman's body lay over their grandmother's like a gelatinous blanket, getting thicker each second.

"Grandmom, help me," Brenda whispered, stumbling against the bed.

"She can't help you now. I got her nice and tight. Soon she be gone; then we have a good time," Mrs. Johnston said, her body filling out, the spectral skin stretching.

Angelique prayed inside, wanting to close her eyes, but could not.

Brenda's lips moved, but no sounds came out; tears streamed down her face.

"Mommy," Brenda blurted out. The gold light traveling from her to Mrs. Johnston turned lighter in color; green light streaked its edges. Brenda suddenly remembered a picture of her mother in a silk gown that same color of green. It was her mother's favorite color.

"Help me, Mommy."

"Stop that." Mrs. Johnston twisted back and forth as the green light increased, pulling from Brenda's arms and chest. "Stop, stop, stop . . ." Her body inflated larger like a balloon.

Angelique snapped loose from her control and staggered away from the bed. When she took a step toward Brenda, a soft voice whispered in her ear, "Wait." Angelique took one step toward Brenda. The voice pleaded gently, "Stay here; it will be all right." The voice was like her mother's but softer. In her heart she could feel it wasn't Mrs. Johnston. Brenda stood taller, her eyes closed, her mouth moving silently as if she was calmly talking to someone.

The outline of Mrs. Johnston's body thinned as the green light filled her form and spiked out in fine lines to the walls. She changed into a two-headed dog, but still the light stabbed through her; the dog's mouth open in an unuttered howl. A huge snake coiled over their grandmother's body, the light slicing through it in rings. The snake shape changed into a gigantic bird, snapping at the lines of light penetrating its body. No matter what she became, the green light continued eating holes in her form. Mrs. Johnston returned to a human shape, slowly deflating.

"You shoulda been mine," she said in a tiny voice, before the aspect of her body slid to the floor and disappeared.

Angelique ran to Brenda, catching her as she wobbled against the bed. A sheen of sweat covered Brenda's face. "Mommy?" she asked.

"You did it, Brenda; you made her go away," Angelique said.

"It wasn't me."

A moan from the bed made them turn toward their grandmother. Her eyes flickered open. "Brenda, honey," she said slowly.

"Grandmom," they both said, hugging her.

"How?" she asked.

"I've been studying online," Brenda said. "I taught Angelique what I know. And she taught me some things I didn't know last night."

"I should have guessed there was too much power between the two of you to ignore," Grandmom said.

"It was Mrs. Johnston; she used us to get to you," Brenda said. "But Mommy helped us push her away."

"Oh, my babies. You didn't know what you were doing." She shook her head. "They found Shelia's body in her house, two weeks ago. She'd been dead a long time. I didn't want to upset you."

"Shelia is Mrs. Johnston? You knew each other when you were young?" Brenda asked.

Their grandmother closed her eyes for a moment. She squeezed their hands and looked at them. "Yes. We were like sisters once, but a man drove us apart." She shook her head. "Love can be a tricky thing. Or lust." She held their hands over her heart. "Don't let that happen to you."

"No, Grandmom, never," Angelique said, taking Brenda's other hand.

"No one will come between us," Brenda said.

The doctor and Larry walked into the room. Larry ran to the bed and hugged her and the girls. "I knew you were too strong to let anything keep you down," he said.

"Not that hugs are bad, but I need to check my patient," the doctor said. "Could you wait outside a moment?"

"Just for a few minutes, because I've got a lot of work to do at home," Grandmom said. She slipped the nation bag back to Brenda, and the gris-gris to Angelique.

The doctor and Larry walked through the green and gold light that splashed and shimmered in the room without seeing it. Brenda and Angelique waved to their grandmother from the doorway, knowing she was safe now, surrounded by the power.

Red

Rickey Windell George

Bleeding a man dry—bleeding him dead—was easy; it was keeping him alive to be bled another day, making a resource of . . . making cattle of him, that was the hard part.

What a horrible notion that was, and yet it floated there, buoyant on the stirring sea of Lex's mind.

But why? These were not her thoughts.

Had she heard someone say those awful words?

Had she dreamed someone speaking such atrocities?

Her dreams were tricky, but not so confused as her waking moments of late. The real trick was in telling the two apart. This very instant she could not discern if she was slumbering or awake, or if maybe these things she was seeing and hearing and thinking were memories, fragments of the life the fever had stolen from her.

The halls were long where she walked, and the ceilings quite high—this of course where there were ceilings at all. In many places the ornately crafted walls, with their etchings and murals and glinting gold moldings, stood roofless. Gazing up, she could see all the way to the fringes and clumps of African jungle trees—leaves more black than green, so densely packed together that the spaces between the snarled branches were cavern-dark—and farther still to a stewing gray sky emblazoned with tatters of red. Lex thought it looked as though someone had taken a dagger to heaven's throat and left it bleeding all over itself. She thought this and then wondered why such an ugly concept had crossed her mind.

Bleeding a man dry—bleeding him dead—is easy . . .

This place, this palace, was her home, or so someone had said. Yet she was lost, with no clue as to the nature of the elaborate floor plan, and not the slightest shimmer of warm familiarity or comfort or safety. She couldn't fix the reality in her memory, but she didn't feel as though she'd ever known the kind of affluence and position that typically befell the sort of person who dwelled in an exotic manor as such, at least not in this lifetime.

What Lex did feel, was watched.

In every nook stood a great statue carved of dark wood, no two of them the same, taller than any man but not representative of men in every case. Grinning daggers and staring with striped pupils, they welcomed with open arms and splayed, taloned fingers. Each watchful carving was unique, and though many had arms and legs—the complement of humanity—not a single one appeared entirely human. They were naked in every case, a great many of them masculine, with scales for skin and venomous vipers jutting out between their legs. Others were female, with rounded hips and weighty breasts, but these had the sharpest and fiercest claws, and eyes where nipples should have been. Many of the tikis had no legs or arms at all. These were freaks of a sort Lex could not even describe. Hurrying past them as quickly as she was capable, she didn't try to understand.

Between the unsettling sculptures were tall doors, beyond which massive rooms awaited. It was in such a room that she'd heard those disturbing words spoken in the boom of a man's commanding voice.

"Bleeding a man dry—bleeding him dead—is easy," he'd said, and now Lex could feel hot breath on the back of her neck, and strong fingers on her shoulders, directing her to turn. "It's keeping him alive to be bled another day, making a resource of . . . making cattle of him, that is the hard part."

The man, the unseen speaker, had turned Lex toward the rear of the room. There, through a glass wall as crisply transparent as thin air, her eyes found the bleeders.

God help them, that's what they were called.

They were men for the most part, every one of them nude and inverted, suspended like sides of beef, dangling from the hooks that were looped through the meat of their ankles. Each was snaked full of tubes, with leads in the wrists and in the jugulars, in the large blood vessels of the groin and in the small circulatory passages of the penis, too. There were hoses siphoning arteries at the armpits, and others tapping into the bleeders' intestinal tracks. Every hose flowed red, leading to the huge glass cylinders that were the size of household water heaters at the rear of the chamber, filling those man-high cylinders with hot, stolen life.

A tear rolled down Lex's cheek, and her unseen host caught it, brushed it away with the slightest touch before it had a chance to fall or even to cool.

It was the creak of a tricky floorboard that woke Lex.

It had been blazing hot and vivid-bright outside when the headache had taken her down. She'd retreated into bed, drawn the canopy, and shut her eyes against the pain, but still it had throbbed behind her lids until sleep rescued her.

Though the sun had retired, it was still blazing hot. Beyond the window screens the night was as black as deep-earth oil.

The floor creaked again, and this time Lex focused toward the foot of the bed.

There, standing in the murky light of a few overburdened candles, was Mugambi. He was lighting a final flame atop the dresser even as her eyes found his long, coal black body, nude and lithely muscled, with salient buttocks that were hairless and smooth as a baby's. Lex felt herself go wet between the legs, and knowingly he turned, as if the scent of her heat had summoned him. Perhaps it had.

He fixed his thick lips—purple in this light—into a smile and peered through the canopy at her.

She wondered how well he could see her.

She wondered if she looked all right having just woken, having been so sick just days before. She wanted to look good for him, wanted to look perfect.

She was wearing only a sliplike satin wrap that, in the fit of her sleep, had ridden up around her waist to bare everything below. The mouth of her shaven vagina watered for him, and there was no question at all now that he'd caught both the sight and the scent.

His penis, which at first had bobbed between his thighs like a sleeping cobra, had heard the song of her sex and was charmed indeed. The head pressed against the veil of the canopy a few beats before the man parted the panels. The candlelight found him more fully, revealing a greasy red tint to his skin.

Lex reached for him, finding his body oily to the touch and sweet-smelling. She hauled him toward her, on top of her. She drew his fingers to her lips and kissed, and then licked, and then sucked. There was an oil of some sort all over him—kinky bastard—that was both sweet and salty. It smelled of flowers and honey and man and meat. It was intoxicating. She licked his fingers clean and made her way up the length of his arm to his shoulder, along the line of his collarbone, down the greasy surface of a pec, and finally to a nipple. There she suckled until she felt warm fluid running over her vaginal lips and smelled the meaty-sweet fragrance of Mugambi's oil redouble. In his hand he had a flask of the stuff, turned up, the contents emptying between her legs.

When the bottle ran dry, he tossed it aside and set upon teasing with his fingers till her moisture and that of the oil were one, till she writhed on her back in the sheets. With spasms already shaking her spine just from his touch, he raised her rear effortlessly in his hands— her thighs gyrating on either side of his head, her heels gently knocking his back—and began to eat.

She screamed before he was done, as if she were being murdered, but she'd have gladly died again and again if each time she was to feel the way she'd felt when those blood-freezing cries had slipped her lungs.

The angles changed as beasts moved in the night outside the windows.

The bed was red and sticky, sopping from the mix of sweat and Mugambi's oil by the time Lex took him into her mouth. She didn't actually take him in so much as use him like a lollypop. Her mouth was small, and the head of his endowment—his tip—enormous. He was comfortably hung in terms of length, but it was the head of his erection that defied her jaws. It was like a tennis ball, she thought, black and bottle-cap shaped, but big as a tennis ball. And if that image was an exaggeration, it was not by much. The swollen head of his member was so large that it appeared odd, bobbing at the end of an otherwise normal dick. She could not get it into her mouth; she'd tried and she'd given up. She was contented instead to work around it, lapping the dome, kissing the glans, licking up under the ridge—every surface of it sweet and sticky.

When he entered her vagina, she shrieked at the instant orgasms that fired through every corner of her anatomy. His tongue had made her scream, but his penis, the head in particular, made her shriek as a virgin being deflowered.

How long had it been?

How long had she suffered that fever?

He'd been by her side all the while, nursing her back to health. He'd told her about it, how she'd fallen ill on their wedding night, and how he'd so desperately longed to touch her. She couldn't remember much, but there was an image in her mind of his eyes as seen through a fever haze. The look had been desire. She'd been too weak then to fulfill the promise in his stare, and perhaps she was not fully recovered yet.

Between her legs it felt as though a balled fist, or bigger, was being driven inside her—lovingly, yes, but forcefully still. The shaft was incidental; it was the head she felt moving—rolling, she imagined, as a fleshy black tennis ball would—bowling over her clitoris, grinding against her walls.

Was she a virgin?

God, no! Though her memory was practically a blank, she knew better than that.

Was she a virgin to Mugambi?

That might be the case.

How long had their courtship been? Had they abstained, waited till this very moment? It felt odd and wrong not knowing, not remembering her newlywed husband. And there was absolutely nothing forgettable about this man. Lex doubted that even the hottest fever could fry the memory of his sex from a woman's brain cells. So perhaps this was their first-ever lovemaking, she thought.

She wanted to ask him but couldn't fix the words on her lips.

How would he feel, knowing that their shared memories were lost to her?

Lex cried out both from pain and pleasure, confusion and delight. She ground her teeth, bit her lower lip, and fought back tears of ecstatic rapture as she thrashed against his thrashing. His scent enveloped her; his taste lingered on her tongue, and in some corner of her subconscious she knew these things. Though the fever had made her mind slippery, the space inside her remembered the way in which he filled her.

This was not their first time together.

When he looked at her, his eyes said he'd known her forever, and something in his face, the configuration, made her eyes wish to echo the same.

When he touched her, it was clear that her body was as familiar to him as his own; and the slippery hot shapes her hands sought, gripped, and clawed were familiar to her as well.

The recollection of shared times was lost, but her flesh and her soul knew this man more intimately than she knew herself.

When it was done, she could barely breathe. Threads of the satin wrap hung off her body—the few tatters Mugambi had not torn away with his teeth.

With the side of her face rested upon the sticky-slick surface of his bosom, following the rise and fall of his breaths, he said: "It's almost time, Lexsandra."

Still high off the drug of him, Lex fixed up into his eyes. "Time for what?"

"The gathering," he said.

Much was a mess inside her head these days, but this she did recall. "The reception?"

He nodded. "You shower and I'll have Farisa freshen the room."

It seemed an unreasonable mess to ask the cleaning woman to deal with, but Lex didn't argue. She walked as best she could to the double doors and into what they called the queen's bathroom. She heard Mugambi a beat later, padding across the wood floor. Spying out through a sliver, she saw him—lights on now—red-smeared from head to toe, upon every body surface, and in every nook and cranny.

Standing in the bedroom's great arched doorway, at the end of a trail of footprints the color of rubies that could be followed back to the bed, he shouted, "*Anu fobo, boco kente!*"

He summoned in his native tongue, and Lex did not possess even the faintest notion of the meaning behind the music of it. Farisa, however, entered in a hustle, cloaked as a mummy, as a ninja-fem, or perhaps a nun, draped head to foot in billowing dark fabric. Only her eyes were revealed, eyes that knew only how to serve. In sharp contrast, more naked than the day he was born—for there was much more of him now—Mugambi never so much as thought of a robe. He fanned in the direction of the bed and then made his way to the king's bathroom as the cleaning woman went immediately and dutifully to stripping off the red-soaked, sex-soaked sheets.

Lex eased shut the door to her bathroom and latched it. The room seemed for a second to blur out of true, as if seen through a great depth of shifting water. She didn't understand the customs here. More likely, she just didn't remember the customs—her own customs. There was so much she didn't remember in these days following the fever that it was maddening.

Turning then, jumping as her stare fell upon the mirror, it took her a moment to recall herself. Her brown skin was universally crimson-smudged. Her long satin hair was matted to her scalp, sticky and crimson, too.

She stared for a long while, trying to name the emotion she felt. It wasn't till the shower spray was in her face that she recognized the knots in her stomach as disgust.

"Too much?" Lex eyed her reflection in the ornately framed full-length mirror that adorned the bedroom's eastern wall. She held the bridal shroud up before her curves and waited for the looking glass to respond. When it did not, she brought the fabric to her face and felt the silky skin of it slip past her cheek, and then her eyes were in the mirror afresh.

Red lipstick.

Red nails.

The entire room had been red just a short while earlier, but the workers were a force to be reckoned with, and now only the faintest meaty-sweet scent lingered to tell the tale.

It's probably too much, Lex thought, examining the outfit—red everything. It was the oddest fabric, bizarrely textured, red upon red, the subtly differing hues interwoven in a pattern that brought to mind a serpent's skin. "It's just right," she said after a while. Though she could not name or even recall the custom, this was the appropriate garb. She would not complain. What's more, Mugambi would love it. The color was his favorite, she knew. (God, it felt good to know some small something, to remember even that little detail.) Tonight she would oblige him, though not nearly so acutely as he'd obliged her just a short while earlier.

"Thirty minutes, my queen," the servant's voice sounded in the hall.

"Thank you, Farisa," Lex shouted through the closed door, and the effort made her head swim. For a moment the room seemed to be rotating. The grand canopy bed went by. The massive oak dresser that was cut into the shape of a baby elephant joined the parade as well.

Lex used the elephant to steady herself and sat on the freshly made bed when that failed.

At the bedside window the curtains—patterned after the hide of some fantasy zebra whose fur was the color of rose petals with ebony stripes—billowed in a wind that was sticky and tropical and void of any comfort.

Lex thought to take her medicine, plenty of which poked out beneath the mattress from when she'd decided to stop swallowing the stuff. She thought to have some now because it might settle her head, but then she thought better of it. There was something about those herbs that she didn't like. They made her thoughts so slippery. Mugambi said the fever had left her that way. How had he described it? "Clouded," he'd said. He'd also said the medicine would help her feel herself again. The more she'd taken it, however, the more clouded her mind had become, until she'd been living from day to day not recalling events less than twenty-four hours old. So, against the doctor's advice and Mugambi's advice and Farisa's advice, she'd stopped.

Doctors didn't know everything. Sure, she sometimes had dizzy spells, but just this morning she'd remembered her mother's name. Before then she might have been hatched, for all she could recall of her childhood—that fever, whatever kind of fever it was, had been a bitch. Slowly, though, she was regaining herself. There were other names and faces circling in the soup of her mind that would no doubt solidify soon as well.

"Ten minutes, my queen." Farisa was outside the door again.

"All right, Farisa. I'm coming."

Lexsandra was a vision of unbelievable beauty, of radiance, as she descended the spiral stairs en route to the grand hall. All throughout, tables were set and pleasant faces were sitting at the placements. There had been a murmur of chatting and socializing as she traveled the upstairs hall prior to her descent, but as she appeared at the top of the staircase, the voices had fallen hushed and all eyes turned to her.

Mugambi's grand hall was spacious, well beyond two thousand square feet and more than three American stories high, at least. Giving proof to this were the great jungle trees growing up through cutaways in the floor, more than twenty feet high with still room to spare between their ambitious tops and the arched glass ceiling. Torches burned as centerpieces, mounted through each dining table. At the outskirts of the room ancient carvings of African gods stood well taller than any man present (Mugambi included, and he had nearly seven feet to boast). They watched over the gathered.

Lexsandra's waist was small, her bustline generous, and her hips nicely rounded. The shroud of both shimmering and deep reds wrapped her body, was pinned and wound into place, and appeared like a form-hugging gown complete with a flowing crimson train traveling after her. It began at the bust, leaving her exquisite collarbones and the upper spheres of her breasts to catch the light. It fitted every niche of her body as though it were an extension of her firm, ripe flesh, and as she descended those steps, mesmerizing—no, commanding—the gathering, any residual question why Mugambi had to have this woman vanished.

He was at the bottom of the steps awaiting her, dressed to match. His shroud started at the waist, the same intricate reptilian hidelike pattern of interlocking reds, falling in a ripple of skirts around his legs, flowing as Lexsandra's flowed, a dragging length behind his strides. From the navel up his skin was bare but for a few symbols painted upon his chest. As his bride took his arm, the room erupted with applause and cheers. Lex surveyed the guests, all dressed for the occasion, enwrapped in grand lengths of fabric. The males' garb draped as togas from one shoulder; the females' wear hung as Lex's dressing did but in less vivid color and with head wraps to match. Every face in the crowd was swollen with jubilation.

Perhaps Lex should have been happy, but all she could think was that it seemed a bit much. She looked quizzically to Mugambi as he escorted her to the family table. *This is all so overdone,* said her eyes. In America no one would put up such a show over a woman, even a beautiful one. All she'd done was come down the steps, for Christ's sake. Perhaps the hoopla was because she'd been sick and was well now.

Mugambi sat her beside his mother and said, "Isn't she lovely?"

The older woman rolled her eyes and curled her lips in a savage grin. "Delicious," she said.

Lex gave a hard stare in return and looked back for Mugambi, but found him heading off already, toward the center of the room, toward a podium that looked to be carved from ivory and emblazoned with rubies the size of a man's fist.

"It's a pleasure to meet you," Lex said.

"Oh, we've met before, dear," said the mother.

"Have we?"

"The fever has you forgetful, but you trust Mother—we've met."

Lex looked down at the empty bowl in its saucer in front of her. There were empty glasses and a set of wooden spoons as well. What about a fork? What about a knife? When was the liquor coming out? She was in need of a drink. The appetizer was no doubt going to be a soup of some kind. She was sick to death of soup.

So strange this place was, not like America at all.

America? Yes, suddenly Lex realized she was American. She could remember ripped jeans and sneakers and T-shirts, too. She could recall a street and a series of houses. Pennsylvania was her home state. She lived right outside Philadelphia, or at least she had. Christ, how long ago was that?

Lex rubbed her temples with both hands. She remembered a church now, a Baptist church. Who were these gods surrounding her, embodied in their wooden effigies? Her god, Christ her savior, did not have claws and animal teeth.

"We're gathered here tonight," Mugambi began, "to eat a good meal and to celebrate an end to a lifelong search."

Lex's eyes were shut. She could hear Mugambi somewhere very far away, but in her mind's eye she was traveling that street outside Philadelphia, making her way up the sidewalk, toward the house that was her home—her real home.

"I'd like everyone to raise their glasses in a toast to my queen, to Lexsandra."

Lex's lids fluttered wide—only Mugambi used her full name—to discover all eyes on her and all glasses raised. Mother was extending a glass to her. Either she'd missed a servant filling it, or Mother had done it. A clear liquid shimmered in the crystal goblet.

"Drink," Mother said.

Lex turned the glass up, pulling the fluid into her mouth. She was trying to smile when her eyes stretched at the awful, fetid flavor. The urge to purge swelled in her throat, and it was all she could do to keep down the foul mix, to keep from spitting a film of it across the table. Her every feature locked up in the effort, but she managed to force the fluid down her gullet. Slamming the glass onto the table hard, she would not drink again.

"It cleans the palate for the main course," Mother said.

Servants were moving about now, invisible in their robes, reduced to serving eyes. They were steering great domed platters seated on wheeled tables the size of gurneys. The first covered dish was brought to the family table, requiring two servants to lift the tray and set it squarely before them.

"There will be food tonight, and drink," Mugambi boasted. "Though not our way to waste, it is a special night and we shall have entertainment as well." A roar of praise rolled through the dining hall. "Everyone, share in my joy, the joy Lexsandra has brought to my life."

Outside there was cheering and applause, whoops and congratulatory howls.

Inside, in Lex's mind, she'd reached the front door to the place she was swiftly remembering as home. She turned the knob, and as it opened, a man's face greeted her with warmth in his eyes. She thought at first she was remembering her father, but he was too young. She thought perhaps a brother, but the look in his eyes was not the brotherly kind of love. There was heat and desire, and she could feel the same stirring inside her. The man was a lover, and he was not Mugambi.

A drumbeat began.

Lex opened her eyes to find Mugambi taking his seat beside her. At the room's center a show was taking shape. Beneath a great green monster tree that was tall with weeping branches and woody leaves, two men wearing nothing but paint in the design of scales were pounding tom-toms, their heavy pectoral muscles and genitals bouncing as they beat away. Entering the scene after them were four females with nothing more than pythons coiled about their naked bodies—wound around their necks and around their torsos and down, down, farther down, between their legs and around one or the other of their thick thighs. Two of the ladies pushed the great ivory podium out of sight, while the remaining two dragged an enormous veiled object twice their height and as big around as one of the dining tables into view.

"I'm famished," said the mother.

Lex was thinking the same when something on the platter, beneath the reflective steel dome, moved. She looked toward it, meeting her reflection in the curve of the lid as it moved again—not just a twitch but a discernable kick this time. There was a metallic thud, and the dome jerked. Startled, eyes bulging, Lex lurched in her seat, squirming backward.

Mugambi caught her in his embrace.

"Something moved under there!"

"It's all right," he said. "Don't be afraid."

Lex glared wildly. It was not all right. "Something kicked," she said, and the mother broke into giggles.

The drumbeats doubled in pace.

"Everyone is waiting for us, Lexsandra; we're to uncover our dish first."

Lex's heart rate quickened to compete with the drums. What the fuck was under that dome? She looked around the room, and once again every gaze was trained toward their table, toward their still-covered platter, toward Mugambi's new queen.

"You lift the lid," he said.

Shaking her head, she looked over her shoulder and into his stare with pleading eyes. "Something kicked," she said. That something was moaning now, ever so slightly, sobbing in the dark beneath the dome.

Mugambi leaned in close, kissing her earlobe and running his tongue into the nook of her ear. "Do it for me."

She could feel him then, as she'd felt him not more than two hours earlier, pushing the bulb of his big-headed erection inside her, squeezing every orgasm out as he wedged his way in. She could taste him, smell him; she would lift the lid; it wasn't so much to ask.

The drums beat a fevered rhythm as the veil was snatched off the item at the room's epicenter. Three of the ladies belly-danced with their great serpents while the fourth turned a crank at the intersection of the hourglass. It took Lex a moment to realize what she was seeing, but sure enough, it was a giant hourglass, full with sand at the top, and on the bottom full with a naked, screaming, fist-pounding man. His cries were muted. His raw-knuckled assaults on the glass made not so much as a whisper on the outside. The sand, silent also, seeped down from the upper chamber, poured over his head, spilled over his shoulders.

Lex had pulled the dome off their meal, but was so compelled by the man in the hourglass that she'd not even looked down to see the kicking feast. When her gaze finally lowered, summoned by a twitch upon the plate, her heart ceased up in her chest and would not beat again until a shriek startled it into action. The shriek was her own, as her hands flew to her mouth, as she stared into the teary-eyed face of a child—their meal.

Whoops and howls filled the room as covers were snatched off platters left and right, as other meals (men, women, and children) came into view. They were alive, these victims, drugged so that they were all but fully paralyzed, jabbed a dozen times over with intravenous tubes that were running into their blood streams, capped and waiting— nightmare straws.

Lex threw herself backward from the table and would have fallen over in her chair if Mugambi hadn't caught her. "I've got you," he said.

"Get off me!" she screamed.

In the hourglass, the man, who had to squat because the compartment wasn't high enough for him to stand, continued to pound the glass. He screamed and he strained, and his caramel-colored skin turned purple in the throes of terror. In the cinema of her mind, the man from the hourglass kissed her passionately. He and the man from her home outside Philadelphia were one and the same. He was her husband, her real husband, whom she'd married in the little Baptist church of her newly surfaced memories, and his name was . . .

"Darnell!" Lex screamed, reaching.

Holding her tightly now, Mugambi said, "Sit down, Lexsandra; you're embarrassing me."

She would not sit, however; she fought against him as best she could. The grains were up to Darnell's knees and rising all the while.

In her mind she was still on the stoop of her home outside Philadelphia, staring warmly into Darnell's eyes. Looking into the shadows around his legs revealed a little man in his father's image.

"Help me," the boy on the platter begged just above the slurping sounds.

Mother had already uncapped a tube and was drinking the life, fresh and hot, from his jugular. Mugambi's younger brother had a tube off an artery in the left arm that he'd just uncapped, and Mugambi's aunt was slurping from a hose anchored to the boy's groin.

"Sit, Lexsandra!" Mugambi demanded, and sat her in her chair himself.

As her brain was jarred in her skull, she saw herself in the vast room of her dreams, peering through that glass wall. It was Mugambi who stood behind her, directing her to look upon the bleeders.

"Bleeding a man dry—bleeding him dead—is easy," he'd said. Lex could feel hot breath on the back of her neck, and strong fingers on her shoulders, directing her to turn. "It's keeping him alive to be bled another day, making a resource of . . . making cattle of him, that is the hard part."

Naked bodies, dark and light, swayed on the hooks that were driven through the bones of their ankles. Familiar faces, these were. Hanging inverted behind the glass were tour guides and friends, the spoils of a tour camp ambushed. Everywhere the eye could fall were tubes running in networks that looked like complex crimson orb webs, at the center of which man-high cylinders were filled to the brim with stolen life.

"What the hell are you?"

"Your abductor. Your lover." His voice boomed.

The thought moved in her to fight, to break away, but just the strength in the grip of his fingers upon her shoulders told her that any effort would fail. A tear rolled down Lex's cheek, and her host caught it, brushed it away with the slightest touch before it had a chance to fall or even to cool.

"Don't waste your hot tears on them, my sweet. You are a queen, while they are only fit for meat."

He was a devil of some kind, she'd known, and yet something in his voice made her feel as though she were in a dream awake. Something in his touch made her flesh tingle in places too deep to name. Some aspect of his hot breath tickling her neck made her want to forget herself and simply dissolve to his whims. Some aspect of the geometry she could feel hard against her backside, hot even through the American denims she'd still been wearing, made her wish for the fabric to dissolve and for herself again to be a slave to his whims.

His hand was still upon her cheek when the waking dream proved itself a nightmare. Beyond the glass, two stout servants carried Darnell, kicking and screaming, into the bleeders' room. They flipped him like a rag doll, fighting limbs flailing in every direction. They readied his heels for the hooks from which he would hang, and put him up like a screaming hunk of choice beef. They readied the needle-ended tubes for the job of piercing his flesh and siphoning his life, and began by puncturing his jugular. Lex screamed then and made a move for the glass, as if she might leap through it, but Mugambi had her. His palm clasped over her face, and more than just his magnetism made her weak in the legs now. Something doused on his palm, smelling of chemicals and of poison, infiltrated her nostrils and burned upon her lips.

"You will remember," she heard Mugambi say, and then there was dark.

Shrieking as she'd cried out that day in the bleeders' observatory, as she'd shrieked with Mugambi inside her just a short while earlier, Lex began snatching at the tubes. She groped Mother's loose from her son's neck with a pop, and almost felt the pain herself as a geyser of his little-boy blood fired high. The fallout sprayed her, hot in the face. It shocked her. Even as Lex was trying to clear her eyes and pool her senses, the spray struck Mugambi as well. More shocking than the blood was what Mother did. Moving with animal quickness, almost sexually, she lapped the red spillage from her eldest son's cheek with a savage forked tongue.

At another table the woman on the platter cried out, not a whimper but a shrill scream. And inside the hourglass Darnell had stopped screaming. The grains had reached his buttocks and droopy scrotum, and as if a button had been pressed, the fight had gone out of him. He was just squatting there, panting, staring out at the insurmountable nightmares on every side. Turning his face upward, he caressed the curve of his prison all the way to the place where the sandy rain came down. He was going to die in there.

Lex had not seen the change happening all around the room; she could not see much besides the terror and the pain in the eyes of her husband and child. The dome under which her son had first kicked to alert her of his condition was the weapon she raised. Grabbing it, standing, whirling like a typhoon, she slammed the steel dome into Mugambi's face, making a great *bong* sound with it. Caught off guard he toppled in his chair, and then she was climbing onto the table and claiming her pitiful child. Half rolling and half falling, they ended together on the floor on the other side. Tubes were snatched loose from a half-dozen thirsty lips. The boy groaned. Paler now than he'd been at birth (jaundiced and premature), he spilled blood from the many hoses, leaving red puddles and rivers across the floor.

Mother was up, eyes rolling back in her head to show only vomit yellow, lashing out a serpent tongue, hissing as her ears turned in on themselves and her hair withdrew into her scalp. Mugambi burst out from under the table skirt then, grasping after Lex, something more than human now. If she'd been just a beat slower, he'd have had her, but she was gone with her son in one arm and the steel platter cover in the other.

Mugambi's chest had puffed out, and his skin was ripening into scales, more with every second. Through a flylike seam in his skirts the big-headed appendage found its way to light. Mugambi groaned as it moved, as it writhed and wound in ways that suggested interior skeletal structure and vertebrae. It was more than a penis that reared out of the dark folds of fabric between his legs, and he was more than a man, and all this came to proof as the excess of foreskin blossomed into a hood such as would befit a cobra's head.

Lex was not more than five strides from the hourglass. The rising sand had covered Darnell up to the neck and was but a few precious moments from consuming him. Sweat and blood wet Lex's face; her stomach churned, and her head pulsed, and all at once the room was spinning. Slowing though there was no time to slow down, staggering, with the images around her warping out of their real shapes, it was all she could do to keep standing.

* * *

All this had begun as an innocent anniversary trip to Africa, "to the mother country," as Darnell had put it. She'd been complaining for years that they never went anywhere, and so he'd made all the arrangements and surprised her with plane tickets and champagne and candlelight.

The sights had been breathtaking, the wildlife amazing, and the safari thrilling. She had only been able to focus incompletely, however, for all the while she was there she'd felt she was being watched—and that much had come to prove true amid a night so dark that the devil might have feared to walk alone.

She'd been squatting in the brush, still near enough to the camp to smell the cook pots and see the glowing embers of the bonfire, but far enough to have privacy in the dark. The first time she'd seen him, her pants had been down around her ankles, and the spatter of urine in the leaves beneath her had been the sound track.

She'd thought herself hallucinating, dreaming, or going mad.

Recessed in the dark, hunkered wide-legged upon a low-slung branch, naked and dark as the jungle night behind him, with a huge-headed organ between his legs that moved unnaturally and hypnotically, as a backboned thing, as a snake moves to a charmer's tune, was Mugambi.

"I've been waiting for you, Lexsandra," he'd said from his perch.

That moment had been the first time she'd heard his voice in real time, and yet she'd been certain she'd dreamed it before. That was the first time she'd seen his long black body, and yet she'd known it (the mole just below his left buttock, and the scar upon his upper back on the right side).

Feeling both chills and hot flashes, she'd answered, "I've been waiting, too."

Present-day reality returned.

She had all but completely remembered herself, and she was within striking distance of the hourglass. The bottom chamber was full, and the only sign of Darnell was an eye, a bit of cheek, and a nostril pressed to the glass, hungering after the last drop of air. There was no time to scream or to sob; hisses filled the air on every side of her. The drummers and the dancers grinned razors and stared with cold reptilian eyes but continued to drum and dance. They could not stop, for this was ritual. The dinner guests, however, were not so bound by custom. They were coming across their tables in a blur of billowing red shrouds.

At her back Mugambi grunted as his face began to shrink inward on itself, as though he were inhaling all his features. His thick lips, his eyes, and even his ears—all were pulled into the black pit where his nose had already gone. His head was shriveling, wrinkling like a raisin, deflating like a balloon with a slow leak, down, down into nothing between his shoulders. His sinewy arms were twitching convulsively and readying to recede into his trunk even as his trunk readied to sink into his pelvis, all this transpiring to allow the phallic cobra to become a giant.

The mass of Mugambi's body was redistributing.

The man was deflating, and some kind of African devil-snake was rising in his place. In the end there would be nothing like a man left at all.

Amid all these nightmares everything came clear for Lex.

The heavy platter lid dropped to the floor with a metallic, gonglike sound.

Lex Weathers had been wedded to the man who was vanished now in the hourglass; she had been mother to the child who convulsed in her arms this instant, whose blood was on her face.

Lexsandra, however, had lived another life before that, one she'd forgotten even before the fever had taken the last, one she'd been able to catch snatches of only in dreams. One that had returned to her now.

Lifting a palm to the seething tide of dinner guests, a palm that split down the center and dripped yellow venom, she spoke: "Stop, or know the wrath of your queen." Her voice had changed. Gone were the timid tones. Ultimate memory had put power and bass in her larynx. A forked tongue fired from her mouth and lavished in the red drink that was splashed upon her face.

The dinner guests—her subjects—froze, each in midstride, eyes wide.

"On the floor," she demanded. "Have you forgotten your manners?"

As an army responds to a general's command, so they followed Lexsandra's order, obedient and silent but for the thunderous and unanimous thud of knees striking the hard slate floor.

Mugambi's metamorphosis slowed, stopped, and reversed a touch until his upper body was restored upon the serpent's lower extreme. Bloomed around his woolen head was a cobra's ornately scaled hood, a crown befitting a king. Slithering near, smelling Lexsandra with his forked tongue as she returned the gesture, a tear rolled from his right eye.

"Lexsandra," he said. "You remember?"

She answered in the strong syllables of their native tongue and what the music of her words meant was, *Even if forever were to come and pass, I could not forget you.* Her head rose up then upon a serpentine neck, so that she could get to his height and kiss him.

Still in her arms down below, the half-breed's body shook with violent spasms. "Mommy," it sputtered. "Make it stop . . . Mommy."

Lexsandra grinned down, her yellow snake eyes full of ancient knowledge. "Silence," she commanded in a voice that shook the grand hall. "Silence from the meat," she said, and struck. Her snake neck thrashed, bringing her mouth to the child's throat. Lips parting in a fissure lined with jagged cutters, she sank down to the bone and beyond. When she was full, she threw the carcass to her subjects as any good queen would.

They swarmed on the thing in a red tide of scales and fangs, so many that in the end little Manny was invisible, for all the shrouded feeders feasting on him.

Lexsandra did not watch, nor did she think anymore about the man who had suffocated in the hourglass. He'd been nothing but a diversion in a moment of forgetfulness. After seeing Mugambi that first time, she'd known that she and he were creatures of the same will. But she'd fought it; she'd given over the camp, but she'd regretted; she'd agreed to marry him but lamented the fate of Darnell and Manny. She'd known they were creatures of the same will, but excluding a few vague dreams and an indefinable magnetism, she could not recall the life, eternal in its span by human comprehension, that they'd shared.

The fever had been the result of Mugambi's venom, spilled from his palm, pressed to her face; and those magical herbs were not intended to remind her of a current life, but of a past one in which she'd been a queen.

Lexsandra was no commoner; she was royalty, perhaps a reincarnation, perhaps a bloodline descendant of the original; she was also more than human. Whatever kind of hybrid she was, the memories of that life were hers again. The boy, little Manny, had been a half-breed and an abomination fit only for meat. His father had been just a man, incapable of satisfying the queen for obvious reasons now. He'd been good entertainment.

Returning to his Homo sapiens form, the king stood naked beside Lexsandra, fitted in her shroud, boasting new shades of red where fresh blood had plastered the fabric to her breasts.

It was she who addressed the guests, their subjects.

"*Anu kike, bo bo, fon be,*" she said. *I've not been myself for a long while, but I am home.*

Cheers and applause abounded at every corner of the great room. Stopping to kiss her king and then addressing the crowd once more, she said: "Eat, enjoy, and drink to us, to endless love."

Again they kissed as they made their way to the family table for a brief exchange—an apology for earlier behavior—with Mother. Then the king and queen were off to the bedchamber.

Love was in the air . . .

And on the floor . . .

And everywhere in between . . .

The color of love was red.

Siren Song

Francine Lewis

"She sit 'pon da seawall, mon, an' comb she long, long hair in da moonlight wit' a comb a' solid gold—velvet midnight she hair be, long and pruttie, mon," Jo-Jo said over the muted thumps and clatter of the men playing dominoes in the corner of Jackson's Bar. His dark brown eyes were enchanted with the very thought of his fantasy woman.

"Come on, Jo-Jo," Jackson scoffed, breaking the spell. "Don' tell me you believe in all dem old fisherman tales? Mon, you too damned gullible fo' yoh own good use!"

But Jo-Jo always had a way of capturing them, spinning sailor stories and old wives' tales so well, that when they were little boys—ten, eleven years old—he'd had them believing in jumbies, obeah women, and *Treasure Island*. Even now, he could get grown men to waste their time listening to his wild stories, and it made Gaby mad.

"How much Jack Iron you have to drink? Dat shit done rot yoh brain," Gaby taunted maliciously, leaning against the bar as he looked out over the docks and the new wharf. Jackson Caufield had chosen the perfect place to build his shop—even sailors who hadn't caught anything despite being out for days could always spare a couple of dollars on a beer.

But in school, it was Jo-Jo who was always ahead of everyone, got firsts in every subject, got all the scholarship money and made everybody feel like a dumb-ass. He sure got his comeuppance, though; kicked out of his fancy Canadian university in his first year for drugging and boozing, he'd slunk back to the Island with his tail well up between his

legs. His mother had died of shame and a heart attack when she found
out. What a waste of money! All the old people had pinned their hopes
on him becoming a doctor or a lawyer—something worthwhile.

But even after he came back, fishing and shopkeeping were too far
beneath Joseph Belvedere. He didn't want to lower himself to take no
pissant job for no "measly sixty dollars a week!" His big break was always just around the corner.

Well, he lowered himself soon enough, Gaby thought with a snarl,
*right into a two-dollar bottle of Jack Iron rum! How the mighty have
fallen.* He sniggered as Jo-Jo took another slug from the grimy bottle.

Now, fifteen years later, Jackson had this little shop and a disco
down the beach for the tourists, and he, Gabriel Macintosh, was captain
of his own fishing boat, *Lady Belle.* He also had a little carpentry business on the side, outfitting fancy tourists' yachts with mahogany cup-
boards and the like. Not that there were many tourists coming to the
Island nowadays, and most of those who still came were downright
stingy.

He'd wanted to study to be an architect, and not even at a fancy
high-priced school, just across the reef to Barton's College on Big
Island. But even Barton's College cost more than his family could hope
to pay, so he went to work on a fishing trawler straight out of high
school.

Gaby remembered how proud his *own* mother had been of Jo-Jo at
their graduation, and the day Jo-Jo had flown off in the little nine-seat
Liat on his way to Big Island, the first stop on the journey to Canada.
Even the little school band that usually played only at a few school cer-
emonies—on account of that only tone-deaf, rhythm-blind kids ever
tried out—had been bussed all the way to the airport strip on Hangman's
Point to see him off. Now here he was, in clothes he probably hadn't
changed in weeks, reeking of alcohol, sweat, and piss. A beggar hustling for his next bottle of booze.

"Ah tellin' da truth!" Jo-Jo insisted stubbornly, fumbling to set the
empty bottle down on the bar. "Dere's a marmaid down in Calabash
Bay. She sing to me every night—tell me what she want an' ah go get it
for she. An' she pay me if ah do a good job."

"Don' look like she pay you much," Gaby sniggered as Jo-Jo wiped
his mouth with one grimy sleeve cuff.

"She does give me 'nuff," he muttered.

"Yeah, whaddevah," Jackson said, wiping down the portion of the countertop in his shop that served as the bar. Gaby could tell that he was getting tired of Jo-Jo's stupid games. "If you done with dat, den get movin', Jo-Jo."

Jo-Jo mustered an indignant look—a pitiful look. "Hey, ah wants to buy 'notha bottle!"

Jackson glared at him in annoyance. "You know ah don' sell dat crap!"

"Go hustle Fat Albert for yoh usual, Jo-Jo. Ah hear he lookin' fo' somebody to shovel out his latrine," Gaby put in with a disdainful smirk as he sipped his Heineken. "Da concrete cover 'pon his mama's fancy American shit tank done broke."

There was a handful of other men in the bar besides the domino players, scattered at four or five tables, and they all roared with laughter. Ten, twenty years down the road, Geraldine Beauvais's overflowing septic tank would still be the butt of many jokes.

But say what you wanted about fat old Ms. Gerry, when it came to her son, no other man on the Island was number one. She'd been one of the few school board members who'd openly protested the decision to give Jo-Jo all the scholarship money; Albert had wanted to be an accountant or maybe a banker. Even when Fat Albert got five years in prison on Hangman's Point for smuggling (this only a week after smuggling Judge McAllister's new fridge in from Miami), she'd insisted her boy was as pure as the Virgin Mary herself!

And unlike all the other old biddies, including my own mother, Gaby thought sourly, *who felt compelled by "Christian charity" to give the worthless bum handouts from their kitchens when he came around, Ms. Gerry had once picked Jo-Jo up and thrown him out of her yard.*

He knew better than to darken *her* doorway!

"Ah don' want no Jack Iron," Jo-Jo said, holding Gaby's mocking gaze. His haggard face became a black blot—blacker than the sky on a moonless night—and the bulging whites of his malevolent stare were no longer bloodshot. Gaby looked away, wondering why he hadn't noticed that before. With the amount of rotgut Jo-Jo poured down his gullet, his eyes were usually riddled with bloody veins.

"Ah don' want no Jack Iron," he repeated. "Ah wants a bottle a' yoh best Johnnie Walker Black—"

Laughter erupted from Gaby's throat and echoed in rapid-fire bursts around the room as the men stared at Jo-Jo in disbelief.

"He want a bottle a' Johnnie Walker!" Gaby laughed hysterically at the reeking scarecrow before him. "An' what you goin' to pay fo' it wit'?

Ev'ry'ting you own is been sittin' at da bottom a' dat Jack Iron still down in Ms. Gerry's cellar fo' da last ten damned years!"

Jo-Jo's eyes narrowed, and as Gaby's mirth dried up under the other man's steady gaze, he wondered if Jo-Jo remembered that night ten years before—the night he went from being simply a pathetic laughing-stock to being the Island's most notorious drunk. The night that had cost him the only job he'd held for any amount of time, the friendship of an old man who'd trusted him—and it had cost him Trudy.

A coin glinted in Jo-Jo's palm, appearing as if by magic. Gaby shook his head, blinked hard, and blinked again. The laughter died. The polished gold coin gleamed in the grimy hand, shiny and solid in the dim light. Jo-Jo slammed it down on the countertop, like a man slamming down his last domino to win the game and take the pot. A pure, clear sound rang out against the hardwood, filling the suddenly silent room.

"Dat ain't no *damned* chocolate covered wit' no tin foil," he snarled, moving his hand away as Jackson stared speechlessly at the coin. Finally, Jackson picked it up and held it to the light—as if he were some expert on gold.

Gaby leaned over the bar to get a closer look. It sure as hell looked like a real gold coin to him, not perfectly round and a little warped— but then, what did *he* know?

"Where'd you get dat!" he demanded, turning back to Jo-Jo.

The insufferable smirk he hadn't seen on Joseph Belvedere's face for over fifteen years was there now.

Jo-Jo eyed Gaby bitterly. "Nobody listens to da sea no more; all you evah do is piss in it. You can't even find yoh way outta da reefs wit'out dat fancy sonar 'pon yoh boat—an' none a' you sure can find no fish wit'out it. Ah done tolds you," he said, his voice suddenly devoid of its usual alcoholic slur. "A marmaid—she does pay me to do t'ings fo' she."

"What kinda t'ings?" Peter Caufield, Jackson's first cousin, asked, eyes hard with speculation as his hands shuffled the domino tiles.

"Anyt'ing she want," Jo-Jo said proudly. "She ask an' ah gets it fo' she. After all, wit' da reefs all broke up an' da pollution from all da bilge water an' dat oil spill a couple years ago—well, she does gots to do she grocery shopping 'pon land like ev'rybody else," he said as if it were the most reasonable thing in the world.

"Aw—come off it!" Gaby exploded angrily, still looking at the coin in Jackson's hand. "Who you expect to believe you got it from a marmaid? Dere ain't no such t'ing!"

"Ah wants ma bottle a' Johnnie Walker," Jo-Jo said obstinately, looking at Jackson again.

Jackson nodded, reached up, and took a large bottle of Johnnie Walker Red off the shelf. He handed it to Jo-Jo. "Ah don' have no mo' Johnnie Walker Black," he said almost apologetically as Gaby stared at him in disbelief.

Jo-Jo grunted his reply, picked up his lantern, and stalked out of the shop without a backward glance.

"You outta yoh mind, Jackson?" Gaby demanded.

His friend shrugged and slipped the coin in his pants pocket. "He done paid fo' it," he said, watching Jo-Jo weave down the road and disappear into the night. "An' ma cousin Beverly, over 'pon Big Island, say dat some tourist paid two hundred dollars U.S. fo' one gold coin some kid find 'pon a beach over dere. Ah figure dat was da most expensive bottle a' whiskey ah evah sold," he said seriously. Jackson was always serious when it came to money.

"Hey, maybe it be like one a' dem American shows Zagada does catch 'pon sata-lite," Dan Curry said, picking up his dominoes and studying them. "Da ones dat show dem white guys who do divin' and snarklin' an' da like fo' treasure from sunk Spanish ships. Somet'ing prob'ly wash up from dat storm we had last week and Jo-Jo find da coin. 'Nuff a' dem ships takin' gold to Englan' an' Spain an' dem places done sunk around here."

Gaby took a last disbelieving look around the bar and drained his beer. "All you's as crazy as Jo-Jo," he said in disgust, handing Jackson three dollar bills and pocketing his billfold. "Good night!"

He was outside before the ragged chorus of "good nights" reached his ears. The wind off the water was cool and heavy with salt and the scent of another storm. Most of the tourists were gone during the rainy season—lean months for him until they came back in the height of summer—but he always made sure he had enough to tide him over till then. And with the job he got from Judge McAllister's pretty, bubblehead wife to build her fancy cabinets, he'd make out all right if he was careful. Janet McAllister—or *Jeanette*, as she called herself now—was as dumb as a post (having paid him nearly two hundred dollars up front), but that pretty face and tight, round ass more than made up for it whenever the judge went over to Big Island.

The wind swept black clouds across the dark, moonless sky, blotting out the stars and the feeble light they gave, as Gaby left the few lights of Town behind. It was after midnight, and all the houses along Old Sea

Road were in darkness, tightly shuttered against the coming storm. He didn't mind; his feet knew the way home.

As he rounded the side of the hill, he cut down the goat path to the seawall. The road, built for cars, meandered too far inland, away from the rocky coastline, and Gaby didn't feel like adding fifteen minutes to his walk home. Sometimes he wondered why he didn't just move up to Town and get it over with, instead of staying in the same fisherman village where his parents and family still lived.

A light flickered in the distance, then disappeared. It reappeared a moment later; the flickering flame of a kerosene lantern made slow, erratic progress across the mangrove swamp down toward the beach. Unbidden, Dan Curry's explanation of how Jo-Jo had come by the coin rose in Gaby's mind. He stood on the seawall listening to the distant surf and watching the dancing light recede into the distance. It stood to reason that if the storm had washed up one coin, it might have washed up more. And mermaid or not, it had washed up right into the lap of a drunk who had just pissed away two hundred dollars on a bottle of whiskey!

His feet found purchase on familiar rocks before he'd even made the decision to move. The wet mud of the swamp sucked at the ankles of his sturdy boots. The putrid stench of rotting leaves and animals blotted out the clean smell of the sea. Most of the water from the storm had drained away in the last two days, but over the years more fools than he cared to count had broken their legs in ill-placed crab holes. And after each storm, one or two stupid cows or sheep were always found dead, half-eaten by crabs, and stuck in waist-deep mud because they hadn't been staked well enough in their upland pastures. Frightened by the thunder and lightening, the animals would blunder into the swamp and perish.

Gaby knew the swamp, but he was glad when he felt the firmer ground beneath his feet. As he emerged onto the beach, the crisp salt sea air overpowered the stink. Silhouettes of palm trees swayed in the wind, looking like something off a postcard. The white sand gleamed dully against the black of water and sky. He looked around for the lantern light and a moment later felt stupid for his folly. The tide was rising quickly, leaving only a narrow strip of sand that disappeared into the tangled mangrove swamp.

A match flared beneath a coconut palm ten feet away. Jo-Jo was sitting on the ground, leaning against the tree. He lit a cigarette and shook out the match. "What you doin' here, Gaby?" he asked quietly.

"Where'd you find dat coin, Jo-Jo?" Gaby demanded, stepping closer, fists balled. "An' don' give me no bullshit about no marmaid!"

Jo-Jo looked at him, the whites of his eyes glowing in his black face. "Nobody listens to the sea . . . Ah was sure it'd be Jackson tonight on account of the gold," he said. "But no matter; all you's the same. Fo' gold, Jackson will come a-sarchin' in his own sweet time."

Gaby hesitated. "What's dat supposed to mean?"

"You always hafta be grudging a mon a little fortune, ain't you, Gaby?" he said almost sadly. "You nevah satisfied unless ah be down in da mud licking yoh boots. You din't even wait till Trudy left me before you started in sniffin' around she—did you."

Gaby couldn't hide his surprise; he didn't think Jo-Jo had been lucid enough in those days to even know that Trudy had left him, much less that she and Gaby had had a brief affair before she'd taken herself and her guilt back to Big Island.

Jo-Jo barked a bitter laugh. "My good friend Gaby—did you screw her dat night before you come buddy-buddy 'pon me wit' dat bottle a' Bacardi, while Jackson an' Zagada an' da rest a' dem cleaned out Old Man Findlayson's place an' burned it to the ground?"

"You got what was comin' to you!" Gaby sneered in contempt. "An' Trudy got sick an' tired of breakin' she back scrubbin' people's floors only to have you piss she money away on booze an' big talk about how you was goin' to get yoh big break. What a laugh!"

"Sure musta been funny dat night—ah remember you smilin' all da time, sittin' dere pourin' me cup after cup. But funny, ah don' remember the flames," he said quietly. "Ah don' remember the flames." Jo-Jo reached out and flicked up the lantern shade. Light spilled onto the unopened bottle of Johnnie Walker Red lying in the white sand. Gaby was surprised; knowing Jo-Jo, it should have been half empty by now.

"Where's dat gold?" Gaby asked again, his voice low and tight with rage.

Jo-Jo lifted the lantern wearily and pointed to the little outcropping of rocks toward the edge of the mangroves. "The chest be over there."

Again Gaby stopped and stared at the other man, wary in his surprise. Tears ran down Jo-Jo's face.

"Remember that hidey-hole we all found when we were ten, Gaby? You, me, Jackson, Dan, Zagada, Albert and the rest—remember the year we all read *Robinson Crusoe*, *Treasure Island* . . . remember *Swallows and Amazons* and how we were going to be them except without the sissy girls?"

Gaby's surprise turned to scorn as Jo-Jo rambled on. Snatching the lantern away, Gaby hurried over to the small cairn, where the sea or man must have deposited the rocks ages ago. He remembered exactly where the little cave was. He dropped to his knees and began to clear the loose stones and debris concealing the entrance.

Jo-Jo's ramblings washed over him as he reached into the mouth of the black hole and found one handle of the chest. "Mon, they had to go spoil a good story with a bunch of silly girls."

As he pulled the chest out, Gaby thought he heard Jo-Jo's same complaint in a high, fluting ten-year-old voice. And he heard the answering giggles and splashes from the other boys as they pushed one another into the water, playing pirates walking the plank—a short piece of two-by-four tied to the side of an old rowboat they pretended was a mighty schooner.

Gaby's head snapped around. Jo-Jo was still leaning against the coconut tree, but now he was guzzling back the whiskey. Gaby shook his head and pulled the old chest farther out of the cave.

Christ, it was heavy!

His heart pounded as he lifted the lid. It was full of gold—coins and goblets and thin plates with animals etched into the edges. He dipped both hands as deep as they would go into the coins—a pool of gold in the lantern light. It felt as if there were no bottom. God—what he could do with it all!

"Shit! I'm rich!" he laughed hysterically. The wind rose, whipping his clothes, stirring up loose sand as he held a coin up to the light.

From behind him, "Oh, you are, are you?"

Gaby froze, jaw clenched. He'd forgotten about Jo-Jo, but there was no way in hell that he was going to share that chest with *anyone*! Especially not with Joseph Belvedere. He would have to kill the worthless, good-for-nothing piece of shit. No one would miss Jo-Jo. In the morning they would find him facedown in the mud with the other animals and his bottle, and *know* what had happened.

It'll take me all night to get the chest home, but first things first, he thought, picking up one of the rocks at the mouth of the hidey-hole.

Jo-Jo's voice came again over the wind, hard and bitter, strange without the alcoholic slur and Island patois. "Didn't I tell you there would be no stupid cow—no scrawny *sheep*—tonight? Don't I always treat you right?"

Gaby turned to him in confusion. Jo-Jo was standing at the edge of the surf now, taking another slug from his bottle.

And as the wind swept the last wisps of clouds from the bright stars, out of the black water she rose, midnight hair streaming, flowing out behind her and floating on the water. She blotted out the stars as she reared up against the sky on her scaled belly, her long, sinuous tail lashing the waves, and her cavernous mouth open wide in song, white teeth glinting like stars.

The song caressed Gaby's skin like the mist of sea spray carried on a breeze. It permeated his pores, intoxicating him as she swayed rhythmically above him. Gaby's mind deserted him as long, boneless appendages reached for him. The beauty of that rotting mouth was unmatched, her perfume an unimaginable bouquet.

Jo-Jo's triumphant laughter broke the spell at last. Gaby screamed, scrambling back in uncomprehending terror as one cold, monstrous tendril brushed his arm. Gathering his wits, he pelted headlong into the mangroves.

"Next time, Mistress, it'll be a fat, old, self-righteous *cow*!"

Jo-Jo's laughter pursued him like the siren's sweet song on the foul wind that stung his sinuses, bringing tears to his eyes as he ran. Gaby's lungs burned as he fought his way through the mud—away from the madness pursuing him.

The silhouette of the seawall loomed high above, and for a moment he entertained the thought that he might actually make it. Then he took that last step into the crab hole, felt his right ankle twist in the mud—and *snap!* As he tried to break his fall, his left arm skidded on the thick, slimy surface, and he bellowed over the wind and rain at the explosive *crack!* when shards of bone broke the skin.

Through his pain, he heard the siren's windsong calling to the storm as she moved inland. Crabs scuttled out of their holes and across the surface of the swamp as she came. Gabriel Macintosh sank down into the mire, unable to move—unable to escape the sucking sounds as she slithered into the swamp, her pretty long black hair dragging the roaring sea behind her.

Granddad's Garage

Brandon Massey

"Look at all of this junk," Craig said. Frowning, he stood amid a jungle of old car tires and warped hubcaps. He kicked a hubcap; it rolled like a giant coin across the dusty floor, struck a paint can, and crashed to the concrete. "Granddad was a damn pack rat. It'll take us forever to go through this crap."

"You know how Granddad was, always collecting things," Steven said. He ran his fingers through his short hair, brushed out a cobweb that had attached itself to his scalp when he'd walked through the door. No one had been in the garage since Granddad had passed three weeks ago, and spiders and who knows what else had begun to reclaim the dank space. If Mama had not asked him and Craig to sort through the garage, months might have passed before anyone crossed the threshold. Steven would have avoided entering because the garage triggered bittersweet memories; Craig would've stayed out, Steven guessed, because he didn't feel that anything in there was worth his time. Craig had precious little time for anything that didn't make him money.

Steven swept his gaze across the garage. A mounted deer's head hung from the wall, above a dirt-filmed window flanked by flimsy, ragged curtains. Gray afternoon light struggled through the glass. A pair of naked lightbulbs that dangled from the rafters provided additional light. Still, shadows ruled the musty, junk-filled corners of the chamber.

"What a mess," Craig said, his brown face puckered in a scowl. Standing beside an old manual push mower, he spit on the floor. "I can taste the dust in here. Can we raise the door or open the window to let in some air?"

"They won't open," Steven said. "They haven't worked in years."

"Are you serious? What the hell kind of sense does that make? Why have a garage if you can't raise the door to park a car inside?"

"Granddad never parked in here. I thought you knew that."

"I never had time to figure out that old man's crazy habits," Craig said. "Some of us have real careers and lives to lead."

Steven opened his mouth to come back with something to salvage his pride, but a chirping sound cut off his response: a cell phone. Like a quick-draw gunslinger, Craig unsnapped the phone from its holster on his hip and placed it against his ear. "Hello? Hey, girl, how ya doing? I ain't doing nothing now, just chilling with my baby brother at my granddad's place. What's up with you?" Winking at Steven, Craig walked outside, his voice drifting away as he chatted with one of his countless women.

Steven wondered, not for the first time that day, why their mother had bothered to ask Craig to accompany him to Granddad's house. Although he and Craig were adults—Craig was thirty and he was twenty-eight—in family matters she insisted upon their doing things together, as if they were still children and unable to function independently. Granddad had served as a father to both of them (their biological father had fled the responsibilities of fatherhood after Steven's fifth birthday), but Craig had seemed to resent the role that Granddad had played in their lives. "You can't tell me what to do; you ain't my daddy!" had frequently been Craig's answer to Granddad's request that Craig help mow the lawn, rake the leaves, or shovel the snow. If Craig had railed against assisting Granddad when he had been alive, why did their mother assume Craig would want to help now that Granddad was dead? Steven had been prepared to clean Granddad's garage on his own.

And there was a lot of cleaning to do. Craig was right: Granddad really had been a pack rat. The garage was large, able to accommodate three cars, and even if the roll-down sectional door had worked, there would not have been enough free space to allow a single car to park inside. The area was filled with two long, wooden tool benches laden with screwdrivers, wrenches, hammers, paintbrushes, and other assorted items; a chest-style freezer that lay like a coffin against the far wall, the top covered with empty cans of oil and pour spouts; an old-fashioned Speed Queen washing machine with a wringer to roll clothes through; a couple of lawn mowers; an old Schwinn bicycle; and a bewildering jumble of auto parts, tool boxes, gardening implements, rusty appliances, pipes, buckets filled with junk, milk crates teeming with more junk, and more. More items than Steven could catalog.

He looked toward the ceiling. He saw pipes, fishing poles, and boxes poking out between the rafters, resting on plywood sheets.

"Well, Granddad," Steven said to himself, "you sure took advantage of every nook and cranny in here." Grief twisted through him. Weak-kneed, he sat on a short stepladder.

He'd known that coming back to Granddad's place would be difficult for him. Louis Miles had always seemed to Steven like a redwood tree, a fantastically solid and eternal creation of nature. Granddad was supposedly eighty-six when he died. For years, there had been a rumor in the family that Granddad was much older than his reported age, but no one could verify it, because Granddad said he'd lost his birth records decades ago, and he had no brothers or sisters to provide a point of reference. Steven, for his part, would've estimated that Granddad was actually younger than he claimed to be. Granddad had the bounce, smooth, dark skin, and sharp mind of a man thirty years younger—facts that made it hard for Steven to accept that Granddad was gone. He seemed too damn healthy to die.

But he was gone. Granddad had willed his property to Steven's mother. And Steven's mother had charged her sons with maintaining Granddad's home until she found a renter or one of them decided to move in. At any rate, their maintenance was to begin in the garage.

Steven heard Craig roving around outdoors, chatting nonstop on his cell phone. Clearly, Craig was not pressed to help him.

"Whatever," Steven said. He began sorting through a pile of items near him: an old clock radio, floor tiles that looked like giant slices of old cheese, a milk crate full of screws and bolts, a wooden toolbox secured with a shiny padlock . . .

Perhaps it was the apparent newness of the padlock that caught his attention. He dropped to his knees to take a closer look at the weathered red box, which served as the foundation for the junk pile.

He grasped the lock, tugged. It was clasped tight.

He chewed his lip. Why would Granddad put a new lock on an old tool chest? Granddad had been a purposeful man and never did anything without a good reason.

Steven went inside the house. In the kitchen, beside the refrigerator, a peg board hung on the wall, and enough keys to please a jailer dangled from the hooks. He scooped the smaller keys into his hands and returned to the garage.

His brother was pacing around the driveway, yapping like an auctioneer.

Steven removed the articles from the top of the toolbox. A strange but familiar design was carved in the center of the wooden lid, outlined in black: a circle the size of a half-dollar, and within the circle, a series of tiny hieroglyphic characters.

Granddad used to wear a silver pendant around his neck that bore the same inscrutable symbols. Whenever Steven had asked him what the characters meant, Granddad would answer, "It's from Africa," which only increased Steven's confusion and curiosity—and only convinced Craig that Granddad was just a weird old man.

But it was certainly weird to find the identical design emblazoned on a toolbox.

Steven looked at the keys in his hand. He tried them in the padlock. The third one worked.

When Steven raised the lid, the hinges creaked, reminding him of an old door in a haunted house.

Come on. Don't let your imagination run away with you. There's probably nothing but junk in here.

A light blue, velvety sheet concealed the contents. Slowly he pulled away the fabric.

He didn't know what he had been expecting. If not junk, maybe a stash of gold coins. What he found instead were books. All hardbacks with dark covers, they were stacked in neat columns, perhaps twenty books in total. They had the look of age, of old, forgotten classics that littered garages, attics, and basements across the world.

A different man might have closed the box in disgust, but Steven had been an English major at Illinois State and occasionally took a stab at writing mystery stories (and, less often, poems for women he liked). He plucked a book out of the chest. He examined the cover.

Invisible Man, by Ralph Ellison. Okay, he'd read this one in high school. He opened the book.

"Whoa," he said.

A signature in black ink was scrawled across the title page: *Ralph Ellison, May 2, 1952.*

Steven checked the copyright page. This book was a first edition.

"Well." The air seemed to have been sucked out of his lungs. He wasn't an expert collector, but he estimated that this edition had to be worth a thousand dollars at least.

He carefully set aside the volume and looked at a few of the other books.

Native Son, by Richard Wright. *Their Eyes Were Watching God*, by Zora Neale Hurston. *Harlem Shadows*, by Claude McKay. *Narrative of the Life of Frederick Douglass*, by Douglass himself. *Poems on Various Subjects*, by Phillis Wheatley.

All of them appeared to be authentic first editions, in mint condition. All of them were autographed.

Wheatley's book went back to 1773.

"Impossible," Steven said, breathing hard. His thoughts seemed to have derailed like a train on greased tracks.

Outside, birds chirped and dogs barked, normal neighborhood sounds on a weekend afternoon.

Rational thought, when it returned to Steven, exploded back into his consciousness. Where had these books come from? How had Granddad come to own them? Why had he kept them in here? He was afraid to think of the monetary value of these volumes, sitting here as if they were worthless pulp fiction paperbacks, not national treasures. What if someone stole them?

He replaced the books in the chest. Bending down, he lifted the box. It was heavy, about fifty pounds, but he only needed to carry it inside the house, somewhere safe. His arm muscles straining, he hefted the chest out of the garage, climbed the short flight of steps in the breezeway, and shouldered his way through the door. He placed the box on the floor beside the kitchen table.

As he was about to flip up the cover and dig through the rest of the texts, Craig's footsteps clapped up the breezeway stairs. Quickly, Steven slid the books underneath the table.

"Hey, bro," Craig said. "I'm gonna pick up a six-pack and some rib tips. Want anything, like some spring water or something? Warm milk?" Craig chuckled; he found it amusing that Steven wasn't a drinker.

"I'm fine, thanks," Steven said. "I'm going to keep working in the garage. There's a lot of . . . stuff in there."

"Weird." Craig shook his head. "When you get old, I bet you're gonna be like Granddad. Fill a garage with junk and leave it to your family to clean it up when you kick the bucket. That was so goddamn inconsiderate."

"Yeah, the nerve of Granddad not to have cleaned up his garage before he passed."

"He had to know that he'd die soon. Shit, he was eighty-six, right? At that age, you start making preparations. Get your house in order. Know what I'm saying?"

Steven only looked at him. He had to restrain himself from launching himself at Craig and busting his disrespectful mouth.

"Anyway," Craig said, "I saw old Mr. Jackson across the street, watching me like a damn vulture. You know how nosy he is; you might want to go talk to him before he rolls over here and you can't get rid of him. I don't feel like talking to him."

"Okay," Steven said. Craig's suggestion that he talk to Mr. Jackson was perhaps the smartest comment he'd made all day. Mr. Jackson had lived across the street from Granddad for thirty years, and the men had been close friends. Mr. Jackson might know the story behind the rare books.

Craig left the house and zoomed away in his Lincoln Navigator, cell phone once again pressed against his ear.

Steven crossed the street to talk to Mr. Jackson.

"It's gonna storm soon," Mr. Jackson said. A lean, mahogany-skinned man, he scanned the cloudy sky, perched in his wheelchair like a bird in a nest. He turned to Steven. "I ain't talked to you since Louis passed. How're you holding up, youngblood?"

"Fine, I guess." Sitting in a wicker chair on the veranda, Steven sipped at the lemonade that Mr. Jackson's daughter had brought for him. "We're cleaning Granddad's garage today. Granddad sure collected a lot of stuff." Steven watched Mr. Jackson closely for his response.

"Yep, he sure did." The old man stared into the distance. "Louis had a peculiar knack for finding antiques. Hell, sometimes we'd be on a fishing trip, he'd see a sign for a rummage sale, and he just had to stop and check it out. He'd find the damnedest things, Louis would."

"Like books," Steven said.

Mr. Jackson stared at him.

A current of understanding passed between them, like electricity.

"Like books," Mr. Jackson said. "And other items."

Other items. Steven wondered if more amazing valuables awaited him in the garage, hidden under a heap of apparent junk.

"Granddad picked up all of those things at rummage sales?" Steven said.

"Sure. Rummage sales, flea markets, junkyards. Sometimes I don't know where he got them. Things had a way of kinda falling into his hands." Mr. Jackson looked at his own wiry, weathered hands as if an ancient treasure might be found within his leathery palms. "Louis called it his mission."

"If it was his mission, why didn't he open an antique shop?" Steven said. "Instead of running that delivery business like he did?"

Mr. Jackson looked again at the darkening afternoon sky, paused. "Youngblood, it might be my mission to go fishing every week, but that don't mean I want to open a bait-and-tackle shop. Some things you do out of love. Some things you do because you have a gift. And some things ain't supposed to be sold." He looked at Steven squarely. There was a warning in his black eyes. Mr. Jackson was in his late seventies, and both his legs had been amputated due to his diabetes—but at that moment he was as forceful and forbidding as a spirit that guarded a cursed Egyptian tomb.

"It's a big garage," Steven said, hoping to lighten the mood. "It'll take me a while to go through everything."

"That it will. Louis had been collecting for a very long time. All of his life."

Distantly, thunder grumbled. Ghostly fingers of lightning plucked at the horizon.

"How old was Granddad?" Steven said. "According to what he said, he would've been eighty-six when he died, but there was always a rumor in my family that Granddad was older."

"What makes you think I'd know?" Mr. Jackson seemed more amused than annoyed.

Steven shrugged. "You and Granddad were buddies. I thought you might have an idea."

Mr. Jackson appeared to be mulling over an answer when the front door of his house opened, and his daughter, Anne, appeared, saying that her father needed to come inside before the rain started. Anne smiled at Steven; then she grasped the handles of Mr. Jackson's wheelchair and began to roll him inside. Before Mr. Jackson disappeared inside his home, he winked at Steven.

"Every man got a secret, youngblood. Your granddad wasn't no exception."

As rain hammered on the roof and thunder shook the walls, Steven explored the garage with the fervor of an archaeologist combing through a dig. He found, secreted throughout the garage, several more boxes and chests of various sizes, colors, and makes. Usually concealed beneath ordinary heaps of junk, swaddled within cobwebs, and filmed with dust, the boxes were constructed of steel or wood, all of them secured with padlocks. Strangely, all the locks could be opened with the same key that he'd used earlier to uncover the books. But the strangest fact of all was that each box bore the same enigmatic hieroglyphic design on the lid.

Clouds of dust swirled around him, but Steven ignored the filth and dug up the artifacts with trembling hands.

In one box he found a collection of pristine-condition letters addressed to various people he'd never heard of; the only name he recognized on each was the name of the author, Paul Robeson.

In another, Steven discovered a beautiful, vibrantly colored quilt that depicted a scene that, at first guess, came from a Biblical story: a bearded man feeding fish to a line of people. A label attached to the underside of the lid read, in what Steven recognized as Granddad's handwriting: *Harriet Powers quilt, 1887.*

Another contained vinyl records in their original jackets: recordings by Dizzy Gillespie, Louis Armstrong, and Josephine Baker. The respective artist had signed each album.

Still another had a piece of sculpture in excellent condition: it portrayed a man and a woman embracing, and broken chains lying at their feet. The label read: *Edmonia Lewis, 1881.*

Yet another long box was lined with cool velvet and full of gold pieces: coins, necklaces, rings, and other ornaments. There was even an item that appeared to be a staff, crafted of gold. A label attached to the underside of the box's lid read: *Musa reign, Sudan, circa 1320.* Musa, Steven recalled from his African history classes, was the best-known ruler of ancient Sudan, renowned for his wealth.

Sweat poured from Steven's brow and into his eyes. He wiped away the perspiration with the back of his hand, leaving a streak of dirt in its place.

You didn't find treasures like these at rummage sales, in junkyards, or at flea markets. Not these days. Steven refused to believe such a thing.

He thought about the hieroglyphics engraved on the boxes and on the silver pendant that Granddad had worn. He thought about the perfect condition of the artifacts in a less-than-ideal storage environment. He thought about the family rumor that Granddad was much older than he claimed to be.

Every man got a secret, youngblood. Your granddad wasn't no exception.

Who was Granddad—really?

Steven could not draw a rational conclusion. Every theory—that Granddad was hundreds of years old, that he lived through the centuries randomly collecting valuables, that he preserved the artifacts using African magic—was utterly crazy. Steven was a logical man, an ordinary man, a high school English teacher who might not live the flashy life of his attorney brother but who compensated with his loyalty, dependability, and common sense. Common sense, most of all, would help him arrive at a sensible solution to this mystery.

"Hey, what the hell are you doing?"

Startled, Steven shot to his feet—and in his haste, his legs bumped the open chest in front of him, knocking the box sideways and spilling coins on the floor. Steven half-turned to see Craig staring at him; then he spun to set the box upright. He snatched up the coins, too, praying under his breath that Craig assumed he was only picking up more junk.

"What do you have there, man?" Craig hurried forward. In one hand, he clutched a half-filled bottle of Heineken. "Gold coins?"

Steven slammed the lid shut, but the contents hadn't escaped Craig's greedy gaze.

"It's only junk," Steven said. His hands were filled with coins; he slid them into his pockets. "Screws and washers, stuff like that."

"Don't lie to me. I saw money in there." Craig took a swig of the beer. "Open it up and lemme see."

"Seriously, Craig, it's only junk. That's all that's in this garage. Worthless junk."

"Open it, Steven." Craig's eyebrow twitched, a sure sign that he was getting angry. His grip tightened on the beer bottle. "Open it now."

Steven stared at his brother, who was older and had always been taller, wider, stronger. In the past, Steven had always wilted under Craig, had let Craig take his toys, his money, his candy. It was part of being the little brother. Big brother always got whatever he wanted, and he got the leftovers.

But Steven was not going to budge. Not this time. The stakes were too high. He had stumbled upon an incredible store of amazingly valuable artifacts, and he would not let Craig plunder them to sell to the highest bidder. Granddad never would have wanted it that way. For a reason that Steven had yet to learn, these treasures had fallen into

Granddad's hands, and he was certain that they were not meant for sale. He was willing to bet his life on it.

He drew in a breath and held his ground against Craig.

"No," Steven said.

"What?" His eyebrow twitching, Craig took a step backward. "You're not going to let me look in there?"

"You heard me, Craig. No."

Craig's shoulders drooped. He turned away as if to leave—and then he swung the Heineken bottle at Steven. Steven was caught off guard. The bottle thwacked into his shoulder, driving a shard of pain down to his marrow and instantly numbing his arm. Craig seized him by the front of his shirt. Steven grabbed his arm, and they were suddenly in a wrestling match: grappling, pushing, tugging, grunting, and cursing.

But it didn't take long for the big brother to assert his physical dominance. Craig had been a wrestler in college, and he'd remembered some of his techniques. He wrapped Steven in a painful headlock and twisted him up like a noodle. Steven's face was mashed against the floor, his nose sticking in an oil spot. Craig's knee slammed into his kidney; agony buckled through him, and he felt his lunch erupting up his throat in a hot, putrid rush.

Craig left him there on the floor, vomiting and gasping.

"Boy, you should know better than to show out with me," Craig said, getting to his feet and cleaning his hands on his jeans. "I only wanted to see what was in the damn box. I know I saw some money."

Steven flopped onto his back as Craig walked toward the chest. He couldn't get up to continue the fight. The pain that had begun in his kidneys had spread like a throbbing cancer throughout his body. *Sorry, Granddad. I tried.*

"I wouldn't be surprised if Granddad had kept his life savings in here," Craig said. "A nutty old man like him would do something like that. Bad enough that he gave the house to Mama, and we both know she'll give it to you. I deserve my share, dammit!"

Craig put his hands on the lid. He raised it.

And screamed.

Even from where Steven lay on the floor several feet away, he heard the sound issuing from the chest. It was louder than Craig's chilling scream, louder than the thunder and pounding rain.

The furious buzzing of a swarm of bees.

Steven never again wanted to witness an incident like what happened in those few, seemingly endless minutes after Craig opened the box: the dark mass of bees emerging like a shark's mouth from the depths of the chest, swallowing Craig whole; Craig howling and tearing out of the garage, blindly bumping into walls, falling over his grandfather's junk, finally escaping through the door, but unable to evade the angry cloud of insects; Steven finally struggling to his feet and running outdoors into the rain to follow his brother; Craig fleeing down the sidewalk and into the street, directly into the path of an Oldsmobile; the impact of the automobile smashing into Craig like a boom of thunder . . .

Sometime later, after the ambulance had rushed Craig to the hospital and loved ones had been called, Steven went back to the garage. He approached the chest full of gold that had spewed a swarm of bees onto his brother (amazingly, no stings were found on Craig's body when the paramedics arrived, and Steven never mentioned them).

Heart thrumming, Steven opened the box.

The same golden objects that he'd seen earlier lay within.

He sighed, closed the chest.

The mysterious circle full of hieroglyphs carved on the lid seemed to glimmer.

Or perhaps that was his imagination.

"How's your brother doing?" Mr. Jackson said. They sat on the old man's veranda. Both of them had glasses of lemonade close at hand.

"He finally pulled out of the coma," Steven said. "But he's paralyzed from the waist down. The doctor doesn't think he'll ever walk again."

Mr. Jackson looked down at his own wheelchair and shook his head. "A terrible thing to happen to such a young man. A shame."

"Some things ain't meant to be sold," Steven said. "A wise man once told me that."

Mr. Jackson nodded, his face grim and drawn.

Steven sipped his lemonade. He reached into his jacket pocket and removed two photographs. He placed the photos near Mr. Jackson's hand.

Mr. Jackson brought the pictures close to his eyes. "Where did you find these, youngblood?"

"In Granddad's garage, of course," Steven said. "I'm sure you've noticed that I've been spending a lot of time in there the past few weeks. I'm moving into the house soon."

Mr. Jackson laughed—a high, thin sound. Steven had rarely heard the old man laugh, and hearing his laughter made him laugh, too.

"You know, youngblood, you always favored your granddaddy," Mr. Jackson said. "Spitting image of the man."

"That's what everyone says," Steven said. Mr. Jackson gave him the photos. Steven finished off the lemonade and stood.

"Leaving already?" Mr. Jackson said.

"I have a lot of work to do. But I'll see you around."

"Youngblood?" Mr. Jackson said when Steven had turned.

"Yes, sir?" Steven said.

"Louis made a good choice in you. You'll do fine. Lord knows, you'll have plenty of time to learn."

Steven smiled. "Thank you. I appreciate that."

Steven returned to the garage. Although he'd spent all his free time in there lately, he hadn't done much cleaning. Cobwebs still ringed the windows, dust covered the floor, and junk filled the garage in no evident order.

But, of course, it wasn't all junk. His recent findings—and he seemed to discover more each time he explored—led him to believe that he stood on the humble threshold of one of the most magnificent museums in history.

He slid the photographs out of his pocket. The first was a black-and-white shot of two black men sitting on the stone steps of what appeared to be a brownstone, in a neighborhood that was most likely Harlem. Steven guessed Harlem because the younger man was Langston Hughes, a famous writer from the Harlem Renaissance period. The older man, who appeared to be in his fifties, was Louis Miles, Steven's grandfather.

Granddad looked the same as Steven had remembered him shortly before his death, and the photo was probably taken in the 1920s. Steven discovered the picture between the pages of a signed first edition of Hughes's *Not Without Laughter.*

The second black-and-white showed Granddad and four other black men, standing under a tree. They were dressed in the uniforms of Union troops. Granddad didn't look to be any older than thirty. Steven found the photo inside the pages of a Civil War soldier's diary.

In addition to the pictures, Steven located Granddad's pendant. He'd assumed Granddad had been buried wearing it, but either he was mistaken—or this one had been created solely for him. Attached to a silver necklace, the pendant had dangled from a tool-laden peg board on the garage wall. It was crafted from a piece of silver the size of a half-dollar. On one side, the intricate array of hieroglyphics had been inscribed; on the other, words engraved in English read:

> *Thou shall preserve what would be lost, destroyed, or sold for selfish gain.*

When Steven had slipped the necklace over his head, a strangely pleasant chill rippled down his spine, and a feeling of rightness settled over him like a comfortable blanket.

Standing on the threshold of the garage, the pendant resting against his heart, Steven exhaled a deep breath.

"Thank you, Granddad. For trusting me."

He locked the garage door and went to his car, which he'd parked in the driveway, a used but reliable Chevy. He got behind the wheel and started the engine. Quickly he rolled onto the street and pulled away.

He'd spotted a rummage sale earlier that afternoon, and he didn't want to miss it.

Wild Chocolate

Patricia E. Canterbury

"Madam", the tour guide said, gesturing toward a blue pushpin at the edge of a large map, "this identifies a village, deep within the jungles of northern Brazil, that practices the ancient customs from the Old World. The women live to be very, very old. I'm sure that they have secret potions that help them fight disease. These elders do not have much contact with outsiders; even we Brazilians don't see them in our villages. It has taken me years to get them to allow me to bring tourists to them."

The hotel guests nodded and smiled. Marguerite and her husband, Ramon, were especially pleased to begin their first trip to an authentic African village that was, to their knowledge, the only one of its kind in South America.

Marguerite prided herself on her knowledge of native customs. She couldn't believe that she would be fortunate to meet real Africans in the middle of the Brazilian jungle. What treasures could she bargain for? After all, as a curator of major exhibitions on the West Coast, she knew a thing or two about what to export and how to speak to natives. She didn't actually *speak* to the natives. She did not have an ear for languages. Ramon, on the other hand, was fluent in seven.

Marguerite's passion was her gift and eye for colors and patterns. She could combine Caribbean, Mexican, and Portuguese rugs, pottery, and paintings in a mixture all her own. She used to brag to her friends that she was born in a Bedouin tent and learned about colors and textures before she could crawl. She and Ramon were in Brazil searching for wooden bowls to add to their collection. But what else might they find?

Both she and Ramon were excited about this trip to the deepest part of the Brazilian jungle.

"I'm having some of the strangest dreams," Ramon told her as they packed before their last night in the tourist hotel. "It's like I'm coming home or visiting an old friend. Isn't that strange? Of all the places we've traveled, I've never felt like this before."

"It could be because the village may have descendents from your original tribe from Africa. The guide has assured us that these natives still live, worship, and practice the old ways."

"Maybe."

"You know some magic is extremely powerful, and we do have many artifacts at home."

"You and your magic."

"Don't you believe in magic?" she teased.

"I believe in the magic of us," Ramon replied, pulling her close and kissing her neck.

"I think that some people have certain powers. That's all I'm saying. Maybe it's because we're some of the first African-Americans to visit. We're probably already in tune with the vibrations from the elders." Marguerite laughed; her skin glowed with excitement.

"This is the village that you want," the guide said as he steered the ten-passenger bus into a clearing near a group of thatched huts. The heat was intense. Marguerite and Ramon were the only northern African–Americans on the tour. Marguerite took it upon herself to point out the birds, flora, and fauna. Her fellow tourists were all new to jungle camping even if they were housed in a stilt hotel and slept on feather mattresses and under netting so fine that even no-see-ums couldn't fly through. She also identified the night calls. Marguerite loved the monkeys' high-pitched chatter. The guide acted like an enchanted guest and savored her words. He never once contradicted what she said.

Marguerite was in her element. She looked and acted like royalty. Yes, she was a queen, especially when she wore her white cotton traveling shirts and shorts and sturdy hiking boots that accented her milk chocolate skin. Her short, dark curls hugged her small head and curled around her small pierced, silver-studded earlobes. The huge tortoiseshell sunglasses covered her large, dark eyes. She always walked with her head held high. Her long neck sported an ever-present silver-beaded choker.

The heat caused everyone's glasses to fog up after they exited the

air-conditioned bus. Marguerite was the only one not adversely af-
fected by the heat. She could see the neat rows of huts clearly through
her unclouded sunglasses.

The guide helped Marguerite, always the first off the bus, down the
steps. Just looking at her, one knew instinctively that she was a daughter of pharaohs, so of course, the heat wouldn't affect her.

"Let me take your picture," the guide said as he pointed the yellow
disposable camera at Marguerite and Ramon. Ramon had his arm
around her.

"Madam, this village has a matriarchal system. As I told you earlier,
the women live an extremely long time," the guide said, pointing to a
dark-chocolate-colored woman with a heavily lined face, full lips, and
blue-black hair with a snow-white streak sweeping across the front.
Except for her hair, she looked to be in her nineties. She was seated in
a large ornately carved wooden chair in front of a small hut only a few
feet from the bus.

Marguerite took a few steps toward the village elder, stopped, and
called out, "Ramon, please come here and help me. Your gift of language would be helpful." Turning once again toward the old woman,
she said, "Greetings." Marguerite put her hands together and bowed
slightly in the manner of the Senegalese. "This is my husband, Ramon . . ."
Marguerite's words faded as she looked first at the woman, then at
Ramon as he made his way through the tightly packed tour group. The
old woman was in front of him. She got up slowly and smoothed the
front of her clean, worn cotton dress with both hands. Her schoolgirl
smile showed perfect teeth. They stood transfixed, staring at each
other much like lovers who'd been separated for months.

"Ramon? Ramon, do you know this woman?" Marguerite asked as
she shooed away a red dragonfly.

Ramon appeared distracted. He looked around the tightly grouped
huts, turned toward his wife, frowned as if awakening, and said,
"What? Oh, no. It's just . . . its just . . ." He shook his head and walked
closer to the old woman, then took her hand, which she held out for him.

"Pleased to meet you," he said in an ancient Portuguese dialect, one
that he hoped the woman would understand. Marguerite observed the
old woman staring at Ramon. They whispered something that
Marguerite could not hear.

"You've returned," the old woman said as her eyes filled with tears.
She stared at the tall, walnut-colored man with deep dimples and a

bright smile who stood before her. The Levi's white cotton shirt and inch-long dreadlocks gave him the appearance of a man ten years younger than his thirty years. The man in front of her resembled a boy she remembered from many, many years ago.

"You must have me mistaken for someone else. This is my first visit to this part of the Amazon," Ramon said, blushing deeply. Marguerite noticed that his dimples not only deepened but also darkened when he was embarrassed. Why was he blushing? He still held the old woman's hand.

"What is she saying?" Marguerite asked.

"She said, 'You've returned.'" the guide answered.

"Returned? Does she think that she knows my husband?" Marguerite asked. "Ramon, have you met this woman before?"

The old woman glared at Marguerite and mumbled something under her breath. She let go of Ramon's hand, or he let go of hers. They reluctantly parted.

The old woman turned and entered her hut without another word to the newcomers. She began to speak softly to herself:

"My love, I almost didn't recognize you. It has been so long. I remember when I laughed at the old priestess, so many years ago, who said if we really loved each other we would have to wait. I didn't know she meant nearly a century. It's almost exactly a century since she sent you away. But you don't know me, do you? You look the same as when I last saw you in ... When was it? Yes, 1904. It's magic ... something that I should not question. Why are you here in this village? Why are you with another woman? Oh, oh, more questions ... I must be patient ... She looks like the priestess's granddaughter. The one who wanted you back then. The others have had you for nearly a hundred years. Now it is our turn together. I must prepare myself."

After a few seconds, the old woman began to chant aloud in a language almost as old as the earth. To those with hearing keen enough to decipher the words, they seemed like a jumble of vowels; "*Iiaeejy, iiaeejy ... iiaeejy.*" The old woman's chants grew louder even though one still had to strain to hear her. She stood in the middle of her hut's barren floor and looked at her reflection in a very large wooden bowl of rainwater in which cacao leaves and tiny buds floated. She dipped her fingertips into the cool water and began to chant louder. She removed her clothing and slowly began to wash her face. The red dragonfly sat on the edge of the bowl, then dipped its wings in the water.

"Yes, he's returned," the woman said to the dragonfly. She smiled, then poured the water over her head and body. As the water flowed to the dirt floor, the lines, sags, and wrinkles washed to the floor and mixed with the dirt. In a matter of seconds she again stood straighter, firmer, younger. She was the teenager she had been in 1900. In another, smaller bowl, also filled with rainwater and the leaves of the cacao tree, she dropped broken pieces of manufactured bitter dark chocolate, then placed the bowl on a small stove. She stopped chanting, then took a sip of the chocolate-flavored water. The bitter flavor caused her to shudder. She took another sip; then, as she swallowed, she bowed to the four winds. She wrapped herself in a dark blue cotton blanket and slipped out the rear of the hut and into the jungle.

"That's strange. Usually she's very friendly. She sure liked you, Ramon," the guide teased. Then he turned to the group and said, "Believe it or not, there is a lot to see around here. Follow me to the market." He walked between two huts and entered a square filled with food lying in wooden bowls on colorful blankets. Stacked to the right of the food were more wooden bowls, which were covered with drawings of mythical animals and rare plants.

The odor of chocolate was almost overwhelming.

"Is there a candy factory nearby?" Marguerite asked; her mouth watered from the smell of the chocolate.

"No. Do you wish to visit a candy distributor?" the guide asked.

"No, don't you smell the chocolate?"

"No."

"Honey, it's probably the heat," Ramon said. "I don't smell chocolate. Actually, it is very fresh and clean out here. I feel years younger just breathing the fresh air." He picked up a blue bowl with three-eyed dragons and flying fish etched on the edge.

"Let's buy this," Ramon said.

The scent of chocolate was so powerful that it made Marguerite feel ill.

"I feel faint. I think I'll go to the bus. I can sit on the shady side."

"Do you want me to stay with you?" Ramon asked.

"No. As you know, the heat doesn't usually bother me, but . . ." Marguerite let the words linger in the stifling heat. Sweat gathered in the hollow of her throat. She wiped perspiration from her face. "What's wrong with me?" she asked as she stepped into the slightly cooler bus.

She looked around for Ramon. He had not looked back to see if she'd made it to the bus. She found a seat on the bus that was shaded by a large tree. A red dragonfly hovered near her window. Marguerite dozed off. She woke up when Ramon opened the door to the bus. He'd brought her some fresh fruit.

"Thanks, but I'm not hungry. You go and have fun and let me rest here. You seem right at home." Ramon gave her a soft kiss. She felt herself melt against him. He slowly pulled away and returned to the villagers and tourists. She felt drained even though she'd drunk three bottles of water and smoked a half pack of cigarettes. She dozed off again.

A young woman who resembled the village elder walked to the window where Marguerite sat sleeping. "You can keep him until the new century," the woman whispered into the breeze.

Marguerite brushed the words from her ear in her sleep; then she woke with a start. "What? Strange dream . . ." Marguerite opened her eyes for a second, then drifted back into her half sleep. The dragonfly remained just outside her window.

Marguerite noticed her first white hair as she brushed her hair before getting ready for bed in the air-conditioned hotel at the edge of the jungle. Later she dreamed of snow.

"Marguerite, come out and play in the snow," she heard Ramon say. Snow in Oakland? Wait, they were still in Brazil, near the Amazon. It couldn't be snowing. She was dreaming. It was so hot, she felt as if she were melting. Usually, she and heat were the best of friends. She looked out the window; it was a large bay window just like the one in her home in the Oakland Hills. It was really snowing heavily. She tried to see the Golden Gate Bridge, but something was blocking her view.

"Ramon, we're in Brazil. Near the equator. It can't be snowing." She woke up with her heart pounding as if she had run a long way. She was drenched, and she felt as if she were stuck to the bed.

The old woman from the village whispered strange sayings in a language totally foreign to Marguerite. She danced above the snow and called to Marguerite. Marguerite tried to move, to run, but she couldn't; she was still asleep.

The rest of the week was uneventful—the tourists spent their money on trinkets, and Marguerite spent her time looking over her shoulder for the old woman who invaded her dreams. She always said the same thing: *"He belongs to me. You've can only have him until the new century."*

The next day the tour was to leave for Rio. Marguerite and Ramon drank coffee as they sat on the hotel patio. A woman who looked vaguely familiar walked past their table.

"You can only have him until the new century; then he returns to me," the girl whispered as she slipped a note to Marguerite.

"What?" Marguerite asked as she turned in the direction of where the girl had been. It was the same phrase the old woman used in her dreams.

"Who are you talking to?" Ramon asked.

Marguerite hid the note in a pocket of her skirt. *Why did I do that?* she thought. She looked up toward the girl, but she had disappeared.

"No one. It's the heat—I must be imagining things. I haven't been sleeping well and . . . it's . . . it's nothing. I'll be glad when we're back in the States." Marguerite felt the note. It felt strange, soft, and spongy, like melted candy.

"I can't breathe here . . . the chocolate . . ."

"What chocolate? All I smell are the gardenias," Ramon said as he inhaled deeply.

"It's the heat. I'll be happy to get back to the fog."

Marguerite packed the note in with her sweaters so that she could read it again once they were home.

Once Ramon and Marguerite were back in Oakland, they tried to continue their lives as before, though they regaled their friends with tidbits of their wonderful trip to Brazil. Late at night and early in the morning, or after Ramon had left for work, Marguerite took the note out of her bedroom drawer and reread the words that continued to haunt her:

He recognized me. He still loves me. He belongs to me and I will have him back forever.

A chill went through Marguerite as she looked up and saw the image of the old village woman fill the mirror of their bedroom. The image gradually faded until only Marguerite's face and her bedroom were reflected in the polished mirror.

"Silly woman. You've spent too much time in Brazil. The heat and all the talk of magic has gotten to you even here in the fog-shrouded hills of Oakland." She took the note, which no longer had the spongy feel to it, and dropped it into the fire in the fireplace. The flame grew light green, then orange, then burned out. There weren't any ashes left to throw away. Instead there was a dark stain much like melted chocolate on the bricks below the wood grate. She thought she heard the flutter of dragonfly wings, but it was late fall. It must be her imagination.

Marguerite and Ramon had now been home for four months. It was a few days before New Year's, and the memory of the old woman and the girl came flooding back. What had the note said about the end of the century? Marguerite tried to remember, but nothing came to her. She was alone at the end of the day. Ramon would be home soon. They'd have dinner and perhaps watch a movie on the television, then finalize their plans to visit her mother in South Carolina. They loved spending New Year's on the East Coast.

Marguerite brushed cigarette ashes from the yellow raw-silk pantsuit she'd received on Christmas Day. It complemented her milk-chocolate skin. She looked around her spacious home, glanced at the clock on the mantel above the brick fireplace, frowned, then got up and poured a glass of white wine. The wine usually warmed her, but today, in the late afternoon, she felt chilled to the bone.

She walked barefoot across the muted multicolored antique carpets as she always did, even in the dark days of winter, to the large picture window, through which she had a breathtaking view of the Golden Gate Bridge. The fading sun shone on the silver bracelets on her small, dark wrist. A cool breeze blew through the pleated pale lavender gauze curtains that partially covered the west windows. She inhaled and frowned as the breeze blew in a faint hint of chocolate. Chocolate—who would be baking with that much chocolate in the Oakland Hills? The last time she smelled chocolate that strong was in late summer, during her and Ramon's trip to Brazil. She turned, listening; someone was whispering nearby; she couldn't make out what the people were saying. Nonsense, she was alone. The odor of chocolate was getting stronger.

Chocolate, that's what had been bothering her all day. The slight hint of chocolate where there shouldn't be any—she shook her head. She was imagining that she could smell chocolate.

"Ramon, where are you?" she asked as she looked over the edge of the balcony that defined her hilltop home. She picked up the cordless phone and punched in his cell number. The phone rang and rang.

"Honey, it's me. Call and let me know when you'll be home." She rang off, and returned to the living room.

The wind picked up. The gauzy curtains normally blew flimsily into the room, with so little weight that they didn't stir papers that lay on the dresser. This time, however, the curtains scattered papers and knocked over a silver-framed picture of Marguerite and Ramon, taken in the Brazilian village where all the old women lived.

"Strange," Marguerite said. She had begun talking aloud to herself lately. It seemed that the house was too quiet, even with the kitchen radio on the local talk-news station. She couldn't explain the whispering. Someone was talking just below her conscious hearing level.

Marguerite picked up the picture that had fallen facedown on the rug. She ran her slender fingers over the ornate silver frame and turned it over. She looked at her smiling face in the photo, screamed, and dropped the picture. The frame bounced on the edge of the rug and hit the hardwood floor, shattering the glass.

The photo that a second earlier held a picture of her and Ramon now showed only her smiling face, with a streak of white that ran down the left side of her hair.

"Ramon?" She stepped over the broken glass and picked up the cordless phone and pushed Redial. "What's happening to me? I'm beginning to look like a younger version of the old village woman. Ramon!" she screamed over the mechanical voice of the phone's recording.

"ABC Wireless, the number you've entered is not in service at this time. If you're sure that the number is correct, dial it again."

"NO!" She pushed Redial and heard the "not in service" message again. Then she pushed each number individually: 5-5-5-5-7-1-0. The recording replayed.

"Ramon? Where are you?" she screamed, and raced from the living room down the stairs to the master suite and opened the large walk-in closet. Rows of colorful dresses, hats, shoes, short leather jackets, and a bright orange raincoat greeted her. There wasn't any men's clothing hanging on the side that belonged to Ramon.

She ran into the bathroom. Bath salts, candles, makeup, lipstick, and perfume lay on the large marble vanity. Her pale blue hairbrush and yellow toothbrush were in their places.

All of Ramon's things were gone.

The king-size kente cloth black-and-white bedspread covered the bed. The bright throw pillows covered with fabric from Africa, the Caribbean, Portugal, and Brazil complemented the stark white walls. The book Ramon had been reading the night before was missing.

"What's happening? Where are you?" Marguerite ran from room to room. Nothing of Ramon's was in the house. The odor of hot cooked chocolate was getting stronger and stronger. She ran around in circles, first upstairs, then down. She looked in the garage. As she'd expected, only her car was there, but none of Ramon's tools were lying about.

She went upstairs just as the afternoon mail was dropped through the mail slot and onto the floor. She ran to pick up the mail. The mail carrier had already walked next door. The letters and magazines were addressed either to Miss Marguerite Mason or "Occupant." Nothing was addressed to Mr. Ramon Beauregard or Ms. Marguerite Beauregard.

The mail carrier . . . next door . . . Surely the carrier would remember delivering mail to Ramon. Their next-door neighbor . . . a redhead—what was her name? Something about liquor—Grenadine? Dina? That was her name, Dina. She'd remember Ramon. They spoke to each other every morning as they left for work.

Marguerite ran after the mail carrier. She stubbed her toe on the post next to where the mail truck was parked. Hobbling, she walked to the truck.

"Good afternoon. My name is Marguerite Beauregard. I live at twenty-one Bakwel Place. You delivered these letters addressed to me under my maiden name. I've been Marguerite Beauregard for a while." *Remain calm,* Marguerite said to herself as she took a deep breath.

"Pleased to meet you, miss, but you need to make the name change at the post office proper," the carrier stated as he slid into the truck.

"But . . . but you don't understand. I don't have any mail for my husband."

"Guess no one wrote to him today. Lady . . . I have to complete my rounds." With those words the mail carrier drove away. As he was driving away, a bright red PT Cruiser drove up the driveway and into the garage of the house immediately to the left of Marguerite and Ramon's home.

Marguerite took a step and cried out in pain. Her left toe felt broken. It had turned dark. She walked slowly on her heel toward her neighbor's home and rang the doorbell.

She heard the chimes echo throughout the house. A short redheaded woman answered the door.

"Yes?"

"Ah . . . I know it sounds strange, but do you know me?" Marguerite asked.

"Yes . . . you're Marguerite Mason. You invited me over for a glass of holiday wine last week." The redhead smiled and moved away from the door she was holding open. "Come in. Oh, did you hurt your foot?" She looked down at Marguerite's swollen toe.

"Ah . . . yes, I . . . I think I broke it." Marguerite stumbled inside.

"Sit down. I'll get something to wrap it in." The redhead disappeared, leaving Marguerite seated on an oatmeal-colored sofa in the middle of a room filled with dozens of ornamental eggs.

"Sorry to take so long. This is all I have." The redhead pulled out a yard of white bandages and began to wrap Marguerite's foot.

"Thank you. I . . . I came to ask you about my husband."

"Husband? I didn't know you were married."

"Yes, Ramon. You say hello to him every morning when he leaves for work."

"Are you sure that you don't have me confused with your other neighbor? I don't remember saying anything to anyone in the neighborhood when I leave for work," the redhead replied.

"Ramon, my husband. I think that something's happened to him. He doesn't answer his cell; he should have been home an hour ago, and all of his things are gone from the house. Wait . . . you don't remember him?"

"Sorry, no . . ."

Marguerite began to feel dizzy. "I . . . I . . . don't feel well. Perhaps if I laid down . . . " She stood up. A pain shot through her foot. She took a deep breath and held on to the arm of the sofa.

"Do you want me to walk you home?" the redhead asked.

"No, now that I'm up I can make it home. Thanks, I feel so foolish, but I can't seem to remember your name."

"It's Dina."

"Of course, Dina. I remember it now. I'm having difficulty remembering a lot of things. Perhaps I'm coming down with the flu. I can't fly to the Carolinas if I'm sick . . ." Marguerite rambled as she hobbled next door to her own home.

"Um . . . what smells so good?" Ramon asked as he walked into a kitchen filled with copper pots and pans, red bowls, and sheets of ginger cookies. The girl—she looked so familiar. Had he seen her in Brazil? Could she be the one from the café? She turned toward his voice and took a tray of cookies from the stove. She smiled and moved the cookie sheet to the chopping block table in the middle of the room.

He'd had momentary lapses when he would forget where he was, ever since he'd returned from Brazil. He looked around; yes, he was in his own kitchen.

He shook his head. Whoa! What was that? He stared at his wife,

Jolene. There were times when he thought he didn't know her at all, and other times it seemed that they'd been together for a million lifetimes.

"You can't have any until they cool," Jolene said, playfully slapping his hand as he stopped to pick up a cookie.

"This is my great-grandmother's recipe for milk-chocolate ginger cookies. She likes to shape them in the form of people."

"I don't know about eating *people* cookies," Ramon teased, nuzzling her neck. "Besides, you know I love bitter dark chocolate better than sweet milk chocolate."

"They're not *people* cookies. They're cookies shaped like very beautiful people. This one looks like a model or a pharaoh's daughter, don't you think? Yes, she's a pharaoh's daughter, in celebration of your African heritage."

"What's wrong with her foot?"

"I couldn't get it right. I kept taking it in and out of the oven. I even sprinkled powered sugar on her. She looked uncomfortable, so I had to blow all of it off and make her over. Just when I had everything just perfect, I hit her foot on the edge of the rolling pin. I tried to fix it, but nothing looked right. Look, I think I put too much frosting on it."

Ramon looked down at the milk-chocolate gingerbread woman with white frosting on her hair and a large mound of frosting on her left foot.

"I wanted this one to be special just for you. See, I gave her beautiful clothes and these silver beads for her necklace and bracelet. Even though her foot is broken, I think I'll keep her. I'll put her in the freezer again. I had her there for a while to harden the frosting, to keep her foot on."

"She's beautiful, just like you." Ramon kissed Jolene's neck. "Are we going to give these cookies away at your mother's New Year's party?"

"No, I want to keep Marguerite here in California. She's special."

"Oh, oh . . . you've named the cookie? Now I know that I'm not eating any of them."

"Of course they have to have names. We can preserve the cookies and keep them for our children, then our grandchildren, and they can have the cookies to welcome the next century in correctly. And on the correct day."

"Preserving cookies? Now, that's one of the stranger things you've said lately."

"I was joking. We'll have them later."

Ramon smiled and walked out of the kitchen. Jolene laughed and put Marguerite in the plastic freezer bag.

Jolene stuck a pin in the side of the bag and wrote, *Marguerite, rest in peace*, on the freezer bag. Then she drew a circle around the cookie figure, chanted a spell in her native language, smiled, and put the bag as far back in the freezer as possible.

Cum Onn, It'z Lovely Whether

Anthony Beal

Night winds shimmered with snow as toxic and black as Barber felt inside. First time he'd seen snow this early into the season since he was a kid. Whether this anomaly posed a good omen or a bad one remained to be seen.

Below the icy perch atop the Wyndham New Boston Hotel, from which he surveyed the rust-colored sky, New Boston winked at him, a sprawling whore whose prime was long lost to posterity. Barber consulted his wristwatch as the screaming began on the avenues below. He and the others didn't have long to wait.

Straining to hear over the rising gale winds, Barber noted the pervasive rumble of New Boston's annual Dasher stampede. The ageless one's minions were running. Charging, in fact. *Weeding out the faithful,* as the lord of broken promises put it to his people. Barber and a few like him knew better, though—that there was more to it than that. The ritual "Running of the Dashers" was the greedmonger's preferred method of paring the unmanageable populace, extending the reach of what meager rewards he brought to offer the people whose happiness depended upon his slightest expression of favor.

New Boston Common gleamed with a garish brand of elegance, like a diamond lying in a mud puddle. It was where the ritual drop was made every year. The wonderland of capering children and scaled renderings of global architectural wonders carved from black ice offered up a target too obsequious to be denied.

Barber's brown, salt-and-pepper-dusted cheeks tightened. His broad brow furrowed with something like revulsion as he scanned the streets through binoculars. He didn't have much more use for his fellow citizens these days than he did for the sort of plastic glad-handing on which they thrived. Idiots. Capering about wearing mistletoe in their hair with the same pride with which men of his days wore purple hearts. It irritated him to see so many people so willing to lick the boots of a flagrant megalomaniac like the ageless one. That was why he and those fighting alongside him intended to end the immortal's reign tonight. If they failed, then those among them to meet swift deaths would be considered the fortunate ones.

The horror was beginning anew. Same damned story every Christmas Eve. Dashers, with their noses so bright, torched the city just for spite. And people shouting out tonight did so without the faintest hint of glee. Instead, they did it with bloody throats that dared not stop singing.

Were people really so blind? Madeleine wondered, flipping the hood of her tunic up to protect the crimson spikes of her hair from the elements. It was a perfunctory gesture, the sort performed out of habit rather than need. Not only didn't dead girls have to contend with wet hair when it snowed toxic sludge, but they also didn't catch the colds usually brought on by such exposure.

People around her were singing a Christmas carol. People around her were burning, dying on their feet and knees and backs. The flames didn't discriminate between beggar and bureaucrat. The flames hated all unworthy ones equally, even those still praying to earn a crumb of mercy by trying to sing as their mouths filled with flames.

The ageless one, the Crimson Christ, had selected "Sleigh Ride" as this year's decreed carol. To those few New Bostonians blessed enough to own televisions fell the advantage of being able to tune into any of three available channels and join the citywide sing-along from its outset, before carrying the song out onto the streets in praise of the immortal. And God help those whom the Dashers caught outside with throats too weary to sing.

"Please don't!" Madeleine heard behind her. A half-dozen Dashers had cornered an aging gent with skin as wan and gray as the rags he wore. His voice was a croak, barely audible. On his knees, his upraised hands pleaded with the air as the Dashers advanced. Madeleine shuddered. The reanimated reindeer corpses had lost none of their power to horrify the deceased spirit watching them administer to the man. Dead girls were not without fear.

Their every step flexed large slabs of shiny meat that stank of decay as the undead creatures closed in. Glistening tendons crawled across the sooty craniums of the skinned reindeer affectionately dubbed "Dashers."

They pawed the cobblestones with charred, bleeding hooves. Fibrous adhesions sewed impossibly red tissue like keloids to the hardness of skulls that still housed remembrances of fanciful reindeer games. Tiny phosphorescent flames roared from the blackened bone nostrils, illuminating the yellow-black pulp beyond the eyeless sockets. Their glow lit the way for what carnage they would unleash.

"Please," the old man rasped, "I had to feed my family. I couldn't afford the decorations this year."

Madeleine noted for the first time that this man's clothing went unadorned by the metallic tinsel and shiny ornaments worn by other citizens who had come out tonight to welcome the immortal to New Boston. Stitching boughs of holly along one's coat sleeves and pant legs and skirt hems was this year's holiday fashion fad, but no holly bedecked this man's outer garments. His pallid cheeks remained undaubed by the red or green greasepaint being hawked from every street corner. No bells jingled at his fingers or toes.

Another sacrifice to the ageless one's mania, Madeleine thought. Unless she could stop it. The Dashers, she'd learned from experience, could see her. Humans could not, and so the old gent's failure to thank her, or better, chastise her for interfering in his affairs came as no surprise to the ghost as her courage galvanized her and sent her diving for him.

The Dashers synchronized their assault, spewing monstrous bursts of fire from their black bone nostrils. Madeleine flung her tunic over her head and face as she landed huddled in front of the old man, praying absurdly for the soft wool to guard her against the cleansing flames.

Behind her, she heard the old man's tortured wail.

Dead girls made poor fire shields.

The old man began his death dance, swaddled in incandescent splendor, twisting to the roaring groove of white-hot flame jets that cared nothing for how tight money was this year. They cared even less for the protests of mocha-skinned ghost girls who possessed no flesh with which to challenge them. The Dashers and their cleansing fire would sear his financial woes away.

Madeleine scrabbled toward the old man, falling through him when her attempt to drape her tunic over him failed. Her nose slid through his liver, mired amid his intestines. Cooked to the bone, he was. What

hurt her worse than knowledge that her incorporeal form had pre-
cluded any conventional rescue was the realization that seconds were
all it had taken for the Dashers to send this man beyond all need to be
delivered from their wrath. Over sixty years' worth of wisdom and experience, stolen in less time than it took to boil an egg.

Still, she pleaded with the Dashers. She demanded. She cursed. She
kicked at them with her ghostly feet, swatted at them with her brown
ectoplasmic fists, no more disturbing their activity than plunging those
same nothing hands into a rushing river would impede its progress.
For all her courage, Madeleine could do little except weep over the
charred meat and ashes left behind after the murderers had gone.
Rising night winds defiled these, scattered them among the ashes of
other unworthy souls dispatched by the Dashers tonight.

Christmas hadn't always been like this. Surely there'd been a time
when it hadn't been like *this*, although it got more difficult for
Madeleine to remember with each passing year.

People around Madeleine were burning to death on their feet and
knees and backs. People around Madeleine were singing "Sleigh Ride."

All of them, with that same joyless terror filling their eyes.

Barber adjusted the U-chip device fastened behind his left ear. The
intelligent technological design in the devices worn by him and his com-
rades not only kept Barber and his party in remote contact but also featured automatic frequency alteration. This allowed the U-chip devices
to independently switch communication channels the instant a security
breach was detected. It would keep Barber and his crew from being
eavesdropped on.

"Hey, Barber," he heard as he watched the streets burn below. New-
mark had that tone in his voice again, the dangerous one that made
Barber's shaven scalp itch. He'd stationed the kid atop the Charles
Street Inn.

Although Newmark wasn't his ideal choice of mission mates, Barber
felt he could continue liking the pale, spindly twenty-four-year-old as
long as the kid delivered when it counted. This translated to keeping
his mind on the job at hand, and it remained to be seen whether he'd
maintain his focus once the shit hit the fan.

But he was willing. That was more than enough to satisfy Barber.

"Go ahead, kid," Barber replied, hoping it would be something important, but knowing Newmark far too well to expect it.

"How can you tell if the ageless one has a high sperm count?"

Barber sighed loudly, the sound of genuine suffering. "I give up."

"Special K has to chew before he swallows." Peals of the kid's laughter stung Barber's ear, summoning a grudging smirk to the lips of the older man more readily than the joke had.

"I wish you'd quit calling it 'Special K,'" complained a female voice entering the conversation. "That's more than it deserves. Nothing special about the ageless one's main henchdemon."

"I stand corrected and awed by your sense of political correctness, Angelica," Barber heard Newmark capitulate. He didn't have to see him to know that Newmark's pierced, tattooed lips were curled into a grin that mocked even as it adored. Newmark possessed all the subtlety of a charging rhinoceros when it came to his affection for the statuesque black woman twelve years his senior.

"Joke all you want," Barber told Newmark. "Just don't drop the ball. There's a lot at stake tonight."

"Octavio, what's your status?" Angelica asked, rehearsing the button sequence she would soon activate in the remote control device she held.

None of them knew much about the fourth and eldest member of their party. Octavio hardly spoke unless spoken to, and although none had ever seen him smile, he seemed happiest with a vodka tonic in hand. This Christmas Eve had afforded him no such amenities yet, and so his tone sounded as dour as one might expect.

The old man under the black beret switched off the autorepeating minidisk player in his pocket. The Dashers, having done their work, were departing, and therefore, so did the need for the Andy Williams rendition of "Sleigh Ride" he'd recorded and kept blaring on speakers hidden on his person to spare himself having to carol like the rest of the populace to avoid incineration.

"I'm standing in the Common, near the Old Boston Massacre Monument, hoping this is no night for history to repeat itself," Octavio replied. The monument carried ominous weight on the brightest of sunny days. On a night like tonight, it bore too much resemblance to a massive tombstone with Octavio's name on it.

"What's the scene like down there, old man? Bad as it looks?" Barber asked him.

Octavio huffed in disgust. Even his bushy gray mustache seemed fixed in a dissatisfied frown. "You ever smelled burnt human flesh, son? Well multiply that by a thousand, and if you can guess how fuckin' delightful the aroma is, then that's what the scene is down here.

Goddamned Dashers just finished doing a number on the crowds here. But they've started backing off in the past few minutes. You all know what that means."

"The Krampus is about to address the masses," Angelica said.

"All right. Time to give the Crimson Crank's number one cheer-leader something to cry about," Newmark crowed.

Barber adjusted the telescope on his Swiss Sig-Sauer SSG 2000 a final time. Through its crosshairs, Boston Common writhed with throngs of the worthy faithful. The desperate and hungry. The gladly blind. Were such people even worth risking his and his team's life to save? When the dust was settled, would they welcome their emancipators with flowers or with bullets? It was a hell of a gamble, but one worth taking.

Barber quietly told his compatriots, "Look sharp, everybody. One way or another, it ends tonight."

The Krampus, immortal torturer and executioner for the Crimson Christ, grinned through the window of the ruined Arlington Street Church, with scraps of human tendon lodged between its several rows of needle-fine teeth. The maggot populace couldn't see this from where they gathered below by the thousands to pledge their pious lives to it and the Crimson Christ. Fools.

Shrugging into ceremonial robes of iridescent green-red silk, the immortal goat cast a backward glance at the torn heap of nude human-ity bleeding into the pile of straw that was as much of a bed as whores deserved. To think that people still existed who believed that the wretched unworthy could turn to the church for refuge from the Dashers . . .

Drawing resplendent gold-embroidered sleeves along onyx arms, the goat-creature licked the last taste of human cunt and cock pulp from its hairy jowls. This had been no silent night they'd spent beneath the brawny beast to whom they'd been more than eager to trade their complete coital subservience in exchange for respite from the Dashers and their flames. They'd squealed like the pigs they were, every one of them, if not at making first acquaintance with the demon's cock, then at the first taste of its scalding lava erupting across and into their most in-timate physical regions.

"So much wasted potential," the demon sighed, turning from the blood-splashed straw pile to draw black, sack-sized gloves of human skin over its talons. Sooty chains and blackened jingle bells chimed from the glove cuffs. The Krampus pushed the iron D ring on the leather strap cinched around its cock through the rusted padlock it always wore chained around its furred barrel of a chest, and clacked it shut. Bad publicity, its blood-slick demonhood dragging along the stone balcony when it stepped out to address the filthy cockroaches waiting to hang on its every word.

With its phallic helmet chained securely beneath its chin, the goat god straightened the green-red shimmer draping it and strode onto the balcony, every fall of its hooves reporting like antiaircraft fire.

Trumpet fanfare greeted the demon upon first appearance. Flash photography. Flowers. Tossed strings of popcorn, Christmas ornaments, mistletoe. Shrieks of "Ooh, I saw him! I saw him!" and "It won't be long now!" detonated throughout the caroling masses.

"Amen! Amen, I say to you worthy souls! All on your knees!" the Krampus bellowed theatrically through its jagged rip of a mouth. The demon lived for this shit.

"The Crimson Christ bids a Merry Christ Mass to all!" the demon continued amid a storm of tinsel and strings of dried cranberries. A few of these it looped over the great bone horns jutting from its temples.

The demon proclaimed, "Into thy hands, oh Crimson Christ, do your humble ones commend their blood and spirits! To thee, oh Red Redeemer, do they lift their carols of praise! To their purest, grant the gift of your favor this night! Grant them an audience with their Lord of excess!"

Snowy winds whipped its shiny robes to and fro as if in reply. On their knees, people watched the sky for streaks of red.

The Dashers had departed. Madeleine heard the Krampus begin its annual address heralding the arrival of the Crimson Christ in the Common. Snow continued skirling down out of the night's void. The sky looked like a pile of wool suffused with rusted water. Breathing, she imagined, probably felt like having icy water poured up one's nose. She'd never know. Never again.

Madeleine watched them flock toward the Krampus and its frigid lies, and remembered her last night breathing. How many years ago tonight was it?

With one last bit of Christmas shopping to be done, on that night she'd foregone her typical routine of heading straight home after school. Instead, she'd detoured down to Olde Faneuil Marketplace, where the extravagant in this Depression-era city still hunted for the occasional amenity in addition to life's necessities. She'd selected a gift for her stepdad (always the last person left to shop for on her list, since, as a police officer and decorated World War III veteran, the man already had every cool gadget, artifact, or keepsake imaginable) and purchased it before noticing that toxic snow had begun to fall outside.

The olive-colored wool tunic was a loaner from the ponytailed shopkeeper, a veteran friend of her stepfather's, who'd noticed the girl's uncovered head and insufficient jacket. At least, he told her, the tunic had a hood and was one hundred percent wool. She could return it to him after the holidays. Madeleine wondered why he didn't distrust her with the garment he'd lent her for free, and so she had to ask.

"I've known your stepfather since he and I were your age," the old shopkeeper had told her, "and I know *you*. Just like I know that you're meant to go places, and right a lot of wrongs in the world. Lending a warm coat to a champion of souls is the least a guy with bones as old and tired as mine can do for the future."

She figured the guy had to be a nut. But he was a friend of her stepdad's, and on a night as arctic as that one, a warm coat was a warm coat. She'd promised to return the tunic in immaculate condition. Then she'd stepped out into the chill night, and the Dashers had taken her. They'd roasted her on her feet, right there on the sidewalk where some frightened citizen fleeing the wrath of the beasts had paused in the course of his escape long enough to shove Madeleine into the path of their whitehot flames. In her last second of life, Madeleine realized that in donning the tunic right over her clothes and jacket, she'd inadvertently hidden the gaudy tinsels and bells ornamenting her outerwear, offering the Dashers one more soul to deem unworthy for not displaying Christmas love for the Crimson Christ.

Madeleine hadn't breathed since. She hadn't needed to.

She got to her feet. There was nothing more she could do for the dead man at her feet, or for what Christmas had become, and this she wept over.

"It wasn't always like this," she assured the crumbling corpse as memories rose within her of childhood Christmases, hugs and wreaths and good food and family surrounding her. Sometimes family finances allowed for more presents, sometimes fewer, but kisses and carols and falling asleep watching Christmas movies on the sofa between her mom and stepdad never cost a thing. She wanted it back for everyone. She wanted it back for herself. Dashers and Crimson Christs and demon-led masses—these things weren't Christmas and never would be.

Sleigh bells jingled overhead. Faint. Distant, but nearing. A familiar convoy hovered toward Boston Common, heralded by the oohs and aahs of the kneeling masses. They floated in overhead, bearing gifts in their metal arms. At their center, drifting in as slowly as a storm cloud and as red, came a familiar new god.

"It's going down!" Barber barked into his U-chip, noting the approaching convoy. "Angelica, wait for my signal, then light up their lives. Come back?"

"Roger that, Barber. You say the word and I'll burn us some sky."

To Newmark: "Kid, be ready to do your thing. You'll only have one shot at it. Come back?"

"I'm ready," came the reply. Barber took the absence of flippancy as a sign that maybe the kid would be all right after all.

"I'm ready, too," Octavio grumbled into his U-chip. "Let's do this, already."

Barber took studious aim with his sniper rifle, training crosshairs on the heart of the Crimson Christ. *Disgusting*, he thought. The false messiah's protuberant stomach jiggled like a bowlful of jelly as he sat grinning his tight-lipped grins through that mouth drawn up like a bow. The self-righteous bastard.

"And to all a good night," Barber said to himself, finding the trigger.

Madeleine watched the E.L.F. brigade fan throughout the town. The Eminent Liaison Floater, affectionately dubbed the E.L.F. by the people of New Boston, remained the Crimson Christ's preferred automaton. The hovering monstrosity of nickel-plated steel and circuitry required no salary and never tired. It worked in any kind of weather and required no sleep. It functioned with equal aptitude at safeguarding the Christ as at menial labor. These were qualities that the ageless one appreciated, and so he utilized scores of them every Christmas Eve. Dozens of them flanked his chariot's final approach to New Boston. They hovered throughout the town, depositing the ageless one's gifts in the Common, removing the charred bodies of the worthless, managing the overwhelming crush of worshippers.

She almost didn't notice the filamentous blue material, like gossamer mucus threads, that trailed her phantom fingers when she forgetfully sought to caress the dead man's brow but instead passed her hand through it. Madeleine started at the sight of the luminescent ectoplasm, confusion grappling with terror for control of her next act. She drew her tunic about her as the stuff wafted upward like smoke, congealing into a sphere that roiled like flame. It bobbed to eye level with her, and though desperation seared her conceptual stomach, something kept her from fleeing this phenomenon. Something that wasn't fear, something closer to an overpowering sense of pity.

"What are you?" she whispered, lamenting that she found herself forced to speak to the eerie candle. The flame roiled. Had she caught a flash of the dead man's face in the dancing light? The thing imparted no heat to the fingers with which she reluctantly reached for it. Was it the man's soul? If so, did he remember how he died? Did her disembodied spirit appear to it as a blue flame, too? Fascination slowly gained ground on her fear.

Within the tunic's voluminous inner pocket, Madeleine found the gift she'd chosen for her stepfather. She didn't know what instinct had caused her to reach for it, but she withdrew the antique hammered-metal lantern, which somehow remained wrapped in sheets of newspaper bearing the date of her death, and held it up by its chain. The shopkeeper's accolade occurred to her, and tempted her to try something just foolish—and arrogant enough to work.

. . . *you're meant to go places, and right a lot of wrongs in the world* . . .

"Come with me," she told the blue sphere, unlatching the lantern's tiny glass door. The blue flame sphere floated into the lantern and glowed.

Madeleine shut the door and smiled through the lantern's glass walls at her newfound friend.

The Crimson Christ's chariot hovered near the balcony where Krampus stood, and the two exchanged greetings. Barber gave the signal, and Angelica punched the sequence of buttons intended to launch the artillery shells and skyrockets she and the others had spent the day stashing on rooftops surrounding the Common. That no one have any idea where the fireworks were coming from was crucial. If their crew got discovered too soon, all was lost, and the Crimson Christ would likely reign forever.

Octavio seized a pause in the Krampus's benediction as opportunity to carry off his phase of Barber's mission. "Fellow worshippers! Look! The Crimson Christ showers us with fire from heaven!" shouted the old man stationed amid the throng in the Common. The kneeling pop-

ulace followed his gnarled finger skyward toward the sound of fireworks.

Angelica let twelve dozen Whistling Breakers fly from the roof of
the abandoned financial district building, and launched nine dozen four-
color bursts from the ruins of the John Hancock building. From the
roof of the Boston Park Plaza Hotel, she detonated eighteen 88-
millimeter mortar shells that burned them some sky, just as she'd
promised. Corpulent clouds glowed with tulips of red light and blue
spark cataracts. Orange-yellow comets sailed toward heaven and
rocked the world with explosive cracks.

Below, the masses smiled and gasped at the spectacle above them,
believing that it marked some planned aspect of the Christ's visit. The
Crimson Christ likewise observed the sky, coldly beaming with the satisfaction of a monarch whose peons were immolating themselves for his
amusement.

Through his telescope, Barber watched the snowy-bearded devil
exchange knowing glances with Krampus. His diversion had performed swimmingly, so Barber gave Newmark the signal.

The fireworks' sound showers would provide the sound of Barber's
solitary gunshot more than sufficient cover. Newmark launched the
single e-bomb he'd been entrusted with. Its detonation would release
electromagnetic waves over a radius of five miles, successfully render-
ing useless the circuitry driving every E.L.F. within range, along with
every appliance bearing *any* kind of microchip. This would leave the
grinning Red Rogue unguarded and neutralize any E.L.F. units that
would investigate the attempt Barber was about to make on his life.

Barber knew things had gone his way when one E.L.F. veered into
a building before crashing to the street below. Another spun out of control, shattering on impact with the Common, collapsing a black-ice ren-
dering of the leaning tower of Pisa. Another E.L.F. followed suit. One
by one, the compromised E.L.F. brigade disintegrated, dropping like
green steel flies. Soon all within view would lie broken and burning,
scattered about like tin toys left behind by a colossal, ill-behaved child.

Barber pulled the trigger.

Madeleine opened the lantern door, admitting the ninth persecuted
soul inside with the others she'd spent the past half-hour collecting. So
many dead and dying littered the streets. So many stolen dreams still
haunted their flesh. How would her lantern ever hold them all?

She held the thing before her face, watched the glowing flame undulate, growing brighter with every soul added. What she intended to do with them remained an unsolved riddle. All Madeleine knew was that the dead girl in the green tunic was doing okay for herself for the first time since she died. She had friends now, and with each one collected, she grew less afraid for herself and for them and for Christmas. Besides, the spirits seemed to gravitate toward her. When the spirits beckoned, what champion of souls, living or dead, could say no?

"Are you an angel?" asked the horribly burned child over which she knelt. The fact that he could see her told Madeleine that he didn't have long left to live.

Madeleine surprised herself with the answer she gave. Her mouth seemed to reply independently of her brain. "I'm the new G.C.P."

"Hm?" Even through the third-degree burns ruining his face, she could read his confusion.

"The Ghost of Christmas Past."

The child tried to furrow his cracked brow in ponderance of this, wincing at the pain wrought by folding scorched skin. Then he asked, "Can you bring it all back? Back to the way my dad says things used to be?" This kid had never known any Christmas except that over which the Red Fiend presided! Madeleine's rage shook her, knotted in her throat, momentarily making it difficult to speak.

"I'm trying."

"Cool."

It was the last word the boy would ever say. Madeleine rested the lantern beside his body and drew out the tiny luminous web of his soul.

"Go toward the light," she whispered to the tiny blue flame that hovered above his black-edged nostrils. The tears in her eyes obscured her vision a bit, but the sphere appeared to obey her. It entered the lantern, and Madeleine closed the door behind it.

The Crimson Christ's chariot hovered toward the Common, directly above the piled crates of gingerbread and fruitcake that New Boston's Messiah had brought for the starving masses. Even after his E.L.F. brigade began falling away in the wake of Newmark's e-bomb, the bastard had the temerity to continue waving at the grown men and women approaching him on their knees, hoping for their Red Redeemer to look their way. Barber's bullet was aimed for his heart, and pulling the trigger felt better than any twelve orgasms Barber had ever experienced.

It satisfied him right up until the red chariot canted left, throwing the fat man out of the projectile's range.

While the Crimson Christ's sorcery drove most of the chariot's functions, others relied on the same microcircuit technology that powered the E.L.F. brigade—the same technology crippled seconds ago by the e-bomb. Barber's bullet fragmented the vehicle's windshield and, if nothing else, alerted Krampus and the Crimson Christ that someone was shooting at New Boston's Savior.

The masses scattered. Some sought personal safety. Others dove for the chariot, as if seeking to shield the hulking hovercraft from further injury. He fired again. And again. And again. The Red Fiend couldn't slip through his fingers. He *couldn't!*

The bullets tore through the hood, the grill, the rear seat cushion of the fallen chariot, as the Crimson Christ scrambled free of its driver's seat. The fat bastard could really haul ass when he meant to. Barber didn't have to guess where he was headed. He watched through his telescope as the ageless fucker hobbled through the broken door Krampus opened, and into Arlington Street Church.

Barber hadn't been to church in years. Tonight was a nice night for it.

Madeleine didn't suppose God had anything against ghosts in church, and so she made her way to Arlington Street because it was the closest. Perhaps there, she could pray on what to do with the souls she'd collected. She wondered what had made her identify herself to the boy as the Ghost of Christmas Past. Surely it sounded less distasteful than "Specter Collector," the first thing to spring to mind. But now that her collection was going along swimmingly, what was she to do with it?

As she approached the church, she wondered whether the Krampus and The Crimson Fiend would be able to view her. If so, she hoped they'd not object to her presence there. Even if they did, the chances that they could do anything about it seemed slim enough for her to seek guidance there anyway. What harm could be brought to a dead girl?

Barber's U-chip lay underneath a parked station wagon, where it had landed when he cast it away. The e-bomb had rendered the thing useless. He didn't bring the others along, because it wasn't their vendetta and never had been. They were just three people he'd saved in the line of duty from a hostage situation a few weeks ago, just three brave souls who'd meant it when they told him, "If I can ever do anything to repay you, let me know"—and who believed, as he did, that the time had come to depose the Crimson Christ. He'd not endanger their lives any further.

The ruined Arlington Street Church menaced as he approached it. The building seemed very much like a sentient entity inhaling gusts of passion and color and life from everything and everyone surrounding it, and breathing out contagion and malice and panic. The sort of stuff that thrived on blind need. The sort of stuff that took you out of yourself. If you breathed it long enough, you grew accustomed to it, and then there was simply no more "you" to be had or offered to the world.

The church doors hung open, battered by Newmark's e-bomb, so Barber stepped inside quietly. Most of the pews had been splintered, overturned, bashed to tinder against the walls.

His rifle rested in the bend of one arm, relaxed and ready. His finger stroked the trigger, poised to pump a hot one into whichever of the two devils he came across first. Between the two of them, the Krampus would surely be the more difficult takedown, and so Barber prayed to meet the demon before running into the fat ageless one. The Crimson Christ, called Santa Claus, didn't appear to offer much in the way of physical confrontation. But the demon would be unstoppable if Barber were to get separated from the rifle.

No, he told himself, *keep thinking along those lines and you're as good as smeared.*

"We wondered if you'd show your face here," Barber heard. The voice came from nowhere and from everywhere. Acoustics made the speaker's position impossible to pinpoint.

"Where is he?" Barber demanded.

The demon grinned. "It's after midnight and his work is finished. He's on the first magic carpet back home. No microchips in a magic carpet."

"Liar," Barber snarled before noting the faintness of the Crimson Christ's laughter outside, receding into the falling snow. The temerity of the smug bastard's "Ho, ho, ho . . ." left Barber feeling murderous. He'd lost him.

The Krampus told Barber, "You've been bad, black. Real bad. The Crimson Christ knows it. And he doesn't forget."

"He might wear Crimson, but he ain't no Christ," Barber called into the cavernous dark.

"And who are you to judge? Sniping at us from a concealed location. Does it feel righteous, seeking to execute a man who's brought such joy to so many people? Does it help you sleep at night?" Again, spoken from nowhere.

Barber stepped cautiously in the dark, approaching the pulpit. "How does your false messiah sleep, knowing all the lives snuffed out in his name? How does he dream, knowing children have been trampled and burned in the name of the Crimson Christ?"

"They weren't worthy," the Krampus said, "but since you apparently feel you are, here's something to help you sleep, you self-righteous berk."

The Krampus rose to full height behind the pulpit. Even from twenty feet away, the creature looked larger than life. It was as wide as Barber was tall. It stood naked, its chest looking like the black-carpeted hood of a Buick. It stank of blood and burning death. And what the devil was that veined cathedral column jutting out in front of it?

Barber squeezed off a round as the demon wrenched the pulpit free of the floor and hefted it overhead, seeming to have no more trouble than if it were lifting a loaf of bread. The act hadn't taken two seconds. It hefted the torn-free pulpit at Barber like a hell-bound fastball. Unlike the demon, the rotted structure seemed to drift toward Barber in slow motion. Panic kept him from moving quickly enough to dodge it, and although the thing burst into kindling several feet in front of him, a hunk of it large enough to jar the rifle from his hands struck his chest and head. The next moment found Barber falling on his ass in the dust while the demon laughed.

A heavy talon smacked him across the face, ripping flesh. There and gone in the blink of an eye.

From the darkness, Barber heard, "On your feet, human! You will not water down this victory for me by making it too easy!"

Barber laughed because he'd learned from his bar-fighting days that laughter made it hurt less. He struggled to his feet, shaking off the pain, talking to distract himself from it and to keep the demon talking.

At this point it was all he could do. He had no idea which direction his rifle had flown off in.

"Are you afraid of me, demon? Is that why you hide in shadows? Why don't you show yourself?"

Talons tore through Barber's jeans, shredding the tenderness of his right knee. He went down again. The Krampus moved with such unreal speed that when it wasn't altogether invisible in that darkness, its movements blurred because the human eye simply could not keep up with it.

"Why don't you *make* me, Sambo?" the demon snickered.

Something terrible was going down inside the Arlington Street Church. Madeleine had heard the crash from a block away. She stepped up the pace, cradling the lantern against her bosom to avoid dropping it. Her tunic rode the wind as she sprinted up the crumbling steps and into the darkness.

"Oh, my God," Madeleine gasped, reeling on discorporate legs that had never felt weak before this moment. Pinned against a wall of the church, hefted several feet off the ground by one of Krampus's arms, was her stepfather.

"Daddy!" she shrieked, rage sweeping her initial fear out the door. "Let him go, you fucking monster! You're going to kill him!"

"Give me one good reason why I should," the demon told the intruder, leering through black eyes that bore no pupils. "Better yet, come over here and wipe *two* good reasons across my tongue." The language it spoke had not approached a human ear in over two thousand years. Somehow, Madeleine understood every word it said, and that it hadn't wanted Barber to know what was being discussed.

Something snatched at Madeleine's breasts. Something cruel and invisible. Madeleine's shocked yip thrilled the demon like a kiss, and it roared with laughter that shook dust from the beams overheard. The demon had the power to touch her! It was the first time the dead girl had been physically caught off guard.

Confused, Barber managed to croak, "The fuck you laughing at?" His head was going fuzzy in the monster's grip. He'd failed New Boston, and failed his stepdaughter and failed himself. He wished the Krampus would go ahead and snap his damn neck already. It had been years since he'd had anything left to live for.

"Quiet! The condemned have no right to speak!" the Krampus answered in English.

"Please!" Madeleine pleaded. "Let go of him! Now!"

"What am I offered for him? Make it good. Daddy's life depends on your offer."

"Anything. Anything you want." The demon knew she meant it, and grinned at her.

"Fine. I want to hear you squeal like the pig you are!" The demon tossed Barber aside and headed for Madeleine on those hooves as big as oak stumps. The big man sailed at least fifteen feet before landing against an adjacent wall with a heartbreaking sound. Barber's unconscious, bloody heap slid to the floor and didn't move.

The Krampus stalked toward the terrified dead girl, its monumental phallus jutting several feet ahead of it, scraping the floorboards. It resembled a gigantic, blood-engorged leech and looked rigid enough to break sidewalks. Madeleine scrambled away from the Krampus, loathing the implications of its erection. The thing bulged nearly as wide as Madeleine herself.

The invisible talons took another thoughtless swipe at her breasts. She wondered how the Krampus was doing it, but now was hardly the time to ask.

The lust behind its eyes would not be abridged by her questions. Or her screams. What would happen to her once the demon was finished? Would she die again? Simply fade away into nothingness? What happened to supernatural beings who got savaged beyond anything an ordinary human could survive? Madeleine was afraid to find out.

The lantern occurred to her. She'd forgotten she was holding it the entire time. The Krampus grinned at her with a thousand teeth as Madeleine's last-ditch effort came into play. She whispered a prayer and opened the lantern's tiny door.

"Take him!" she bellowed to the souls inside. The lantern's light exploded outward, snaking along the demon's cock and arms. Blue rage pooled about its hooves, clinging to furred legs. Consuming. The vengeance of persecuted souls screamed through the decaying structure, deafening ghost and demon alike.

The Krampus burst into swirling sapphire flames and began to shriek.

Barber awoke just before sunrise. The Crimson Christ was long gone. He stood, stretched aching joints, and started toward the front of the church, toward the place he'd been pinned by the Krampus. The demon was still there, but its state was cause for much confusion.

The beast's body had been burned hairless. Its splintered ribs burst through the crackling flesh of its chest. It lay facedown, stinking of burning death, roasted carrion. Dried ichor crusted black-edged wounds torn in the leathery parchment skin. Its desiccated erection lay cracked and impotent between meatless thighs. The Krampus looked as if it had lost an argument with a horde of Dashers.

"Hello, Daddy," Madeleine said gently, approaching him from behind. He seemed as disoriented as any man would under what Madeleine now knew to be his circumstance.

Barber heard her. He knew that voice. Jarred by recognition and remembrance of loss, hoping for even a faint echo of the stepdaughter he'd lost to the Crimson Christ's demented games, he turned in search of the girl he knew better than to expect.

And Madeleine stood before him. Impossibly, she stood there smiling at him, as chaste and beautiful as he remembered her.

"Maddy?" Barber croaked as time withered to a standstill and reality changed shape inside his mind. "Baby?" He dared not hope for such redemption. Second chances of this magnitude rarely touched men like him, so he'd long since outgrown his ability to hope for them. He didn't deserve them. His role in the grand scheme of the universe was inconsequential at best. If this were untrue, Madeleine would never have been taken from him in the first place.

"I love you, Daddy. I've missed you."

But he believed in his own two eyes, if not in redemption, and hope he did, just like a fool, and reached for his dead stepdaughter where she stood beckoning to him with outstretched arms. He wondered fleetingly if this was what it felt like to be driven insane. Perhaps despair had finally sent him tumbling into that abyss. If so, then insanity was bliss.

Tears sprang to Barber's eyes. "It's not you. It can't be. It can't—"

Barber closed his arms around the ghost girl. And all was calm, all was bright and for an instant, he could feel Madeleine filling his arms, then passing through them as if the two of them were twists of smoke.

"This won't be easy to explain," Madeleine told him. "Come with me, Daddy."

Madeleine lifted the lantern and collected the swirling blue flame that was her father's harvested soul.

Christmas Eve. The Dashers were running, showing the downtrodden a hot time in the cold town tonight. The Red Redeemer would soon hover into town with crates of fruitcake and gingerbread and hand-painted cedar baubles.

Nothing ever changed. It had always been like this.

The hooded figure approached the dying stranger with the molten prosthetic knee. The Dashers were nothing if not efficient murderers.

"My name's Sarah. I couldn't run any farther," rasped the stranger. It sounded like an apology.

"Shh," the Ghost of Christmas Past told her. "Don't try to talk. My name is Madeleine. I'm here to escort you home to yesterday."

Drawing the spirit free of the smoldering flesh, Madeleine opened the lamp and watched the spark float inside. Madeleine rose and continued along East Berkeley Street. It was starting to snow.

The first thing she noticed was her hips: two full, flesh-and-blood hips. Her prosthesis had ceased to exist. Perhaps it never had.

Her name was Sarah, and at the time she materialized in the lavishly decorated parlor room, her murder by the Dashers was only hours old. She found herself dressed in a bodice and overskirt of exquisite peacock blue silk. White ruching bedecked the front of the bodice down to its waistline and along its bottom and sleeves. At her back, a large bow drew the garment close to her waist. Nine blue silk buttons fastened the front.

She felt relaxed, as if she'd returned home to convalesce from some tedium in a faraway land. Giggles like crystal chimes perfumed the air. Small, grinning children toddled after each other. Sarah stepped backward to allow them passage, and collided lightly with the tallest, greenest Christmas tree her eyes had ever fallen upon. Ornaments of gold and pearl decorated its every bough. Although Sarah didn't recollect how she'd come to this place festooned so generously with mistletoe and cranberry wreaths and colored lights, the Edwardian furnishings of the parlor felt oddly familiar.

From an adjacent hall, a towering black gentleman emerged, smiling when he saw her. Judging by the salt-and-pepper shadows upon his cheeks, Sarah guessed him between fifty and fifty-five years of age. His gray wool top hat and matching coat resembled something out of a Rockwell greeting. Had he known she would be arriving?

"Welcome," Barber said to the new arrival. "Merry Christmas."

In the palatial dining room behind him, people milled about with steaming mugs or tiny plates piled high with fruit and cheese and exotic meats. The scent of apple cider pervaded the air. Sarah noted the faintest hint of a snowfall beyond the room's expansive windows, painting the landscape a magnificent white.

"Christmas . . ." Sarah repeated. The memory of her former life under the reign of the Crimson Christ was already fading. In time, no memory of the suffering to which she and thousands of others had yearly been subjected would remain.

"It's Christmas morning. It's always Christmas morning here." His eyes were kind. His smile seemed to invite her into some sort of family.

Always Christmas morning? How could this be? And why had the word sent initial shivers of misgiving down her arms? Even as she pondered this, her apprehensions ebbed. Christmas was a wonderful season. One to be enjoyed.

"Yes. Yes . . . Merry Christmas to you."

Barber told Sarah, "Welcome home. Come meet the others." When he offered her his spectral arm, the deceased woman took it, her fingers slipping through his sleeve, and allowed the big man to unhurriedly escort her in to meet the rest of the new arrivals.

Back in the land of the living Christ, a ghost girl in a green tunic made her way along Bowdoin Street, feeling contented and warm despite the night's rising chill.

The Gray Riders

B. Gordon Doyle

It was funny how he came to be there, bleeding, his life trickling away and dripping onto the carpeted floor of the Metro subway car. It wasn't *ha-ha* funny, like when his son, Laron Junior, all of twenty months old, tried to wear his Timberlands and looked just like a Bigfoot cartoon. It was another kind of funny. Funny the way some fool leave his ID sittin' on the counter at the liquor store after he done capped the cashier, or funny the way the Orangehats dime five-oh on a domestic and the dumb-ass cops go to the wrong crib, but walk out with a couple pounds of Jamaican sinse anyway, 'cus it turns out that the nigga' up there was dealin' quantity.

Funny that way. Funny, but ain't nobody laughin', 'cus it's dumb shit like that get a nigga' locked up or dropped.

Big Ron lamped that nigga' Schawan struttin' hard up to his mom's place, a scabby two-story brownstone at Eighth and Taylor with bars on all the windows and graffiti on the stairs. Ron had just rolled up to the corner in his brand new Taurus when here come that nigga' Schawan, bold as you please. He was thinkin' that the nigga' gots to be packin', or maybe he didn't make Ron in the fresh ride, 'cus if he did, Schawan would sure be duckin' low. Ron had a beef with that nigga', goin' back to summer last when Cool Deuce got smoked an' wouldn't nobody step up an' cop to it. Big Ron knew it was Schawan's crew what did it, even though they didn't brag on it none.

Didn't brag on it 'cus they knew payback was comin'. They just didn't know how. Or when.

Big Ron decided right there. *When* was *now*.

He waited for his mark to move into the house and then whipped the Taurus into a tight U-turn, tires screeching. Ron drove back to the small apartment he shared with Denita and Laron Junior, and moved quickly to the back hall closet. Luckily, the two of them were out. He searched frantically until he found his hammer, wrapped in oilcloth and stashed away in a Nike shoe box. It was a jinxed .38 police special revolver, all snub-nose and blue steel, the barrel scored with an awl; serial numbers burned off with industrial acid. There were two notches on the crosshatched grip; this piece had history long before he'd put up fifty dollars and a quarter ounce of lovely for it. The gun was untraceable, but hotter than a tar roof on the Fourth of July, and just for show.

Thirty-eight cal. don't do shit. Ron saw in the paper where some narc in Miami was still walkin' 'cus a folded Racing Form inside his jacket stopped a thirty-eight.

But it would be enough for this. Good enough for close in.

The plan was to ring up a couple of his crew and ambush the nigga' comin' out his mom's. Ron was parked out front, across the narrow street, watching for Schawan and tryin' to raise a posse on his cell phone when the first bullet tore through the car roof and buried itself in the backseat. The second and third shots found him; from his vantage point on the second floor of his mother's house, Schawan had sussed out the ambush and flipped it. One bullet shattered the driver's-side window, burned into Ron's meaty shoulder, and tore free. The other came through the door panel, flattened on his ribs, and slid through muscle and flesh until it came to rest below his left lung.

It was the third shot that sledgehammered Ron across the Taurus's seat, smashed him into the passenger door, rammed his foot down on the accelerator, and sent him roaring down Eighth Street. Ron knew he'd been hit, that somehow he'd tipped his play and that nigga Schawan had busted him. The street was a blur as the numbness receded; the car fishtailed, slammed into a mailbox on the curb, and stalled. There was a black iron band around his chest that kept him from drawing a clean breath. Through a fog of pain and confusion, Ron saw red, realized it was a stoplight, and restarted the car.

The Taurus leaped through the intersection, lurching and rocking like a wild bronco. Ron could hear sirens in the distance, and risked a glance at his side mirror; a fourth and final shot had punctured the left rear tire. He made a series of turns, arbitrary, instinctual, as he pushed the accelerator to the floorboards and tore heedlessly down the avenues, wanting only to escape, to live . . .

And blackness. Ron snapped back from the void. He opened his eyes, acknowledged the pain with a low moan. His side was afire.

The street was deserted, a wasteland of darkened office buildings and windblown debris. The Taurus was on the sidewalk, rear wheels in the gutter, unmoving. Ron had no idea where he was or how long he had been unconscious. He felt light-headed and couldn't seem to focus his thoughts. Curious images flickered in his mind's eye: a plastic toy soldier, a girl unbuttoning her confirmation dress, a single fat line of coke on a mirror. A large, white letter "M" floated in the air in front of him. . . .

It was the street marker for the Waterfront Metro station. Somehow, the Taurus had found its way to the subway. Ron pushed open the driver's-side door and tumbled onto the sidewalk, the shock of impact blinding him with red agony. The void beckoned, again.

No! Not goin' out like this.

Ron bit down on his tongue until he could taste blood. The new pain cleared his head as he stood and staggered down the escalator, left arm folded awkwardly against his wounded side. Now he could feel the wet stickiness on his back, the throb in his shoulder, the weakness in his legs.

There was no Metro attendant in sight, in the kiosk or at the turnstiles. The pistol was heavy in his hand. Ron pushed past the EXIT ONLY swing-through and gingerly shook down his sleeve to cover the gun. In moments, he was on the train platform and stumbling onto a waiting train.

The first dead nigga' that Big Ron ever saw was Sweet P. It was six weeks before Ron's twelfth birthday. Him an' June an' Li'l Skip were tightening the brakes on June's new mountain bike, had it wheels-up on the sidewalk in front of Packer's Carry-Out, when they heard the telltale *pop-pop-pop* that meant drive-by.

Sweet P, light-skinned, handsome, was on the corner up a ways, slingin' a pocketful a' twenty rocks, when a black Jeep Cherokee rolled up and left him for dead.

Ron was by his side before the cordite smoke had cleared. It was a known fact that sometimes when the hardboys got hit, when they thought their time was up, they'd be tellin' shit. Like where all the cake was stashed up, or the bodies buried or such. Sometimes, they mommas' upbringing would show through and these street-corner boys, these gangsters, would be confessin' and cryin' like they was locked outta church at Judgment.

But not Sweet P. He'd pulled himself up to a sitting position, his back against the door of an abandoned storefront. There were two saucer-sized red stains spreading across his chest.

"Laron," he grimaced, "I'm a'ight, young. Get nine-one-one."

The boy pushed closer. Sweet P's white Raiders jersey was soaked through, the 9mm pistol in his waistband forgotten.

"C'mon, nigga. I said I'm a'ight. Get nine-one-one . . ."

And died.

Didn't blink. Didn't cough. Just died.

Quiet-like.

The bulkhead door at the far end of the Metro car rattled open. The din of air horns and brakes and screeching wheels cascaded over him like a wave. The tunnel air was moist and cool; it smelled of old piss and high voltage.

A Metro engineer in an oversize shirt moved slowly past him, up the aisle. The key rings on his belt jingled like spurs.

Ron was tucked into a ball on a seat in the middle of the car, his legs pulled up beneath him. His head rested against the window. He tried to focus, tried to give the engineer a hard look as he went by, but could only manage to close his eyes.

Sweet P was seven years gone. Laron could still see his face.

The train rumbled, slowed. The lights of the station strobed through the windows on either side of the car. Ron could hear hushed voices all around him as the train halted and the doors hissed open.

"Green Line train to Greenbelt," said the intercom, a disembodied voice crackling with static. "Next station, National Archives and the Navy Memorial."

The pain in his side was unbearable now. Ron gritted his teeth and squeezed his eyes tighter. Tears ran down his face, mingled with the fever sweat of his agonies. His baggy jeans were full of blood.

"Been gored?"

A whisper, so close. Across the aisle. The voice was comforting. Familiar . . .

NO!

Ron's eyes snapped open. He looked across the aisle, incredulous.

Cowboy.

"Naw. You ain't dead yet. But you're ridin' hard for Boot Hill, Shortlegs. An' there ain't two ways about that."

Cowboy.

"Lookit you! Dumbstruck! Y'oughta see yourself, boy. It's to laugh out loud."

Cowboy. Full grown at six foot even, all worn denim and rawhide and a Colt Peacemaker slung low on his hip. Black leather vest with silver conchas. Silk bowler hat with two eagle feathers in the band.

"Laron! Who left that milk out all night?!"

"What happened here with your daddy's good shirt?"

"Who took my last two dollars off the kitchen counter?!"

Cowboy.

"Boy, you best quit all that make-believe and tell the truth . . ."

But it wasn't me. It was Cowboy. It really was.

"Cowboy," Laron whispered aloud, sure that he was dead. It didn't matter that he could feel the bullet in his side and hear his own voice. He was certain. "You're all in my head. 'Cus I'm dead."

The rhyme made Ron laugh; cursing, he grabbed his chest and coughed blood.

"Naw," Cowboy began as he pulled out a suede tobacco pouch and cigarette paper. "You just *wishin'* you was dead; then that hole in your side wouldn't pain you so."

Ron pushed himself up, steadied himself against the train window. The glass was cool on his hand.

"YOU . . . AIN'T . . . REAL!" he said slowly, emphatically.

"Well, I wouldn't know about all that. But I'm sittin' right here. Right where I've always been. It was you what moved on. You might give pause to recollect . . ."

Laron remembered. He remembered racing pell-mell down the sidewalks on Sunday mornings, digging forts in the park, tossing a basketball up from half-court. He remembered monkeybars and Redskins cards. He remembered silver coins and Intendo and teaching himself Chinese checkers alone in a darkened stairwell.

No. Not alone. Never alone. Cowboy was there. Cowboy was always there, a little older, a little faster, always better. Ron could never beat Cowboy at anything. Never ever.

And one day, he stopped trying. He didn't care who could run the fastest or throw the farthest or hold his breath the longest. It was stupid. It was young and stupid and weak to have a fake, invisible friend called Cowboy.

Cowboy! What kind of name was that, anyway?! Did all the other li'l niglets have imaginary friends named Space Man or Pirate or Caveman?

Hell, no.

And suddenly, he couldn't see Cowboy anymore.

Until now.

Cowboy tapped his fixin's into his palm, rubbed his hands together, and lick-sealed the finished cigarette. Smiling, he hefted the tobacco pouch. His teeth were perfect.

"Reckon I can't fairly call you Shortlegs no more; you all stretched out now. It's a wonder you reached this ripe old age. A proper wonder."

The train was slowing again. Laron glanced toward the doors.

"Naw. They can't see me. Like before, don't nobody know about me but you. Can't see me, can't hear me, can't touch me mostly. Like when we was just shavers . . ."

The train stopped; the doors opened. Two white girls, one busty and dark-haired, the other slim and blond, sat down together on the seat directly in front of Ron. The blonde had waist-length yellow hair; she turned around to look at him quickly, then flipped her long mane over her shoulder with a dismissive wave of her hand.

Ron felt a flush of sick heat wash over him. His mouth was dry as dust.

"This . . . this is hell," he rasped, then coughed more blood. "Fuckin' hell!"

"No need to cuss out loud, son. Just move your lips, the way we useta."

Fuck you, said Ron's lips.

"Back atcha, pardner. That lead feelin' frisky . . . movin' round a mite?"

Ron sank back down into the seat. As he wiped the tears and sweat from his face, he found himself nodding in response to Cowboy's query. It was pointless to ask the whys or wherefores. Cowboy had come back.

"The veil between is thin, Little Brother. Thin as smoke."

Cowboy lit up with a wooden match, reached across the aisle, and held the cigarette to Laron's lips.

"Breath deep. It's Injun medicine."

All around him, people were oblivious. Ron inhaled, held the smoke, and exhaled with a gasp. He felt something popping inside his chest; then the pain that had been with him since Eighth Street receded. There was a cloud of smoke filling the Metro car. He felt like he was floating on it.

"Next stop, Gallery Place," the intercom crackled. "Transfer station for the Red Line to Glenmont and Shady Grove."

"That ought t'take the edge off," Cowboy began. "So's you're an out-law now. On the run with blood on your boots and a pistol in your hand. Bet your mama's proud."

Fuck you, Ron's lips repeated.

"Have it your own way, Shortlegs. I done my best by you," Cowboy said sadly. "Guess I'll be moseyin' on . . ."

"WAIT!" Ron screamed aloud, suddenly afraid.

He could feel everyone's eyes on him. Startled, the fair-haired girl in front of him stood up, ready to move to another seat, but her friend grabbed her hand and tugged her back down.

"City girl. Plenty spunk there," Cowboy observed wryly. "I'd wager *she* knows how to ask nice to get her way."

Please, said Ron's lips. *Please stay*.

Cowboy brightened. He dropped the butt into the tobacco pouch, held it up for Ron to see. He cupped his hands around it and blew into the space between his thumbs.

The pouch was gone. In its place, Cowboy held up a flattened slug of grayish metal.

"Learn't that trick at the Raven's Grin. You know what this is?"

Laron nodded slowly. He'd seen spent, misshapen shot before. Lots of times.

"Two summers past. You was standin' outside that dance hall on Georgia Avenue . . ."

Laron couldn't remember, couldn't think straight. Two years was a lifetime ago. Two lifetimes ago.

". . . bushwhacker was all set for a back-shoot. Had you in his crosshairs. He got off a single shot 'fore he lost heart an' took to wing."

Ron shook his head. So long ago.

" 'Course, you might not recall, 'cus this bullet never reached ya'. On account'a me SHOOTIN' it out THE VERY AIR!"

Cowboy leaped up and slapped leather for effect; whipping the Colt off his hip, he spun it twice around by the trigger guard and slipped it back into his holster.

Ron laughed then, laughed out loud. The pain in his side was no more than an itch, a pinprick. There was a moment of panic when he realized that he couldn't feel his breath, but it passed. Cowboy was full of shit.

The train slowed, fluorescent lights inside flickering like quiet lightning, and stopped. The doors opened with a hiss. There was some small commotion in the middle of the car as a squat black woman wrestled with an overloaded baby stroller, but Ron ignored it. He felt like he was at the bottom of the ocean—sounds were muffled and distant, and the light curled and eddied in waves.

"Green Line train to Greenbelt. Next stop, Mount Vernon Square and the University of the District of Columbia."

As the train lurched forward into the tunnel, Ron heard the telltale rattle of the bulkhead door at the end of the car. Cowboy climbed up onto the seat as the Metro engineer rushed down the aisle and past him, returning to the front of the train. Cowboy watched him pass, frowned.

"We're gettin' pressed here, Little Brother. Time to speak plain . . ."

Ron nodded dreamily.

"The long an' short of it is right simple. I come for your gun."

Concealed under his jacket, the .38 spasmed in Ron's grip, his hand tightening involuntarily. He slowly shook his head.

"I'm sayin' we got no more time for this," Cowboy continued, exasperated, "You known me all your life. Now I'm tellin' you why I'm here. Hand me over that iron an' be quick about it."

"NO!" Laron muttered aloud. "Let them come get it."

The two girls in front giggled at Ron's mumbled rantings as the brunette rolled her eyes and tipped back a phantom bottle.

"*Bo-racho!*" she laughed, swaying with the motion of the train car.

The train braked and stopped, passengers shuffling in and out. Cowboy slipped easily between them, moving wherever they weren't.

"Green Line train to Greenbelt. Your next station stop is Shaw and Howard University."

Cowboy lifted his eyes to the intercom, then leaned over until he nearly covered Ron, still curled up in the seat. As the Metro train began to move, sounds began to break through, loud and sharp. Impossibly loud.

"No more palaver, Shortlegs. We're fresh out of time." Cowboy reached down and covered Ron's eyes. "I'll have to show you . . ."

With the darkness came terror.

Suddenly, Ron was falling. All he could feel was the weight on his eyes and the dull ache in his side, and falling. He reached up to pull Cowboy's two hands away from his eyes, but there was nothing to grasp on to. There was only his curled, bleeding body, falling through the darkness.

Falling. Tumbling. And then, from far beneath him, a tiny bit of light. Then another. And another. Moving upward to meet him like campfire sparks rising into the night, continuing past him, these wisps grew larger and brighter until he could see them, focus on them as he fell.

The bits of light were his life. There were hundreds of them, bright scenes like snapshots, fluttering past him in the darkness. There was his grandmother's funeral. There, his first fistfight. A used syringe in the gutter. A bandaged knee. His mother waving a lottery ticket. A bloodstain on the sidewalk. A brick thrown from the roof.

A pistol recoiling in his hand.

"See it plainly, boy!"

Cowboy's voice came through the darkness, howling like a whirlwind. The weight on his eyes pushed Ron down, faster and faster, falling. He was filled with fear and gripped the pistol with ferocious strength.

And silence. He felt the weight lifted from his eyes.

Ron gasped aloud. The train was gone. Everything, gone.

He was standing on a gray plain that extended, featureless and flat, for as far as he could see. Ron turned around, turned again. He was alone beneath a black sky. He felt a twisting in his chest unlike anything he'd ever felt before, and knew it was the darkness moving within him. He hadn't fallen through it; the darkness had fallen into him. The darkness, the gray plain and black sky—all these things were inside him.

"It's all on account a' you pullin' down the barrel, Shortlegs."

Ron turned full about, and there was Cowboy. A beautiful white horse was beside him, mane billowing though there was no breeze.

"All that dope and liquor stole your mind, boy. Let me refresh you. It was springtime, and you was all a' fourteen years old and drunker than an Irishman on Christmas Eve. There was bit of a dustup at a fiesta, and you and your boys got shown the door . . ."

Ron suddenly remembered. Standing on the curb, looking back at the house.

". . . and somebody put a boot pistol in your hand and told you to light 'em up. You turned and fired five shots."

He remembered screaming, and breaking glass. Some blood.

"Five shots into a crowd, Shortlegs. And hit nobody. Some folks said it was a miracle. But we know better . . ."

"I-it was a thirty-two. I pulled down the barrel. Just bounced the shots off the sidewalk." Laron whispered, "I made my name that night. Nobody ever fucked with me again."

The horse whinnied, and Cowboy stroked her neck.

"You ain't no kind of bad man, Laron. You ain't got enough of this darkness in your heart. Granted, you've a gutful. But not a heartful."

"You sayin' I'm weak!" Ron blustered, feeling the dead weight of the sky.

"I'm sayin' the foolishness is over. This gray place is what's waiting for you. The only way outta' here is to ride her, an' you're gonna need your good hand to guide her."

Ron smiled.

"Didn't know you could rap like that, Cowboy."

"The gun, boy," Cowboy pleaded. "You got one chance now. One choice. Give me the gun."

Suddenly, the sound of air brakes filled Ron's ears. In the short distance, three rows of seats hovered above the gray plain. A window appeared, then the bulkhead door at the far end of the car. It opened.

Ron looked away, raised his eyes to the sky. There was nothing there except gray. And black.

It seemed to him it went on . . . forever.

"You win," he said, as he drew back and tossed the pistol into Cowboy's waiting hands. He felt naked.

"You don't know the half of it. Here, lemme getcha leg up . . ."

In a moment, Ron was atop the white mare. There were bloody handprints where he touched her.

"Straight ahead, and don't let go of her mane. Whatever happens, don't let go . . ."

Forever.

"Cowboy," he said, and suddenly, he was crying. "Am I dead?"

"Don't let go, boy. It's a long, hard ride back. But you're gonna get there."

"I don't wanna be dead," Ron sobbed. "I don't understand . . ."

"No matter now. Grab hold a' that mane, and don't let go."

"Cowboy . . ."

"Soon enough, Little Brother. *Adios.*"

Ron reached out and dug his fingers into the thick, yellow mane as Cowboy slapped the mare's flank. She reared up, forelegs flailing . . .

And screamed.

* * *

"... thought he was cuttin' her throat! Christ!"

District of Columbia Police Detective John Lewis unbuttoned his oversize Metro engineer's shirt. There was never room underneath for a Kevlar vest when he worked the trains undercover, but he'd figured out a way to wear one anyway. Size XXL.

"Lucky bastard's gonna make it. You had a clear shot, shoulda put him down ..."

The two Metro uniforms, first on the scene for backup, were huddled with Detective Lewis by the elevator. As the three of them watched, an emergency medical team wheeled the gurney past them and up, out of the Metro station. Out and above, to the waiting surgeons in the Howard University Hospital emergency room.

Laron smiled at them as he went by. Smiled at them like he knew a secret.

"Next time, perp," Lewis said simply, then turned to the uniforms. "We knew he was on the train; surveillance cameras caught him comin' in at Waterfront. We knew he was carryin'. We were waitin' to get everybody into place, EMTs, hostage teams, backup. 'Cus these days, you never know."

"Yeah, we heard the squeal. Coulda gone either way."

"Fuck, yeah. But before we can pull into the station, he grabs her. Just reaches right out and grabs a handful of that yellow hair in front of him an' won't let go. She's screamin' an' her girlfriend's screamin' and I know he's strapped, and he's yankin' on that hair and I'm runnin' up an' I'm just about to drop him ..."

"Yeah. And then ..."

"God*damnedest* thing ..." Lewis paused. Cops loved this stuff. "Over everything, the yellin' an' screamin' and everything, I hear this voice, clear as a bell. Like some guy's standin' right next to me in the aisle. Over everything, I hear, 'There's the gun. There's the gun!' and I look down and the goddamn piece is right there, on the floor between my feet. Outta nowhere. It's just there."

One of the uniforms laughed aloud. It was an odd laugh.

"Freaky shit. And lucky."

"No. Here's the freaky part. I swear to God, he said *'sheriff.'* He said, 'Sheriff, there's the gun.'"

Danger Word

Steven Barnes and Tananarive Due

When Kendrick opened his eyes, Grandpa Joe was standing over his bed, a tall dark bulk dividing the morning light. Grandpa Joe's beard covered his dark chin like a coat of snow. Mom used to say that guardian angels watched over you while you slept, and Grandpa Joe looked like he might have been guarding him all night with his shotgun. Kendrick didn't believe in guardian angels anymore, but he was glad he could believe in Grandpa Joe.

Most mornings, Kendrick opened his eyes to only strangeness: dark, heavy curtains, wooden planks for walls, a brownish-gray stuffed owl mounted near the window, with glassy black eyes that twitched as the sun set—or seemed to. A rough pine bed. And that *smell* everywhere, like the smell in Mom and Dad's closet. Cedar, Grandpa Joe told him. Grandpa Joe's big, hard hands had made the whole cabin of it, one board and beam at a time.

For the last six months, this had been his room, but it still wasn't, really. His Spider-Man bedsheets weren't here. His GI Joes, Tonka trucks, and Matchbox racetracks weren't here. His posters of Blade and Shaq weren't on the walls. This was his bed, but it wasn't his room.

"Up and at 'em, Little Soldier," Grandpa Joe said, using the nickname Mom had never liked. Grandpa was dressed in his hickory shirt and blue jeans, the same clothes he wore every day. He leaned on his rifle like a cane, so his left knee must be hurting him like it always did in the mornings. He'd hurt it long ago, in Vietnam.

"I'm going trading down to Mike's. You can come if you want, or I can leave you with the Dog-Girl. Up to you." Grandpa's voice was morning-rough. "Either way, it's time to get out of bed, sleepyhead."

Dog-Girl, the woman who lived in a house on a hill by herself fifteen minutes' walk west, was their closest neighbor. Once upon a time she'd had six pit bulls that paraded up and down her fence. In the last month that number had dropped to three. Grandpa Joe said meat was getting scarce. Hard to keep six dogs fed, even if you needed them. The dogs wagged their tails when Kendrick came up to the fence, because Dog-Girl had introduced him to them, but Grandpa Joe said those dogs could tear a man's arms off.

"Don't you ever stick your hand in there," Grandpa Joe always said. "Just because a dog looks friendly don't mean he is. Especially when he's hungry."

"Can I have a Coke?" Kendrick said, surprised to hear his own voice again, so much smaller than Grandpa Joe's, almost a little girl's. Kendrick hadn't planned to say anything today, but he wanted the Coke so bad he could almost taste the fizz; it would taste like a treat from Willy Wonka's Chocolate Factory.

"If Mike's got one, you'll get one. For *damn* sure." Grandpa Joe's grin widened until Kendrick could see the hole where his tooth used to be: his straw-hole, Grandpa Joe called it. He mussed Kendrick's hair with his big palm. "Good boy, Kendrick. You keep it up. I knew your tongue was in there somewhere. You better start using it, or you'll forget how. Hear me? You start talking again, and I'll whip you up a lumberjack breakfast, like before."

It *would* be good to eat one of Grandpa Joe's famous lumberjack breakfasts again, piled nearly to the ceiling: a bowl of fluffy eggs, a stack of pancakes, a plate full of bacon and sausage, and homemade biscuits to boot. Grandpa Joe had learned to cook in the Army.

But whenever Kendrick thought about talking, his stomach filled up like a balloon and he thought he would puke. Some things couldn't be said out loud, and some things *shouldn't*. There was more to talking than most people thought. A whole lot more.

Kendrick's eye went to the bandage on Grandpa Joe's left arm, just below his elbow, where the tip peeked out at the edge of his shirtsleeve. Grandpa Joe had said he'd hurt himself chopping wood yesterday, and Kendrick's skin had hardened when he'd seen a spot of blood on the bandage. He hadn't seen blood in a long time. He couldn't see any blood now, but Kendrick still felt worried. Mom said Grandpa Joe didn't heal as fast as other people, because of his diabetes. What if something happened to him? He was old. Something could.

"That six-point we brought down will bring a good haul at Mike's.

We'll trade jerky for gas. Don't like to be low on gas," Grandpa said. His foot slid a little on the braided rug as he turned to leave the room, and Kendrick thought he heard him hiss with pain under his breath. "And we'll get that Coke for you. Whaddya say, Little Soldier?"

Kendrick couldn't make any words come out of this mouth this time, but at least he was smiling, and smiling felt good. They had something to smile about, for once.

Three days ago a buck had come to drink from the creek.

Through the kitchen window, Kendrick had seen something move—antlers, it turned out—and Grandpa Joe grabbed his rifle when Kendrick motioned. Before the shot exploded, Kendrick had seen the buck look up, and Kendrick thought, *It knows*. The buck's black eyes reminded him of Dad's eyes when he had listened to the news on the radio in the basement, hunched over his desk with a headset. Kendrick had guessed it was bad news from the trapped look in his father's eyes.

Dad would be surprised at how good Kendrick was with a rifle now. He could blow away an empty Chef Boyardee ravioli can from twenty yards. He'd learned how to aim on *Max Payne* and *Medal of Honor*, but Grandpa Joe had taught him how to shoot for real, a little every day. Grandpa Joe had a roomful of guns and ammunition—the back shed, which he kept locked—so they never ran low on bullets.

Kendrick supposed he would have to shoot a deer one day soon. Or an elk. Or something else. The time would come, Grandpa Joe said, when he would have to make a kill whether he wanted to or not. "You may have to kill to survive, Kendrick," he said. "I know you're only nine, but you need to be sure you can do it."

Before everything changed, Grandpa Joe used to ask Mom and Dad if he could teach Kendrick how to hunt during summer vacation, and they'd said no. Dad didn't like Grandpa much, maybe because Grandpa Joe always said what he thought, and he was Mom's father, not Dad's. And Mom didn't go much easier on him, always telling Grandpa Joe *no*, no matter what he asked. *No*, you can't keep him longer than a couple weeks in the summer. *No*, you can't teach him shooting. *No*, you can't take him hunting.

Now there was no one to say *no*. No one except Grandpa Joe, unless Mom and Dad came back. Grandpa Joe had said they might, and they knew where to find him. They might.

Kendrick put on the red down jacket he'd been wearing the day Grandpa Joe found him. He'd sat in this for never-ending hours in the safe room at home, the storage space under the stairs with a reinforced door, a chemical toilet, and enough food and water for a month. Mom had sobbed, "Bolt the door tight. Stay here, Kendrick, and don't open the door until you hear Grandpa's danger word—NO MATTER WHAT."

She made him swear to Jesus, and she'd never made him swear to Jesus before. He'd been afraid to move or breathe. He'd heard other footsteps in the house, the awful sound of crashing and breaking. A single terrible scream. It could have been his mother, or father, or neither—he just didn't know.

Followed by silence, for one hour, two, three. Then the hardest part. The worst part.

"Show me your math homework, Kendrick."

The danger word was the special word he and Grandpa Joe had picked because Grandpa Joe had insisted on it. Grandpa Joe had made a special trip in his truck to tell them something bad could happen to them, and he had a list of reasons how and why. Dad didn't like Grandpa Joe's yelling much, but he'd listened. So Kendrick and Grandpa Joe had made up a danger word nobody else in the world knew, not even Mom and Dad.

And he had to wait to hear the danger word, Mom said.

No matter what.

By the time Kendrick dressed, Grandpa was already outside loading the truck, a beat-up navy blue Chevy. Kendrick heard a thud as he dropped a large sack of wrapped jerky in the bed.

Grandpa Joe had taught him how to mix up the secret jerky recipe he hadn't even given Mom: soy sauce and Worcestershire sauce, fresh garlic cloves, dried pepper, onion powder. He'd made sure Kendrick was paying attention while strips of deer meat soaked in that tangy mess for two days and then spent twelve hours in the slow-cook oven. Grandpa Joe had also made him watch as he cut the deer open and its guts flopped to the ground, all gray and glistening. "Watch, boy. Don't turn away. Don't be scared to look at something for what it is."

Grandpa Joe's deer jerky was almost as good as the lumberjack breakfast, and Kendrick's mouth used to water for it. Not anymore.

His jerky loaded, Grandpa Joe leaned against the truck, lighting a brown cigarette. Kendrick thought he shouldn't be smoking.

"Ready?"

Kendrick nodded. His hands shook a little every time he got in the truck, so he hid his hands in his jacket pockets. Some wadded-up toilet paper from the safe room in Longview was still in there, a souvenir. Kendrick clung to the wad, squeezing his hand into a fist.

"We do this right, we'll be back in less than an hour," Grandpa Joe said. He spit, as if the cigarette had come apart in his mouth. "Forty-five minutes."

Forty-five minutes. That wasn't bad. Forty-five minutes, then they'd be back.

Kendrick stared at the cabin in the rearview mirror until the trees hid it from his sight.

The road was empty, as usual. Grandpa Joe's rutted dirt road spilled onto the highway after a half-mile, and they jounced past darkened, abandoned houses. Kendrick saw three stray dogs trot out of the open door of a pink two-story house on the corner. He'd never seen that door open before, and he wondered whose dogs they were. He wondered what they'd been eating.

Suddenly, Kendrick wished he'd stayed back at Dog-Girl's. She was from England and he couldn't always understand her, but he liked being behind her fence. He liked Popeye and Ranger and Lady Di, her dogs. He tried not to think about the ones that were gone now. Maybe she'd given them away.

They passed tree farms, with all the trees growing the same size, identical, and Kendrick enjoyed watching their trunks pass in a blur. He was glad to be away from the empty houses.

"Get me a station," Grandpa Joe said.

The radio was Kendrick's job. Unlike Dad, Grandpa Joe never kept the radio a secret.

The radio hissed and squealed up and down the FM dial, so Kendrick tried AM next. Grandpa Joe's truck radio wasn't good for anything. The shortwave at the cabin was better.

A man's voice came right away, a shout so loud it was like screaming.

". . . and in those days shall men seek death and shall not find it . . . and shall desire to die and death shall flee from them . . ."

"Turn that bullshit off," Grandpa Joe snapped. Kendrick hurried to turn the knob, and the voice was gone. "Don't you believe a word of that, you hear me? That's B-U-double-L *bullshit*. Things are bad now, but they'll get better once we get a fix on this thing. Anything can be beat, believe you me. I ain't givin' up, and neither should you. That's givin'-up talk."

The next voices were a man and a woman who sounded so peaceful that Kendrick wondered where they were. What calm places were left?

". . . mobilization at the Vancouver Armory. That's from the commander of the Washington National Guard. So you see," the man said, "there *are* orchestrated efforts. There *has* been progress in the effort to reclaim Portland, and even more in points north. The Armory is secure, and running survivors to the islands twice a week. Look at Rainier. Look at Devil's Wake. As long as you stay away from the large urban centers, there are dozens of pockets where people are safe and life is going on."

"Oh, yes," the woman said. "Of course there are."

"There's a learning curve. That's what people don't understand."

"Absolutely." The woman sounded absurdly cheerful.

"Everybody keeps harping on Longview . . ." The man said "Longview" as if it were a normal, everyday place. Kendrick's stomach tightened when he heard it. ". . . but that's become another encouraging story. Contrary to rumors, there *is* a National Guard presence. There *are* limited food supplies. There's a gated community in the hills housing over four hundred. Remember, safety in numbers. Any man, woman, or teenager who's willing to enlist is guaranteed safe lodging. Fences are going up, roads barricaded. We're getting this under control. That's a far cry from what we were hearing even five, six weeks ago."

"Night and day," the cheerful woman said. Her voice trembled with happiness.

Grandpa Joe reached over to rub Kendrick's head. "See there?" he said.

Kendrick nodded, but he wasn't happy to imagine that a stranger might be in his bed. Maybe it was another family with a little boy. Or twins.

But probably not. Dog-Girl said the National Guard was long gone and nobody knew where to find them. "Bunch of useless bloody shitheads," she'd said—the first time he'd heard the little round woman cuss. Her accent made cussing sound exotic. If she was right, dogs might be roaming through his house, too, looking for something to eat.

". . . There's talk that a Bay Area power plant is up again. It's still an unconfirmed rumor, and I'm not trying to try to wave some magic wand here, but I'm just making the point—and I've tried to make it before—that life probably felt a lot like this in Hiroshima."

"Yes," the woman said. From her voice, Hiroshima was somewhere very important.

"Call it apples and oranges, but put yourself in the place of a villager in Rwanda. Or an Auschwitz survivor. There had to be some days that felt *exactly* the way we feel when we hear these stories from Seattle and Portland, and when we've talked to the survivors . . ."

Just ahead, along the middle of the road, a man was walking.

Kendrick sat straight up when he saw him, balling up the tissue wad in his pocket so tightly that he felt his fingernails bite into his skin. The walking man was tall and broad-shouldered, wearing a brick red backpack. He lurched along unsteadily. From the way he bent forward, as if bracing into a gale, Kendrick guessed the backpack was heavy.

He hadn't ever seen anyone walking on this road.

"Don't you worry," Grandpa Joe said. Kendrick's neck snapped back as Grandpa Joe speeded up his truck. "We ain't stoppin'."

The man let out a mournful cry as they passed, waving a cardboard sign. He had a long, bushy beard, and as they passed, his eyes looked wide and wild. Kendrick craned his head to read the sign, which the man held high in the air: STILL HERE, the sign read.

"He'll be all right," Grandpa Joe said, but Kendrick didn't think so. No one was supposed to go on the roads alone, especially without a car. Maybe the man had a gun, and maybe they would need another man with a gun. Maybe the man had been trying to warn them something bad was waiting for them ahead.

But the way he walked . . .

"No matter what," Mom had said.

Kendrick kept watching while the man retreated behind them. He had to stop watching when he felt nausea pitch in his stomach. He'd been holding his breath without knowing it. His face was cold and sweating, both at once.

"Was that one?" Kendrick whispered.

He hadn't known he was going to say that either, just like when he'd asked for a Coke. Instead, he'd been thinking about the man's sign. STILL HERE.

"Don't know," Grandpa Joe said. "It's hard to tell. That's why you never stop."

They listened to the radio, neither of them speaking again for the rest of the ride.

Time was, Joseph Earl Davis III never would have driven past anyone on the road without giving them a chance to hop into the bed and ride out a few miles closer to wherever they were going. Hell, he'd picked up a group of six college-age kids and driven them to the Centralia compound back in April.

But Joe hadn't liked the look of that hitcher. Something about his walk. Or, maybe times were just different. If Kendrick hadn't been in the car, Jesus as his witness, Joe might have run that poor wanderer down where he walked. An ounce of prevention. That was what it had come to in Joe Davis's mind. Drastic measures. You just never knew; that was the thing.

EREH LLITS, the man's sign said in the mirror, receding into a tiny, unreadable blur.

Yeah, I'm still here, too, Joe thought. And not picking up hitchhikers was one way he intended to *stay* here, thanks a bunch for asking.

Freaks clustered in the cities, but there were plenty of them wandering through the countryside nowadays, actual packs. Thousands, maybe. Joe had seen his first six months ago, coming into Longview to rescue his grandson. His first, his fifth, and his tenth. He'd done what he had to do to save the boy, then shut the memories away where they couldn't sneak into his dreams. Then drank enough to make the dreams blurry.

A week later, he'd seen one closer to home, not three miles beyond the gated road, *not five miles from the cabin.* Its face was bloated blue-gray, and flies buzzed around the open sores clotted with that dark red scabby shit that grew under their skin. The thing could barely walk, but it had smelled him, swiveling in his direction like a scarecrow on a pivot.

Joe still dreamed about that one every night. That one had *chosen* him.

Joe left the freaks alone unless one came at him—that was safest if you were by yourself. He'd seen a poor guy shoot one down in a field, and then a swarm came from over a hill. Some of those fuckers could walk pretty fast, could *run*, and they weren't stupid, by God.

But Joe had killed that one, the pivoting one that had chosen him. He'd kill it a dozen times again if he had the chance; it was a favor to both of them. That shambling mess had been somebody's son, somebody's husband, somebody's father. People said freaks weren't really *dead*—they didn't climb out of graves like movie monsters—but they were as close to walking dead as Joe ever wanted to see. Something was eating them from the inside out, and if they bit you, the freak shit would start eating you, too. You fell asleep, and you woke up different.

The movies had that part right, anyway.

As for the rest, nobody knew much. People who met freaks up close and personal didn't live long enough to write reports about them. Whatever they were, freaks weren't just a city problem anymore. They were everybody's problem.

"Can you hold on, Dad? My neighbor's knocking on the window."

That's what Cass had said the last time they'd spoken, then he hadn't heard any more from his daughter for ten agonizing minutes. The next time he'd heard her voice, he'd barely recognized it, so calm it could be nothing but a mask over mortal terror. "DADDY? Don't talk—just listen. I'm so sorry. For everything. No time to say it all. They're here. You need to come and get Kendrick. Use the danger word. Do you hear me, Daddy? And . . . bring guns. Shoot anyone suspicious. I mean *anyone*, Daddy."

"Daddy," she'd called him. She hadn't called him that in years.

That day he'd woken up with alarm twisting his gut for no particular reason. That was why he'd raised Cassidy on the shortwave two hours earlier than he usually did, and she'd sounded irritated that he'd called before she was up. "My neighbor's knocking on the window."

Joe had prayed he wouldn't find what he knew would be waiting in Longview. He'd known what might happen to Cass, Devon, and Kendrick the moment he'd found them letting neighbors use the shortwave and drink their water like they'd been elected the Rescue Committee. They couldn't even *name* one of the women in their house. That was Cass and Devon for you. Acting like naive fools, and he'd told them as much.

Still, even though he'd tried to make himself expect the worst, he couldn't, really. If he ever dwelled on that day, he might lose his mind . . . and then what would happen to Kendrick?

Anytime Joe brought up that day, the kid's eyes whiffed out like a dead pilot light. It had taken Kendrick hours to finally open that reinforced door and let him in, even though Joe had used the danger word again and again. And Kendrick had spoken hardly a word since.

Little Soldier was doing all right today. Good. He'd need to be tougher, fast. The kid had regressed from nine to five or six, just when Joe needed him to be as old as he could get.

As Joe drove beyond the old tree farms, the countryside opened up on either side; fields on his left, a range of hills on his right. There'd been a cattle farm out here once, but the cattle were gone. Wasn't much else out here, and there never had been.

Except for Mike's. Nowadays, Mike's was the only thing left anyone recognized.

Mike's was a gas station off exit 46 with Portapotties out back and a few shelves inside crammed with things people wanted: flour, canned foods, cereal, powdered milk, lanterns, flashlights, batteries, first aid supplies, and bottled water. And gas, of course. How he kept getting this shit, Joe had no idea. "If I told you that, I'd be out of business, bro," Mike had told him when Joe asked, barking a laugh at him.

Last time he'd driven out here, Joe had asked Mike why he'd stayed behind when so many others were gone. Why not move somewhere less isolated? Even then, almost a full month ago, folks had been clumping up in Longview, barricading the school, jail, and hospital. Had to be safer, if you could buy your way in. Being white helped, too. They said it didn't, but Joe Davis knew it did. Always had, always would. Things like that just went underground for a time, that's all. Times like these the ugly stuff festered and exploded back topside.

Mike wasn't quite as old as Joe—sixty-three to Joe's more cumbersome seventy-one—but Joe thought he was foolhardy to keep the place open. Sure, all the stockpiling and bartering had made Mike a rich man, but was gasoline and Rice-A-Roni worth the risk? "I don't run, Joe. Guess I'm hardheaded." That was all he'd said.

Joe had known Mike since he first built his cedar cabin in 1989, after retiring from his berth as supply sergeant at Fort McArthur. Mike had just moved down from Alberta, and they'd talked movies, then jazz. They'd discovered a mutual love of Duke Ellington and old sitcoms. Mike had always been one of his few friends around here. Now he was the only one.

Joe didn't know whether to hope his friend would still be there or to pray he was gone. Better for him to be gone, Joe thought. One day he and the kid would have to move on, too, plain and simple. That day was coming soon. That day had probably come and gone twice over.

Joe saw a glint of the aluminum fencing posted around Mike's as he came around the bend, the end of the S in the road. Although it looked more like a prison camp, Mike's was an oasis, a tiny squat store and a row of gas pumps surrounded by a wire fence a man and a half tall. The fence was electrified at night: Joe had seen at least one barbecued body to prove it, and everyone had walked around the corpse as if it weren't there. With gas getting scarcer, Mike tended to trust the razor wire more, using the generator less these days.

Mike's three boys, who'd never proved to be much good at anything else, had come in handy for keeping order. They'd had two or three gunfights there, Mike had said, because strangers with guns thought they could go anywhere they pleased and take anything they wanted.

Today, the gate was hanging open. He'd never come to Mike's when there wasn't someone standing at the gate. All three of Mike's boys were usually there, with their greasy hair and their pale fleshy bellies bulging through their too-tight T-shirts. No one today.

Something was wrong.

"Shit," Joe said aloud before he remembered he didn't want to scare the kid. He pinched Kendrick's chin between his forefinger and thumb, and his grandson peered up at him, resigned, the expression he always wore these days. "Let's just sit here a minute, okay?"

Little Soldier nodded. He was a good kid.

Joe coasted the truck to a stop outside the gate. While it idled, he tried to see what he could. The pumps stood silent and still on their concrete islands, like two men with their hands in their pockets. There was a light on inside, a super-white fluorescent glow through the picture windows painted with the words GAS, FOOD in red. He could make out a few shelves from where he was parked, but he didn't see anyone inside. The air pulsed with the steady burr of Mike's generator, still working.

At least it didn't look like anyone had rammed or cut the gate. The chain looked intact, so it had been unlocked. If there'd been trouble here, it had come with an invitation. Nothing would have made those boys open that gate otherwise. Maybe Mike and his boys had believed all that happy-talk on the radio, ditched their place, and moved to Longview. The idea made Joe feel so relieved that he forgot the ache in his knee.

And leave the generator on? Bullshit.

Tire tracks drew patterns in hardened mud. Mike's was a busy place. Damn greedy fool.

Beside him, Joe felt the kid fidgeting in his seat, and Joe didn't blame him. He had more than half a mind to turn around and start driving back toward home. The jerky would keep. He had enough gas to last him. He'd come back when things looked right again.

But he'd promised the kid a Coke. That was the only thing. And it would help erase a slew of memories if he could bring a grin to the kid's face today. Little Soldier's grins were a miracle. His little chipmunk cheeks were the spitting image of Cass's at his age.

"Daddy," she'd called him on the radio. "Daddy."

Don't think about that don't think don't—

Joe leaned on his horn. He let it blow five seconds before he laid off.

After a few seconds, the door to the store opened, and Mike stood there leaning against the doorjamb, a big, ruddy white-haired Canuck with linebacker shoulders and a pigskin-sized bulge above his belt. He was wearing an apron like he always did, as if he ran a butcher shop instead of a gas station. Mike peered out at them and waved. "Come on in!" he called out.

Joe leaned out of the window. "Where the boys at?" he called back.

"They're fine!" Mike said. Over the years, Joe had tried a dozen times to convince Mike he couldn't hear worth shit. No sense asking after the boys again until he got closer.

The wind skittered a few leaves along the ground between the truck and the door, and Joe watched their silent dance for a few seconds, considering. "I'm gonna' go do this real quick, Kendrick," Joe finally said. "Stay in the truck."

The kid didn't say anything, but Joe saw the terror freeze his face. The kid's eyes went dead just like they did when he asked what had happened at the house in Longview.

Joe cracked open his door. "I'll only be a minute," he said, trying to sound casual.

"D-don't leave me. Please, Grandpa Joe? Let me c-come."

Well, I'll be damned, Joe thought. This kid was talking up a storm today.

Joe sighed, mulling it over. Pros and cons either way, he supposed. He reached under the seat and pulled out his Glock 9mm. He'd never liked automatics until maybe the mid-80's, when somebody figured out how to keep them from jamming so damned often. He had a Mossberg shotgun in a rack behind the seat, but that might seem a little too hostile. He'd give Kendrick the Remington 28-gauge. It had some kick, but the Little Soldier was used to it. He could trust Little Soldier not to fire into the ceiling. Or his back. Joe had seen to that.

"How many shots?" Joe asked him, handing over the little birder.

Kendrick held up four stubby fingers, like a toddler. So much for talking.

"If you're coming with me, I damn well better know you can talk if there's a reason to." Joe sounded angrier than he'd intended. "Now . . . how many shots?"

"*Four!*" That time, he'd nearly shouted it.

"Come on in," Mike called from the doorway. "I've got hot dogs today!"

That was a first. Joe hadn't seen a hot dog in nearly a year, and his mouth watered. Joe started to ask him again what the boys were up to, but Mike turned around and went inside.

"Stick close to me," Joe told Kendrick. "You're my other pair of eyes. *Anything* looks funny, you point and speak up loud and clear. Anybody makes a move in your direction you don't like, *shoot*. Hear?"

Kendrick nodded.

"That means *anybody*. I don't care if it's Mike or his boys or Santa Claus or anybody else. You understand me?"

Kendrick nodded again, although he lowered his eyes sadly. "Like Mom said."

"Damn right. Exactly like your mom said," Joe told Kendrick, squeezing the kid's shoulder. For an instant, his chest burned so hot with grief that he knew a heart attack couldn't feel any worse. The kid might have *watched* what happened to Cass. Cass might have turned into one of them before his eyes.

Joe thought of the pivoting, bloated freak he'd killed, the one that had smelled him, and his stomach clamped tight. "Let's go. Remember what I told you," Joe said.

"Yes, sir."

He'd leave the jerky alone, for now. He'd go inside and look around for himself first.

Joe's knee flared as his boot sank into soft mud just inside the gate. Shit. He was a useless fucking old man, and he had a bouncing Betty fifty klicks south of the DMZ to blame for it. In those happy days of Vietnam, none of them had known that the *real* war was still forty years off—but coming fast—and he was going to need both knees for the real war, you dig? And he could use a real soldier at his side for this war, not just a little one.

"Closer," Joe said, and Kendrick pulled up behind him, his shadow.

When Joe pushed the glass door open, the salmon-shaped door chimes jangled merrily, like old times. Mike had vanished quick, because he wasn't behind the counter. A small television set on the counter erupted with laughter—old, canned laughter from people who were either dead or no longer saw much to laugh about. "EEEEEEE-dith," Archie Bunker's voice crowed. On the screen, old Archie was so mad he was nearly jumping up and down. It was the episode with Sammy Davis Jr., where Sammy gives Archie a wet one on the cheek. Joe remembered watching that episode with Cass once upon a time. Mike was playing his VCR.

"Mike? Where'd you go?" Joe's finger massaged his shotgun trigger as he peered behind the counter.

Suddenly, there was a loud laugh from the back of the store, matching a new fit of laughter from the TV. He'd know that laugh blindfolded.

Mike was behind a broom, one of those school custodian brooms with a wide brush, sweeping up and back, and Joe heard large shards of glass clinking as he swept. Mike was laughing so hard, his face and crown had turned pink.

Joe saw what he was sweeping: The glass had been broken out of one of the refrigerated cases in back, which were now dark and empty. The others were still intact, plastered with Budweiser and Red Bull stickers, but the last door had broken clean off except for a few jagged pieces still standing upright, like a mountain range, close to the floor.

"Ya'll had some trouble?" Joe asked.

"Nope," Mike said, still laughing. He sounded congested, but otherwise all right. Mike kept a cold six months out of the year.

"Who broke your glass?"

"Tom broke it. The boys are fine." Suddenly, Mike laughed loudly again. "That Archie Bunker!" he said, and shook his head.

Kendrick, too, was staring at the television set, mesmerized. From the look on his face, he could be witnessing the parting of the Red Sea. The kid must miss TV, all right.

"Got any Cokes, Mike?" Joe said.

Mike could hardly swallow back his laughter long enough to answer. He squatted down, sweeping the glass onto an orange dustpan. "We've got hot dogs! They're—" Suddenly, Mike's face changed. He dropped his broom, and it clattered to the floor as he cradled one of his hands close to his chest. *"Ow! SHIT ON A STICK!"*

"Careful there, old-timer," Joe said. "Cut yourself?"

"Goddamm shit on a stick, shit on a stick, goddamn shit on a stick."

Sounded like it might be bad, Joe realized. He hoped this fool hadn't messed around and cut himself somewhere he shouldn't have. Mike sank from a squat to a sitting position, still cradling his hand. Joe couldn't see any blood yet, but he hurried toward him. "Well, don't sit there whining over it."

"Shit on a stick, goddamn shit on a stick."

When Mike's wife, Kimmy, died a decade ago, Mike had gone down hard and come up a Christian. Joe hadn't heard a blasphemy pass his old friend's lips in years.

As Joe began to kneel down, Mike's shoulder heaved upward into

Joe's midsection, stanching his breath and lifting him to his toes. For a moment Joe was too startled to react—the what-the-hell reaction, stronger than reflex, which had nearly cost him his life more than once. He was frozen by the sheer surprise of it, the impossibility that he'd been *talking* to Mike one second and—

Joe snatched clumsily at the Glock in his belt and fired at Mike's throat. Missed. *Shit.*

The second shot hit Mike in the shoulder, but not before Joe had lost what was left of his balance and gone crashing backward into the broken refrigerator door. Three things happened at once: His arm snapped against the case doorway as he fell backward, knocking the gun out of his hand before he could feel it fall. A knife of broken glass carved him from below as he fell, slicing into the back of his thigh with such a sudden wave of pain that he screamed. And Mike had hiked up Joe's pant leg and taken hold of his calf in his teeth, gnawing at him like a dog with a beef rib.

"Fucking *son of a bitch.*"

Joe kicked away at Mike's head with the only leg that was still responding to his body's commands. Still Mike hung on. Somehow, even inside the fog of pain from his lower-body injury, Joe felt a chunk of his calf tearing, more hot pain.

He was bitten, that was certain. *He was bitten.* Every alarm in his head and heart rang.

Oh, God, holy horseshit, he was bitten. He'd walked right up to him. They could make sounds—everybody said that—but this one had been *talking,* putting words together, acting like . . . acting like . . .

With a cry of agony, Joe pulled himself forward to leverage more of his weight, and kicked at Mike's head again. This time, he felt Mike's teeth withdraw. Another kick, and Joe's hiking boot sank squarely into Mike's face. Mike fell backward into the shelf of flashlights behind him.

"*Kendrick!*" Joe screamed.

The shelves blocked his sight of the spot where his grandson had been standing.

Pain from the torn calf muscle rippled through Joe, clouding thought. The pain from his calf shot up to his neck, liquid fire. Did the bastards have venom? Was that it?

Mike didn't lurch like the one on the road. Mike scrambled up again, untroubled by the blood spattering from his broken nose and teeth. "I have hot dogs," Mike said, whining it almost.

Joe reached back for the Glock, his injured thigh flaming, while

Mike's face came at him, mouth gaping, teeth glittering crimson. Joe's fingers brushed the automatic, but it skittered away from him, and now Mike would bite, and bite, and then go after the Little Soldier—

Mike's nose and mouth exploded in a mist of pink tissue. The sound registered a moment later, deafening in the confined space, an explosion that sent Mike's useless body toppling to the floor. Then Joe saw Kendrick just behind him, his little birding gun smoking, face pinched, hands shaking.

Holy Jesus, Kendrick had done it. The kid had hit his mark.

Sucking wind, Grandpa Joe took the opportunity to dig among the old soapboxes for his Glock, and when he had a firm grip on it, he tried to pull himself up. Dizziness rocked him, and he tumbled back down.

"Grandpa Joe!" Kendrick said, and rushed to him. The boy's grip was surprisingly strong, and Joe hugged him for support, straining to peer down at his leg. He could be wrong about the bite. He could be wrong.

"Let me look at this," Joe said, trying to keep his voice calm. He peeled back his pant leg, grimacing at the blood hugging the fabric to flesh.

There it was, facing him in a semicircle of oozing slits: a bite, and a deep one. He was bleeding badly. Maybe Mike had hit an artery, and whatever shit they had was shooting all through him. Damn, damn, damn.

Night seemed to come early, because for an instant Joe Davis's fear blotted the room's light. He was bitten. And where were Mike's three boys? Wouldn't they all come running now, like the swarm over the hill he'd seen in the field?

"We've gotta get out of here, Little Soldier," Joe he said, and levered himself up to standing. Pain coiled and writhed inside him. "I mean now. Let's go."

His leg was leaking. The pain was terrible, a throb with every heartbeat. He found himself wishing he'd faint, and his terror at the thought snapped him to more alertness than he'd felt before.

He had to get Little Soldier to the truck. He had to keep Little Soldier safe.

Joe cried out with each step on his left leg, where the back of his thigh felt ravaged. He was leaning so hard on Little Soldier, the kid could hardly manage the door. Joe heard the tinkling above him, and then, impossibly, they were back outside. Joe saw the truck waiting just beyond the gate.

His eyes swept the perimeter. No movement. No one. Where were those boys?

"Let's go," Joe panted. He patted his pocket, and the keys were there. "Faster."

Joe nearly fell three times, but each time he found the kid's weight beneath him, keeping him on his feet. Joe's heartbeat was in his ears, an ocean's roar.

"Jump in. Hurry," Joe said after the driver's door was open, and Little Soldier scooted into the car like a monkey. The hard leather made Joe whimper as his thigh slid across the seat, but suddenly, it all felt easy. Slam and lock the door. Get his hand to stop shaking enough to get the key in the ignition. Fire her up.

Joe lurched the truck in reverse for thirty yards before he finally turned around. His right leg was numb up to his knee—*from that bite, oh, sweet Jesus*—but he was still flooring the pedal somehow, keeping the truck on the road instead of in a ditch.

Joe looked in his rearview mirror. At first he couldn't see for the dust, but there they were: Mike's boys had come running in a ragged line, all of them straining as if they were in a race. Fast. They were too far back to catch up, but their fervor sent a bottomless fear through Joe's stomach.

Mike's boys looked like starving animals hunting for a meal.

Kendrick couldn't breathe. The air in the truck felt the way it might in outer space, if you were floating in the universe, a speck too far in the sky to see.

"Grandpa Joe?" Kendrick whispered. Grandpa Joe's black face shone with sweat, and he was chewing at his lip hard enough to draw blood.

Grandpa Joe's fingers gripped at the wheel, and the corners of his mouth turned upward in an imitation of a smile. "It's gonna be all right," he said, but it seemed to Kendrick that he was talking to himself more than to him. "It'll be fine."

Kendrick stared at him, assessing: He seemed all right. He was sweating and bleeding, but he must be all right if he was driving the truck. You couldn't drive if you were one of them, could you? Grandpa Joe was fine. He said he was.

Mom and Dad hadn't been fine after a while, but they had warned him. They had told him they were getting sleepy, and they all knew getting sleepy right away meant you might not wake up. Or if you did, you'd be changed. They'd made him promise not to open the door to the safe room, even for them.

No matter what. Not until you hear the danger word.

Kendrick felt warm liquid on the seat beneath him, and he gasped, thinking Grandpa Joe might be bleeding all over the seat. Instead, when he looked down, Kendrick saw a clear puddle between his legs. His jeans were dark and wet, almost black. It wasn't blood. He'd peed on himself, like a baby.

"Are you sleepy?" Kendrick said.

Grandpa Joe shook his head, but Kendrick thought he'd hesitated first, just a little. Grandpa Joe's eyes were on the road half the time, on the rearview mirror the rest. "How long before your mom and dad got sleepy?"

Kendrick remembered Dad's voice outside of the door, announcing the time: "It's nine o'clock, Cass." Worried it was getting late. Worried they should get far away from Kendrick and send for Grandpa Joe to come get him. Kendrick heard them talking outside the door plain as day; for once, they hadn't tried to keep him from hearing.

"A few minutes," Kendrick said softly. "Five. Or ten."

Grandpa Joe went back to chewing his lip. "What happened?"

Kendrick didn't know what happened. He'd been in bed when he heard Mom say their neighbor Mrs. Shane was knocking at the window. All he knew was that Dad came into his room, shouting and cradling his arm. Blood oozed from between Dad's fingers. Dad pulled him out of bed, yanking Kendrick's arm so hard that it popped, pulling him to his feet. In the living room, he'd seen Mom crouching far away, by the fireplace, sobbing with a red face. Mom's shirt was bloody, too.

At first, Kendrick had thought Dad had hurt Mom, and now Dad was mad at him, too. Dad was punishing him by putting him in the safe room.

"They're in the house, Kendrick. We're bitten, both of us."

After the door to the safe room was closed, for the first time Kendrick had heard somebody else's footsteps. Then, that scream.

"They stayed for ten minutes, maybe. Not long. Then they said they had to leave. They were getting sleepy, and they were scared to come near me. Then they went away for a long time. For hours," Kendrick told Grandpa Joe. "All of a sudden I heard Mom again. She was knocking on the door. She asked me where my math homework was. She said, 'You were supposed to do your math homework.'"

Kendrick had never said the words before. Tears hurt his eyes.

"That was how you knew?" Grandpa Joe said.

Kendrick nodded. Snot dripped from his nose to the front of his jacket, but he didn't move to wipe it away. Mom had said not to open the door until Grandpa Joe came and said the danger word. No matter what.

"*Good* boy, Kendrick," Grandpa Joe said, his voice wavering. "Good boy."

All this time, Joe had thought it was his imagination.

A gaggle of the freaks had been there in Cass's front yard waiting for him, so he'd plowed most of them down with the truck so he could get to the door. That was the easy part. As soon as he got out, the ones still standing had surged. There'd been ten of them at least; an old man, a couple of teenage boys, the rest of them women, moving quick. He'd been squeezing off rounds at anything that moved.

"Daddy?"

Had he heard her voice before he'd fired? In the time since, he'd decided the voice was his imagination, because how *could* she have talked to him, said his name? He'd decided God had created her voice in his mind, a last chance to hear it to make up for the horror of the hole his Glock had just put in her forehead. "Daddy?"

It had been Cass, but it *hadn't* been. Her blouse and mouth had been a bloody, dripping mess, and he'd seen stringy bits of flesh caught in her teeth, just like the other freaks. It hadn't been Cass. Hadn't been.

People said freaks could *make noises.* They walked and looked like us. The newer ones didn't have the red shit showing beneath their skin, and they didn't start to lose their motor skills for a couple of days—so they could run fast, the new ones. He'd known that. Everybody knew that.

But if freaks could talk, could recognize you . . .

Then we can't win.

The thought was quiet in Joe's mind, from a place that was already accepting it.

Ten minutes, Little Soldier had said. Maybe five.

Joe tried to bear down harder on the gas, and his leg felt like a wooden stump. Still, the speedometer climbed before it began shaking at ninety. He had to get Little Soldier as far as he could from Mike's boys. Those boys might run all day and all night, from the way they'd looked. He had to get Little Soldier away . . .

Joe's mouth was so dry it ached.

"We're in trouble, Little Soldier," Joe said.

Joe couldn't bring himself to look at Kendrick, even though he wanted to so much he was nearly blinded by tears. "You know we're in trouble, don't you?" Joe said.

"Yes," the boy said.

"We have to come up with a plan. Just like we did at your house that time."

"A danger word?" Kendrick said.

Joe sighed. "A danger word won't work this time."

Again, Kendrick was silent.

"Don't go back to the cabin," Joe said, deciding that part. "It's not safe."

"But Mom and Dad might . . ."

This time Joe did gaze over at Kendrick. Unless it was imagination, the boy was already sitting as far from him as he could, against the door.

"That was a story I told you," Joe said, cursing himself for the lie. "You know they're not coming, Kendrick. You said yourself she wasn't right. You could hear it. That means they got your father, too. She was out in the front yard, before I got inside. I had to shoot her, Little Soldier. I shot her in the head."

Kendrick gazed at him wide-eyed, rage knotting his little face.

That's it, Little Soldier. Get mad.

"I couldn't tell you before. But I'm telling you now for a reason . . ."

Just that quick, the road ahead of Joe fogged, doubled. He snapped his head up, aware that he had just lost a moment of time, that his consciousness had flagged.

But he was still himself. Still himself, and that made the difference, right? He was still himself, and just maybe he would stay himself, and beat this damned thing.

If you could stay awake . . .

Then you might stay alive for another—what? Ten days? He'd heard about someone staying awake that long, maybe longer. Right now he didn't know if he'd last the ten minutes. His eyes fought to close so hard that they trembled. *There'll be rest enough in the grave.* Wasn't that what Benjamin Franklin had said?

"Don't you close your eyes, Daddy." Cass's voice. He snapped his head around, wondering where the voice had come from. He was seeing things: Cassie sat beside him with her pink lips and ringlets of tight brown hair. For a moment he couldn't see Little Soldier, so solid she seemed. "You always talked tough this and tough that. Da Nang and Hanoi and a dozen places I couldn't pronounce. And now the one damned time in your life that it matters, you're going to sleep?" The accusation in her voice was crippling. "We trusted you, and you walked right into that store and got bitten because you were laughing at Archie Bunker? I trusted you, Daddy."

Silence. Then: "I still trust you, Daddy."

Suddenly, Joe felt wide awake again for the last time in his life.

"Listen to me. I can't give you the truck," Joe said. "I know we practiced driving, but you might make a mistake and hurt yourself. You're better off on foot."

Rage melted from Kendrick's face, replaced by bewilderment and the terror of an infant left naked in a snowdrift. Kendrick's lips quivered violently.

"No, Grandpa Joe. You can stay awake," he whispered.

"Grab that backpack behind your seat—it's got a compass, bottled water, jerky, and a flashlight. It's heavy, but you'll need it. And take your Remington. There's more ammo for it under your seat. Put the ammo in the backpack. Do it now."

Kendrick sobbed, reaching out to squeeze Joe's arm. "P-please, Grandpa Joe . . ."

"*Stop that goddamned crying!*" Joe roared, and the shock of his voice silenced the boy. Kendrick yanked his hand away, sliding back toward his door again. The poor kid must think he'd crossed over.

Joe took a deep breath. Another wave of dizziness came, and his chin rocked downward. The car swerved slightly before he could pull his head back up. Joe's pain was easing, and he felt stoned, as if he were on acid. He hadn't driven far enough yet. They were still too close to Mike's boys. So much to say . . .

Joe kept his voice as even as he could. "There were only two people who could put up a better fight than me, and that was your mom and dad. They couldn't do it, not even for you. That tells me I can't, either. Understand?"

His tears miraculously stanched, Kendrick nodded.

READ REVELATIONS, a billboard fifty yards ahead advised in red letters. Beside the billboard, the road forked into another highway. Thank Jesus.

The words flew from his mouth, nearly breathless. "I'll pull off when we get to that sign, at the crossroads. When the truck stops, *run*. Hear me? Fast as you can. No matter what you hear . . . don't turn around.

Don't stop. It's twenty miles to Centralia, straight south. There's National Guard there, and caravans. Tell them you want to go to Devil's Wake. That's where I'd go. When you're running, stay near the roads, but keep out of sight. If anyone comes before you get to Centralia, hide. If they see you, tell 'em you'll shoot, and then do it. And don't go to sleep, Kendrick. Don't let anybody surprise you."

"Yes, sir," Kendrick said in a sad voice, yet still eager to be commanded.

The truck took control of itself, no longer confined to its lane or the road, and it bumped wildly as it drove down the embankment. Joe's leg was too numb to keep pressing the accelerator, so the truck gradually lost speed, rocking to a stop, nose down, its headlights lost in weeds. Feeling in his arms was nearly gone now, too.

"I love you, Grandpa Joe," he heard his grandson say. Or thought he did.

"Love you, too, Little Soldier."

Still here. Still here.

"Now, go. *Go.*"

Joe heard Kendrick's car door open and slam before he could finish.

He turned his head to watch Kendrick, to make sure he was doing as he'd been told. Kendrick had the backpack and his gun as he stumbled away from the truck, running down in the embankment that ran beside the road. The boy glanced back over his shoulder, saw Joe wave him on, and then disappeared into the roadside brush.

With trembling fingers, Joe opened the glove compartment, digging out his snub-nose .38, his favorite gun. He rested the cold metal between his lips, past his teeth. He was breathing hard, sucking at the air, and he didn't know if it was the toxin or his nerves working him. He looked for Kendrick again, but he couldn't see him at this angle.

Now. Do it now.

It seemed that he heard his own voice whispering in his ear.

I can win. I can win. I saved my whole fucking squad. I can beat this thing . . .

Joe sat in the truck feeling alternating waves of heat and cold washing through him. As long as he could stay awake . . .

He heard the voice of old Mrs. Reed, his sixth-grade English teacher; saw the faces of Little Bob and Eddie Kevner, who'd been standing beside him when the bouncing Betty blew. Then he saw Cassie in her wedding dress, giving him a secret gaze, as if to ask if it was all right before she pledged her final vows at the altar.

Then in the midst of the images, some he didn't recognize.

Something red, drifting through a trackless cosmos. Alive, yet not alive. Intelligent but unaware. He'd been with them all along, those drifting spore-strands gravitating toward a blue-green planet with water and soil . . . filtering through the atmosphere . . . rest . . . home . . . grow . . .

A crow's mournful caw awakened Joe, but not as much of him as had slipped into sleep. His vision was tinged red. His world, his heart, was tinged red. What remained of Joe knew that *it* was in him, awakening, using his own mind against him, dazzling him with its visions while it took control of his motor nerves.

He wanted to tear, to rend. Not killing. Not eating. Not yet. There was something more urgent, a new voice he had never heard before. *Must bite.*

Panicked, he gave his hand an urgent command: *pull the trigger.*

But he couldn't. He'd come this close and couldn't. Too many parts of him no longer wanted to die. The new parts of him only wanted to live. To grow. To spread.

Still Joe struggled against himself, even as he knew struggle was doomed. Little Soldier. Must protect Little Soldier. Must . . .

Must . . .

Must find boy.

Kendrick had been running for nearly ten minutes, never far from stumbling, before pure instinct left him and his mind woke up again. Suddenly, his stomach hurt from a deep sob. He had to slow down because he couldn't see for his tears.

Grandpa Joe had been hunched over the steering wheel, eyes open so wide that the effort had changed the way his face looked. Kendrick thought he'd never seen such a hopeless, helpless look on anyone's face. If he had been able to see Mom and Dad from the safe room, that was how they would have looked, too.

He'd been stupid to think Grandpa Joe could keep him safe. He was an old man who lived in the woods.

Kendrick ran, his legs burning and throat scalding. He could see the road above him, but he ran in the embankment like Grandpa Joe had told him, out of sight.

For an endless hour Kendrick ran, despite burning legs and scalded throat, struggling to stay true to the directions Grandpa Joe had given him. South. Stay south.

Centralia. National Guard. Devil's Wake. Safe.

By the time exhaustion claimed Kendrick, rain clouds had darkened the sky, and he was so tired he had lost any certainty of placing his feet without disaster. The trees, once an explosion of green, had been bleached gray and black. They were a place of trackless, unknowable danger. Every sound and shadow seemed to call to him.

Trembling so badly he could hardly move, Kendrick crawled past a wall of ferns into a culvert, clutching the little Remington to his chest.

Once he sat, his sadness felt worse, like a blanket over him. He sobbed so hard he could no longer sit up straight, curling himself in a ball on the soft soil. Small leaves and debris pasted themselves to the tears and mucous that covered his face. One sob sounded more like a wail, so loud it startled him.

Grandpa Joe had lied. Mom had been dead all along. He'd shot her in the head. He'd said it like it hardly mattered to him.

Kendrick heard snapping twigs, and the back of his neck turned ice-cold.

Footsteps. Running fast.

Kendrick's sobs vanished, as if they'd never been. He sat straight up, propping his shotgun across his bent knee, aiming, finger ready on the trigger. He saw a small black spider crawling on his trigger wrist—one with a bloated egg sack, about to give birth to a hundred babies like in *Charlotte's Web*—but he made no move to bat the spider away. Kendrick sat primed, trying to silence his clotted nose by breathing through his mouth. Waiting.

Maybe it was that hitchhiker with the sign, he thought.

But it didn't matter who it was. *Hide.* That was what Grandpa Joe said.

The footsteps slowed, although they were so close that Kendrick guessed the intruder couldn't be more than a few feet away. He was no longer running, as if he knew where Kendrick was. As if he'd been close behind him all along, and now that he'd found him, he wasn't in a hurry anymore.

"I have a gun! I'll shoot!" Kendrick called out, and this voice was very different from the one he'd used to ask Grandpa Joe for a Coke. Not a little girl's voice this time, or even a boy's. It was a voice that meant what it said.

Silence. The movement had stopped.

That was when Grandpa Joe said the danger word.

Kendrick's finger loosened against the trigger. His limbs gave way, and his body began to shake. The woods melted away, and he remembered wearing this same jacket in the safe room, waiting. Waiting for Grandpa Joe.

There had never been a gunshot from Grandpa Joe's truck. Kendrick had expected to hear the gunshot as soon as he ran off, dreading it. Grandpa Joe always did what needed to be done. Kendrick should have heard a gunshot.

"Go back!" Kendrick said. Although his voice was not so sure this time, he cocked the Remington's hammer, just as he'd been taught.

Kendrick waited. He tried not to hope—and then hoped fervently—that his scare had worked. The instant Kendrick's hope reached its peak, a shadow moved against the ferns above him, closer.

"Breakfast," Grandpa Joe's watery voice said again.

ABOUT THE CONTRIBUTORS

Zane is the *New York Times* bestselling author of *Skyscraper, Nervous, Dear G-Spot*, and many more novels. Visit her on the web at www.eroticanoir.com.

Robert Fleming is the editor of *After Hours: A Collection of Erotic Writing by Black Men* and *Intimacy: Erotic Stories of Love, Lust, and Marriage by Black Men*. His collection of horror stories, *Havoc After Dark*, was published by Kensington in March 2004. He lives in New York.

Chesya Burke has been writing within the horror genre for a little over three years. She has had stories published in a variety of publications, such as *1000 Delights, Horrorfind, Dark Angel Rising, Deviant Minds*, the anthologies *Hour of Pain* and *Genre Noir* as well as many others. She lives in Atlanta with her husband, four daughters, two dogs, a cat, and a hamster.

Kalamu ya Salaam is a New Orleans-based writer, editor, filmmaker, and teacher. He is the founder of the Nommo Literary Society, a black writers' workshop, and co-founder of Runagate Multimedia publishing company. He also serves as leader of the Wordband, a poetry performance ensemble, and moderator of e-Drum, a listserve for black writers. He can be reached at kalamu@aol.com.

Joy M. Copeland is a native of New York City but has spent the last twenty-five years in northern Virginia. Until her recent retirement, she worked as an executive for a major corporation, one of many roles in the chain of careers that has taken her through Capitol Hill, the intelligence community, public policy, systems consulting and finally to corporate systems management.

Joy has written a number of short stories and has just completed her first novel, a supernatural suspense tale, entitled *Borrowed Destiny*, which she hopes will be published soon. She holds undergraduate and graduate degrees from Howard University. Now, her focus is writer's education. As a retiree, she devotes her time to her passions—writing and traveling to the settings that serve as backdrops for her stories.

L. R. Giles is a Virginia native, an alumnus of Old Dominion University, and a book reviewer for *Elemental Renaissance*, a Hampton-Roads hip-hop magazine. He made his publishing debut at the tender age of eight after winning his elementary school's Young Authors' Competition with a tale entitled "Giant Dinosaur Inside," about a boy who pulls a monster T-Rex out of his cereal box. His penchant for the strange revealed, he continued to write fantasy, sci-fi, and horror for more than a decade and a half and is currently hard at work on his first novel, *Necromance*, as well as the construction of his online home for the weird, www.LRGiles.com. Contact him at LRGiles@cox.net for feedback or general horror chitchat.

L. A. Banks (a.k.a. Leslie Esdaile and Leslie E. Banks), is a native Philadelphian and dean's list graduate of the University of Pennsylvania, Wharton Undergraduate Program. Upon completing her studies in 1980, she embarked upon a career in corporate marketing and sales for several Fortune 100 high-tech firms. In 1991, and after a decade of working in the corporate environment, Esdaile-Banks shifted gears and began an independent consulting career assisting small businesses and economic development agencies.

Leslie Esdaile-Banks soon found a hidden talent, fiction writing, which has led her on a successful trajectory toward becoming one of the nation's premier African-American authors capable of deftly crossing literary genres. Successfully graduating in 1998 from Temple University's Masters of Fine Arts Program with a degree in Film and Media Arts, she adds the dimension of filmmaking and visual media (with a portfolio of strong documentaries) to her artistic and business endeavors. Drawing from her urban environment, Esdaile-Banks uses both life experience and a vivid imagination to create new landscapes in print. Each of her many works, from classic horror to suspense/thrillers, to women's fiction, and even within the romance genre, all contain a paranormal, otherworldly slant. At present, she is broadening the scope of her work to include a series of projects for St. Martin's Press (the Vampire Huntress Legend series to be authored under the pseudonym, L. A. Banks), and a series for Pocket Books (Soul Food, a novel series based upon the ShowTime/Paramount Television Show, under pen name, Leslie E. Banks). Ms. Esdaile-Banks lives and works in Philadelphia with her husband and children.

Ahmad Wright is a transplanted New Yorker from the D.C. metropolitan area. He is interested in the psychological intensity of the macabre and the chaos that it brings to light within our own selves. His fiction has appeared in *African Voices Magazines* and *A Place to Enter*. He is a 2003 participant of the Hurston/Wright Writer's Week. His nonfiction credits include a host of magazines including *Vibe*, *Maxim*, *Publishers Weekly*, and *Trace*. He is currently a contributing writer for *Upscale Magazine*.

Lawana Holland-Moore received her B.A. in journalism and history from George Washington University. She was a freelance writer and graphic designer for eight years and wrote for publications such as *YSB Magazine* before concentrating on writing full-time. Due to her Washington, D.C. ghost hunting website (www.dcghosts.com), she has become one of the nation's foremost experts on ghosts and hauntings of the D.C.–metro area and is one of the few African-American ghost hunters in the country. She has been featured in radio interviews and articles in numerous U.S. publications and media such as *The Washington Post, Washingtonian, USA Today*, and cnn.com. Due to a Reuters news story, she has also been featured in international media such as *The Times of India Online* and the *Bahrain Tribune Daily*. Also writing as part of the collaborative team Ellen Kay, she lives with her husband in Washington, D.C.—a city whose people and daily life are a constant inspiration for her work.

Christopher Chambers is a former U.S. Department of Justice attorney. He has penned two Random House hardcover thrillers, *Sympathy for the Devil* and *A Prayer for Deliverance*, both optioned for cable television. He's authored several acclaimed short stories, and the upcoming historical novel *Yella Patsy's Boys*, based on the true story of the MacDaniel Brothers and the burning of Washington, D.C. in 1814, and the nonfiction hardcover *Uncle Joe's Cabin*, about the journey of African-American Communists from Harlem to Stalin's Russia during the 1930s. He lives in Maryland. Visit him online at www.chrischambersbooks.com.

D. S. Foxx, in her words: "My family hails from Jamaica and Barbados. For the most part, I write romances to order, where even the hair color can be changed on a whim, let alone heritage; it was great fun being able to write something closer to home."

Terence Taylor was born a child, and has remained one for most of his adult life. Originally from New York City, he spent his youth traveling the United States and Europe as an Air Force brat, giving both Terence and his work a universal point of view. For almost two decades he has specialized in children's television, writing and producing for live actors, on location and in the studio, puppets, costume characters, animation (traditional, stop motion and CGI), in comedy, drama, and documentaries. His efforts have been recognized with a New York Emmy and awards from the International Film and Television Festival of New York and the Chicago International Film Festival.

He has written for East and West Coast studios: Nickelodeon, Disney, Universal Cartoons, Marvel Animation, Hanna-Barbera, The Children's Television Workshop, DIC, Scholastic Television, Film Roman, ABC, Jumbo Pictures, Porchlight Entertainment, Lancit Media, Don Cornelius Productions, Hearst Animation Productions and Sun Woo. His work has appeared and continues to air on PBS stations WGBH, WQED, WNET, KCET, SCETV and on HBO Kids, Fox Kids, the Learning Channel and Nickelodeon. He has contributed his talents to programs for pre-schoolers—*Gullah Gullah Island, Jay Jay the Jet Plane, Dooley & Pals, I Spy, The Puzzle Place, Pinwheel House*; for middle school ages—*Arthur, Gadget Boy* and *Heather, 101 Dalmatians, The Woody Woodpecker Show, Sonic Underground, The Book of Virtues* and *3-2-1 CONTACT*; and for teenagers—*Spiderman, Mortal Kambat, You Can't Do That on Television, Dumb and Dumber, Sherlock Holmes in the 22nd Century* and *Livewire.*

He has also written industrial/educational films for such corporate clients as Ballpark Franks, Parkway, Lincoln Mercury, Bank of America, the American Heart Association, and Domino's Pizza. He has twice been a granting panelist for ITVS, the Independent Television Service and judged children's shows for the ACE awards. Terence won his New York Emmy for co-creating and writing *High Feather*, a nutritional series for children and an International Film and Television Festival of New York award for his work as a producer of promotions and fund-raising at WNET-13. In addition to his writing work, Terence has also worked extensively as a graphic artist/designer and digital animator. He was creative director, graphic artist and digital animator on CD-ROM adaptations of five Mercer Mayer children's books, and has designed and produced animation and interstitial video elements for Microsoft, Parkay and Ballpark Franks. Terence Taylor is a member of the Writer's Guild of America East, and received a B.S. in communication arts and science from St. John's University, where he graduated Cum Laude.

Linda Addison is the first African American to receive the Horror Writers of America Bram Stoker award for her latest collection of poetry, *Consumed, Reduced to Beautiful Grey Ashes*, published by Space & Time. Her science-fiction story, "Twice, At Once, Separated," in the award-winning collection *Dark Matter: A Century of Speculative Fiction from the African Diaspora*, was listed on the Honorable Mention list in the Year's Best Science Fiction. Her poetry and stories have been listed on the Honorable Mention list for the annual Year's Best Fantasy and Horror for four years. She also is a member of SFWA, SFPA, and HWA. She's a member of a writing group, Circles in the Hair (CITH) that has been meeting every other week since 1990.

Rickey Windell George was born in Port Chester, NY, twenty-eight years ago. Rickey Windell George recalls his hometown as just a tiny place wedged between Greenwich, Connecticut, and Rye, NY. He is married to a wonderful woman, Lavern, with whom he has two children, Bryce and Bryanna.

By day he is manager and a technical architect for one of the big-four accounting firms. There he develops enterprise-level applications and mutlitier web platforms. His hobbies include a religious workout regimen and nutrition plan, some dabbling in art, reading, and a deep appreciation for the cinema. The author is ever quick to point out the fact that "Writing is not a hobby, writing horror is who I am and always have been." His published work includes the story collection, *Sex & Slaughter & Self-Discovery*, and stories published in *Blasphemy, Peepshow, Scared Naked*, and many others. Visit him online at www.thedeathcollection.com.

Francine Lewis is a Toronto-born writer who spent her first eight years on a small island in the Caribbean. She received her bachelor and masters' degrees at the University of Toronto and did post-graduate studies at McGill University. Her poetry has been published in

Existere, Just Us magazine and *Sensations Magazine,* while her first short story. "To Feast on Royal Jelly," appeared in the children's science fiction anthology *Tales from the Wonder Zone: Odyssey,* published by Trifolium Books and edited by Julie Czerneda.

Patricia E. Canterbury is a native Sacramentan, an award-winning poet, an award-winning short-story writer, novelist and political scientist. Her first published novel, *The Secret of St. Gabriel's Tower,* is the first of a proposed juvenile mystery series, "The Poplar Cove Mysteries." *Carlotta's Secret,* the first of her children's mysteries in "The Delta Mysteries Series," was published in February 2001. Patricia won the First Annual Georgia State Chapbook contest in 1987 for her poetry chapbook, *Shadowdrifters . . . Images of China.* Pat is the assistant executive officer of the Board for Professional Engineers and Land Surveyors. She lives in Sacramento with her husband, Richard, and pets: two cats, a red Doberman who thinks he's a cat, fresh and salt-water fish, and a very mean parakeet. She is hard at work on a future Poplar Cove Mystery *Carlotta and the Locke Ghost Mystery,* scheduled for publication in 2004. Her essay, "The Color of Childhoods" was published in the winter 2001 edition of *Obsidian III.* Pat is also hard at work editing her first speculative fiction novel, *The Geaha Conflict.* Visit her online at www.patmyst.com.

Anthony Beal has sold his fiction and poetry to dozens of publications such as *Space and Time* magazine, *Dark Muse, Dark Angel Rising, Cthulhu Sex* magazine, *MillenniumSHIFT* magazine, and *Brutal Tales.* He co-authored the extreme erotic horror anthology *Sex and Slaughter and Self-Discovery,* published in 2003.

B. Gordon Doyle

Born and raised in the Empire State,
The son of the son of a preacher.
A dark horse, a falling star
The last of the Dunbar Apache.

Knave of ravens, reluctant magician.
Out of the blue and bold as love,
I go walking after midnight along
The moonlight mile.

Steven Barnes is the author of more than a dozen science fiction novels, including *Lion's Blood* and *Zulu Heart*. He lives in Washington.

Tananarive Due is the author of *The Between*, *My Soul to Keep*, *The Living Blood*, and *The Good House*. She lives in Washington with her husband, novelist Steven Barnes.

ABOUT THE EDITOR

Brandon Massey was born June 9, 1973 and grew up in Zion, Illinois. Originally self-published, *Thunderland*, his first novel, won the Gold Pen Award for Best Thriller. His second novel, *Dark Corner*, a tale of vampires that takes place in rural Mississippi, was published in January 2004.

Brandon currently lives near Atlanta, where he is working on his next thriller. Visit his Web site at www.brandonmassey.com for the latest news on his books and tours.